# CORMAC: THE SEERS

Dwina Murphy-Gibb was born in Kilskeery, Co. Tyrone, in the North of Ireland. She was educated in Ireland and England. Her interest in mythology and history started from the moment she could read and draw as is evident from her paintings and early writings.

She was co-founder and editor of *Celtic Dawn*, the international literary journal. She has been the recip????? ?ous poetry and art awards. Dwina founded the Yea?? ?ub, which sponsors international competitions for poets. *Erg? On The Rye*, her first volume of poetry, has aroused great interest and is now in its second edition. Her short stories ha?? ?ppeared in a number of magazines.

Dwina Murphy-Gibb has written and recorded *Any Old Yarns*, a series of satirical Irish dialogues which have been broadcast on radio in the U.S. and Australia.

Dwina lives in Oxfordshire and Florida with her husband Robin, son Robin-John, her dog and two chinchillas. She spends as much time as possible in Ireland where she is the owner of a splendid white bull called Cormac.

*Also by Dwina Murphy-Gibb in Pan Books*

## Cormac: The King Making

# DWINA MURPHY-GIBB

# CORMAC THE SEERS

PAN BOOKS
LONDON, SYDNEY AND AUCKLAND

First published 1992 by Pan Books Limited

This edition published 1994 by Pan Books Limited
a division of Pan Macmillan Publishers Limited
Cavaye Place London SW10 9PG
and Basingstoke

Associated companies throughout the world

ISBN 0 330 32723 2

1 3 5 7 9 8 6 4 2

A CIP catalogue record for this book is available from
the British Library

Phototypeset by Intype, London
Printed and bound in Great Britain by
Cox & Wyman Ltd, Reading, Berkshire

*For ROBIN, who gives me love, humour, freedom and inspiration.*

# ACKNOWLEDGEMENTS

I wish to thank . . .

Michael Eaton whose gift of a book on Irish High Kings started the wheels turning;

Richard Ryal and his psychic guide, Dyah, who made it possible for me to *see*, and whose long hours of proofing I will not forget nor forgive easily;

Starr Mahe de Berdouaré and Lady Anna Lee Porter for their invaluable friendship and enthusiasm. They introduced me to Robert Lacey who led me to the world of agents and publishers.

I am also indebted to . . .

The Old Grey Woman of the *Sidh-Beanh* who saved my life and started my studies in Irish mythology;

Christine Falls for her assistance with my research in Ireland, help with the Irish language, and for her love and support;

Liam de Paor for spending some of his own precious time showing me exhibits in the National Museum in Dublin, discussing his archaeological excavations at Tara and the nature of metal artificing. He enlightened me about the sacred white bulls with the red ears;

Gabriel Rosenstock whose knowledge of Old Irish and ancient Irish poetry is second to none;

Muriel Ludden, (Mrs P.) a fellow countrywoman and poet, who has a fine command of the English language and whose editing skills cannot be matched; and Bonnie too!

Terence DuQuesne, shaman and scholar of all things ancient, whose studies of wild dogs and wolves heped me enormously;

Donna Serpe for her long hours, personal assistance and ready ear;

Phelim Lunny for showing me Knocknarea and helping me with the Irish names;

All my friends and family, at home and abroad, for their great eagerness and optimism.

My deepest appreciation and respect I reserve for:

Maharaj Charan Singh Ji and Swamiji Saraswati;

The likes of Seamus Heaney, Derek Mahon, Gabriel Rosenstock and Seamus Deane who brought me gentle respite with their poetic writings;

The writers of the hundred or so books I used in research. (Now I know what it is like!);

My father and mother for being Irish;

And my son, Robin-John, who delightedly traipsed over Ireland in mid-winter with me, finding tombs and stone circles, visiting crannógs and climbing high mountains.

Lessons for us all.

# GLOSSARY

Over the centuries, many of the Irish words have been changed and spelt in different ways. Neighbouring European cultures (whether embraced in Ireland, or not) have created their own interpretations, pronunciations and speech rhythms, in the seeking of a common language for purposes of communication. This glossary is aesthetic in value only to those who wish to read and understand the old ways in the original Irish language. It is perfectly all right to pronounce the names and italicized words phonetically as written in the book, and probably a lot easier for some, as the old Irish is difficult for the non-Irish ear and throat.

Achtán . . . (Aught-awn) . . . Name.

a chroí . . . (Ah Kree) . . . Oh, heart, my heart (an endearment).

a chuisle . . . (Ah Koosh-la) . . . Oh, pulse, my pulse (an endearment).

a chuisle mo chroí . . . (Ah Koosh-la mo Kree) . . . Oh, pulse of my heart.

Arch-Druid . . . (Arch Drew-id) . . . Elder, head of Druids, high-rank priest; worshipper of nature, the oak tree is sacred to him; master of nature and all natural things; teacher.

Ard Rígh . . . (Ard-Ree) . . . Sometimes spelt Ard Rí; High King.

Art Aenfar . . . (Art Ayne-are) . . . Name meaning the solitary one, one alone, the lonely one. The *F* is silent. Art Aenfar is the same as Art the Lonely.

Art mac Conn . . . (Art mawk Konn) . . . Art, son of Conn, the same person as Art Aenfar.

a stór . . . (Ah St(h)ore) . . . My treasure.

Athair . . . (Ah-hir) . . . Father.

Bal or Bel . . . (Baal) . . . A fire-god.

Baldur . . . (Boal duhr) . . . Tree-god, Fire of the Oak.

Baltinne . . . *see* Bealtaine.

Bealtaine . . . (Bwall-tinn-eh) . . . Mouth of the Fire. The spelling has changed over the centuries – Beltaine, Baltinne, Beltinne; it is a major fire-festival which spans May Eve and May Day, the beginning of summer.

Beith . . . (Bee-ith) . . . Birch tree (ogham).

Bel . . . (Bwall or Belle) . . . A fire-god.

Bláth . . . (Blaw) . . . Name; flower.

bodhran . . . (Baw-rawn) . . . Circular hand-drum usually stretched with aged goat-skin.

Bothán . . . (Buh-hawn) . . . dwelling, circular hut.

Brehon Law(s) . . . (Brey(h)-awn) . . . Brehon law-givers made special laws for the communities to live by, and these laws covered every conceivable problem which arose between families or strangers. There was a famous wise law-giver by the name of Brighid (Brigit).

Bréifne . . . (Bray-if-nay) . . . Name of place.

Brighdal . . . (Bree-dal) . . . of the goddess Brighid.

Brighde Brighid (Breed or Bree-sh-de) . . . Name of the goddess Brighid (Brigit). The name has changed through the ages.

Briugu . . . (Bree-ugoo) . . . A special nobleman appointed to oversee the Chieftain's lands and herds of cattle.

cairn . . . (Kern) . . . Burial mound usually covered with stones.

Carmel . . . (Karr-mell) . . . Name.

Cauldron of Dagda . . . Bottomless cauldron of the god Dagda, which is never empty and is constantly all-giving.

céird . . . (Kay-erd) . . . Master smith; metal-artificer; tradesman.

ciorbolg . . . (Keer-bolg) . . . Comb-bag.

Cleitech . . . (Clee-tey) . . . Name of place.

Cnoc Sidhe . . . (Knock Shee) . . . Hill of the Faeries.

coll . . . (Kawl) . . . Hazel tree (ogham).

Conn of a Hundred Battles . . . Name of famous king who is Art the Lonely's father and Cormac's grandfather.

Cormac mac Airt . . . (Kormack mack Art) . . . Name, Cormac, son of Art.

crannóg . . . (Kran-nawg) . . . Special lake structure or man-made island, upon which are various dwellings; lake settlement.

Cred . . . (Creth) . . . Name – *D* in Old Irish is *Th*. From Creidné (Creth-nay or Creed-nay), goldsmith to the Tuatha De Danann.

Cromlach . . . (Krum-lough(loch) or Krum-a-lough) . . . Name.

Cruachu or Cruachan . . . (Kruah or Kru-an) . . . Place in west of Ireland where an idol of the god Crom Cruach (Krum Kruah) was erected.

Crom means *hunched* or *the bent one*.

Cruach means *peak* or *stack*.

cú . . . (Koo) . . . Hound, wolf or wild hound.

Dagda . . . (Dag-da) . . . Father of all gods.

Daire . . . (Dare) . . . Name; dair . . . oak.

Dairine . . . (Dare-een) . . . Name.

Danaan . . . *see* Tuatha de Danann.

delg . . . (Dell-ge) . . . Brooch or clasp, usually for fastening a cloak or mantle.

Devin . . . Pronounced as spelt . . . Name.

Donal Rua . . . (Dohn-all Roo-ah) . . . Name meaning Red Donal (usually referring to the colour of hair).

dreuth . . . thirst.

Dorcha . . . (Dorr-a-ha) . . . Name; dark.

Draoi . . . (Dra-oy) . . . Druid teachers.

Drui-én . . . (Drew-ehn) . . . Bird of the oak, the Druid bird, thought to have been a wren.

duir . . . (Doo-ear) . . . Oak tree (ogham) . . . dair . . . oak.

Dulem, Rig Na n-Dul . . . (Dool-em, Ree Nah-in-Dool) . . . Dulem, King of the elements.

Dún . . . (Doon) . . . Stronghold; fortified place.

Dún Hall . . . (Doon Hall) . . . Large meeting hall at the Dún.

Éiriú . . . (Aye-roo or Eh-roo) . . . Name for Ireland; a modern variation on this is Eirinn.

Emer . . . Pronounced as spelt, but the name derives from the older name Éimhear . . . (Ave-err).

Eógan . . . (Oogan) . . . Name.

faoi gheasa . . . (fa-ey gay-es) Under obligation.

feis . . . (Fesh) . . . Fair, festival.

Fergus . . . (Fair-gus) . . . Name.

Fert . . . (Fair-te) . . . Grave.

Fiachrae Cassán . . . (Fay-hra Cass-awn) . . . Name.

filé . . . (Feel-eh) . . . Poet who trains for twelve years; privileged poet.

Finann . . . Pronounced as spelt today, but the older name is pronounced Shin-ann. Slender vowel following *F* makes a *SH* sound.

findruine . . . (Shin-drew-een) . . . White bronze.

Fire of Dagda . . . Fire for the Father of all gods.

fire-wheel . . . A wheel of fire constructed at midsummer (summer solstice) and rolled down a steep hill as part of the sun ceremony and celebration.

gahbar . . . (Gavh-ar) . . . Goat.

gadhar . . . (Gaar) . . . Dog.

gessa or geas . . . (Gay-es) . . . Taboo; prohibition. Faoi Gheasa . . . under obligation.

gráinne . . . (Grawn-ye) . . . Name.

Í-Bhreasail . . . (Ee-Verr-asill, Ee-Ver-ra-sill) . . . Isle of the Blessed; a faery isle or an isle of souls, thought to have been somewhere off the west coast of Ireland, a place of no time where one became ever-young.

Imbolc . . . (Imm-bolk) . . . Festival for the dawning of spring when the ewes let down their milk for their lambs; when the Earth Mother makes the sap rise into the trees and plants to bring forth their blossom and leaves, returning the green to the earth after the long spell of winter; the awakening; the first of February; Candlemas.

kirtle . . . (Kirr-til) . . . Article of clothing.

Knocknarea . . . (Cnoc-na-ray) . . . Name of a mountain in Sligo where there was once a neolithic settlement. There is a cairn on top of this mountain borrowed by Queen Maev (Medb) for her burial tomb. The mountain is known as the Hill of Kings.

koad . . . (code) . . . Sacred grove, grove sacred for the dead.

Laighin . . . (Lie-on) . . . Old name for the district of Leinster in Ireland today.

Laighin Theas . . . (Lie-on Thee-as) . . . The south district of Leinster.

Lugaid . . . (Lu-ee or Louis) . . . Name.

Lúgh . . . (Lew) . . . Name of a god; Lúgh of the Long Arm.

Lúghnasadh . . . (Lew-na-saa) . . . Name of special harvest festival on the first of August, named after the god, Lúgh, a major Druid festival.

Lugnae Fer Trí . . . (Lew-nay Fer-T(h)ree) . . . Name.

Luis . . . (Lew-is) . . . Rowan tree (ogham).

Macha, Badb, Morrighan . . . (Ma-ha, Ba-ab, Morri-an) . . . Three names of the triple goddess, darker side of the Earth Mother.

Mag Muccrime . . . (Mag Muck-creem-ay) . . . Battle-plain where Art the Lonely fell.

máthair . . . (Maw-hir) . . . Mother.

Misha . . . Pronounced as spelt . . . Name; the old word for goat was Minseach (Min-cha).

mo chroí . . . (Mow Kree) . . . My heart, my pulse.

Mogh . . . (Maw) . . . Name of ruler of southern half of Ireland whom Conn slew in battle.

Mora nee Derga . . . Pronounced as spelt . . . Name . . . But the old Irish is Mora ní Derga, Mora, daughter of Derga.

Morann . . . (Mawr-ann) . . . Name.

niam-lann . . . (Ne-am Lann) . . . A band of metal worn around the forehead, usually of burnished gold.

óenach . . . (Oh-in-ah) . . . Ceremonial mantle for a king.

ogham . . . (Owmm or Om) . . . Tree alphabet, a form of writing making scratches and notches in stone or wood.

Olc Aiche . . . (Olkee) . . . Name.

ollam . . . (Oal-lam) . . . Fully-fledged poet who trains for twenty years; high rank poet.

Ollathair . . . (Oal-ah-hir) . . . All-father.

Phagos . . . (Faig-aus) . . . Beech tree (ogham).

ráth . . . (Raw) . . . A fort; a raised settlement.

rí . . . (Ree) . . . King.

saille . . . (Sal-ya) . . . Willow tree (ogham).

Samhain . . . (Sough-in or Sow-in) . . . This is the first day of winter, a special turning point of the Irish year; this festival is the old Celtic New Year, the first of November.

Scath . . . (Ska-ath) . . . Name.

scian . . . (Skee-ann) . . . Small sharp hunting knife.

seer . . . (See-er) . . . Someone who has a special gift of looking into the future or reading the minds of others.

sennight . . . (Se'en nite) . . . Seven nights; one week.

Serb . . . (Sir-ba) . . . Name.

sidh . . . (Shee) . . . Faery-folk; otherworld beings.

solstice . . . (Sauls-tiss) . . . Division of the year, when the sun is in a particular position in relation to the earth; the summer solstice is the longest day of the year, the winter solstice is the shortest day of the year; major festivals take place on these turning points which were sacred to the Druids.

straif . . . (Stray-if) . . . Blackthorn tree (ogham).

Tachta . . . (Taa-(h)ta) . . . Name.

Teamhair . . . (Tauw-er or Twaw-eor) . . . It is difficult to give the phonetics of this word. The initial *T* is a slender sound, so *Tower* is probably the nearest modern equivalent. The modern name for Teamhair is Tara, the place of the High Kings.

tinne/tine . . . (Teen) . . . Fire.

tuath . . . (Tua) . . . Territory (tribal).

Tuatha De Danann . . . (Too-ha-day-Dan-ann) . . . Name of a faery race who are tall and blond, mystical people with great spiritual powers who can slip in and out of the unseen world; people of Dana, Tribe of Danu.

Tula . . . (T(ch)oo-la) . . . Name.

uilleand . . . (Ool-lay-and) . . . Honeysuckle (ogham).

Varda . . . Pronounced as spelt . . . Covered wagon; traveller's cart (Romany).

NB Usually when an *H* appears in a word the consonant before the *H* renders the two letters silent, e.g. Bla*th* is pronounced *Bl-AW-*. *BH*, however, is pronounced as *V*, as in *Í-Bh*reasail . . . (ee-*v*err-asill).

# PROLOGUE

The *Ard Rígh*, the High King, Art mac Conn, the single one, the lonely one, remembered.

His memories burnt a dark hole like a gaping pit in his mind, and the white flesh on his arms quivered as he felt himself falling inwards, crumbling like stone to dust in an avalanche.

He tasted blood in his mouth, felt a warm, sticky fluid pour from his loins, and knew that the sickle of death had severed him. The Corn King was falling. Stains of crushed red poppies danced on his bare unblemished skin. The war-drum droned and thumped with his heartbeat.

"The *Ard Rígh* has fallen! He has fallen!"

He heard the flurry of feet and muffled shrieks echo in his head like bat-wings escaping into the night. The wild eyes of horses rolled in fright as their hoofs thundered, churning the ground, and still they tried not to trample the fallen men, their nostrils flaring at the sickening stench of battle-sweat and open wounds. A wolf howled. The raven cawed close by, startling Art the Lonely.

It reminded him of his father, Great Conn the warrior, Conn of a Hundred Battles, Conn of the wolf, Conn of the raven.

"The wolf runs with me, Art, and the raven flies over my head. They were there at my birthing and they will also be there at my passing over. Where I am, they are, and where they are, so am I. Remember that, Art."

His father, Conn, who had ruled the northern half of Éiriú for so long, had slain Mogh, ruler of the southern half. Conn had, by unfair means, attacked Mogh in the dead of night before the battle-day. Out of remorse, he had given his daughter Sabia in marriage to Mogh's son. So Éiriú had been united by the merging of families and peace had ruled until Conn was assassinated at his home in Teamhair. He was long gone, but Art felt he was here with him now. He could smell him in the peat of the earth, in the blood of the battle. Had the Great Conn not always smelt of the battle-blood in his comings and in his goings, that sickly-sweet smell that Art had always hated?

He felt his body heaving and tried to get rid of it but it welled into his throat and invaded his nostrils like something unwanted and yet familiar. He had suffered the same scents when his two brothers had been slain by his uncles. Conn had told him then that his favourite brother had sailed away to Í-Bhreasail, the land of spirits, to live with the Faeries, and so he would never return.

Art's companions from that day onwards were desolation and loneliness. He preferred his own company, spoke little and thought a lot, so earning him the name of Art the Lonely.

He spat the red sweetness from his mouth like a fountain and knew that the stain on the earth was the well-spring of his being. He cast his gods away from him.

"Not now . . . I am not prepared," he muttered, glad that his head was still with his body . . . his nephew, Lugaid Laga mac Conn, son of his sister, Sabia, had not taken it for his belt yet.

Art moaned and thought of his sister. Was Sabia aware that her own son, Lugaid, had just taken her brother's right to life and the rulership of Éiriú? Art did not want to accept his defeat yet. No, there was more to think through. He had to resolve it before his gods came for him and he passed over.

Delv, his wife, loomed into his mind, beautiful Delv, whose hand he took, despite the knowledge that her mother, the sorceress, would die at their coupling. Harsh was the cruel laughter of the sorceress, like the cackle of the black crow, before she was slain, but her last terrible curse remained with them. Delv did not fall with child, not with his anyway.

Art shook his head to take away the loud ringing, no longer the clash of iron swords and spears, but a gong of iron against the anvil. And so he remembered the Druid smith, Olc Aiche, with whom he had spent his last nights before this terrible battle; Olc Aiche, the Druid Elder, who made him drink the milk.

"By what sorcery?" he had murmured, knowing as he drank

the milk that it had that strange taste, not unlike the sacred well of blood within his throat now.

He had first seen her standing by the byre. She was Achtán, daughter of Olc Aiche, and she was the most breathtakingly beautiful young woman he had ever set eyes upon, even fairer in face than Delv. Her hair, black as soot, trailed to her ankles, and catching her gaze was like falling into a sea of clear blue water, drowning, drowning.

Her pail was overflowing with the creamy after-milk strippings she gathered for her father each night.

Art's servant had asked her for a drink.

"Who seeks the drink?" she said, her voice like the song of a bird, her cheeks flushed, pink petals of a wild rose.

"Art, son of Conn, *Ard Rígh* of Éiriú," answered the servant.

"Let one of you come to carry it," she said, dimpling merrily.

No one could lift it. She carried it on her own and offered it to them. Art drank it. The others refused.

The servant caught the girl's arm.

"Fortune would be propitious if you would but give yourself to the King."

"I am unable to do that," she murmured, her eyes bright, "but if you will wait, my father will listen to your request."

Olc Aiche had come in, looking for his drink. He demanded his milk. She filled the vessel with new milk.

"This is my vessel but the first milk is not here. This is not my milk. Where is it?"

The girl informed him of what she had done and repeated the request of the servant.

"What did Art's servant convey to you, daughter?" he asked, surprised.

"He said to me: 'Fortune would be propitious if you would but lie with the King.' "

Olc Aiche had then stared at them in such a way that their spirits trembled within.

"It were better," said he, "that you went with him, Achtán."

"I should like that too, if you but approve, Father." And Achtán's eyes had swept boldly and appraisingly over Art, so that his body began to shake with desire for her.

"Good will come of it," said Olc Aiche. "Save what you bear he will leave no progeny, and the progeny that you bear will be Kings of Éiriú until doomsday. Let a feast be prepared by you for the *Ard Rígh* and his men and for his ally Eógan and his men, to wit: fifty oxen, fifty boars, five thousand loaves, and fifty vats of wine. Give him, in addition to them, fifty horse bridles and fifty cows."

On the morrow, the girl Achtán went with fifty other girls and distributed the milk and food to Art and to Eógan, his ally.

Special chambers were set up and tented around, hidden from the others. And Achtán had the will to sleep with the *Ard Rígh*, Art the Lonely. And the Druidess, Monchae, with Eógan. There was no resistance.

Art tasted the sweetness on his lips again and this time it was the soft honeyed kiss from the gentle lips of Achtán, her hair falling like a shadow upon him, and the shadow of his own death looming there also.

He sighed and the sound of her laboured breath whispered in his ear, the gasps of his own dying, being at one with her.

The beauty of her pale flesh melting under his own weight pierced him, so that his heart pained with an exquisite ecstasy. He knew that the spawn he spilled was going to be his last. His mouth was unsealed and words, the secrets he had told to no other, were unleashed into her.

She had been stirred then, weeping silently at his words, and somehow he felt that the knowledge he gave her had gone with his seed, embedding itself deep within her, to grow for another day, a day he knew was gone for himself.

"The progeny you will bear will be Kings of Éiriú until doomsday." Olc Aiche's voice hummed to the sound of the war-drum.

"He is going to Í-Bhreasail! The *Ard Rígh* has fallen!"

Someone beside him was sobbing. Art forced himself to turn his head. His eyes fell on the dark curls of the minstrel who had flung himself upon the battlefield beside him and was smearing the blood of his king over his face. The strings of the harp slung across the boy's back rang out discordantly like the sounds of women weeping and keening.

Art waited, but still his gods did not come.

"No! No!" wailed the boy.

Art followed the petrified gaze of the minstrel, and, looking up, caught the eyes of Lugaid mac Conn, his own nephew. Lugaid was wielding a battle axe, swung high above him, glinting in the sun, a shaft of light that spun and froze upon the bloodied blade as it descended.

The shadow was black, like the long dark hair of Achtán, and Art closed his eyes at last and let her image swim before him. So this was the shadow of death. He had known it. Had he not slipped the gold thumb-ring off his hand and given it to Achtán? She had laughed as it rolled between them off her tiny white thumb and on to her belly.

"It will belong to him one day!" she whispered, as she stroked her belly, her dimples like crescent moons upon her face.

He grabbed her to him suddenly, overcome with her charm and aware of his own sadness in the knowledge that he would never see his only child. Her response was immediate, soft and caring, full of gentle passion, her lips yielding against his own, the tip of her tongue, feather-soft, teasing his mouth.

"My father will care for the ring for him, Art Aenfar," she had murmured. "And our gods will look after you."

He inhaled her breath, the fragrant breeze of summer flowers.

"I answer only to one god, above all others, being of them and encompassing them all." He had said this into her hair, pulling it across his face, winding it around his neck. "Achtán, my love, I surrender myself to him and if this be indeed my last night, I will be embraced by him and do my duty for him."

This terrible secret had aroused a passion in her that caused her to cling to his white, muscular body. With awe, she realized that she, alone, held the heart and mind of the *Ard Rígh* within her own mind, and now, part of his spirit within her body. She knew him, above all other men, in one brief, loving encounter before the biggest battle of his life. She wanted him to know everything about herself, but her secrets were small.

"I have been in fosterage with a clan in the West. I will not take the vows of the Druidess," she said shyly. "My name there is Gráinne, and a Druid hermit is giving me the sacred teachings of the gods but I have not heard him speak of one god above all others. His wisdom is not of the King and an Ard Rígh utters a Truth surely."

Art the Lonely remembered this, felt a blackness engulf him and then, suddenly, he was free, running with the wolf, the wings of the raven flapping above his head, rushing, rushing across plains and fields. There was Teamhair, his beloved home! He was going fast, faster than the wind, running with the wolf towards the sun, Achtán's small feet chasing him, her tinkling laughter like a song in his head. He heard bells and drums and the clang of the great anvil and then, there it was . . . the sea and the island of light shimmering upon it . . . Í-Bhreasail . . . the land of his god. A great joy and peace came upon him as he ran towards the light to merge with it, the sound of the anvil far behind him. He knew she stood on the shore, her feet wet with the lapping waters, her hair caressing her ankles, and within her belly the tiny seed of life, that part of himself which would grow and flourish again to have what was rightfully his. And the wolf sat beside her. And the raven perched upon her shoulder.

Lugaid mac Conn kicked the weeping boy aside.

"Nay! Do not slay the little minstrel! It will be an ill deed!" yelled Dadera, one of Lugaid's Druids. But Lugaid did not, or chose not, to hear.

His battle axe, already bloodied from the slaying of the *Ard Rígh* and countless others, now sliced through the strings of the harp and the boy's back as one, stilling their voices for ever.

His other hand swung down to grab the long pale curls of Art the Lonely. Bellowing a great harsh laugh that drowned the last echo of the broken harp, he hoisted the dripping, severed head into the air and then tied the hair on to his belt. His prize. Cheers rang out from his allies and they flung themselves at his feet.

"Hail the new *Ard Rígh* of Éiriú! Hail Lugaid Laga, Lugaid mac Conn!" they shouted as one.

Lugaid limped, another new wound upon an old, back to his chariot, an imperfect king, going to claim Teamhair for his own after a long exile from these shores. No good could come of it . . . no good at all.

# THE SEERS

# CHAPTER 1

# KNOCKNAREA

*As the earth breathes, so do we.*
*As the fire leaps, so do we.*
*As the water flows, so do we.*
*As the air swirls, so do we.*

Gráinne pushed back her wild hair, black as sloe, black as the deadly night-berries. She twisted it into a thick coil and tied it in a knot which she knew would not hold for long. It was too heavy and sleek. She hurried on her way up the mountain, her feet stumbling into natural spring outlets and sometimes into the pinched imprints of goats' hoofs in mud. Her woven linen tunic was not going to stay clean at this rate but she didn't think that Cromlach would mind that, or even notice, or care; such was the way of Cromlach.

Cromlach had exiled himself from the tribe long ago and also from the Druid Elders more recently, much to their surprise. No one knew the exact reason for his chosen hermitage and even the poets had kept quiet about it. For several seasons he had disappeared into the deep forest and no one knew if he had managed to survive the last fierce winter.

In the springtime, Finann the goat-herd had discovered his dwelling half-way up Knocknarea Mountain, where a multitude of spirits was known to reside. At the top of the mountain there was a huge cairn built of stones, each one of which had been carried up from the valley. Finann had told Gráinne that each stone on the cairn had been carried up there by the Elders to mark the passing over of someone in the settlement, but that it had been done for centuries before. He had taken her breath away when he had told her that he had heard Queen Maev was

3

buried in the tomb and that it was now sealed, away from prying eyes.

Gráinne had never been to the cap of Knocknarea but she knew in her heart that one day she would be able to go up there. The Druids guarded it fiercely as their own, not with any visible malice or laws but with an unspoken force. The Elders had adopted it for most of their sacred rites and the people were unable to go beyond the Hill of the Well, which was the green mound covered in mists, the last step of the mountain before the steep incline that led to the cairn. The Druids called it the Hill of Mists. There was a sacred well here with healing waters. Cromlach had his dwelling near by, it was said.

"He is like the Guardian of the Well now," thought Gráinne, "and the Keeper of the Stones."

She stopped to regain her breath.

"Wind, give me air," she gasped, putting her head down to her knees to expel her ragged breath and then stretching up to the sky to inhale deeply of the crisp breeze.

She gazed back along the path she had trodden and marvelled at the sudden turning of the path into a trickling stream at the bottom. Most people would not venture walking upstream to join a pathway which was pitted with holes and which disappeared at random in the stepped hills of the mountain. Only those with determination and the spirit of will or madness would get as far as she was now, and certainly no woman who was with child would attempt such a climb.

Gráinne felt the butterfly-flutter within her and she smiled warmly, her hands covering her belly protectively.

"Only a little way now and we shall see Cromlach. He will tell me all about you."

She glanced at the Dún below, the turf-sod huts and the few structured *bothán s* strung together like round beads on a circular necklace, small, far away. Spirals of pale grey smoke tainted the reddening sky.

"A red sun to bed and a clear day to rise," whispered Gráinne as she picked her way carefully up the next leg of the mountain.

A thin, shredded mist came swirling towards her at eye level, startling her as her eyes struggled against the glare of it. It seemed to pass through her in layers so that even when she moved forward she felt like she was standing still or about to fall backwards. She blinked the moisture from her eyes like glistening teardrops and felt her heart begin to thud. A chill tugged at her spine, washing her with her own fear, and she wanted to run. These were the spirit mists, the veils that sheltered her from, and invited her to, that other world. Her mind struggled against the horror that threatened to envelop her and she caught her breath sharply when she saw a cowled figure crouching on the ground, peering at something in front of him. He was still some distance away but he looked haunched and old, not at all like Cromlach. She turned to flee and froze instantly, fear now charging through her veins. Before her stalked a wolf, one of the biggest she had ever seen, his amber eyes glowing through the sheets of hovering mist. He must have been tailing her. She stared back at him, unreasonable anger welling up to override her terror. Her blue eyes pierced his yellow as he padded to a stop, suddenly unsure of her. His hackles rose on his neck.

Gráinne was rooted to the ground. The wolf bared his teeth in a low snarl but she remained still, her heart drumming loudly and painfully. She was angry that she should be confronted by a wolf now when she was with child. He was a deadly threat to her unborn. She would fight him with her will. She would bite and claw him to the death if he as much as breathed on her.

His gaze wavered and his eyes screwed up suddenly as he sniffed the air. He sat down abruptly, threw his head back and howled, a long mournful wail.

She started to shake, suddenly weak, her strength crumbling, then she almost leapt out of her skin when an answering howl echoed right behind her.

A voice spoke hoarsely and she cried out with relief when she heard Cromlach's deep, rasping tones.

"Do not look around, Gráinne. Back towards me slowly. Do not take your eyes off the wolf. Slowly now, slowly."

She nodded and backed up the hill as slow as she dared. Another howl from the wolf rang out over the mountain, causing her spine to tingle and Cromlach answered the call yet again, this time closer to her.

"Come, c'mon, you're close by me, slowly, slowly, there . . . there."

His arm touched her shoulder and as they made contact, the wolf suddenly turned tail and ran back down the hill as if he'd had a sudden fright himself.

Gráinne collapsed against the old man, burying her head in his long woven cloak. The smell of turf and gorse engulfed her, evoking familiar memories of his old wattle *bothán*, dried herbs and roots hanging from the eaves, clay pots full of potions and broths always on the boil, sods of turf burning slowly on his hearthstone making one pine for the comforts of a wise man's fireside.

"I've missed you, Cromlach," she whispered. "We've all missed you."

He was not listening. His eyes stared down the hillside, following the path of the wolf. His ears listened intently to the noises around him. His mind swept the countryside searching for an answer. So far from the forest, why had the wolf ventured so far from the forest and so far from the lower pastures on the mountain where Finann had the goats? He tried to blend his mind with the wolf's but he could not, not when Gráinne was holding on to him, not when her emotions were calling him for response. He had seen the tracks of the wolf earlier, near his dwelling by the well, and the tracks crisscrossed and backtracked each other. The animal had been pacing back and forth, watching, waiting, waiting for something. For Gráinne? Why Gráinne?

Cromlach stared at the upturned fresh face of the young woman and saw the tumbling dark hair like a river rolling over gleaming black rocks as her knot undid itself. He peered into her eyes, blue as the still pond reflecting the sky, blue as ice-crystals in winter at the top of the mountain and he knew. Suddenly, he knew. Only a woman with child had that simple clarity in her gaze, that snowy glass in the whites of her eyes and that anger that had rooted her to the spot, in a moment of danger, to face the wolf. He had watched her bristle with the wolf. Of course. Only a mother shielding her child or her unborn baby would react with that fierce, protective spirit he had seen in her.

"You are with child." His voice was a statement, spoken not with a reprimand or a proud indulgence in his own keen perception but with the directness of truth. Had she not believed she was with child, she would have nodded anyway, knowing he was right. Cromlach was always right.

He was silent, contemplative, then he drew his cloak around her just as she shivered slightly in the evening air. He guided her wordlessly through the last veil of mist. As the air cleared she saw the tyings of cloth and bits of flapping rag that covered a bush by the well. This was the healing well, visited by pilgrims once a year who traipsed up the mountain, led by the Elders, to partake of the waters. They passed it and Gráinne bowed her head reverently to the spirit of the well, then she was led into the tiny *bothán* near by, Cromlach's home from home.

There was a large flat smooth hearthstone inside. She wondered where he had found that on the grassy mountain which had great elbows of rock jutting out at peculiar angles every so often, no smaller flat stones in sight. He could not have carried the stone all the way up here. Then she remembered about the cairn of stones at the top.

As if he had read her thoughts he said: "It was the only stone there without a voice, the only one the wind did not whistle to or the spirits whisper with and it rolled freely down the mountain, glad to feel the fire again," Cromlach smiled, "as I will too, some day."

"You mean you will return?" Gráinne was excited but he caught her hands and rubbed them between his coarse brown fingers, gently massaging some warmth into them. Turning away from her abruptly, he threw a turf and some bracken on the fire and it crackled into life.

"Not yet, not until your son is born."

"That long?"

"That long."

"A son?"

"Yes, a son."

7

Gráinne closed her eyes happily for a moment, visualizing a little boy kicking his sturdy legs and smiling at her. She let the vision linger, hesitant to let it go.

"Will you *see* for me, Cromlach?"

He nodded, only too willing to do so, now that they had encountered the wolf. He wanted to know himself who this child was. There was something very special about him for such a strong totem to make itself known so early in child-growing.

"You have had a fright, *a stór*, so we will eat and we will sleep," he said. "You cannot return down the mountain tonight. Finann will go with you tomorrow, especially with this wolf about. We will see to the other matter at dawn. I have to prepare some things. Now tell me of my people, the *tuath*. Finann does not have the tongue of a woman nor a flair for observation of people. His mind is only for his goats, so I know nothing. Tell me it all, Gráinne, and leave none of it out."

As Cromlach prepared a broth for them both from the new shoots and the last of the winter root-vegetables, Gráinne made some flat quern breads from the sack of meal kept near the hearth. The meal was warm and dry. It felt like coarse grains of sand and looked not much different. She found the goat's milk in a stone-lipped vessel immersed in a wooden pail of water. The water was as cold as a mountain stream and kept the milk from curdling. Her hands deftly worked the cornmeal with the milk into a sticky dough, then she soaked some dried berries in the water to soften them and added them to the dough for sweetness. Her fingers pressed and rolled, turning and tossing the dough with some finer corn until it was nearly pliable. She then flattened it out in a crude circle and threw it on a flat griddle iron which Cromlach placed over the fire.

As she did this, her voice chattered incessantly about the settlement and the Dún. Cromlach placed the black pot of broth on the side of the hearth, then he used some smith's iron tongs to grope in the flames for a warming stone. He placed the smooth, round stone in the broth to keep it hot.

"We have a new goldsmith and Lugnae says he is the best metal-artificer yet. We are so fortunate to have a king like Lugnae Fer Trí. He fostered me and now he has fostered the boy. His name is Cred and he is also staying at the Dún and his workings in gold have surpassed everything we've ever had before . . . anything I have ever seen before, even better than my fa – but I shouldn't say that, or even think it."

"You are not being disloyal to your father, *a stór*. He is a very fine smith, one of the best in the land, a better *céird* there has not been than Olc Aiche but each kingdom has its own best metal-artificer and now in Lugnae's kingdom we have a challenge for the others. It keeps the standards high, Gráinne, and the spirits true to the craft. Let it be. Now, this Cred, what favours his face? Is he dark or fair?"

Cromlach was curious. A smith with such an aptitude for the crafting of metal did not appear every day and certainly not at the court of Lugnae. He was more likely to be farmed out to Teamhair to serve his fosterage in the *Ard Rígh*'s household if he indeed did possess such a talent. He must have served an apprenticeship with a smith such as Olc Aiche and there were few Druid smiths in the land as talented as Gráinne's own father. It was said that even the *Ard Rígh*, the High King, did not have a *céird* as good as Olc Aiche. Was it possible that Cred the boy had had his training in secret or that he was sent to Lugnae in preparation for some event, sent by the Elders or the Tuatha De Danann themselves? Why? Cromlach had no answer to the stirrings of his own mind.

"He is tall for his age and fair. His skin is as pale as milk, his hair as burnished as corn and his eyes are as grey as a thunderstorm, but he does not talk much and although he has a pleasant enough way about him, he does not appear to befriend one easily. He ignores me, save to nod in the morn when I walk by the forge or to say: 'It looks like rain,' or some such thing. He has a gift for reading the sky, so Lugnae says."

"And he would know, of course," said Cromlach glibly. Gráinne looked up quickly, sensing some sort of emotion searing through Cromlach. She was surprised. It was not at all like the old man to give away his feelings or to stand in judgement of anyone either by thought or deed. Their eyes met and he could not face that blue honesty comfortably. She had always had a way of cutting through to his innermost feelings. He busied himself with ladling out the broth into two horn bowls and handing one to her.

"Let us sup, *a stór*, and partake of the bread before we lay our heads down. The morrow will be here soon enough."

# CHAPTER 2

# CROMLACH'S VISIONS

*I've seen you where you never were
And where you never will be;
And yet within that very place
You can be seen by me.*

The night descended upon Knocknarea in a blanket of black stillness.

Only the soft sighs of Gráinne's breath disturbed the inner peace of the *bothán*.

Cromlach sat in front of the foundering fire and stacked it up with the dry grass-sod and bracken twigs. It flew and sparked into life again and he gazed into the flames, hot, searing, licking flames. He saw the lolling tongue of the wolf, the yellow dancing eyes, the grey bracken fur and he caught and held the image until his eyes hurt from the strain. He blinked and his gaze wandered over to the girl, curled up in the woollen plaid covers he had draped over her. He studied her face. Her eyelids flickered as she delved into some wayward dream. She stirred slightly but was too far enveloped in her sleep to wake up.

He wondered about her, about the coming child and about her family so far away. He had been gone for at least three *Samhains*, and missed the spectacular celebrations for the turn of the year now, on these three occasions. He had seen the beacons flaring on the distant hills and knew that the Elders had lit a fire above him at the Cairn.

The last winter was the coldest yet, the biting winds and snowdrifts having been a hardship to sorely overcome. He almost starved. Had it not been for the old stray deer conveniently meeting his death in the jaws of a hungry wolf at his door, he, himself, would surely have passed over. The gods were generous

11

to him then, even though the meat was tough and lean, but the small amount of fat gave him the strength he needed to survive. The wolf had not devoured all of the deer and Cromlach often wondered why.

He missed no one from the tribe but Gráinne. She was always very special to him, from the first day she arrived, escorted by Olc Aiche, her stern father, smith and Druid chieftain from Cruachu. It was the custom for children to enter fosterage and be schooled in the arts and crafts of other tribes. Royal children, nobles' and chieftains' children were given a special place at the settlements they were farmed to, as was Gráinne in the Dún.

Her eyes had gazed fearfully around the waiting throng when she arrived. She directed the blue challenging surveillance at all of them and when her eyes rested on himself, he had the distinct sensation of both falling and being uplifted at the same time. She was definitely her father's daughter, possessing the ability of touching one's soul and discerning one's character with one sweeping look. She had the way of the Druid.

Her smile, faint and tremulous, only for him, had made his old heart tug painfully with her pain, his mind absorbing her fear as he watched her take leave of her father, tears dropping silently off her dark eyelashes. The tough Olc Aiche was visibly moved.

"Her name is Achtán," he had said, "but from now on, she shall be known as Gráinne."

As he spoke, he dropped three grains on the earth in front of Lugnae Fer Trí, her new foster father, and then he ground them into the dirt with his feet.

No one would have dared to go against his workings and from that day onwards she was known as Gráinne.

Cromlach watched the three corn-grasses grow from the earth, sprouting tall from the place where the grains were planted by the feet of the Druid. One night, he collected all the offspring grains and burnt the grasses before anyone really took any notice.

Each day was a joy then to Cromlach. Gráinne treated him like a substitute father, much to the chagrin of Lugnae, her foster-father. Cromlach taught her as much as he dared, about the trees, the *ogham* writing, the plants, the herbs, the stars, the ways her own father would have shown her. It broke his heart when he knew he had to leave, but he did not want to think about that now.

Now, the light of the fire formed black shadows within the *bothán* and Cromlach felt it was time.

He fingered his totem bag which hung from the side of his long kilt. Opening the bag, he shook out some of the grains carefully from their resting place within. Various precious stones and a small serpent wood-carving also spilled out. He placed the precious objects on a stretch of smooth pale linen that he unfolded and laid out in front of him.

Somehow, he knew when he had carefully collected the grains that he would have a use for them one day. There was a secret somewhere, something Olc Aiche had known would occur, something the Druid smith saw in his own divinations. That day he had thrown the grains down and trampled them into the ground, he must have known that only another Druid would have realized what he had done. The planting of seeds at the change of one's name was a very powerful magic. The girl's destiny was contained in the offspring seeds of the growth, and only a Druid *seer* who had witnessed the event would be able to read them. Olc Aiche knew that he, Cromlach, was an Elder and he must have seen the smile that had passed between Gráinne and himself, must have felt the healing when the pain had been absorbed, must have deigned it so that, although it appeared to everyone that Gráinne was being passed into the protection of Lugnae, it was obvious that the keeper and care-taker of her destiny was to be Cromlach himself.

Cromlach stripped off his top and reached for a small dark bottle, one of his most prized possessions. He poured the oil from it on to his palm. The well of pungent liquid in his hand emitted a woodland scent that permeated the *bothán*. The red woody night-berries had been picked when the leaves just started to fall from the trees, before the winter had begun. The little purple flowers with their yellow eyes and red berries were grow-ing profusely then. He always loved the smell of the berries after they had been squashed and left to soak in the oil for several months in the dark. It increased their potency.

He slapped the well of oil on to his chest, massaging it thoroughly into his body, then he poured out some more to rub on to his arms. There was a thin residue of dirt left on his body, in fine ridges, after he finished the process. He wiped himself down with a wet cloth. The essence of the berries had already filtered through his seven layers of skin to reach his spirit. He waited, anticipation overriding any thoughts or misgivings about what he might be doing. Meanwhile, he set a pot of water on to boil and dropped the few precious grains into it to cook.

The first wave of fatigue swept over him but he fought it with all his mental energy and strong will-power. It was imperative that he did not give in to sleep. Sleep was a very dangerous enemy after he absorbed the berries.

His heart began to slow down, pumping gently in a steady rhythm. He felt his fingers begin to cool and his toes were already tingling with the cold draught which was starting to sweep over his body. He knew that he would experience several of these before the real effects would hit him. He hoped she would not awaken but it was essential that the corn be ready to eat before the paralysis seized him. For once, he was unsure of his timing.

Several long moments crept by as the chills chased one another down his spine. The water was boiling fiercely. He stretched across the world, it seemed, to swing the iron griddle below the pot and to cover the cooking corn with a lid. Several more long moments trailed away. He shivered now uncontrollably. Wrapping himself in his plaid was of no use, his teeth still chattered, his mind was encased in ice. He willed the simmering pot to soften the corn quickly. Shadows deepened around him and different colours began to float before his eyes. The lid stopped popping; the moisture had boiled away and was absorbed by the corn. It was ready. He could hardly move, everything spun in slow, slow motion. He swung the griddle iron off the fire. The pot tumbled but the lid did not fly off. To spill the grain now would have been a terrible omen for Gráinne. He had to be mindful. Righting the pot, he prised the lid off

14

with his hand wrapped in a corner of his plaid. He was no longer aware of hot or cold but he knew he must feed the fire, so he threw on some more turf and sticks with his other hand, then he poured the softened grains, some of which had turned into gruel, into his clay bowl, careful not to drop even the tiniest amount. There was no time to cool it down. He would have to sup it hot and chew it well. Maybe some water would help but he could not test nor measure heat any longer.

It tasted like hundreds of spiders' webs in his mouth as he chewed and rolled the gruel around. He sipped some water and it felt like smooth liquid glass bubbling down his throat. He stuffed the rest of the mixture into him as there was not much time to lose, cleaning the bowl with a horn knife made for just such a purpose, and then licking every scrap up off the sides to make sure that none was left.

The bowl fell from his hands as a sudden, vivid flare of purple flame filled his head cleanly. He pulled the warm plaid around his shoulders and fell to the side of the fire. Curling into the position of a child within the womb, he prepared to face whatever truth revealed itself beyond the purple veil. His vision was not long in coming to him.

A young man lay sleeping, his golden hair curling in spirals on his brow. Beside him lay a heavy sword beautifully wrought by a *Danann* smith, on his hand a gold ring glowed warmly, the finest yellow sun-gold from Laighin Theas, and across his body was the ceremonial *óenach* garb, purple raiment of the finest quality, as only befits the *Ard Rígh*, the High King of Ireland.

Cromlach studied the vision and was reluctant to let it go. He became aware of a strong white bull, the biggest, most magnificent beast he had ever seen. It took his breath away. The bull was in the room with the young man. These were surely not mortal beings he was seeing. A sound of deep chanting filled his ears and he saw four robed Elders spinning their enchantment over the sleeping youth. One of them he recognized as an Arch-Druid, dressed in a splendid saffron raw-silk garment, complete with cowl. They all had pale yellow haloes shimmering around their bodies and as they moved in unison, drawing spirals with their hands above the body, Cromlach thought he had never witnessed such a sacred ceremony before. As quickly as the vision came, it left, and Cromlach tumbled into a dark tunnel, coughing and choking back to consciousness again. He sat up suddenly, back in his *bothán*, back beside the sleeping Gráinne. A grain of the corn was somehow back in his mouth again, regurgitated because of his choking. He chewed and chewed. Somehow the taste was different, not quite so bland, a little sweeter perhaps.

This time, a vivid green field descended before his eyes, so verdant that he could smell the fresh grass, see the wind shake the green stalks, and he could almost touch the three-leafed clovers that grew in bunches between the grasses. A woman ran across the field, stumbling, weeping, clutching something in her hands. She was keening and lamenting, her hair cut off into long black strands which she gripped tightly in her white fists, her mourning cutting through the air like the slice of a sword, her tears gushing like a spring-well on the mountainside.

As Cromlach observed the woman, he thought she was familiar to him. He saw her enter a room full of flax, wherein stood a large spinning wheel. Astounded, he watched as she fed the strands of her hair along with the flax strands and spun the finest linen threads, then she fed those on to the wheel with the most beautiful raw-silk fibres he had ever seen. All the time, her tears fell as she worked, wetting the threads with her sorrow.

Her shorn head was now covered with a roll of linen, wrapped around several times. The scene changed and she was weaving a garment, a cloak of such dimensions as would be an ample cover for a babe, a splendid cloak for a child and a beautiful *kirtle* or cape for a young man. Her undying love was now woven and stitched into it along with her hair and the result was breathtaking.

He then saw the woman, in the garb of a Druidess, take the vows of separation from, and protection of, the tribe. She was accepted by the Elders and known as *the dark one*, but always she cared for the one she had made the precious garment for and always she remembered him until her dying gasps.

Cromlach felt the welling bitter-sweet taste in his throat and tumbled into the dark tunnel, once again choking for breath.

He emerged from the second vision exhausted but knew that when a third grain of corn came back into his mouth, ready for chewing, he would have to brace himself for another journey.

His body felt ice-cold and he tried to huddle nearer the fire but the frozen seizure was already creeping over him. He could not even reach out to feed the flames with a new turf-sod, could no longer sit up nor look to check if Gráinne was asleep or awake. His mind drifted into pitch black this time, a roaring, turbulent cauldron of darkness. Pain seared into his throat and through his chest and he tried to call out but in vain. No word could he utter, no sound at all could he make. He just had to go with the pain and hope it would pass soon. It cut him like a knife so that he thought his gullet was being ripped out. It was excruciating and the visions that came with it were disturbing. He saw a fish, hooked by the throat, flailing and fighting for its life, a fine silver salmon of mammoth proportions, the same which would be served to the *Ard Rígh*.

He saw the Arch-Druid of the province of Laighin and knew him from there because of the blue-green *kirtle* he wore on his robe. The man was pulling the salmon from the River Boyne and he heard the mutterings of the dark enchantment the Elder wove on the salmon. The fish fought with all its power, leaping upstream against the rapids, trying to shake off the curse upon it, until, unable to resist the Druid's will any longer, it succumbed and died.

Cromlach gasped with the salmon, then he saw the *scian* in the hand of the Elder, saw the gleaming, golden blade of the knife as it sliced through the belly of the fish, the sliver of bone that the Druid sliced off the backbone and reinserted into the flesh of the fish, at a peculiar angle to the other bones, and saw how he then sealed the fish by knitting the paper-thin scales together once more with his incantations. The salmon was then taken to the dwelling of Cleitech on the Boyne, where the King, now an old man, sat writing laboriously, his hands gnarled and white, his hair long and pale like gold and silver threads curling down his back and through his beard. Cromlach struggled to warn him, tried to cry out as the old man stretched for the freshly cooked fish that was served to him on a beautiful gold platter, but he could not stop him. He could see that the man had only one eye, one eye of the most piercing blue. As Cromlach stared at the eye, he knew suddenly that the King was no longer the *Ard Rígh*. No one who was imperfect or blemished in any way could hold the title of High Kingship any longer. He also remembered where he had seen that blue before, his beautiful Gráinne had eyes just such as that, and as he stared, he suddenly saw the light go out of the eye, the life-light drain away and Cromlach himself was choking with the well of exquisite sweetness that spread into his own throat. It was like nectar of the first honey of the bees at Teamhair, like a child's first smile, like a first kiss, like everything sacred and healing. His pain subsided as quickly as it had engulfed him but he lay, unable to move with the sadness and intensity of the last vision.

Just as he thought he had experienced the third and final vision, he began to feel a stray grain on his tongue again. He struggled against it but it was persistent, almost with a life of its own, moving around in his mouth. He tried to open his mouth to spit it out, afraid to undertake another journey but his lips were sealed tight. This time a wonderful golden amber filled his head. He sank into it and became swallowed up as if into a honeycomb. It was warm and inviting and he had no fear. There were no dark tunnels, everything was bathed in this glorious, golden light. He felt himself soothed by it, suspended in it and cared for, a great peace wrapped up in his mind, protecting him from the world, and Cromlach knew this was a healing given by the gods. His aches and pains disappeared as he surrendered himself completely. He could have been there for moments or for eternity, it didn't much matter, it seemed all the same; and as he came out of it reluctantly, he could have sworn he saw the same amber eyes of a wolf staring at him, smiling at him, looking at him in adoration, much as the look one would have from a pet hound. He swore the wolf lay down at his feet, laid its head upon its front paws and went quietly to sleep.

The night slipped away silently. Cromlach slumbered deeply, curled beside the fire in his plaid, and Gráinne did not stir until

18

the fingers of the dawn stole into the *bothán*. Outside the *bothán*, the lone wolf stretched himself and bounded off down the mountain, his vigil over.

# CHAPTER 3

# CROMLACH SCRIES

*Let him magnify Truth, it will magnify him.*
*Let him strengthen Truth, it will strengthen him.*
*Let him preserve Truth, it will preserve him.*
*Let him exalt Truth, it will exalt him.*


Gráinne awoke first and busied herself immediately. First, she went outside the *bothán* and stretched her body, then went a little way behind the dwelling to relieve herself. There was a large wooden ewer left outside which was designed to catch rainwater and she slapped some of the cool water on her face and scooped a little over her hands and arms. She would bathe later when she returned to the Dún.

A small kick within her reminded her that she was not alone and also that it was time for breaking the night's fast. She smiled to herself. Today was the day Cromlach would *see* for her. She would have some of her child's destiny revealed for her. She knew there was still a lot she had to tell Cromlach about her own travels, about the visit home she had had during the time of his hermitage and about the father of her child. It was a sad time for her when Cromlach suddenly decided to leave the Dún. Her foster-father, Lugnae, had been angry and distraught when she sobbed every day; in desperation, when her sullenness had continued, he arranged for her to return to her own father's house for a time, even though preparations were taking place for the battle of Mag Muccrime, near her homeplace of Cruachu. After the battle she had been sent back to the Dún of Lugnae and for a time she tried to find out where Cromlach was but no one had known. Now, having found him through Finann, she had no intention of ever losing him again.

She went inside to feed the fire, the last remnants of red-glowing ashes still with enough light in them to flare up again. Thankfully, Cromlach had not smoored the ashes last night but it did seem that he had been cooking whilst she slept. He must have been hungry in the night, the pot smelt like it had been used for grains. There was another scent lingering in the air that puzzled her, a musky smell that was pleasant but unusual. It permeated the plaid that wrapped Cromlach, her own clothing, and just about everything else within the small space. She knew it had not been there before she fell to sleeping, neither had the dark glass bottle. This was something one did not see often but some instinct stopped her from touching it, yet she knew that the strange scent had something to do with it. Maybe it was a herb concoction, a special medicine that Cromlach used. She did not recognize the smell.

Bunches of dried leaves, strung together with grass plaits, hung from the wicker and thatch inside the *bothán* roof. She rubbed some of the leaves between her finger and thumb, then sniffed at her hand to detect which plant she needed to make a strong brew to start the day. She chose a berry-leaf tea, preparing it expertly in the way Cromlach had taught her. Sipping hers gratefully to break the coolness of the early morning, she pondered on whether she should waken him or not as he seemed to be in a restful sleep, the kind of sleep that is dreamless, when one barely breathes. She decided not to and began to work on the other side of the fire from Cromlach, for fear of disturbing him. The flat griddle-cakes she made quickly and then she stretched her hand up for the muslin she knew would be hanging at the back of the *bothán*. This contained the special goat-curd which Cromlach always had on hand, made from the milk of Finann's goats and liberally laced with the wild herbs of the mountain. He always had a bag of it, straining off the whey into a jug, in a cool place in his *bothán*. He loved the griddle-cakes with this special cheese from the muslin and wild blue berries mixed with the whey. The smell of the cooking berries sifted into his spirit and he awoke, hunger ravaging his body, making his belly feel hollow and rumble like a distant war-drum.

"*A stór*, you are up and about? Ah, I see you have found enough for us to break our fast."

21

She jumped up and came around the fire to hug him.

"I've missed you, Cromlach. This is like old times, is it not?"

He nodded, stroking the long dark hair as he had done many times in the past, to comfort her, to allay her fears, to let her know how precious she was.

His hands trailed through the silken strands as he let a wave of warmth wash over her, then he suddenly had a vision of it all shorn off, grasped in her own hands, and the night came back to him. He tried to keep his body from tensing, lest she realize something was wrong. His instinct was to push her away from him as though he could somehow undo the workings of the night before.

She seemed unaware of any change in him. Jumping up, she ordered him immediately to go and attend to his ablutions, then come in and break his fast.

He sighed with relief and got to his feet, at the same time reaching for his precious bottle and returning it to its resting place high up near the eaves.

She pretended not to notice, but when he was outside she stared at the bottle as if in some way she could see into it and know what it was. Some distant memory stirred in her mind, unfolding itself like a little tight bud warming to the sun. She remembered her father, Olc Aiche, shooing her away to play when she had disturbed him squashing little berries, red as blood, into some mixture. At the time, she had been fascinated by the curious see-through brown container that stood tall beside the mortar and pestle. She could not help putting her hand out towards it to touch it but her father had exploded in anger. She ran then like the wind as fast as her little legs could carry her, back to the sanctuary of her mother's arms.

All day long she had been sick on her father's anger, making her mother anxious for her well-being.

"Do not anger him, a stór, he has the way to hurt without meaning to and sometimes forgets to retract it."

After that she took great care not to anger him. He liked to drink milk from cows and she brought his milk to him morning and night. He would drink pails of the fresh frothy milk and there were always young herdswomen only too willing to serve it to him. She tried her very best not to cross him at all but he still managed to discipline her in a subtle way by expecting and encouraging her submissiveness.

She shifted her gaze from the bottle when Cromlach came back shaking the water from his hands and she attended to serving their meal.

Gráinne and Cromlach ate peacefully, enjoying the flavour of the cool cheese and the warmth of the griddle-cakes. The blue berries and whey were sharp and delicious and the tea washed it all down so well that they both felt satisfied with their fare. Then Cromlach gave her a piece of deep purple dulse to chew on.

"For the babe," he said.

"Will you *see* for me now?" she asked eagerly, taking his reference to her child as a sign that he was ready to scry for her. The eagerness in her eyes pained him. He was himself anguished. If he told her everything he had seen in the night, he would be bringing great sadness to her which, in turn, could hurt the child within. The carrying mother must always be kept in a state of bliss whenever possible. He could not tell her that he had already scried for her and yet neither could he lie nor pretend. He decided that the concealment of the greater part of the truth was best and that the truth in its entirety should be dealt to her in portions, little by little, until it was all revealed, but that would take until after the child was born, maybe long afterwards.

He reached for his *ogham*, the tree writings. They were etched on to pieces of wood he had taken and carved from the topmost branches of an alder tree, an alder tree that grew from his own teacher's burial mound, many moons ago. What he was about to do with these runes was not within the boundaries of his own moral code, not within the Laws of the Brehons nor the ethics of the Elder's teaching, but he had to do it for the sake of his dear Gráinne, had to do it for the sake of the unborn child whose destiny he had seen, woven already in the land, springing up like the corn-grass itself.

He threw the sticks before him, keeping his mind blanketed so that he saw the symbols but could not decipher their meanings

23

nor retain them in his memory. Each *ogham* rune he saw, he placed a vivid vision across, so that his mind sailed over them all in a series of his own mental pictures. It was hard work that entailed a lot of concentration. Beads of moisture broke out on his forehead.

He had taught the *ogham* to Gráinne only as symbols for writing but not as a means of divination, so he knew that she could not decipher their meanings herself as a destiny reading.

He began to unravel the truths from last night and sieve a little at a time to her. Everything he spoke he knew he would have to say with the real truth and conviction of a learned diviner, without ever letting his mind slip from producing the visions which would block out the runes. He did this because he knew that if for one moment his guard was down he would have to speak what he saw. His mind had to be blind for the entire reading. It was a trick which had been given to him by his own teacher and one which he had taken half his given life to perfect. It was used to protect the Knowledge, and usually only the Arch-Druids knew how to do it.

"Gráinne, your son is protected by the dog-spirit, the spirit of the wild hound, the spirit of the wolf. If you heed your heart and only go where your heart leads you, you need never fear the wolf. Your son will not fear the wolf. He is charmed."

Gráinne's eyes were bright with unshed tears.

"I know he is charmed, I know it." She covered her belly with her hand and wished for the day she would hold her child close to her. Nothing in life had prepared her for the joy she was experiencing in the carrying of this child. She had had no sickness at all. She knew that most women had the sickness for the first three moons of child-growing. She had been fortunate and she felt that she would be fine for the rest of her time until his birthing.

"Your son will one day make many people happy with his wisdom and judgements. He is a scholar and writer. He has the makings of a good *rí*," Cromlach's voice faltered on the word, "a *rí* who will serve his people well, who will serve his land well."

"A king! I knew it! I knew it!" Gráinne cried out suddenly

24

so that for a moment Cromlach's mental overplay of vision was lost on the rune he had in his hand. He could not control the truth that rolled off his tongue but he managed to block the other runes by visualizing the cairn at the top of the mountain, planting himself firmly there, hearing the rushing whispers of the wind-voices, hoping that his words would not wound.

"I am *Coll*, the Hazel tree. Spawned from me are the nuts of knowledge. Into the pool of wisdom they fall and fodder are they for the silver-blue salmon. Swimming against the tides I am, up to the source of the stream, flowing river, surging tide, to my death for his death as it is decreed. *Straif*, Blackthorn, my companion, hails an ill deed."

Gráinne gasped, her eyes wide with fear. Clutching Cromlach's arm, she bade him tell her what he had seen but he was struggling to contain the reading. Somehow, his mind had started to interpret the *Straif* rune he now knew lay next to *Coll*. He tried to override the image of the other runes that threatened to seep into his head. He concentrated on yellow eyes, calling upon the vision of the wolf and the healing amber glow that had surrounded him earlier. It seemed to help and he was able to placate Gráinne somewhat, for the slip of his mind and tongue.

"*A stór*, do not fear. The *ogham* runes speak of deeds many, many moons away. Your son is to be a great king. He will have much training for his role as guardian of the soul of the land. I will work with the Elders in the preparation of his *gessa*, you know, the rules he must heed to keep his kingship. One of the taboos I will impose will be the eating of flesh from the silver-blue salmon, caught against the tide, on the way to the spawning source."

Cromlach thought to himself that kings die befitting their lives. It was obvious that the king would be swimming against the tide, going against the flowing wishes of the people, one man struggling to get to the source but with the wisdom of the salmon, in harmony with the laws of nature even whilst swimming against the natural order of things. This insight he did not disclose to Gráinne. Neither did he ponder on it too much, knowing what he knew from the night before and also from the reading of the *Straif* in the *ogham*. Someone was going to try to harm the King, someone from Laighin because of the colours on his *kirtle*. This act would be a divine retribution for going against the people. Surely a king of such Truth could not possibly go against the land and the people. It had to be something more than that. Against the Elders? Cromlach had no answer.

He gazed into the imploring blue eyes before him. The reading was over. He did not wish to bring her any more pain. Gathering up the runes without looking down at them, he wrapped them in their linen and put them away, tucking them well into the eaves near the little brown bottle. He knew that she was unhappy and somehow he had to turn that around, especially because she was with child. Telling her about the fate of her unborn child, no matter what age her son might reach before he passed over, was a great burden to put on the mother, even if she might no longer be here when it happened. He could only try his best to comfort her. She relied on his strength and wisdom now, had faith in his judgements.

"Cromlach, is it true? Is there someone who will try to harm him?"

She was trembling, fragile, like dew on the tip of a leaf. He forced himself to smile.

"Gráinne, remember this if you forget all else: there is no greater force than Love and no greater quality than Truth. A *rí* is imbued with both of these. He earns his greatness, is deserving of it. His own protection is in the honour and reverence of the people around him. Likewise, they may walk in safety in the embrace of his mantle. You need never fear, his spirit will be cared for by the Elders and we must not forget my friend, the wolf. For the duration of his kingship, your son will be safe."

"And after?"

"After, he will live to a ripe old age. His destiny will be his then, no longer will he be the property of the people. You and I will probably have passed over by then. We will be with the *Tuatha De Danann* or on Í-Bhreasail, waiting for him to join with us on the Isle of the Blessed. What matter how he gets there as long as he does, eh, Gráinne? The time will be right. Suffice it to know we have the responsibility of doing what is best and correct now, for our land, our Mother, the provider.

26

It is a great honour to be chosen as the parent and guardian of one who will bring good fortune and peace to her."

A smiled played about Gráinne's lips. A surge of joy and pleasure swept through her spine, in the absence of pain or sorrow. No longer was she going to carry the worry of a knowledge that, if harboured, could mar her relationship with her child. She would do her best for him for as long as she lived. Together, Cromlach and she would protect him. They would do it for him and for the Mother.

"I was sent home to my father's house," she bowed her head shyly. "They were tired of my distress after you left. It was my own fault. I had decided when I arrived that you were to be my ' friend and I angered my foster-father by favouring you and not giving him a chance to know me. My foster-mother has so many children, she did not really notice what was happening. The fact that I spent so much time with you made her happy. She had one less child to worry about, one less mouth to feed. Emer is a good woman but she lavishes her love too much on her own wains and has not the time, nor the energy, after a day's lavishing, to devote to others, even Lugnae, her own husband! Not that I wanted any special attention from her but I needed an exchange with someone older, wiser, to feed my own mind."

"And you chose me over Emer," Cromlach chuckled. "Well, I am glad. Why are you telling me all this, *a stór*?"

"Because I want you to know what happened to me after you left the Dún. Many miserable moons seemed to go past before they decided to send me home to my father's house. They timed it so well, can you believe it? Almost on the eve of the battle of Mag Muccrime. Olc Aiche was not pleased at first . . . "

"I dare say he was not," Cromlach murmured, but still he was pained to hear of her sadness.

"Then he changed suddenly with the arrival of the *Ard Rígh*, Art the son of Conn and his ally, Eógan of Munster. All the warriors were staying at various abodes scattered across the countryside near the appointed place for the battle. Art stayed with us. He was a beautiful man, with the fairest golden curls I have ever seen."

Cromlach was startled.

27

"Was? You said *was* a beautiful man? Art the Lonely lost his life in a battle? He is no longer the *Ard Rígh*?"

Gráinne's eyebrows shot up. She looked at him incredulously.

"The Elders did not tell you? No one said anything to you about one of the biggest and bloodiest battles we have ever had? But, of course, no one knew of your whereabouts, did they? Even Finann, did he not say anything when he found you?"

Cromlach shook his head slowly.

"Finann only talks about his goats. Who battled whom and how did Art lose the kingship of the *Ard Rígh*?" Cromlach was almost afraid to hear the answer.

"Art the Lonely was challenged to battle by his nephew Lugaid, who arrived from his exile in Alba with foreign forces. He pitted himself against the *Ard Rígh* and none of the people wanted him to win. My father knew he would though, and he also knew Art would fall in battle so he set a powerful charm on him the night before."

"A charm?" Cromlach was curious.

"Yes. Summoning me, Olc Aiche ordered me to fetch his pails of precious milk and distribute them amongst Art the Lonely and his warriors. He bade the Druidess, Monchae, daughter of the Druid Treth moccu Creccai, to do likewise with Eógan and his men. He watched as they drank it down, then urged me to drink some and lie with Art and asked the Druidess Monchae to lie with Eógan. I had no resistance in me. Neither did Art the Lonely. My father told me on that night that Art mac Conn, Art the Lonely, was the rightful *Ard Rígh* but that Lugaid, because of much assistance from foreign forces, was likely to wrench the kingship from his grasp by foul deed. He must have known then that Art would perish in the battle. Of course, he could not have told him that, or me. After the battle, my father went to the battlefield and helped burn and bury the dead. The ashes were taken back in small yew caskets by the survivors and the relatives, along with any belongings which had not been pilfered. The strangers who were not claimed by the clans were buried, claimed then only by the Mother. The physicians were there to heal those who were wounded and the poets were there to record, had been there throughout the battle too, protected by their mantles and their colours, but you know that anyway, Cromlach. Olc Aiche came home, bearing the sword, the gold ring and the ceremonial *óenach* garb, the sacred purple mantle of Art mac Conn. Apparently Lugaid had fled, riding triumphantly for Teamhair, sporting Art's head on his belt. He had not taken the ceremonial regalia for the kingship. Olc Aiche said he was going to make sure they went to the rightful heir of Art's."

Cromlach leaned forward and stroked Gráinne's face.

"They will go to the rightful heir, Gráinne, they will. Don't you see what has happened? Olc Aiche, your father, had the *sight* to see. He knew that you, *a stór*, would bring through the rightful heir. We can now restore Teamhair to its rightful king."

Gráinne's eyes were glassy and bright. She threw her arms around Cromlach and buried her face in his long silver beard.

"I do love you, Cromlach. You are like my brother, my father, my physician, my philosopher all in one. I do not feel alone away from my home any more and I no longer feel alone with this new knowledge that I have now, of my unborn child. Olc Aiche must have known that you would always be here for me."

"He did that, Gráinne, *a stór*, he did that and he still does," whispered Cromlach, as much in awe of Olc Aiche as Gráinne was.

A sound of feet scuffling the gravel outside the *bothán* disturbed them.

"Are you in, Cromlach?" The voice was low and had a soft lilt.

Cromlach got to his feet and patted Gráinne on the head.

"It is our friend Finann and he has timed his visit well, has he not?"

"Cromlach?" The voice was a little louder.

"I am here, Finann. Come in, boy. How fare your goats today?"

"Oh, grand! Grand!" Finann came through the doorway, his dark curly hair tousled and his brown eyes shining. He wore a rough brown tunic belted with a broad tan leather belt. It had the most wonderful gold buckle on the front that caused an audible gasp to come from Gráinne. The sun caught it as he entered and the glare from it danced through the *bothán*. His leggings were tied with long plaited strands of the same leather. Although his clothing befitted that of a goatherd, the workmanship on his belt was worthy of any nobleman's wear.

Cromlach bade him come closer.

"Finann, you have on the finery of one going to the *Feis* at Teamhair."

Finann stood proudly before them, tucking in his belly with an intake of breath, the better to display his new treasure.

"It was a gift from Cred!" Finann flushed with pleasure.

Gráinne stared at the gleaming gold buckle incredulously.

"A gift? Finann, it is a gift for a king!"

"That is what he told me but he said I was by far more deserving of it and gave it to me. I had only brought him a pail of goat's milk too."

"But you bring it to him every day, Finann. You were the first to show him kindness when he came to the Dún and you are the only one he converses with in words of more than two syllables!"

"We talk only of the weather. We both have the knack, you see, of reading the sky."

"And the land too, Finann, if I know you." Cromlach put out his hand to finger the delicate gold spirals on the buckle. "This is the finest workmanship I have ever laid eyes on," he continued, murmuring more to himself than to Finann. "Tell me, have you seen the prints of a wolf hereabouts on the mountain?"

"That I have, that I have! Strange thing though, he hasn't come after the goats and I have four kids in the herd now, more to come too. This is the time to look out for the wolves and foxes, they're hungry and lean after the winter, but this one has stayed up on the higher slopes. I am surprised you have not seen him. He has surely been to your door and left his footprints all around here. I dare say he's skulking for easy food rather than trying to stalk a kill. Unusual for a wolf and there doesn't seem to be a pack around. I have the goats on the lower slopes now for the new grasses as it is still too crisp up here for them yet."

Cromlach nodded. It was just as he had thought. The wolf was alone. It was probably the same wolf which had enabled him to survive the winter by dragging the deer to his door after consuming only half of it for himself. It was the same wolf which had confronted Gráinne, the same in his vision in the night. The token of the wolf that would protect a king, a king spawned of Art the Lonely who, in turn, was spawned of Conn of a Hundred Battles, Conn of the Wolfhound. Éiriú was going to see some changes. Lugaid had won the battle of Mag Muccrime, so Art had fallen in battle and lost the kingship of the *Ard Rígh* for his branch of the family, the true direct blood from Conn. Lugaid might not be a popular king, might not be a just king, but he was now the *Ard Rígh*, and as such demanded a certain reverence. This fine gold buckle with all its beautiful spirals and gold lacework was definitely a gift crafted for a king, a High King, an *Ard Rígh*. Cred had made it for Lugaid, Cromlach felt sure of that, so what had happened to make him give it to Finann? It was true that Finann was definitely more deserving of such a prize but such an act of defiance from Cred was bound to cause ripples which Cromlach hoped would not get back to Lugaid's ears. It would be a dreadful insult to the *Ard Rígh*.

As if Finann had read his mind, he said: "My lips are sealed. Only you and Gráinne know it for a king's buckle."

"It is well kept that way, Finann, well kept that way."

"Right now, I wear it up here in the hills with my goats as my sole companions. No one to bother me, no one to care whether I drape myself in gold or not," said Finann, pausing for a moment. Then he changed the conversation lightly. "Cromlach! I almost forgot my purpose here. I have some supplies with me to keep you in good humour and well fed."

He disappeared outside and reappeared carrying a wicker creel full of goods.

"You are very popular: you see I have here some of Emer's matured cheese, fermented for seven moons, so says she. I did not tell her where you were, only that I had found you . . . and I have some bread from the best grain grown by Scath the

31

Druid. Mora nee Derga made a hot-pot which has since gone cold but I am sure you can heat it up again with the fire-stones and, of course, I have your milk here with *my* blessings."

"My blessings on you, Finann. Tell me, how did you carry the creel up the mountain?" Cromlach asked.

"Ah, a good question and an even better answer. I have trained Misha to carry the creels. She has the surest feet of all my goats. Come and have a look at her. See for yourselves."

They all traipsed out of the *bothán* and there, standing as still as a little donkey, was Misha. Finann was enthusiastic like an excited little boy, his childlike joy spreading to both Gráinne and Cromlach.

"Look! See how well I have trained her. Misha, come here, come here, Misha, Misha."

The goat obediently tossed her head and trotted over. Gráinne leapt forward to hug her.

"She is great. How clever of you, Finann."

Misha had a harness on her body and on one side there was a creel which matched the other empty one that Finann was now strapping on to her. She didn't seem so lop-sided when he had finished. Finann was fairly bursting with pride.

"I made them myself. A person up the mountain has a great deal of time on his hands to spare and so the invention of things to make life even easier comes comfortably to him."

"That rings true," nodded Cromlach. "I dare say we all have needs at times but not always the wit or the wherefores of how to appease them with new inventions. What you have accomplished, Finann, is something they have been doing with mules and donkeys in the East, so I have heard say. But the owners of these beasts of burden are not always considerate of their animals, many of which collapse with fatigue from being over-burdened, and very often the poor creatures are nothing but skin and bone, whilst their fat owners sport nicely filled bellies. They are not at all kind like you, Finann, who would give your eye-teeth to keep your goats happy."

Finann blushed red as a russet apple. He was both pleased with the compliment and astounded that it was not a new artifice thought up by himself but shared by strangers in the East. That such goings-on went on in the world, he was filled with awe. Cromlach was so wise. He knew everything.

Gráinne said, reluctantly, "Shall we sup before we go down the mountain? I will have to return to the Dún before Lugnae Fer Trí gets worried, but I hate to leave you, Cromlach. I will definitely come back to see you."

"No," Cromlach said, "it is much too steep a climb for you, especially now when you are with child, so I shall come to you, *a stór*. Finann will help me on the mountain."

"Oh Cromlach, here we both are, you at the top of Knocknarea, me at the bottom and neither of us too fit for the climb up or down. Would it not be a simple thing if you came back to your *bothán* at the Dún or I came up here to care of you?"

"The time is not right yet, Gráinne. The tree that bears the sweet fruit is worth waiting for, but pluck the fruit before its time and it is a bitter bite. I still have thoughts to think, still have work to do here, but the time will come, maybe a lot sooner than we both anticipate. Now, Finann, because of the wolf-tracks, I think you know what I am going to say . . . "

"Of course, Cromlach. I shall see her safely down the mountain to her abode. No lone wolf dares approach the goatherd. You know I have a reed-pipe with a very high pitch that sends wolves scurrying if they come within a hair's breadth of any of my goats. Did you, by chance, know that?"

"I did not know that, Finann, but I am very glad to hear it."

There was a tearful farewell. Cromlach gently put Gráinne away from him. He told her to go forward and not to look back, they would be together again soon. He watched the two figures with the wobbly little goat start off down the hill, then he went inside the *bothán* to refuel his fire. He gathered up his plaid to fold it and put it away. It had kept him warm in the long night. As he smoothed it with his fingers, he twiddled thoughtfully with a few strands of hair caught in the weave, then examined them closer, his heart thudding excitedly.

Yes, they were definitely the hairs of the wolf! So, he had company last night. The wolf had curled up at his feet, watchful as he slumbered, just as he had *seen* in the vision.

# CHAPTER 4

# THE DÚN

*Purity of hand, bright without wounding,*
*Purity of mouth without poisonous satire,*
*Purity of learning without reproach,*
*Purity of husbandship.*

Gráinne fairly bounced down the mountain with Finann and Misha. The thin trailing mists on the first hill, past the well, did not bother her this time nor did they seem to trouble Finann, so they did not speak about them. She wanted to run, leap, shout aloud with her joy. Instead, she hummed a tune, over and over, until Finann, infected with her good humour, did likewise. Her feet fell on the ground in time with her song and helped her absorb the shock of the sharp stones in the stream, the only pathway down from Finann's slopes. Misha joined the other goats when they reached the herd and Finann did a quick count of the goats before they continued on their journey. The cool water rolled over Gráinne's sandals, getting her leggings wet, but she did not care. She would have loved to have raced the stream down the mountain, such was her exhilaration. There was no sign of the wolf, no sign of any danger at all.

When they reached the bottom, she begged Finann to go back to his goats. She would be fine for the rest of the journey. The Dún was in sight.

"But Gráinne . . . " Finann was unsure.

"But nothing, Finann. Now, go back to your herd lest the wolf be looking for a tasty morsel to break his fast."

Thoughts of Misha being munched for a wolf's meal spurred Finann back up the mountain quickly. He hurriedly bade his farewell and started his ascent upstream as Gráinne headed for the Dún.

34

It was warmer in the valley in the shelter of the mountain. Gráinne put her face up to the sun to bathe in its warm glow. She could not wait to get back to her dwelling to soak in a hot tub and change her tunic. The rest of the day lay before her but she would probably have to attend the class of the Draoi this afternoon. The Draoi were the teachers, the educators of the Druid sect. They taught about the stars and the movement of the planets. They taught the aspiring poets the essential metres and rhythms they needed for their basic training. The Druids knew all the wild flowers and plants, although to heal with them was a different science. Only the best herbal healers were allowed to train as physicians and practise on the seriously ailing or injured. Most mothers had a knowledge of the healing plants. They knew how to suppress fevers and fix the pains in the head, heal twisted ankles, sprained wrists and children's scrapes, but in the cases of broken bones or battle wounds, they left those to the trained physicians.

Fergus the poet was sometimes called out instead of Morann the physician at the settlement. Morann called upon Fergus too if he was having difficulty with a serious wound or a sickness that could not be seen on the body. Fergus had a physic finger, which was inherited. Fergus's mother had been a great healer in her day, and although she had wanted him to become a great physician his calling had been that of a *filé poet*. Nevertheless, he had the physic finger which could pinpoint the source of a pain when all else failed. He had also the gift to spirit-heal. Morann could spirit-heal too, but the ability of locating the site of the disturbance in the body was sometimes beyond him. The Draoi priests had seen the gift in Fergus when he was a young boy but they had also had the *sight* to see the poet, so his training had begun immediately. His memory was phenomenal and he was now one of the most loved and respected poets in the land, although his years of training were not yet completed. It took precisely twelve years to become a *filé* and twenty to become a *poet-ollam*. In time, Fergus knew, he would be an *ollam*, and his life was dedicated to this. He hoped to reside at Teamhair one day and, as befits only the highest-ranking poet in the land, share the King's joint at table.

As Gráinne approached the Dún, she saw Lugnae Fer Tr'"s wife Emer hurrying towards her like a great brown spider scuttling across the path, arms flailing as she gesticulated feverishly in Gráinne's direction. It made Gráinne smile until she saw the red puffed face and the impending doom of her expression.

"Gráinne, Gráinne, where have you been? Lugnae has been up all night, fired out of his mind with worry. He has had two search parties on horseback sent out with fire-spails to look for you in the dark. Cred searched the riverbanks and the lakeside, beating the brush back with a wooden staff. He returned at sun-up and last I saw of him, he was setting out again, heading towards the marshes with a gold sickle. We have been all in a panic since sundown yesterday."

"A – a gold sickle? But only the Druids . . . "

"I know! I know! He was making it for Scath the Druid but he could not find his own scythe so he just grabbed it and ran."

A grey cloud descended on Gráinne. Such a sacred implement should never be used in such a trivial way, especially since she had not really been perishing in the marshlands or by the riversides. She suddenly wished she had been.

"I went up the mountain to see Cromlach."

"You what?" raged Emer. "In your condition, you climbed the mountain! How did you know where Cromlach was?" she demanded.

"Finann told me." Gráinne bowed her head in shame, realizing that she had thought only of herself and it had never crossed her mind that they would have worried so much about her.

"Finann told me too that he found Cromlach, but he did not disclose the location," said Emer. "I sent some cheeses back with him."

Gráinne suddenly thought of something that Emer had said.

"How did you know, Emer, about my being with child?"

"How could I not, having had seven of them myself? You little goose, you have put us all in a tither," she said crossly but affectionately, feeling sorry for the girl who was now very near to tears. She put her arm clumsily around Gráinne's shoulders.

"I will send one of the trappers out to tell the others you are safe."

36

Gráinne nodded, unable to speak for a moment, then she asked: "Does anyone else know of my child-growing?"

"They do now. Cred was like a demon, desperate to find you. Lugnae was beside himself, barking orders left, right and centre, frightening the children. I have never known such a raucous household in my life. It was as if we were going to battle!"

"Oh, no," groaned Gráinne, "please forgive me. I was so happy when I found out where Cromlach was, I could not wait to see him, you understand, Emer? It was as if I had found my father or my brother again."

"Please, please, Gráinne, I understand but do not repeat what you have just told me to Lugnae. My husband is a fair man, a little temperamental but nevertheless fair. He felt he had been lacking in his duty as foster-father to you but it was apparent you preferred the company of Cromlach. That stung Lugnae as he is a proud man. He is good to his foster-children. They adore him, but you, Gráinne, were different right from the first day. You must give Lugnae a chance, Gráinne. He has given you more than that, much more."

Gráinne was despondent.

"I know, I know that now more than ever. I will try, I really will. I have been so selfish. Please forgive me, Emer, how can you ever forgive me?"

"Do not ask it of me, Gráinne. You must make your peace with Lugnae."

They reached the Dún and there was great excitement at the return of Emer with Gráinne. Emer immediately sent one of the trappers to find Lugnae and the search parties that had been back and forth most of the night. She then set about making a hot broth for everyone's return and summoned one of her bond-maidens to stir and watch the soup. The children crowded around trying to ask questions all at once but Emer shooed them outside to play.

Marching purposefully to the back room, which was divided from the main hall by screens of woven willow and windlestraw, she began to pump water into the bathing tub, then filled it with hot water from huge red copper pots. She poured some of her best perfumed oils into it and bade a very grateful Gráinne to

37

disrobe and soak herself. It was the first time that Emer had
ever done anything like this for her, the first time that Gráinne
had been mothered away from home and it made her feel that
changes were going to happen all around. Emer was a natural
mother, and it seemed she had at last accepted Gráinne into
her brood even though Gráinne was old enough now to be a
mother herself, indeed soon would be.

If they only knew what Cromlach and I now know, thought
Gráinne as she slid into the scented tub. Emer had put soapwort
into it so that it became frothy with the least amount of movement. She felt as though she were bathing in a bubbling mountain stream, and closing her eyes she visualized a tall pine tree
stretching to the sky, a weeping willow draping hair into the
water like a woman gazing at her reflection, a hazel bush, strong,
stout, and fruitful, dropping hazelnuts into the stream, and she
saw a salmon leaping joyfully upstream heading for the spawning
pool further up the mountain. She saw the salmon curve through
the air like a flashing rainbow, catching the hazelnuts as they
fell.

Her baby jumped suddenly inside her, startling her out of her
reverie, and she stroked her silken belly with her hand, comforting him, offering him solace.

The children were playing outside, their squeals and excited
laughter ringing in the air and Gráinne thought of her own son
doing likewise one day. She wondered if he would look like his
father and desperately hoped so. Art the Lonely had had the
most beautiful fair curls and a perfectly chiselled face. His body
had been white, pale as snow, pale as dry grass but muscular to
touch, great curves of strength that embraced her fiercely but
took her tenderly. She had not been afraid. He had spoken of
many things that night to her and she listened and conversed
with him into the small hours. It was as if he had to make up
for all the years he preferred his own company. After the deaths
of his brothers he had become reclusive, save for the running
of his kingdom.

His body blended together perfectly with hers and their minds
harmonized like strings on the harp being played by Fergus. She
puzzled now over a faint distant memory of something he had

said to her. It tickled her mind, called to her, but she tried to put it from her. It had been against the teachings. She knew that, but somehow on that night, it made perfect sense. It persisted. What was it he had said?

"I answer only to one god, above all others, being of them and encompassing them all."

He had said this into her hair, pulling it across his face, winding it around his neck.

"I surrender myself to him and if this be indeed my last night, I will be embraced by him and do my duty for him."

She had found that thought exhilarating at the time because of its forbidden nature and she had enjoyed his different way of believing in the gods, seeing them not separately but as one. She had not asked about the goddess, but he made her feel like one that night so it had not mattered. It was as if Art the Lonely imparted some great precious secret to her, unburdening himself on to her by sharing his secret faith with her, something which could have damned him in the eyes of the Druids, and he had imparted that which should have been his alone to an Elder's daughter. It had seemed wild and exotic then with an element of danger which had appealed to her, but she knew that one day it might haunt her.

Emer came into the room with a large soft linen wrap.

Gráinne stepped out of the tub and Emer dried her body, carefully patting her swollen belly.

"Ah, a boy. My mother always said that the inner cradle is large and round for a boy and long and narrow for a girl. You are carrying a boy, Gráinne.'

"I am?" Gráinne smiled. She did not wish to tell Emer she knew already as she wanted the woman to believe she was the first to tell her. She did not know why she felt like this, but suddenly it seemed important to her that she make friends at the Dún. In a way, Cromlach had shown her that it was important not to attach oneself to one person. His disappearance had made her distraught. She would try never to let that happen again.

Emer held another robe ready for her to slip on. It was pale saffron yellow and had beautiful gold skeins coiled and looped into intricate knotwork, stitched around the neckline. The folds of the soft robe fell loosely from below the breasts. It had been crafted especially for a woman with child.

"I made it for you, Gráinne. It is a birthing gift but I thought you should wear it today. Today is the first day we will accept each other as a family, a real clan. Cromlach's disappearance made you realize how you felt about him. Your disappearance last night made us realize how we should feel about you, how we did feel about you."

"But, Emer, what about the time you sent me home to my father?"

"That was different. You were returning to your family to recover from your love-sickness. We could not help you then, but since your return to us you have somehow grown on us and I, especially, have been looking out for you since I noticed the signs of child-growing. I had hoped you would have told me about it but I thought maybe you were afraid."

"Oh, Emer," Gráinne's tears slid down her face, "this is the greatest gift you have given me and I do not just mean the splendid robe. How can I ever repay you for your kindness?"

"Just let us a little into your heart, *a stór*. Now, come, otherwise I shall be weeping like a keening woman too. We are not out of the woods yet. Lugnae has not returned. Ah, but I speak too soon . . . I think I hear the horses outside. Quick, let me dress your hair."

She deftly plaited the long black hair, weaving gold threads into two of the braids and sealing the ends in little gold balls.

Gráinne was flushed and glowing with her child-growing, making her even more beautiful. Emer rushed into her own quarters and returned with the long polished Phoenician looking-glass that Lugnae had traded for when he had first paid court to Emer.

Gráinne stared at the vision of herself in the mirror and the breath was almost taken from her. She turned to look at Emer and it was then that she saw the beauty and the softness of the woman before her. Now she knew why Lugnae had fallen in love with this handsome woman who appeared to be wrapped up with her children all the time. Emer's love was great, once one was embraced within her circle of kindness. Gráinne could see now that the children were hers during the day and Lugnae was hers by night. No wonder Lugnae was so patient with her apparent dismissal of him sometimes. He had a treasure here in this simple, kind, good woman. Never again would Gráinne take someone just at face value.

"Emer! Emer! Where is she?"

"I am here, Lugnae. Gráinne is here. We will be with you shortly."

"Now! I want to see her now!" Lugnae Fer Trí's voice was enraged and Gráinne began to tremble. Emer looked a little uneasy but she smiled bravely.

"He cannot do anything, Gráinne," she whispered. "Sticks may break your back but he is gentle with women, so he will not strike you or harm you. He can only shout long and loud, but it will be as one gasp in a lifetime to you, so do not fear him."

Emer shoved her forward. "Go, speak the truth without malice and all will be well, but do not hurt him with words wilfully. Words are like swords to Lugnae if they are spiteful. Be mindful of the tongue."

Gráinne stood like a noble priestess. There was something bridal about her as well as fruitful. She was the epitome of fertility and growth.

Lugnae stared at her as if he had seen an apparition. The trappers with him all stood with their mouths hanging open. She was like a goddess incarnate. Their harsh clothing and scorn were not fitting for her eyes or ears. They, as one, all became flustered and started attending to their dress and peeling off their leggings and boots which were caked with mud.

Lugnae recovered quickly, remembering the worry she had put him through the night before.

As he opened his mouth to speak, she glided over to him gracefully with her hands extended.

"Please forgive me, Foster-father, for I had no intention of staying away overnight without informing anyone of my where-abouts."

"Where were you?" he demanded gruffly, not biting the bait to hold her hands.

"I went to see Cromlach up the mountain. He is on the Hill of Mists." She rubbed her hands together nervously, fully aware of his snub.

Lugnae's face darkened. He did not like what he was hearing.

"You climbed a mountain while you are child-growing? To see Cromlach?"

"Yes. I wanted him to scry for me. Just as I reached the Hill of Mists, I became frightened and wished to return to the Dún again but I was confronted by a wolf."

"A wolf?!" Lugnae's eyes were round, as were all the trappers' eyes. They all stopped what they were doing and little quivers of excitement and fear coursed through them. The slip of a girl before them looked more ethereal than ever.

"Yes, a wolf. By good fortune, I was beside Cromlach's dwelling and he saw me and frightened away the wolf," she said, not telling them how he had done so. "And then he insisted I stay the night, as it was too dangerous for me either to travel down in the dark or be confronted by the wolf again. We had to wait for Finann to come up this morn to help me back down to the Dún."

"I was thinking of sending you home again when I found you, whether you were alive or dead," said Lugnae firmly. "I thought maybe the disgrace of being sent home a second time would have been enough to teach you the lesson of awareness that there are more people in the world besides Gráinne."

Gráinne's face paled, then Lugnae went on, "Emer told me you were with child and my feelings changed. The anger was not replaced but it was then coupled with concern for your unborn."

"I am sorry. There is not much more that I can say, except that I am sorry," she said, her voice barely audible, her eyes glittering, "but there was nothing else I could do in the circumstances. There was no lithe nimble-footed messenger half-way up the mountain, anxious to outrun a wolf, to give you a message that I was safe!" Her voice ended on a sarcastic note. She genuinely regretted that she had caused them so much trouble but she thought it unfair that he had already meted out the punishment to her in his mind before he knew what her crime was. She had also seen the change in his face at the mere mention of Cromlach's name. Cromlach was right. It was not yet time for him to return to the Dún.

"No, I see why you could not get a message to me, Gráinne," said Lugnae, with a touch of cynicism in his tone, "but that does not detract from the fact that you left here at sun-down, on a quest up the mountain, without thinking of informing anyone where you were going. In this *ráth*, no one leaves here before or after dark without at least one other person knowing their movements. There are wolves, wild boar and bears out there, all hungry after the winter. Let your confrontation with the wolf this time be a firm lesson to you. I am not a harsh man and I am aware of the law of keeping happy the woman who is child-growing, so no more will be said, but a truce must be reached for us all to live in peace. You have spoken your words and I have spoken mine. We offer you our protection in your child-time but you must also be kind to us and not cause undue worry and unrest. Now, let us sit down to a hearty meal to celebrate the coming of your child. It is not often a foster-father has the privilege of doing his duty for two for the agreement of one."

He turned to his men abruptly. "Now, wipe your smiles off and go bathe your bodies. A little purity and fresh air is needed around here."

They scuttled off in the direction of the sweat-hut and Emer dished out fresh linens for them all and clean plaids to put on afterwards. Most of the men were tired from scouring the countryside the night before, so they welcomed a bath and food before resting in the afternoon. Lugnae also went into his quarters to bathe and change, ignoring Gráinne as if he were afraid he would say more.

Emer came over to Gráinne who was standing mesmerized, musing over the event.

"You see, Gráinne, the Truth is best spoken with sincerity and not with malice. We are now kin and our Truth-speaking has cleared away the grey air between us all. Let us enjoy the company, and maybe later, Gráinne, you will sing us a song."

Gráinne looked startled.

"What made you say that, Emer?"

"Aah. A little bird told me you could sing."

"Which little bird?"

"Said you had a voice that would charm any bud to flower."

"Who said that, Emer?" Gráinne was puzzled. "No one here has heard me sing. And they said, did they, that I could charm a bud to flower? Only one person speaks like that: Fergus, but he has not heard even a whisper of a tune from me."

"Oh, but he has and you did not know of it," teased Emer. "He was very taken with your voice."

"But I have not chirped a note since I have been here except maybe this morn when I came down the mountain with Finann."

"No, this was before you came to live with us, when you were younger at your father's house."

Gráinne was surprised.

"Fergus was at my father's house?"

"Once, when he was younger too, he went to visit the great Draoi-poet, Aengar, during his training. Aengar was staying at Olc Aiche's dwelling and then they went to Crom Cruach on the Plain of Magh Slecht."

"For Samhain! Yes, I remember, Olc Aiche made me sing the dirge for the old and the calling for the new, but I cannot remember seeing Fergus there or Aengar, but then there were so many people and we were all intent on keeping warm. Even with the huge fires lit, it was bitterly cold that time. Of course, I was really young, so new poets or bards would not have captured my attention easily."

"But you commanded their attention. Fergus has spoken of your singing voice to me many times, mostly to ask if you have used it," said Emer, as she crossed the hall and struck a small bronze gong three times.

"And yet he never once spoke of it to me," mused Gráinne. "Well, since he likes it so much, I shall surprise him with it one day. Not today though: I sing only when I am happy or when I am sad, but today I am both, and neither one nor the other. My song shall be sung when Cromlach returns to the Dún with the blessing of Lugnae, and my song shall then be not just for Cromlach but for all of us in the *ráth*."

Emer did not acknowledge whether she had heard this or not because her children burst in, as one scrambling mass of arms and legs, making for the ewers in the washroom so that they could attend to their ablutions before they partook of some food. The smells of broth and stewing slivers of badger permeated the hall and the sight of roast wild boar being carried to the table from the hazel-spits made their mouths water. It was not often that such a feast was prepared at midday. The children were settled at an end table, perpendicular to the large oak table. They sat on a carpet of rushes and Emer tied large fawn napkins around their necks. She admonished them for squabbling and bade them stand up again until their father was seated at the large table. All the men came back from the sweat-hut, clean and fresh with dampened hair plastered against their heads. The children obediently stood still until their father emerged, also fresh and scented, sporting a gold torc around his neck and wearing a loose colourful plaid belted at his waist. A sword swung in a scabbard at his side and a small bronze knife lay beside it in a separate sheath. This he pulled out, offered it in the direction of the sun shining through the wicker slats and then he drew the blade sharply down the golden flesh of the boar. Everyone cheered as he ripped off the haunch for himself and sheared an end off it for Fergus, who had just walked in.

"Come, Fergus, share a chief's feast. We celebrate the knowledge of a child-growing."

"Oh?" Fergus raised an eyebrow at Emer, who giggled and shook her head.

"Not me, Fergus. Seven ducks to fly south is enough!"

They all laughed at her bold confirmation of the rumour that she was going to send her own children into fosterage with her relatives in the south.

Lugnae smiled and looked at his wife affectionately, knowing that she would not give up her control of them easily. Her relatives were akin to herself and he guessed she would have many excuses to visit her family often when the time came.

"No, Fergus, it is not my dear Emer, neither is it her bond-maid. It is Gráinne, my foster-daughter."

Everyone clapped as Lugnae Fer Trí gestured for Gráinne to sit next to him. Lugnae was pleased that for once he had access to knowledge before Fergus had. It was worth the drama to see the expression on Fergus's face. He was astonished, that was clear.

"I hasten to add," Lugnae continued, "that I am not the culprit."

"Neither am I," quipped Fergus, to the delight of all present in the Hall. Gráinne blushed furiously and hung her head, uncomfortable with the way the converse was heading. She felt exposed and almost cried with relief when Cred chose that moment to return dramatically, carrying a brace of the finest golden pheasants they had seen and demanding why no one had sought him to inform him that Gráinne had been found.

# CHAPTER 5

# CRED

*Many earths on earth there be,*
*Whom I love my own shall be,*
*Grow, grow willow tree,*
*Sorrow none on to me.*

Cred returned to his forge without partaking of the midday feast. He had presented the brace of pheasants to Emer to show good-will on his part towards Lugnae, lest it be thought that his absence from the meal be deliberate because he had not been informed of Gráinne's return. He made the excuse that he had had to get back to his forge to make some implements for Scath the Druid. This was, in part, correct. He did indeed have to make some new implements for Scath, particularly when he had impetuously grabbed and sullied the gold sickle. No longer was it pure virgin metal. Cred was a perfectionist and he knew how important it was to be nothing less than truthful with the Druids. Any lesser smith might have tried to palm off an implement of inferior quality to them, but Cred knew well the dire consequences of tricking a Druid. He began his work over again. The furnace was hot, making rivulets of sweat cascade off his body. He removed his vest, airing his muscular frame, then, placing the sickle into his vice, he proceeded to smash it with a huge iron hammer. It was extremely satisfying for him to hear the wrench of twisted metal as the blade bent away from the handle. He thumped it with the hammer again and again, feverishly trying to control his anger, trying to make sense of his desires. He knew he would have to disperse his emotional feelings before he could begin to create another sickle as his anger must not tarnish the earth's ore, the fire, or the water that he would use for the new implement. However hard he tried to overcome his emotions, he could not rid himself of his frustrations. He thought maybe it was because he was fatigued from his search for Gráinne the night before that the day stretched long and wearisome in front of him. No amount of work or rest placated his mind, so that he at last laid down his tools and left his forge to seek solace in the Grove.

As he left the *ráth* wherein lay the large Dún and the surrounding dwellings of Lugnae's Clan, he realized there was an unnatural quiet there and very little activity. Most of the trappers and workers had been out searching for the girl too, and so they were all probably asleep in their homes. This suited Cred, who did not want Lugnae to know he was not working in the forge, nor did he want to meet anyone on his way to the sacred Grove. Not that he conversed with any of them much, but today he needed to have his own silence to hear his own answers.

The oaks were stout and gnarled, their thick grey branches like arms outflung to hail his arrival. Their branches formed a canopy at the entrance, the new-born leaves fresh to the eye and the hard green buds of the acorns starting their cycle yet again. There was a scent of juniper and myrtle and wild crocus. Cred inhaled deeply, his body rippling nervously as it always did when he trod on this ground. A willow tree swept the earth's floor with her fronds, and Cred parted the branches full of furred catkins and sat down on a mossy mound, with his back to the trunk of the tree. He shared the shadow of the willow with a sacred spring, hidden under the folds of the trailing branches. The water was still. There were some offerings placed beside the spring: some woven rush-dolls, ears of corn, a pitcher one could use to fill with the water to quench one's thirst.

Cred pulled his knees up to his chest and laid his head to rest upon them. He clasped his hands to his temples and let his anguish flow freely to be absorbed by the tree.

Since his arrival at the Dún, he had been aware of her. He had left his people in the hills of the South, had come here of his own volition, intent upon fulfilling an inner quest. Several times he had had visions of the *light ones*, *their* shimmering lightness, *their* soft breathy voices, tinkling like a linnet's song or a lark's call. *They* guided him, *they* worked his hands upon the precious gold, *they* showed him the art of working with the fire, bending the ore to his will. Always he had known *they* were there, but also he had the need to cloak his gift. He eventually persuaded his father to send him here to the Dún, far away from his home, to serve his fos.erage in a place unknown where he could learn his trade in peace, where he could be with *them* when he willed. But lately he felt *them* drift away, had been aware that *they* were distancing themselves from him and his heart was heavy. He knew it was because his mind had been thrown into a desire of a different nature, not of *their* subtle world, *their* place upon the earth. He had become aware of her, her long black hair sweeping like the willow fronds almost to the ground, her eyes blue as the sky, blue as a crystal lake. He had only been able to watch her, his tongue at once stilled in her presence. He knew her happiness, befriended her pain, and not a day went by that she did not fill his head. When Emer told him Gráinne had not returned to the Dún before sun-down, he had been distraught, fear sweeping over him in great waves. He had begged for a vision, pleaded with his mind for *them* to show him where she was, whether alive or dead.

*They* had not responded and he had been alone with his loss. He traipsed the river banks all night long, trampling the rushes, beating the thick brush back with a wooden staff, cutting his arms on brambles and feeling the vicious sweep of stinging nettles. At first, he applied dock-leaf juice to the angry red weals but then he stopped treating himself and welcomed any pain his search put him through, as if in some way he was being punished to ease his inner pain. He carried burning bog-spails up and down the lakeside in the dark, searching for her white body and her trailing black hair. He returned to the Dún, despondent and relieved that he had not found her, and then Emer met him and told him. His world had collapsed at her words. Emer told him Gráinne was with child, and he felt betrayed. He ran back to the forge, his breath ragged in his throat and he searched for his scythe. Unable to find it, he grabbed the sickle he had been crafting for Scath the Druid and uncaring of how sacred it was, he hurried off to the marshes.

Emer had called after him, demanding to know why he carried the gold sickle and he shouted to her that it was of his own making and if he could not find his scythe, he was entitled to take the sickle, sacred or not. She looked shocked but he cared not. His madness crept upon him so that he destroyed all within his way. He was ashamed. He had vented his raging anger on some poor unsuspecting pheasants in the gorse near the marshes, the first killings he had ever made, being one to abhor hunting. Now, they would grace Lugnae's table and Cred only hoped that Gráinne would not eat any part of them. He did not want any portion of his anger to get to her.

As he thought of all these things, his head emptied of his feelings to be replaced by a pleasant rushing wind sound. He let it fill his being, soothing him with the absence of words or pictures. It was then that he felt *their* presence again.

Faintly, but surely, the outline of one draped in light seemed to be by his side under the willow tree. His joy at this presence was unsurpassed and he recalled how much he missed *them*. He bathed in the light, his whole being elevated in bliss. No worldly thoughts plagued him now, no yearnings equalled his desire at this moment to be with *them*. It was as if he conquered himself.

And then came the vision, the vision that seeped into the front of his mind, that swept through his head like a giant wave, every seventh wave of the ocean tide. His body trembled with the awe of it, his face was dampened with sweat and tears.

He saw the most beautiful shining chalice he had ever seen, composed of gold, silver, bronze, copper, brass and lead. Scrolls of knotwork interlaced in gold were exquisite in their ornamentation and riveted to the silver bowl of the cup. Bands of bronze and gold wire-work encompassed the bowl in patterns terminating in wolves' heads. Dragons and serpents intertwined around the base, and the belly of the chalice was studded with gold plaques inset with pieces of amber and blue glass. Blue glass was also set in the handles and the stem was bronze, with all the metals carved and knotted and attached by a bronze gilt ball to the bowl.

Tablets of amber and green marble were in the foot of it and a large round crystal almost blinded him with light. Hammered with blood and tears, chiselled until hands had blistered and bled in the crafting of it, he knew it to be the most magnificent vessel he had envisaged. The yellow glory of the finest gold dazzled the eyes, making the heart leap with pleasure, the chest burst with longing to hold, to cherish, to sip the ambrosia of the gods from a vessel such as this. It was as if it had been born of Í-Bhreasail, was a treasure of the Tuatha De Danann or alike unto the *Cauldron of Dagda*, that bottomless source of plenty.

His hands itched to create it, etched into his mind as it was. He wished to see it before him as something tangible that he could touch, something great that others could see and touch and know that he, Cred, had made it. He was going to make it for the greatest king that Éiriú would know, a king yet to be born who would be a king above all others. As he thought these thoughts, he marvelled at them, and as the white blinding light lifted off him like a piece of draped silk being removed from a carving, he saw, suddenly standing before him, the girl, she with the long black hair trailing like the willow fronds almost to her ankles. He saw the small swollen belly and he knew, he knew beyond the shadow of a doubt.

He leapt to his feet, shaken by her presence almost as much as *theirs*. He was firmly back to his normal self but with this added knowledge and excitement within him. He knew it would take years to fashion and craft the vessel, a grail like none other and it would be for the King that Gráinne grew within her.

"Cred! I am sorry, I did not mean to startle you. I did not know you were here. I come here too sometimes. I like this tree."

She felt that her words were tumbling too fast from her tongue, but she had been just as shocked to find him here as he had been with her.

He could not speak but mumbled something incoherently, his tongue unable to form his words, so he tried to be silent and nodded.

She caught his hand and her fingers were warm against his, burning into his flesh.

"I want to thank you, Cred, for caring enough to search for me as you did. I am truly sorry for all the trouble I caused for everyone. It upset me greatly that Lugnae's messenger did not reach you this morn and I know about the sickle . . . Emer told me . . . I know the work you must have put into it and the work you now have to do again."

He recovered his voice as she dropped her hand from his.

"How would you know of such things, Gráinne?" He was slightly indignant, still stung by the way he felt he had made a fool of himself. He felt exposed, vulnerable, tainted.

She did not look at him but hung her head and stared at the ground as she answered him softly. "You forget, Cred, my father is a smith and a Druid."

He was at once contrite. Of course she would know of such things. He bit his lip, angry at himself that he did not know what to say to her, and what he said did not come out right. His fair skin flushed with his embarrassment.

She, in turn, felt the fine wall between them and knew not how to cross it or not to see it. She wished with all her heart that she could be his friend. The silence, like a gap or a widening gulf, was becoming unbearable.

They both coughed at the same time, and then both made an attempt to speak again, which flustered them enough to forget what they wanted to say. Then they smiled at the absurdity of their shyness and the wall seemed to crumble.

"This place has always been a special place for me," Gráinne said, directing her blue gaze meaningfully at him. "The Druidesses use it a lot for their *seeing* and healing."

Cred was taken aback. Had she guessed that he had come here for that too? He decided not to tell her anything about his own visions. They were his secret and his alone, to dare, to see, to know and to be silent.

"You are a Druidess?" he asked.

She shrugged, raising her eyebrows, making her eyes wide, making him feel as if he was going to fall into them, great blue pools reflecting the sky.

"By birth I am, by nature I am, and with Cromlach's help I have studied as they do but . . . no, I am alone. I have not taken the vows. And you?"

He smiled and answered, "No, do I look like one?"

She looked puzzled. "Like what?"

"A Druidess?"

She giggled and it reminded him of a bubbling stream. Her eyes were alive and her cheeks were dimpled. She looked mischievous, and he stuttered over his words when he spoke again.

"I . . . em . . . I trained as a *céird* and because of my ability in the smithcraft I had to learn the laws of the ores and the arts of working with fire. This is a Druid craft, as you well know. I – I have not forgotten your father, Gráinne. He is one of the finest smiths in all of Éiriú. Some say he works with the Tuatha De Danann."

"And you don't?" Gráinne said wryly.

"What do you mean?" he asked, startled.

"I mean that your crafting is more than just a hammering at the anvil to produce basic tools, shields, swords, or whatever. You have the power to work the gold, to produce the finest, most intricate goldwork I have ever seen, and remember what you yourself said? You said my father was the best . . . I do not say these things lightly, Cred. One who is better than my father has to have guidance from another source other than the best Draoi craftsmen. One who can craft a buckle alike unto the creation I saw on Finann – and do not fret, he will be discreet, only Cromlach and I know of it – has to have the Danann gift bestowed upon him."

If he had not already known it before, Cred certainly had it confirmed to him now that the young woman standing before him was a fine Druidess. Her perception was keen, sharper than most of the Druid minds he knew. He had not seen Cromlach yet but he looked forward to meeting him, knowing that this Cromlach was Gráinne's mentor, her own Draoi. Emer had told him a lot about Cromlach's wisdom as a teacher and he had longed to have such a one at the Dún.

Cred could not answer. He had nothing to say. She knew him too well. Perhaps because no one had understood him or *them* before, it made him feel in his being a sudden rush of warmth for her.

He longed to sip the fragrance of crushed petals from her lips, wished her hair as silken skeins binding his body to hers. The rush of warmth was pulsating, invading his flesh until he had to break free of the encircling willow, away from her, out of the circle, out of her sight, out of sight of her. His heart thumped as he ran and he could almost feel the breath of a wolf on his heels, such was his need to flee.

Gráinne did not move. She felt immobilized, her body was stiffened, her legs rigid, the babe seemed like a hard knot coiled in her belly. Rooted as the tree, she was powerless to go after him, to call out, to tell him she did not mean to read his private mind, if that was indeed what she had done. He confirmed to her by his actions that he was blessed by the Tuatha De Danann, had definite contact with them. There was something else though that she read in his grey eyes, a kindling of emotion, of desire that made her own heart leap in her breast. He had taken on a rare godlike beauty about his features which had thrown her off-guard. She had not expected it and her body tensed in anticipation. For a wild moment she thought his lips were going to brush hers, but the moment was frozen and lost to eternity. He had not succumbed to the urge, and she had been unable to go after him.

Slowly her limbs recovered. She knelt down by the well. Scooping some of the crystal-cool water in her hands, she drank, savouring the taste of the source somewhere far up the mountain beyond.

She lifted a willow frond that had broken off and lay by the well. Her fingers worked quickly at making a willow-knot, and she pulled out a few strands of her hair to weave into it.

> "Saille, Saille, willow, willow,
> My will to love, my love to will,
> Weave, weave, willow tree,
> May my love return to me."

She cast the knot into the spring and watched eagerly to see if it would float back towards her. It did, but the knot fell apart so that she scooped it out of the well and laid it beside the other offerings there. It was only a child's game anyway. It did not mean anything much. She was thoughtful as she left the Grove to walk back to the Dún.

# CHAPTER 6

# BALTINNE

*The wait is long, his heart beats sore,*
*Faith drags his feet in time*
*Love leaps more when love is strong*
*And traps of spirit unbind.*

The next three moons were the most difficult for Gráinne. She tried to keep up with her classes every day with the Draoi, but she still missed Cromlach. She was separated from him bodily, unable to get up the mountain because of her increasing size, and he was unable to come down, not because of the descent but because of the ascent back up the mountain on his return.

Every other day she saw Finann the goatherd. He came to see Cred regularly at the forge and then came over to her quarters to give her news of how Cromlach was faring. She made bread for Cromlach, little cheeses and lots of fresh berries, made pies, and gave them all to Finann to take back and share with him. She spent hours stitching little motifs and embroidering fine woven rugs for his bedding. It kept her mind from thinking too many thoughts, thinking of long golden hair and grey eyes. She could not understand why Cred avoided her now. No one at the Dún realized he was doing so, as they knew Cred was a man of little words anyhow. But she knew and it bothered her. The odd times that she glimpsed him coming and going, her heart lurched and she wished she had the courage to approach him.

Preparations were being made for Baltinne, the May celebration. Some called it Bealtaine, but Lugnae Fer Trí preferred the name given by the people of the Isles.

Emer was like a busy bee, preparing the feast three days beforehand.

Lugnae had all his trappers out, hunting only those creatures not spawning, carrying young, or weaning them. The hunters culled only the deer who were not parenting. At this time of year the young females of all the species were left alone.

Scath the Druid's daughter, Serb, was chosen as the Spring Queen. Her hair was long and straight, white as the palest oak that has been bleached with the sun. She was young and very excited at having been the chosen one. Her violet eyes danced as she tried on her robe of the sheerest silk, made by Emer. She visualized herself wearing the green garland of mistletoe upon her brow. Emer was going to attach long flowing ribbons to the garland, which Serb knew she would be able to keep afterwards.

Serb was blossoming like a fragile young flower seeking the sun, seeking the bee's probe, unwilling to let anything stand in the way of her desires. She had a young man in her head already whom she wished to procure for her heart. After she danced the maze, she would choose him for her own, her Corn King. He could not refuse, not on that day.

Fergus the poet was going to play the Green Man. It was usual for the poet or one of the Elders to play such a role.

This year, Gráinne would watch the proceedings from the circle around the edges of the field, a field that was marked out by a drystone wall all around it and, of course, the circles of stones within it. These had been placed in a spiral going around and around into the centre of the field to form a maze. The site was used for Baltinne and Samhain, two of the major celebrations in Éiriú.

The day arrived. Gráinne wondered if Cromlach would come but knew he probably wouldn't. She gathered that he would be with the Elders at the top of Knocknarea to light the Baltinne fire.

All the hearths in the land were smoored with ashes and doused with water. No one was allowed to light a fire until the first one at Teamhair was lit. The seven sacred hills would then brandish their fire-beacons, each beacon hill thereafter lighting its fires, right across the land, one after the other until all of Éiriú was aglow with the new spirit.

Every year it happened. This year would be no different.

The Spring Queen from last year stood in the centre of the maze, with the garland of mistletoe ready to be placed on the new Queen's brow. Everyone grasped hands and swayed in a circle around the field, their garments bright and colourful, children with blossoms in their hair, their faces eager and flushed. Scath had the new bright-gold sickle that Cred had made for him tied to his waist. Gráinne caught the glimmer of the gold as he walked past her, and she thought how Cred had sullied the first sickle he had made for Scath.

She caught Cred's eye but he quickly looked down. She stared, willing him to look up, willing him with all her power but he was stubborn. His eyes firmly found a stone in the grass and refused to waver from it.

The chanting began and Fergus started to recite a sacred dance poem:

> "The power of the wheel
> Turning and turning,
> Churning up fevers
> As feet fly their spirit dance
> Across, beyond, between the swords.
> We bow to the sacred humming of the *bodhran*,
> Throw our arms up for Dulem, Rig na n-Dul,
> And lock antlers with a fighting stag,
> Whirling and bucking and reeling
> So that hearts thud and jump,
> Soaring up purple mountains
> To dive down deep green valleys.
> We yearn for the naked truth of it all,
> The call of clan, tribe, one of us,
> The plaid, the pipes, the strings, the drums,
> The stones, the stones, gateways all,
> Laid down by us before
> And so we return, again and again,
> Keeping that flame alive, that memory clear,

Unshadowed by anything within this world.
As the earth breathes, so do we.
As the fire leaps, so do we.
As the water flows, so do we.
As the air swirls, so do we,
Turning and turning, dancing the dance
As the soil is turned for the seed,
As death moves to life,
As the seed turns to the soil,
As the wheel moves, so do we."

Fergus had a magnificent booming voice which resounded and echoed around the circle.

One of the women of the *ráth*, whose name was Tachta, entered from the side. She represented the old woman of the *Sidh*, keening for the death of Bal, and this rose above the chant. Gráinne felt herself pining for the old with her. Then she saw Fergus, dressed as the Green Man, jump and race through the maze, taunting and teasing the old woman until all the people shouted at him. They called for him to renew, not to listen to the song of death that she sang, to think of the birth, see her only as the divine midwife, help her to renew too. The Green Man, covered in branches from the nine sacred trees, then scanned the crowd, searching, searching until he found Serb, Scath's daughter, the new Spring chosen one.

He started to dance through the maze with her. The chanting grew louder, the people swayed around the field, the air was permeated with their urgings and their calls. They had reached the centre, the old May Queen handed the garland to the Green Man and he placed it on the head of the new Queen.

Serb stood still, her blond hair blowing in the wind like waving corn, her robe sheer on her budding body, her lips red as blood, and no one there could say she was not the new May Queen.

As the old woman's keening turned to song, Serb joined in with her sweet young voice, then took over and brought the old into the new.

Everyone cheered her on and then exploded into laughter, singing, shouting and embracing when the beacon fire on top of

Knocknarea roared into life. They joined hands again and raced around the field in one direction and then in the opposite way. Eventually they calmed down and stood waiting for the Queen to choose the Corn King.

Serb danced out of the maze and went around the circle to find her King. Gráinne watched her, remembering when she, herself, had done the same at Crom Cruach. This was a great moment for Serb, one she would never forget. The girl was beautiful in her robes, with the garland of mistletoe on her head trailing long, colourful ribbons. She carried a posy of white May blossom in her hands. Gráinne had seen her many times chatting and laughing with one of Emer's older sons, Donal Rua, so she guessed that she would probably choose him. She glanced over at Emer and saw her nudging Donal Rua with her elbow and laughing, teasing with him, but the swirling ribbons and the flowing robes danced right on past him. Gráinne felt sorry for the crestfallen look on his face. Emer was frowning, her expression unreadable.

At first, Gráinne had not realized what happened, so intent were her thoughts on Emer's son. It was not really until the cheer went up and everyone started pitching blossom, leaves and grain towards the pair that she was aware of whom had been chosen.

She was stricken. Her pulse stopped. She felt herself flush pink as she saw the May posy clutched in Cred's hand, then she blanched whiter than death as he left the circle. Clutching Serb's hand, he clumsily began the dance again with her around the large field. They made a startlingly beautiful couple.

The next thing Gráinne knew, she was swaying with the people but Emer was beside her, supporting her.

"Gráinne, Gráinne . . . are you all right?"

"N-no. T-take me away, Emer."

"We cannot leave," whispered Emer loudly in her ear, "you know we cannot leave until the Green Man dies."

Fergus, the Green Man, was shedding his branches. He was casting off his old body and the branches were being stacked in the centre of the maze. Cred and Serb then lit the fire with a burning bog-spail given to them by Scath the Druid. The revelry began. Everyone shouted and swarmed the maze, anxious to leap the flames and make new wishes and vows for the coming second half of the year. The Green Man, with his white naked body, leapt the first yellow flames with a yell of freedom and rebirth. Then Cred and Serb followed suit and the people jumped after them.

Gráinne turned away, unable to watch, her heart heavy.

Cred soared high through the air with Serb, the raw heat licking his feet. He was being swept by the fever of it all but he was sorry in his heart, sorry that he had not raised his head to meet Gráinne's eyes. He had felt her drawing him, she would have known, if only he had looked up. Now, it was too late, he had been chosen by Serb. Later, Serb and he would have to drive the cattle between twin fires with Lugnae. This would ensure the bounty of the herds and the crops. Then they would have to cut the apples in half across the core, apples left over from last year, to reveal the stars inside. Everyone would grab the apples and eat them to ensure the unity of the tribe. The feast would begin.

Later, Serb would want him, expect him to love her, her first loving. They would be staying in the *Brighdal bothán*. He would be with her for a whole moon-cycle and a day. After that, he had the choice of staying with her or not for one year and a day until the next Baltinne.

She was beautiful, but he did not know how he would last the day, never mind a whole moon or a year. He wanted the girl with the hair of night, eyes of sky, skin of parched silk. He wanted to caress the snow-white belly which was a cradle for a king.

Gráinne lay on the bedding pallet strewn with furs and soft woollen rugs. She was in Emer's quarters. She clenched her teeth to stop herself from sobbing. She must not shed a tear on Mayday.

"Gráinne, do not upset yourself, remember the babe. Gráinne?" Emer was patting her back. "It is not good. I have two spirits in my household not happy with the Spring rites. It is not good. Please, Gráinne?"

But Gráinne remained silent. She did not trust herself to speak, could not move. She heard Emer quietly cross to another quarter in the Dún. She could hear the sobs, the young heart-broken sobs of a young adult boy and she knew his pain, etched in her own breast as it was, piercing like a thorn, emptying her mind. A vacuum of mourning descended upon her. There was no difference between yearning and unfulfilled love. They laced hands. They were one and the same.

Cred was naked, muscular, staring down at the slender, fragile body before him. She was lying on the hides on the floor, the dancing light of the hearth fire making her skin glow. Her long corn-silk hair draped across her breasts and trailed off the hides across the straw-covered floor. Her hair and the straw became one. Her eyes caught his and she opened her slim legs shakily. He knew he had to take her for the sake of the tribe and for the good of the crops in the coming year, but his spirit was somewhere else haunting him.

He saw Gráinne curled up as if in pain, writhing in her sleep, and the vision disturbed him. His hands stretched out tenderly to the one before him. He half-closed his eyes, transforming her face into the one he desired most. He moaned as he plunged himself into her, straining against the resistance of her maiden veil. She cried out, tensing her legs as he burst through. He felt the hot gush of warmth, blood-red as her lips, tight, merciless. He moaned with the pain of his being, his spirit far removed from it all, and he saw her pain and ecstasy without any joy of his own. The mistletoe berries were squashed in her hair but he was dry. He knew he had not planted his seed, could not, but she seemed unaware as she turned in his arms and sighed blissfully.

# CHAPTER 7

# THE PREDICTION

*Dark silence reigns across the land,*
*Black shadows hail a storm,*
*The rape of Earth, ill-fate at hand,*
*And blighted crop is born.*

Cred woke up one morning four sennights later, thinking to himself: "Just one more day, just one more night, and I am free again."

He had tried to busy himself in the forge during the day, spending valuable hours making swords, farm implements such as the new ploughshare that had the iron blade, protective headwear for skirmishes and battles, rivets and anything else he could think of, to keep him from returning to the Brighdal *bothán*.

She was like a beautiful wraith but he did not want her. By this time, she knew the mistake she had made. Cred was uneasy. No good could come of it but there was nothing he could do to change fate. He could not satisfy her totally in the way that she wanted. He felt sorry for her. Everyone was going to await eagerly to see if she would fall with child. It would bring great fortune to the tribe, but they must all wait in vain. No child could he sire with her. He tried, but always at the last moment the pleasure evaded him and he collapsed on top of her, beads of sweat breaking out of his pores. She would try to arouse him again in a quiet desperation but he could not appease her longing in that way. He brought great pleasure to her, she would weep with joy, but when it came to himself, the gods were against it, the goddess had denied him. And he was glad.

He no longer pushed Gráinne from his mind. Instead, he dwelt on impressions of her, letting her image invade his every waking thought. As he plunged the iron in the fire, he thought of her, when he melted the silver and gold he thought of her. When he awoke, she was in his head and before he fell asleep she was there, ready to slip into all his dreams.

As he stepped out this one particular morning he felt uneasy. Something was not quite right about the air. The wind was light and the sky seemed blue enough, just one or two clouds up there, light and fluffy, but there was something not quite right. Everything had a stillness about it. The birds were not singing as usual. Cred examined the dew on the grass to see if it was bright and clear. It was. He listened for any sounds at all and was not surprised to hear the lonely, raucous call of a young rook. He knew it could not be hailing a battle so it had to be for something else. As he searched the tops of the trees for a sign of the bird, he suddenly noticed a wispy, layered cloud appear from behind the mountain, a cloud with long sweeping tails. So this was it! A goat's-hair cloud silently slipping across the sky.

"Ah, you thought I would not see you," he murmured as he noted from which direction it came, where it was going and how long it would take to cross his view.

A storm! It was hailing a storm and one of great proportions. He calculated that it would hit the Dún in about five nights' time.

Cred ran to the entrance of the *rath*. He scanned the horizon for Finann. There he was, far away but running as fast as his legs could carry him. A smile crossed Cred's face. He knew that Finann had also seen the cloud and read it correctly.

"Cred!" Finann said breathlessly. "There is goat's hair in the sky! Look! I would say, a sennight away."

Cred shook his head.

"No, no, five, I would say five nights. We will have to warn Lugnae. And you, Finann, will have to get your goats off the mountain into shelter. Oh, and we will have to bring Cromlach and the Elders back down."

"Cromlach is not there."

"Not there? Since when?"

"For two nights he has not been there. I think he may be staying with the Elders above."

"And you cannot go up there, Finann?"

"No, of course not."

"Then how will we warn them if we do not find Cromlach to mediate for us?"

"Lugnae or Scath the Druid will have to go up. I tried to blow my horn to see if anyone would come down but I suppose they either could not hear it, or else they are so used to hearing it that they did not think it warranted a response." Finann had a glint in his eye as he added, "It's going to be a big one!"

He loved storms, although he feared for his goats. He loved the charge in the air, the fury of the winds, the sighs of the branches. The clouds were huge, dark, ominous, and exhilarating. He was afraid of them and in awe of them at the same time. He knew the hand of the goddess struck out each time they had a storm.

Cred and Finann ran towards the Dún to find Lugnae. Gráinne saw them through the wicker slats and wondered what was wrong. She was curious, even though her breast trembled at the sight of him.

She could not face him, not in her anguish, could not yet bring herself to speak with him nor acknowledge his presence. No explanation at this time, no matter how genuine, would suffice. The fact that Serb had chosen Cred, even if against his wishes, was not acceptable to Gráinne. She tried to reason with herself but to no avail. Some stubborn inner voice would persist and override any rationality that tried to surface. She responded without feeling now. She answered when she was spoken to, she attended the Draoi classes but her mind absorbed the knowledge given to her without the usual rapt pleasure she experienced. Conversations were dull, food was lifeless, Emer's children a constant backdrop of noise and chatter that was an irritation to abide with. Her belly grew larger, more cumbersome, only the precious little kicks within her serving to comfort, console, and remind her that love grew. Regardless of its struggling journey to the light, persistent with the strength to overcome any obstacle, such as a plant has that pierces through stone to reach the sunlight, love grew. This, her one humbling thought, given to her by Cromlach many moons ago, was now her only thread by which she clung to a separate reality that she yearned to possess. No one had told her of the torture of love, newly found and lost. It was as if she mourned a death whilst she carried a life. She was empty and full at the same moment. Yet, in her twilight, in some strange way, she was centred, her happiness and her sorrow hand in hand. This emotional experience was inflicted upon, and absorbed by, the King-boy within her. She knew it in the stretching of her soul, in the keening of her mind, but was powerless to exert any effort to avoid the pain. He was learning about his life before he came into it. His re-emergence and individuality began the instant of his conception and first movement. His recall and re-learning had begun then too.

Gráinne believed these things and knew them to be so. The Brehon Law pertaining to the constant happiness and placating of a child-carrying woman was valid but useless to Gráinne. Her joys and sorrows were born from a single thought within, which was fuelled from the events external. Whoever had control of such a twin-bearing thought had surely a divine nature. These fat old Brehons, the Law-givers, were wise enough to her way of thinking, but knew nothing about the wayward rules of love and the untimely gestures of its emotions, yearnings, ecstasies, spurnings, and tears.

No Law could be attributed to love or capture its divinity. No child within could be exempt from its pull or shielded from its backlash. There was no protection from its force and only strength and beauty would be carved from the understanding of it. Gráinne did not worry about her child.

Emer did though. She became like a great mother hen, protecting, protecting all of the time, constantly watching out for Gráinne and her own son, Donal Rua. He moped around the house all day, stirring up envy and hatred of Cred from his spurned emotions. He did not even blame Serb but thought that Cred must surely have seduced Serb prior to Baltinne. To his mind, Serb would never have chosen as she did of her own volition. Not after the way she had flaunted herself and teased him over the past moons.

Donal Rua was only made more aware of the inadequacies of being young and inexperienced. He determined to be more of a man, becoming aggressive with his younger siblings, trying to assert his strength, so that Emer had to lecture him on more than one occasion. Lugnae bellowed at him a few times. Only Gráinne remained silent, observing.

Now he too watched from his quarters, through the slatted window. He watched Cred approach, much as a young stag would who has been thwarted by a bigger rival, and he determined to be avenged somehow. His anger bubbled under the surface today, as it did every day, all day, growing along with him, waiting for that one chance.

The tears he had shed for Serb would be his last, each one of those having been wrenched from him. He would be avenged for this robbery. His grief smouldered quietly, fuelled by the sight of Serb's chosen one. He ached at every thought of them together.

He saw his father, Lugnae, rein in his horse. Lugnae was returning from an early hunting expedition with the other trappers. Donal Rua was curious now. Everyone seemed very excited and he could hear his father barking orders at his men.

Gráinne had also been observing from her vantage point and now she ran to meet Emer who was entering the Hall. Emer had gone out to see what the disturbance was about.

"Emer, what is wrong? Is it ill news? I saw Finann." She did not mention Cred. "Is Cromlach faring well?" Her voice was tremulous, afraid.

"Oh, *a stór*," Emer answered, "at last you have emerged from your shell . . . no, do not worry. Cromlach, as far as I know it, is faring well. No, this is probably nothing, only news of a storm. It is nothing we have not been through before."

"A storm?" Gráinne was surprised. "But the sky is blue, there is hardly a cloud out there."

"Well, apparently both Cred and Finann saw a goat's-hair cloud, whatever that may be, and they know it to hail a storm, a fairly hefty one as I understand it." Emer smiled and shook her head, "These men, they love to alarm us from time to time. A lot of waffle about a little nothing, if you ask me!"

Gráinne was not so sure. Their weather predictions were not to be scorned.

Lugnae certainly took them at their word. Before the day was through, Daire the carpenter had wedged and staked anything that was loose. He shuttered up any opening. Cred weighted the roof on the Dún dwelling, his grey eyes constantly scanning the Dún Hall and the inner chambers, searching for even a glimpse of Gráinne, but she avoided him by staying on the other side, in the quarters furthest away from where he was working.

His close proximity was disturbing for her, as it was also for Donal Rua, who eventually could not stand it and ran from the Dún.

He passed the other *bothúns* in the *rúth* and saw that the men were at work, securing them as much as possible. Then, taking courage, in a strange mood of elevation, making sure everyone was busy enough not to notice his movements, he furtively made his way to the forbidden territory, the Brighdal *bothún*.

His heart pumped into his throat, his whole being thudding with the drum of it as he entered the sacred dwelling.

"Cred? You are back early, *a stór*," Serb called from the back chamber, her voice hopeful and eager.

Donal Rua bristled with the endearment which should have been his, not Cred's. The sound of her familiar soft brogue swamped him, making a hard knot under his plaid kilt, a hard knot that tightened and lifted, rising with his rage and desire.

He edged himself along the wall, anxious that she not cry out when she saw him. His palms were wet and clammy and he almost could not catch his breath.

"Come in, Cred, please come in here," she called breathlessly, disrobing and lying down on the soft otter skins, trimmed with rabbit and ermine. She knew it might be too late now in her moon cycle to conceive, but she wanted to have a last try before he eluded her for ever. This would be her last day and last night with him. She knew it in her bones that he was in love with another, although she had no notion of the identity of her rival.

What happened next both astonished and terrified her. A figure lunged itself upon her, forcing a rough, clammy wet hand across her mouth so that she could not scream out. She struggled wildly, her body arching to throw off the assailant.

Then she recognized her friend, Emer's son, Donal Rua, and the full horror of the situation seeped over her. He was breaking the oldest taboo of all, against the goddess, bringing shame to his family. Lugnae Fer Trí would kill him if he ever found out his own son was risking the safety and well-being of the tribe.

Serb struggled and writhed with all her strength but it was no use. He had parted her legs. Positioning himself hard against her pelvis, he slammed his body into hers, crushing her into the furs so that she felt the hard ground beneath them, bruising her back. His kilt was rough and hairy against her smooth belly, causing friction burns with his every movement. She felt then the charging violation of her inner sanctum and shuddered as his weight fell on her again and again, his voice hurling and hissing expletives at her with every new thrust. His nails dug deep into her skin. He then lifted his hand from her face and slapped her violently when she tried to yell, punching her when she tried to wriggle free. He plunged his tongue into her open mouth, to silence her, his lips hard and tight against hers. She tried to bite him but she could not move. Instead, she found herself feverishly absorbing him against her will. His sweat-smell invaded her nostrils, his hardness invaded her belly, the rhythm now fast, furious and constant so that her body gushed wet to protect her from that dry pain. She rose as he drew back and fell as he rushed forward. The tension flew out of her body only to tighten again as she drank his mouth, sucking with all her might now, desperate, desperate, her bruised body leaching his, like the mistletoe on the apple tree, anxious to survive, extracting lifeforce from its host to ensure its growth.

His breath was ragged, his pulse beating a war-drum. He spilled within her in waves and she rose with the swell, frantic now, crashing bones and flesh, rippling a tide of fierce ecstasy.

She was quietly crying, limp like a rag-poppet that the children played with. He crushed the sobbing young woman against him, aghast at the enormity of what he had done. He was shaking, his body racked with remorse, but he had no tears. They had all been spent. Her body was red, rubbed raw in places against his clothing. She would be bruised badly. Her lips were swollen. His fingermarks were still across her cheek where he had plastered his hand against her mouth and where he had struck her. Yet, he knew it had not all been resistance.

"I am sorry, Serb," he whispered hoarsely into her ear, gently brushing her fair hair back from her damp forehead, "I only loved you."

He covered her with a woollen blanket, then straightening himself up, he carefully checked that no one would see him leave and he ran, ran as fast as his legs would carry him. He ran to the river and not even bothering to peel off his clothes he threw himself in the cold water, immersing himself completely, surfacing and choking. He was sick, spewing his guts up as if he would never stop. His manhood had been achieved painfully and not by fair means. He coughed and threw his shame out from his body until the thin, burning taste of his bile welled in his throat, scorching his soul, branding him with his own scorn. No amount of water would wash this memory away. He had violated the one he most cared about to avenge himself on the one he now detested. Cred would pay for this. Somehow, some way, some day, Cred would pay.

Cred did not want to return to the Brighdal *bothán*. It was his last night there but he did not want to be with Serb again, though he knew he must keep to the Law.

With a heavy heart, he left the Dún, having tried to catch a glimpse, just one glimpse of Gráinne all day, but she had avoided him.

He walked into the *bothán*, surprised at the silence. Usually Serb was there to greet him, hungry to fulfil her own desires, and to try to overcome his failure to grant the will of the gods, and the people, to make her fertile with child. This was the purpose of Baltinne.

He did not think he could even touch her tonight.

"Serb?"

There was no answer.

He walked into the back chamber divided from the rest by a woven screen.

She was lying motionless, silent in the dark. Cred was aware of something different about her but he could not detect what it was. He could not see her. He lit a beeswax candle from the fire which was dying in the main room. He thought maybe she was asleep but he felt uneasy, something niggled him, tugged at the fringes of his mind.

The light threw great, long shadows against the wicker walls, playing against her still body.

"Serb? Serb, are you awake?"

There was no answer, just a faint sob. She was covered in a woollen blanket. Slowly, she turned towards him and uncovered herself.

He gasped, stricken by what he saw. Her face was distorted, her lips swollen and bleeding. She had been crying and her eyes were red and puffed. Her slender body was bruised and red raw weals laced her belly.

Cred could not speak. He was bereft of words, his mouth hanging open in disbelief.

A fresh flood of tears squeezed from her eyes, her face crumpling pitifully when she saw his expression change to horror as realization hit him. The goddess had been violated.

"Who did this?" he roared. "Who dared to come here?"

His anger spilled over, his face draining of colour. He tried to calm down. She needed help. Her bruises needed tending. He covered her gently again with the blanket and stroked her face, wiping the wet tears away with his fingers.

"Serb, I have to get help."

She caught his arm to detain him.

"No! Please . . . "

"But, Serb, you are hurt. I must fetch the physician, Morann, and Emer or Lugnae."

"No!" she sobbed as she struggled to sit up, pain biting her back as she did so. "You must not! Not Lugnae nor Emer."

"Serb, they have to know. This warrants a severe penalty, you know that."

"No! Please, Cred, please." Her voice was hoarse.

"Why? Who are you shielding? Serb, he hurt you, he has walked on forbidden ground. The Elders must be told."

70

"Cred," Serb whispered imploringly, "if I tell you who it was, you must swear an oath not to speak to anyone of this day. Swear!"

"I cannot do that, you know I cannot." Cred was emphatic.

She panicked, "You must! You must! If you . . . if you try to tell them, I will deny it. They will think it was you! I will say it was you!"

He was shocked. He felt like someone had thrown ice-cold water in his face. If the tribe thought he had maltreated her like this, he would have to leave. He would never see Gráinne again. He could not work as a smith. He would be demoted in social status, unable to live as a nobleman, unable to practise his art for a number of years, whatever penalty the Elders would impose upon him. His face darkened.

"All right, Serb," he said coldly, "I swear."

"By *Brighde*?"

Bridget! The goddess of the smithcraft, of poetry, of the arts, of the fire. She certainly knew how to make him take an oath he could only break with his life.

He nodded. "By Brighde." He thought of Gráinne and his life ahead. He wanted one to blend with the other.

Serb's swollen lips trembled as she uttered: "It was Donal Rua, Emer's son, Lugnae's son."

Cred sat down beside her abruptly. "Are you sure? Serb, this is grave, very grave indeed."

"Yes, of course I am sure." Serb looked at him pleadingly. "Donal Rua was in love with me. Now you can see why we cannot tell Emer or Lugnae. We can never tell them. It would bring dreadful shame to them and the tribe. The knowledge would destroy them both."

"Donal Rua has already shamed himself in the eyes of the goddess," Cred said bitterly. "She herself will exact a price for this, as I speak the truth. Already there is a storm coming. We cannot stay here."

"But what are we to do? I cannot let anyone see me like this, most of all my family! I dare not go to my father's dwelling. Being a Druid, he would insist on a trial and judgement by the Elders. And Lugnae would have to be present."

Cred tried to shut out the feeling of impending doom that threatened to overcome him.

"But the moon cycle for us is finished on the morrow, Serb. We both know we are not suited to each other. You are deserving of much better than this," he said kindly, trying to let her down gently but truthfully. "You have to return to your father on the morrow unless we decide to stay for a year and a day together. You know we cannot do that. A commitment is a commitment, once we take up habitation in the Brighdal *bothán*, we are in the embrace of the goddess, we have to obey her Law, the tribe's Law."

"If I return home to my father on the morrow, Cred, then you will be called before the Elders. I cannot undo my bruises and veil my face from my family. You will have to stay with me until I recover. Once I look better and the marks have gone, I will go back home."

"No," Cred said darkly, "it is the Law that if we pass the first moon and a day, then you must return to your father. If you do not, we are then obliged to pass the next moons to make up the year and a day. If we do not keep this Law, great misfortune may plague the tribe."

She was silent, miserable.

He put his head into his hands.

"There is nothing to be done. We must serve our allotted time together now, for one year and one day. Already we have served one moon . . . " His voice broke on the words. He was unable to continue. He felt trapped, betrayed, as if he was being punished for not upholding the tradition of the Corn King. He had badly let down the gods and this was his just reward. Gráinne seemed like a distant treasure now, remote, untouchable. He could never explain to her why he was staying with Serb. He had sworn not to tell the Truth, therefore he could not say anything. His lips were bitterly sealed. His heart was stone-weighted.

# CHAPTER 8

# THE STORM

*Trees bend low and break their backs*
*In homage to Earth's solemn fury,*
*The waters flow to swell the banks*
*And burst upon the land in glory.*

Scath the Druid had been surprised when his daughter Serb had not returned home, but he was delighted too. Her choice of partner was everything a doting father wished for. Cred was a very talented nobleman, with all the ways of a Druid, although Scath knew him not to be as such. The outcome of the Baltinne festivities could not have made Scath happier.

He had seen the mild flirtations that had gone on previously between Serb and Lugnae's son, Donal Rua. That had pleased him too. One could not go wrong with a chief's son, although Donal Rua, he knew, was temperamental and not very skilled in any of the crafts. He did not command the elements like Cred did and he was younger, not so much in build as in mind. Scath was content with Serb's choice.

Emer, meanwhile, was not so pacified with the outcome. Two nights ago, Donal Rua came home late, did not eat any food or sup from water, milk, or ale, but went to bed immediately. His clothing had been soaking wet as if he had fallen in the river but his face was a bit scratched and bruised. Emer thought he must have had a scuffle with one of the boys in the *ráth* who had got the better of him and ducked him. Emer did not want to humiliate him further by prying or forcing the truth. Whatever lesson it was, or score that was settled, the gods must have deemed him deserving of it. However, she was worried when he moped all day long and walked half the night. Her concern grew as his appetite diminished. A scowl was permanently

73

engraved on his face, and at every opportunity he tried to spoil any fun the little ones were having. He did not like to see them enjoy themselves. He was not good company at present and Emer knew it was way past the time he should have served his fosterage. Now, she considered it. Maybe it would help him get over his lovesickness and Serb's rebuff. She determined to talk to Lugnae about it when they had a quiet moment.

Gráinne was numb with a constant feeling of loss. On top of that, she had a niggling worry about Cromlach on the mountain. The storm was going to be here any day soon, and Cromlach had not come down. Some of the Elders were due back this afternoon, so maybe he would be with them. Gráinne decided to wait and see if he returned.

Finann's goats were already gathered up and in a wooden shelter near by. Finann said he was going to stay with them. He spent all day piling stones around the shelter for added support against the wind. Emer's children and the other Clan children were amazed when they saw Misha carrying the stones in her wicker creels. They ran alongside, laughing and chattering, wanting to help as much as possible. Finann promised the little ones a ride, the first sunny day after the storm was over.

The afternoon came and left and Cromlach was not in the Dún. Gráinne was distraught. She marched off to find Finann, unsucessfully. For once, he was not with his goats. Without thinking, she went over to the forge.

Cred stopped in his tracks, astounded that she was really standing there before him.

"Where is Cromlach, Cred? Do you have news of him? Does Finann know of his whereabouts?" she asked, her words tumbling into each other, her heart thumping wildly as she tried to get them out coherently. "All the Elders are down, but Cromlach did not come with them."

Cred came over to her. He wanted to comfort her but knew he dared not touch her. Instead, he picked up some fire-irons he was repairing and pretended to examine them carefully. He spoke gruffly.

"Finann said Cromlach has not been on the Hill of Mists for

maybe three or four days now. We assumed he was with the Elders above, but obviously if he did not come down the mountain with them, then he is not there."

This did not give any comfort to Gráinne. Cred looked at her. He wished he had good news to impart to her. Her face paled and she put her hand out to steady herself. He rushed forward to catch her, but despite the fact that she was almost fainting she could not bear him near her and shook him off angrily. He felt as if a bee had stung him.

"I need water," she gasped, as she sat down abruptly on a stool he drew up quickly for her. He grabbed a cup and scooped water from a pail clumsily. Half of it spilled out, drenching him, but he did not care. She looked dreadful. Maybe he should fetch Emer. As if she read his mind, Gráinne said: "No, I do not need anyone."

Her hair was lank and uncombed, her face strained and blotched. This was not the Gráinne he knew.

"Gráinne, Cromlach is not on Knocknarea mountain. If he was, Finann would see him."

"Finann did not see him there before, when he was gone for all those moons," Gráinne retorted sharply, after sipping the water gratefully. She felt a hot flush wash over her.

Cred assured her. 'The Elders would not leave him up there. Wherever he is, Cromlach will be safe. He is a *seer*, is he not? Anyway, that is what Finann said, he said Cromlach knows when a storm is about."

Gráinne felt better than she did when she first came in. Of course Cromlach knew that a storm was coming. Maybe he was staying in a *crannóg* somewhere, outside the Dún. Her mind became calm again.

"Thank you, Cred," she murmured, then almost jumped out of her skin as a huge bolt of bright-blue lightning lit up the inside of the forge.

"Quick! Get back to the Dún, Gráinne!" Cred said urgently.

"But what . . . what about you?" she asked, when she had sufficiently recovered her breath.

His face turned red, shiny like the red night-berries.

"I – I have to get back to the Brighdal *bóthan* to get Serb. Lugnae wants us all in the Dún Hall," he finished lamely.

Gráinne was stunned. He had chosen to stay with Serb then, for the year and a day, maybe for ever.

"Gráinne," he went on, seeing her expression, "I need to explain . . . " But there was nothing he could say truthfully except: "I was asked to stay, against my will."

It sounded feeble. He was angry with himself. Life was unjust. He was with a woman he did not want to be with, and pined for a woman he could not have. He worried about bringing Serb to the Dún as her face was still dark, her bruises having discoloured her complexion. Donal Rua was surely going to be there too.

"It is nothing to me what you do," Gráinne said, her cheeks now as deeply red as his own. But her blue eyes betrayed her, they were icy.

A roll of thunder ripped across the sky. The vengeance had begun. It was now upon them.

She rushed into the black evening, large plops of water descending upon her coldly.

She heard him call after her but she had no intention of waiting to hear what more he could say. She was hurrying awkwardly, her belly full and round, her babe kicking wildly within her. Gráinne was returning to the Dún and she vowed not to set foot in the Hall whilst Cred and Serb were there. She knew in her heart that Donal Rua would not either.

The Hall was full of people squatting on the rush-covered floors, lying on wooden pallets covered in skins, or sitting on benches. No one was anxious to stand up. It was as if the closer they hugged the earth, the more protection they had. The Elders started the story-telling and Fergus strummed his harp soothingly. The rain battered the thatch, the wind howled against the shutters, the lightning glared, its fire-bolts being hurled from above as the sky grumbled and crashed its fury upon them.

Gráinne shivered in her quarters. She heard some of the children crying with fright and a mother's gentle voice hushing her baby. The gruff voices of the men and the interception of light laughter and soft chatter of the women drew her attention away from the storm. She was straining to catch familiar voices, hoping to clarify one of them as Cromlach's or if she had but the courage to admit it to herself, Cred's. She thought it highly unlikely that she would hear Cred as he did not normally speak much. She desperately wanted to hear Cromlach, although she knew in the depths of her soul that he was not there, nor was he on the mountain or anywhere in the *ráth*. This, however, made no difference to the workings of her mind which still envisaged him lost on Knocknarea in the dreadful storm. The Hill of the Well, or the Hill of Mists as Cred referred to it, was the most sheltered part of the mountain but she doubted it would afford much shelter against heavy rains and a wild storm. The clouds were probably really low and thick, creating a fog which could make a late descent very treacherous.

All these things passed through her mind but they were not enough to divert her thoughts from returning to the sounds in the Hall, alike unto a hive of bees. She smiled foolishly at the analogy but that was what she heard. She could not go out there into the midst of such torture and noise.

The lightning was striking frequently now, great blue flashes, making her feel quite sick. It was no use closing her eyes, she could still see it. The sky ripped open above her, the howls of the wrath of the gods swamped the Dún. There was a horrific crash. Gráinne heard the screams of the children. She realized she was unable to stifle her own cries as each new tumbling wave of thunder, like a giant boulder, surged and pounded across her roof. Pulling blankets over her head and curling up protectively helped a little, but she still shuddered with the onslaught of sound. She heard trees breaking and falling to the ground as if they had been chopped at their knees or ripped up by the roots and flung aside by giants. The wind was straining to lift the thatch which, fortunately, had been weighted down by Cred with flax ropes knotted into iron land-pegs.

Emer came in and clucked over her like a hen with a chick. Gráinne could tell that Emer wanted to tuck her under her wing. Emer patted the blankets but Gráinne would not emerge.

She merely mumbled that she was fine. "Gráinne," whispered Emer, "I want to tell you something."

Gráinne cautiously peeped her head out. She felt like a mole testing the air at the top of her mound. It was the intense urgency in Emer's voice that coaxed her from her warm sanctuary.

Emer was perturbed.

"Serb is here with Cred."

Gráinne nodded, flinching, her eyes pained in their expression.

"*A stór*," Emer said, frowning, "I am worried. Serb has a wrap around her head and a veil of heavy dark silk pulled across half of her face. She said she has the ache in her tooth."

"Well?" Gráinne was puzzled. "Can Morann or Fergus not heal it?"

"I know. That is what I thought. I heard Serb's father, Scath, speak with Morann but Serb kept saying to them both: 'On the morrow, on the morrow.' I offered a clove to her which she accepted."

"And?" Gráinne was now sitting up, intrigued. Emer was not in here to discuss a mere ache in a tooth.

"And I gave her the clove, whereupon she put it in her *ciorbolg* with her comb. Later, I was behind the screen in my quarters where the bathing tub is, when Serb walked in and went over to my Phoenician looking-glass. She could not see me and I only saw her reflection in the glass. Gráinne, something is not right." Emer bit her lip and paused, then whispered, "Serb dipped her hand in the water-jug, unveiled her face and splashed the cool water on her cheeks . . . but her face . . . it was swollen, not from an ache in the tooth, oh no . . . it was blue, yellow, black, bruised, as if she had fallen or had been . . ."

"Beaten?" Gráinne's eyes were round, suddenly alert, disbelieving. "No, no, that is not possible, Cred would never hurt her."

Emer shook her head and clasped her hands.

"My eyes did not deceive me. The mirror does not lie. Serb would not conceal it if she had fallen. No, she was assaulted, maybe taken by brutal force. I dare to say there are markings on the rest of her body also. It is not good."

Gráinne thought of how often Emer had said things were not good. Recently, it was true enough. She shivered.

Cred would never do such a thing to Serb. Gráinne could not bring herself to believe it of him.

"Are – are you sure?" she asked, feeling a knife of pain somewhere deep inside, twisting and twisting itself relentlessly.

Although she was foster-sister to Cred, she realized she did not really know him. He was quiet, keeping himself very much to himself. But there was something deep sparking and kindling between them, had been for some time. It was a gentle fire, keeping warm, even though, at this moment, she could not bear to be near him or see him. She constantly felt she was being punished by him or by Serb.

All was not right. She wished she was a *seer*, able to detect immediately what was wrong. She also wished that Cromlach was with her now. He would know what to do. Cromlach always knew what to do and what to say to make everything right for her.

She tried to see Cred beating Serb, but the thought was unable to form in her mind. No, he was too gentle to women.

Gráinne thought of his hands running over Serb's body, caressing her, feeling her, his voice whispering in his lover's ear. This image was too strong, able to form much too clearly for Gráinne's liking. She shook it away quickly.

The rain pelting on the roof was constant, a weeping sound which brought no peace to her heart. She sighed quietly, knowing she had to say something to Emer.

"Emer, the Brighdal *bothán* is sacred territory, as you well know. Only Cred and Serb serve the god and goddess, but if she is hurt . . . oh, I cannot bear to believe it, Cred is so quiet and gentle, he works with the spirits of the craft, how could he do such a thing? Do you think they have hailed the storm then?" Gráinne said, uncertainly. "Without meaning to do so? Emer, my sorrow could not do this? Could it?"

Gráinne gripped Emer's arm tightly. Emer patted her head gently.

"*A stór*, stop fretting. It does not fare well for the babe. Perhaps my eyes are not as they used to be, maybe Serb had a few love-nips, or some horseplay caused her to fall over and hit her face on the hearth or some such thing. She may well have an ache in the tooth, if she knocked it out by accident. She still has a young maid's shame and may be afraid we would tease her."

Gráinne nodded, not totally convinced, but she did not want to think otherwise.

There was a mighty bang, then a loud surging sound coupled with an incessant roaring. Gráinne thought she detected some far-away bleating cries but wasn't at all sure if she imagined it or not. She jumped up, feeling an urge to flee somewhere, anywhere to get away from that awful roaring.

Fear gripped Emer suddenly, an icy hand cupping her heart. It held on, sending washes of terror chasing down her spine.

"My children! Oh, Dagda! My children!"

She rushed out of the room into the large Hall. Everyone was either rooted to the spot or nervously pacing the floor. The little ones were clinging to any adult they could hold on to, or as many as they could touch at once, to sap some form of strength to make up for their own vulnerability and lack of size. Lugnae was hugging as many of them to him as he could, trying to decipher the roaring sound himself. He was very happy to see Emer again.

Cred was listening intently. The trappers were already hauling on furs over their skin trousers and leggings, ready to brace themselves against the storm, to go outside the Dún and investigate.

Cred suddenly shouted in a powerful voice, over the hum in the Hall, above the harp strummings and above all the screams and cries of the children. The whole throng stopped and they stared at him incredulously. Cred had never shouted before.

"The river! The river has burst its banks! We must stay here. This is the highest ground!"

Cred suddenly realized with horror that Finann was out there with his goats. He had stayed in the shelter which was not on raised ground like the foundations of the Dún Hall. Cred glanced around. Everyone was in the Hall now. Cred was aware of Gráinne's presence, even as he pulled on extra skins and furs to brave the wind and floods to find his friend Finann.

Donal Rua was skulking at the back of the room. He saw Serb with her head-swathings and knew why she wore them, but his shame had gone, and he was numbed with the pain of losing her. He knew he was inadvertently the cause of Cred and Serb being still together, and his anger brewed within him, against himself.

Now he watched his father, Lugnae Fer Trí, put his hands up to still the murmurings of the tribe. They were afraid and restless, knowing as they stood there that their homes were probably being demolished and swept away by the tide of the river.

"Cred is right," said Lugnae, "we must all stay in here. Our *botháns* can be rebuilt. I will see that everything that can be replaced or restored to you will be done as soon as possible. I will replenish any perished livestock, if I can, from my own prime herd. Hopefully they all, or most of them, will have survived the storm. As they are reared on different pastures well away from the sea-lands, the more inland they are at times like this the better for us all."

Donal Rua saw Cred putting on his furs to go out but he had no idea why Cred should be thinking of facing such a storm. He felt his hackles rise on the back of his neck. His eyes were intense now, like a wild cat lying in wait, stalking its prey. His heart was jumping and jerking within his breast so that his mouth fell open in order for him to gulp air freely into his lungs. He had a choking sensation within his throat, as if a rope was slowly tightening, constricting his breathing passages. The air was pungent with the scent of fear and sweat that circulated throughout the room. Donal Rua was incensed by it. He felt tired, like a warrior on the eve of a battle, unable to cast his eyes away from the territory of the enemy, helpless to move his body or turn away from his scrutiny of Cred. With some consternation he saw Lugnae Fer Trí, the Chieftain, his father, murmuring something to Cred, imploring him maybe not to go, but Cred's eyes were as dark as the thunder and he was shaking his head emphatically, actually defying Lugnae. Donal Rua was astounded. The other trappers were already settling down, obeying their orders to stay, but Cred's face was set with determination.

Donal Rua started edging around the room until he was behind Cred, hidden in the grey shadows.

Emer saw him and felt uneasy. Her son had been acting very strangely indeed, ever since Serb had chosen Cred for the Corn King. His aggression had abated but his face, sullen and pale, was cold. He never smiled. Emer dearly wanted to comfort him but an invisible barrier prevented that. She hoped he would grow quickly out of his sad phase, although she knew there was no cure for the lovesickness. One had to wait until time matured the spirit enough to release oneself from the shackles of sorrow, cope with the rebuff, accept it, and eventually outgrow it.

Donal Rua, apart from the dousing in the river, had not washed his hair or bathed his body for days. His beautiful red hair, for which Lugnae had insisted he was named Donal Rua, was now unruly, the curls oily and tangled. Dark circles framed his eyes because of lack of sleep. His clothing had a fusty smell of sweat about it, which the other tribe members noticed but put down to his growing trauma, which all boys go through in their transition to manhood.

Cred pulled back the iron bolts he had made himself to secure the shutters. The wind charged against the door behind the shutters and Cred's muscles strained to hold it from blowing inwards. One of the trappers leapt to his feet to help Cred. Donal Rua quickly grabbed some furs and belted them around himself. Everyone was concentrating on keeping the children from the entrance and holding firm the door against the battering of the storm. Donal Rua was like a shadow to Cred who was unaware of his presence, and so it appeared to anyone who noticed him that he was just helping.

The door was eased open slowly but it slammed inwards with a huge blast of wind and rain, drenching the families closest to it. There was a great deal of squealing when the torrent of wet air caused plaids and furs to be whipped across the Hall. Cred pulled his own furs across his face and bent his head to face the storm as he headed in the direction of Finann's shelter. Donal Rua had managed to slip out almost unnoticed, side-stepping to hug the outer wall of the Dún Hall, his head and shoulders pressed into the eaves under the thatch.

After he heard the door close and the sound of the bolts being slid across the shutters, he quickly put his head out and squinted into the blinding downpour. Peering in front of him, he could just make out the silhouette of Cred, tall, broad, haunched against the wind. The *ráth* ground was a mass of churned-up mud. As Donal Rua set out to follow Cred, he slipped and fell over. Picking himself up, he slithered over to the nearest tree, which afforded little shelter but a great deal of support. He had no idea how Cred could have covered such a distance in the short span of time since they left the Dún. Donal Rua slid down the scarp side of the bank, half-crouching and belly-crawling for fear that Cred might glance back and discover him there.

The lightning and thunder had now subsided, leaving in their wake a deluge of rain and gale-force winds and this terrible roaring that came from the direction in which Cred was heading.

As Donal Rua reached the flat ground where most of the *botháns* and farmlands were, he gasped in shock. It was one massive tumbling river, with only a few of the dwellings left intact along its banks. Trees and branches were being swept along in the fast rapids. Cattle with round, terrified eyes swam for their lives while some of the new-born calves floated and spun on the currents, their ungainly legs protruding at peculiar angles, their wet bodies swelling with the intake of water. Horses whinnied in fright, their cries coming from one of the shelters which had missed the flood. Mora nee Derga would have to look after these terror-struck animals for a while. Mora had a special way with horses. She would be able to make them forget.

Cred was devastated. His face was streaming with tears and rain. Never had he experienced disaster such as this, after the Spring Rites. This was all his fault, and he knew the guilt would be his bedfellow for ever more. If Finann had perished, Cred vowed he would leave the Dún. Never again could he face the mountain, knowing that his friend was not there, nor look to the sky knowing Finann would never read it again, not as Finann anyway. Cred tried to concentrate.

"Please, please," he pleaded with *them*, "please let him not be dead."

He rubbed his knuckles fiercely against his eyes, willing the water to clear away but it flowed over his hands. It was as if the gods spat at him. He was alone against the elements, alone with his grief. A little goat went floating past, stiff and cold, causing Cred to sink to his knees in the mud by the river.

So the goat shelter had been swept away by the tide. That meant that Finann too had probably gone with it but Cred did not want to give up his search. He hoped Finann had not fallen into the river, as he doubted if the poor man could swim. Cred was an excellent swimmer, having been taught by the island sea-farmers when he was a little boy. They used to make him dive to the bottom of the estuary, where the fresh water met the salt water, to pick up seaweed, clams and oyster shells to see if they contained pearls. In the marshes, he used to wade into the thick waters to collect leeches on his legs, which he would painfully remove afterwards to give to the physicians. Consequently, Cred was accustomed to the element of water. He was a great diver and underwater swimmer, well able to survive in the rivers or in the sea, at any time of the year.

A cow was struggling to climb a bank, to get out of the river, a few feet away from Cred. Jumping up, he went to her aid. Within the next few moments he assisted several animals out of the tide of death. It was then that he saw a goat in the water near the bank. She had two little kids clinging to her shaggy coat. This gave him a glimmer of hope. They were alive, maybe Finann was too. He wished some of the trappers were here to assist him, but the climb back to the Dún to get them would cause him to lose vital time. He helped the goat and managed to drag the family up on to safe ground. The poor animals were bedraggled, frightened and cold, but at least now they had some chance whereas before the current could well have parted them, the river claiming them for her own.

Cred tried to run back up the river alongside the water, into the wind and savage rain. His breath caught as the air whiplashed his face when he called for Finann as loud as he could. His voice drowned in the roar of the water. He thought he saw a movement to the side of him but he brushed it off as his imagination, an animal or maybe even some misplaced spirit. It wasn't any of these, though. It was Donal Rua, watching and waiting, stirring up hate as he foresaw how Cred would be claimed for a hero, even after defying Lugnae. Cred, this tall, blond man, a stranger to the tribe, had dared to steal Serb, the girl who belonged to the son of the chief. Cred had humiliated him before his family, before the eyes of the tribe and in the presence of the gods.

Donal Rua slipped his hand down his leg and into the top of his hide boots. His fingers curled around the handle of a *scian*, the small sharp hunting knife without which he never went anywhere. He had hunted the great red stag with this and gloried in slitting its warm life away. All the trappers had been keen to bag that one and he made Lugnae very proud that particular day. It was his initiation into hunting and the first of many such killings. It came easy to him. Remorse was not in his code and only Emer had managed to stop him from hunting during the breeding season. The Brehons had made it a Law but their Laws did not deter him even though the penalties for breaking them were severe.

Some white trembling flashes of lightning, the last fire-breaths of the dragon, lit up the sky. Cred felt himself in no danger from these. The last grumbles of the gods were now a mere complaint from a distance, the rage of the storm having been spent, leaving in its wake devastation such as Lugnae's *ráth* had never seen before.

Cred's furs were soaked and heavy with the torrential down-pour beating upon him ruthlessly. His feet squelched through the mud, ankle-deep, the damp dirt penetrating right into his skins and leggings, the bottom of his plaid becoming soaked through from swaying along the ground.

His eyes scanned the river, sorting the debris that bounced past on the current, looking for any clue of Finann's where-abouts. He had to be careful. Tree limbs were cracking and falling down around him.

He saw something glinting in the dirt in front of him, a myriad of colours dancing off the glare. This was due to the drops of rain on his eyelashes flashing into rainbows, so that at first he thought the object was green or blue or purple. It was none of these, he discovered on closer examination. It was all too familiar to him, causing his chest to tighten with fear. He clutched the fruits of his own craft in his hands, the beautiful belt he had made for a king but which he had bestowed on Finann for his kindness. That dear young man was far more deserving of such a prize than the *Ard Rígh*, Lugaid. Cred knew that Finann would not part willingly with this gift and so he concluded that some accident must have befallen him.

Donal Rua crept closer to Cred. He slipped behind a huge oak tree and saw the magnificent gold buckle on a belt that Cred held in his hands. So! This was the reason he had insisted on leaving the sanctuary of the Dún Hall. Donal Rua stared coldly at his enemy. Cred was out here to ransack and steal from the people. As son of the Chief, Donal Rua knew what he must do, what was now his duty. The *ráth* would be well rid of Cred once and for all and he, Donal Rua, would be hailed as a hero, his love would be restored to him, and the title of Corn King bestowed upon him in the eyes of the tribe and the gods.

His palms were wet and clammy as he raised the *scian* to shoulder level. The smell of his own sweat filled his nostrils and he was hunting again. He was stalking the great red stag once more. Lugnae was going to be so proud of this kill, so proud. The roar of the river filled his ears, the cheering of the crowd, the appreciation of his tribe. Oh, yes, definitely his tribe, he would rule them one day. The rain pelted down on his head, rivulets chasing over his face, into his eyes, but he did not blink once. Never once did his eyes leave his prey. The wind howled, whipping up a fierce resistance, though not enough to deter his advance.

He was within steps of gaining his prize, claiming his victim. He lunged forward. There was a tremendous crack from behind him at the same time. It alerted Cred, who turned around quickly and threw himself to the side, rolling his body desperately to get away from the danger he had seen. His eyes were filled with terror as he screamed in Donal Rua's direction but the knife left the clammy hand that gripped it and sliced through the air towards him. Donal Rua had hurled it angrily, enraged that his coveted prize was being taken from him. At the last moment, Cred saw the *scian* and threw up the buckle he still held. The knife glanced off the metal and embedded itself in Cred's arm. He roared as a hot flash of pain seared through his muscle but he still pointed behind Donal Rua. Too late, Donal Rua heard the deafening rushing sound of the great oak tree crashing to the ground. He never heard the final earth-shattering thud as it embedded itself into the mud, or the splash of the branches as they bridged the river. He was in the embrace of the gods, tangled in their limbs with his death throes, breathing his last breath in the bosom of the Mother.

Cred struggled to his feet, clutching his arm which dripped with blood, the water diluting the rich red patches on his furs. He pulled at the knife, the pain almost making him pass out. His face was drained, white with shock, his body rigid as he stared at the massive oak spreadeagled over the ground. He could not see Donal Rua but his stomach lurched sickeningly as the full realization of what had just happened hit him. The goddess had indeed exacted a punishment but it was not what Cred wished or wanted for the boy. He ripped the bloodied *scian* from his injured arm, uncaring of the pain he caused himself and he screamed into the elements with the full force of his lungs before he collapsed into blackness.

Finann heard the unearthly screech above the stormy wind and rain, above the loud surge of the river, above the crashing of trees. He felt chills chase down his spine and he held Misha close to him. Her body trembled against him. Finann had managed to round up some of his goats and he was in the Brighdal *bothán* with them. Miraculously, the *bothán* was still intact and it was just far enough away from the others to miss the deluge of the river, the great inundation that had destroyed all within its path. He knew he was on forbidden ground but thought that this was the only sanctuary besides the Dún Hall that might be a haven.

The goddess would not mind. It was not for himself but for his goats which, in turn, served the people by giving sustenance with their milk. No, the goddess would not mind.

# CHAPTER 9

# KEENING

*She knows it in the stretch of her soul,*
*In the keening of her mind,*
*In the scent in the air,*
*In the sway of the wind-song.*

Finann wrapped himself well in some otter skins and furs he found in the Brighdal *bothán*. He realized, when he tried to buckle them on, that the belt that Cred gave to him was gone. Earlier, he thought that the safest place for it was around his waist but during the struggle to get from the shelter to here with whatever animals he could save, he had lost it. His heart was heavy. No one had ever given him a gift like that one, nor was he likely to get one again in the future. Maybe later it would turn up somewhere but how could he claim it for his own unless Cred was there to back him?

Now, though, he had no time to think of such things. There had been a terrible urgency about that blood-curdling scream outside. He hurriedly grabbed a piece of hemp rope and looped it round his waist. Then clicking his tongue against the roof of his mouth to soothe his animals, he left the sacred *bothán*.

The wind almost blew him over as he headed for the river. He found one of his she-goats with her two little kids. They were soaking wet and he fought his way back to the *bothán* with them. It was warm inside there so he locked them in with the rest of his depleted herd and set out once more.

Slipping and slithering in the mud, he followed the widened river and he was devastated by the sight of so much damage. There was a huge oak tree lying across the ground in front of him, the branches forming several bridges across the water. He staggered around the back of the tree to get to the other side and marvelled at the huge hole it had left in the land, hundreds of roots like giant snakes attached to the underside of the trunk. As he reached the far side, he stopped dead in his tracks with shock.

There was a body, swathed in furs, lying injured on the ground. As Finann approached it, he gasped aloud and rushed to the aid of Cred, his beloved friend, but Cred was not aware of anything. Finann turned him over and saw the matted blood around a rip in the furs on his arm. Finann suddenly felt cold, chilled to the bone, though not from any variance in temperature. He shivered. Somehow, he would need help. Cred was too big to be moved or carried even a small distance but the man needed shelter and warmth, and his wound needed tending.

Finann thought that maybe a tree branch had pierced the arm until he noticed the hunting knife, a *scian* of the finest ore, lying on the ground next to Cred. He picked it up, wiping traces of blood away that the rain had not reached, and was astounded to see the Fer Trí emblem, the mark of Lugnae's kin and clan, engraved on the blade.

Finann spun around fearfully, unable to comprehend the situation but he was fully aware that danger could still be lurking about. He stared, unblinking for a moment to concentrate, to try and solve the puzzle but all he saw was the huge oak tree, *duir*, one of the divine trees, felled by the gods.

"Finann," Cred spoke hoarsely but loud enough to be heard by someone next to him, "Help me."

The words were clear, not slurred in any way, and Finann sighed with relief at the sound of his friend's voice.

He crouched down beside Cred and gripped the outstretched good arm.

"I – I keep passing in and out of this world," Cred continued, "I have to get to the Dún Hall . . . but they must not know what happened. Please help me, Fin. I have to t-tell them about Donal Rua."

"Donal Rua? Why? Where is he?" Finann was alarmed.

Cred pointed to the tree. Large bells seemed to clang in Finann's head, the wind was a rushing tempest in his ears as realization struck him like a thunderbolt. The scene played in slow motion in his mind, a vision of awesome proportions that he did not want to see. He knew now that the knife belonged to Donal Rua, who had tried to kill Cred but the gods must have intervened. Finann could not believe what he was hearing and seeing although he felt it as the truth, knew beyond a shadow of a doubt that Lugnae's son lay dead beneath the weight of the oak and that Cred was blessed to be still alive. Finann's face was white, pained with the knowledge.

"Finann," Cred squeezed his hand imploringly, "E-Emer and Lugnae must not know what Donal tried to do. It must be an honourable passing over. Hide the *scian* for now. I – I cannot get it back to him –' he faltered, his eyes filling with tears – 'so I will return it and place it with his belongings in the Dún. Please help me, Finann, I have no other friend. If – if you bind my arm, I'll borrow . . . " Cred's face creased with a spasm of pain, "I'll borrow one of my own furs from you," he smiled ruefully. "So! You went to the Brighdal *bothán*? Finann, I give you gall. It has been a better place for you, indeed. Sometimes the gods *do* smile, then."

"Hush, hush, do not talk so." Finann was perturbed. "Why did he try to . . . ?"

"Kill me? He broke no Law. He just loved Serb." Cred's voice was tired and tears welled in his eyes.

Finann nodded, his mouth hanging open, speechless. Swiftly, he went into action, tearing strips of his own vest beneath the furs. Pulling Cred's furs carefully away from the gaping wound, he let the clean rain fall on it, then hesitantly he used the *scian* to cut a large width of the linen and went over to the fallen oak. He stared at nothing but the gnarled bark, not wanting to see any parts of Donal Rua or bits of his clothing. He sliced away a piece of the grey bark and shredded at the underside of it, catching the powdered wood in the linen. It was crude and not fine enough, but it would suffice for now. He slapped the linen against the wound, binding it tightly with the other strips of his vest.

Later, the physician would tend to it. Finann suddenly realized that Morann the physician might guess it for a knife wound. Fergus the poet, despite his physic finger, could definitely not

91

be called as he was bound by the Law of Truth-giving, so what was Cred to do? A trained healer was badly needed, who could also keep a great secret.

Finann suddenly remembered: "Mora! Of course, Mora nee Derga. She has the way with animals, she has patched me up a few times too. Cred, if you can fool them at the Dún, then I will get Mora to come to you at the Brighdal *bothán* when you return home. I have seen her perform miraculous things on birds with broken necks and lacerated wings, deer with torn limbs and even a wolf once whose leg was injured in a trap. Docile, I tell you, Cred, the wolf was docile in her hands. We can trust Mora."

The more Finann talked, the stronger Cred felt. He was no longer facing this nightmare alone. If only he could get to his feet without passing out with the pain, he knew he would manage to get to the Dún with Finann's help. He would let Finann do the talking, knowing that his own tongue would be stilled anyway when he faced Lugnae and Emer. The shock was too much for him yet. And Serb? How was she to take the news? The reproach would be too much for her to bear. She most certainly would blame herself.

He cast these thoughts from his mind and struggled to his feet. Determination now gripped him like a vice. Donal Rua had passed on. For Donal Rua's pain and sorrow, Cred was going to be strong. He was not going to let the boy down, or Serb, or Lugnae, Emer, or the siblings.

He sent Finann back to the Brighdal *bothán* with the stained furs and the *scian* and during his absence he forced himself to stand alone, fighting the terrible fatigue that threatened to overwhelm him.

By the time Finann came back, the rain was pouring down at a bearable rate and the wind had abated somewhat. Finann threw some new furs on Cred and they set off to go back to the Dún, one step at a time until he had accustomed himself to the unsteady sway. As they fought their way back up the slippery banks, Finann handed Cred a stick to aid him on the journey. It was a very crude long-staff but it did the trick. It made the task in hand easier and preserved his strength for the confrontation in the Dún.

When they reached the Dún, Cred's mouth went dry with fear but Finann squeezed his hand.

"Cred, I will tell them. It is the way of the gods and no one is at fault. You did not fell the tree, my friend."

Before Cred had time to answer, Finann took the staff away and threw it aside, then he rapped hard on the outer door of the Dún Hall. There was a great scurrying and shouting inside, the bolts were drawn back and Cred and Finann were pulled inside with welcoming arms. Cred winced when someone tugged on his damaged arm but he had to grit his teeth and bear the pain. Finann realized what was wrong and placed himself quickly on that side of Cred so that it would not occur again.

Finann called Lugnae over to them and said, "Lugnae, our news is grave. Something has happened."

Lugnae was not surprised to hear that all was not well.

"Whatever it is, Finann, whether it be damaged or gone, it will be replaced. At least we know all of our people are safely accounted for, and now that Cred braved his life to find you, we are a tribe once more. Our *bothâns*, our crops, our livestock, our tools and wealth can all be replenished. I will see to it all personally."

Finann felt his chest tighten. There was a lump in his throat. Lugnae was a good Chieftain, a fine man, and what he had to tell him was going to come as such a shock. Nothing could replace this. He opened his mouth to speak and could not do so. Cred was aware of how Finann felt but he was equally helpless. This dreadful knowledge would rock the Dún family.

Emer was watching. The pit of her stomach dropped and her heart twisted, as a warning bell sounded far away, deep inside her head. She recognized that bell, she knew it for what it was. Her face was stricken as she shuffled forward. Her fingers clawed into Cred's forearm. The pain reflected in his eyes was her pain too.

"Donal Rua?" she whispered. "*A chuisle*, my babe?"

Cred nodded, unable to escape the burning grip, not trusting himself to utter a word. His grey eyes locked with hers, wishing the knowledge to pass to her from himself but he was swaying dangerously. No! He must not fall, he must be strong for Emer, for Donal Rua, for all of them. His face blanched like bone.

"Tell me, please, though it tear my soul, I – I must know," Emer pleaded. "Tell me he did not suffer." Her voice faltered.

Somehow, Cred found his tongue. His words were husky and filled with compassion. Finann was standing, quietly sobbing beside him. He felt he had failed Cred but knew that he could not possibly give them the ill news.

"Lugnae, Emer, your son Donal Rua was claimed by the gods. It happened so fast, he had no suffering. Lugnae," Cred put his hand out to grip the Chieftain's shoulder, "he . . . he died a hero, he saved our lives, saved our livestock. I owe him my own life." Cred uttered the falsehood, unable to bear the dark wash of sorrow that crossed their faces. He had to give them something, had to give Donal Rua some dignity as befits a Chieftain's son. Donal would never have a chance to be a hero in life now, he would never be hailed as the rightful Chieftain of this Clan. Lugnae had already named him as heir to inherit the title and the responsibility of the *ráth*. This young man's future had been cruelly wrenched from him because of nothing more than his lovesickness. Why oh why had Serb chosen *him* instead of Donal Rua? Cred felt sick. He needed to get away.

Emer was rigid. Her face was grey. Her body tensed until she could no longer contain herself. She heard the scream within her, surging, surging from the well of her being, and then it was out, her mouth twisting in a grimace as the wail lifted into the air, keening through the Dún Hall, through everything and everyone who was there. It chilled their souls, it came from the old woman of the *Sidh*, it was a death-cry from the ancestors, something they did not want to hear, never wanted to hear again. The children's lips trembled, their faces crumpled and they sobbed, clinging to Emer's skirts, afraid for their mother, afraid for themselves.

Lugnae had retreated into some other world, a crushed man. He heard his own voice from a long distance away asking how it had happened. He heard Finann reply through his weeping that a tree had fallen, a sacred oak had claimed Donal. By the hand of Baldur himself. They were in the old ways, a sacrifice had been taken.

Lugnae turned his back and walked, hunched and dry-eyed into his quarters. Everything blurred before him. He could not see anyone, not hear anything except that dreadful mournful wailing of some woman. He did not care, the light had just gone out in his life. No more would he see the gentle, laughing face of his eldest son, no more would he see him strain his fingers through that beautiful red hair. He regretted that his last words to his son had been harsh, a chastisement for worrying the little ones. Now he could never talk kindly with him again. Donal Rua was gone and part of Lugnae had gone too. He remembered saying to his people that he could replace anything that was lost to the storm, but this was something he had not foreseen. Nothing could replace Donal Rua.

# CHAPTER 10

# SEEING

*And yet, within that very place,*
*You can be seen by me;*
*For to tell what they do not know*
*Is the art by which I see.*

Finann had taken the trappers to show them the location of the fallen tree. Whilst the trappers started hacking the tree with axes from the Dún, Finann returned for Cred and Serb to escort them to the Brighdal *bothán*.

Meanwhile, Gráinne took charge of the Dún in Emer's place and bade the bond-maid, Deirdre, care for the little ones whilst she looked after Emer. She arranged for food to be prepared and cooked to feed the tribe, then had some bedding brought out to settle everyone who was homeless for the night. Tomorrow, makeshift shelters would be built by the trappers until the *botháns* were rebuilt. The Elders started the vigil and the chants for the journey of Donal Rua's spirit, and the poet, Fergus, prepared his oratory for the records. The place became a hive of activity.

Mora nee Derga slipped away from the Dún Hall, having been told by Finann that she was needed desperately to tend one of his goats. She headed for the Brighdal *bothán* as soon as she could get away.

Serb was quiet on her journey back to the *bothán* with Cred and Finann. She was aware now that poor Cred was injured but she assumed it had something to do with the storm. Finann had indicated as such, so she did not bother to ask any questions. Her mind was still in shock from the news of Donal Rua, her senses numbed. She did not want to believe it and therefore she did not. He was not gone. There had been a mistake, of this she was quite sure, so she put it from her, locked it away, until the error they had made revealed itself on the morrow.

As they crossed the threshold of the Brighdal *bothán*, Serb was less than pleased with the smell of goat-droppings emitting from within. She gasped and held her nose tightly. Cred almost fell over with the scent. For the first time that evening, he felt like laughing. He laughed. It was a hysterical bubbling over, a release of his emotions, strained but totally uncontrollable.

Finann stared at him in disbelief, then he too started giggling. Before long, they all had pains in their bellies as they rocked back and forth, howling with tears flowing freely down their faces, howling and rocking and crying, holding on to each other for dear life. Cred eventually collapsed, quietly curled up with his pain.

The goats were all huddled together in one corner, the little kids sucking furiously for milk, now that their fear had gone and their hunger had returned.

Mora nee Derga arrived and Finann showed her in. She went straight over to the goats.

Finann smiled affectionately and caught her gently on the arm.

"Mora, the goats are all faring well, *a stór*. We brought you here for something else." Finann's voice became low and serious. "Cred is injured badly."

Mora raised her eyebrows in surprise.

"Why did you not call Morann or Fergus? I only have a way with the animals, you know that, Finann. My ways are not the ways of the physician."

"Mora, we have to keep this quiet, you must swear an oath of secrecy. It is very important for the sake of Lugnae and Emer and the family at the Dún," said Finann softly, not wanting Serb to hear, but Serb had gone into the inner chamber to lie down.

Mora nodded, curious now about the situation.

Cred spoke suddenly from his self-made bed on the furs in front of the hearth.

"Finann! Maybe we should not tell her, maybe it is best not to say anything, no offence to you, Mora."

"Never fear," said Finann, "Mora is full of secrets and none of them have come back to me yet, Cred. She must know what has happened to you, if she is to help you."

Cred consented and Finann told Mora all about the events of the day, leaving none of it out. She was astounded and sad but very sympathetic towards Cred. She realized the dreadful responsibility this knowledge brought to Cred and the weight he would have on his spirit for a long time to come. She was only too glad to be of some assistance to him now.

The knife wound was deep. The knife had torn the muscle badly. Mora washed away the bark that Finann had put there earlier, complimenting him on his quick thinking. Bark had great healing power for open wounds. Mora worked fast, brewing her herbs which she always carried in a bag with her wherever she went. She took out a fine bone needle and some linen thread and proceeded to sew up the wound after soaking it with a little of the juice of the night-berries.

"This will take away the feeling in your arm, Cred, for a little while, then you will soon fall asleep. You will have many visions, so I will stay here for fear they cause you to thrash about. I have the herbs and ways to soothe you." She then slapped the brewed herbs gently on his arm and bound them on with some strips of linen cloth. Her hands stroked his head, smoothing his hair as if she were patting a horse or soothing a dog. She clicked her tongue against the roof of her mouth like Finann did to calm his goats. Cred smiled as he fell backwards into a state of forgetfulness, floating on a sea of lapping water, gazing at a blue sky, the bluest sky he had ever seen, watching the dipping and soaring of a white sea-bird riding the air waves. He was at peace and there was no longer any pain.

Emer grabbed hold of Gráinne's hand as she walked past, having brought Emer some food to break the night fast.

"Gráinne, I have something to ask of you. Please do not refuse me, *a stór*, I am asking with my heart."

Gráinne sat down clumsily on the bedding beside Emer. Her belly seemed the size of the moon to her and all the time it fluttered and jumped impatiently. Very soon she would birth her son. She squeezed the hand that held hers.

"Emer, your wish is my bidding. You know I will do anything you desire, if my size permits it now," she said, smiling.

"I – I want you to sing the dirge for Don – Donal when we . . . " Emer burst into a flood of new tears, unable to finish what she was saying.

Gráinne wrapped her arms around her foster-mother as best she could. Her belly was pressed up against Emer and the babe was very active. Gráinne was afraid that it would remind Emer too much of her own child-carrying but there was nothing she could do about that. She buried her face in Emer's hair, her own tears wet on her eyelashes.

"Of course I will sing for you, Emer, for Donal Rua, for all of us." Secretly she added to herself: "And for you, Cromlach."

She was not sure whether he was alive at all after the storm but she hoped he was further inland or else somewhere very sheltered.

The trappers said the damage was of vast proportions out there. Last night they had returned with the poor crushed body of Donal Rua all newly wrapped up in linens. He was placed in a back room divided from the Hall by a red-cedar ornamental Phoenician screen. This place was a small mourning room where recently deceased bodies were laid out. Donal Rua lay here, ready for preparation by the Elders. The Arch-Druid was to keep vigil all night, wearing the wolf mask of the divine midwife. Because of the violent nature of the passing over, Donal Rua was kept hidden from all eyes so that his family would remember him in his perfected state. Only the Druids who kept vigil, anointed him and dressed him, were allowed to see him. All the trappers who had found and released him were forbidden to divulge to the family the nature of his mortal injuries. Red ochre and blue woad – fire and water – were smeared on the body, to help the soul on its journey as the spirit-warrior to I-Bhreasail. The Divine Midwife would then bind and swathe Donal Rua from head to foot in cloth. He was to be carried to his new cairn with the vow of release from Lugnae and Emer, and the blessings of the gods, his totems, and his favourite tools sent with him. A stone would be carried all the way up

Knocknarea to be added to the spirit-stones of all the others who had passed on before.

Sometimes birds and animals were buried with the body. Lugnae always said that when he himself passed over, he wanted his hawk and his wolf-hound to go with him.

Gráinne lifted herself awkwardly off the pallet. She felt a faint twinge in her back when the child kicked out vigorously. Soon she knew she would have to alert Carmel, Morann the physician's sister, who was renowned for her gentle midwifery. Gráinne knew her birthing time was near. Cromlach had said he would move back to the Dún when her child was birthed. She hoped he was going to remember, hoped he still lived.

"Please, please, let it be, let it be so," she whispered, her eyes tightly closed.

She jumped out of her reverie when Lugnae suddenly charged into Emer's quarters.

Lugnae's mouth was grim, his eyes wild.

"They will not let me see him, Emer! My own son, they will not let me see him!" he cried out, his voice broken and rising like a plaintive song. "I demand it! I must see him, Emer! I must!"

Emer's tear-stained face was full of pity. She sat up and opened her arms wide to Lugnae.

"Hush, *a chuisle*, hush, come here. T-they only want us to remember him as he was, not . . . not as he is now." She clucked her tongue and spoke with him much as she would to take away a child's hurt.

Lugnae slumped on the pallet and buried his face in Emer's breasts, drinking in that special smell she had that reminded him of buttermilk or soured cream. He wished he could stay there for ever. He wanted to sip from a cup of forgetfulness to take away the tortures of his mind's thinking and the constant pain of that hollow gap somewhere just below his ribs.

"I want to see him, Emer. I want to see what the gods have done to him! I want to know why! Why did they do it?" He burrowed his head into her, wishing he could be swallowed up by her. She was his only comfort now, dear Emer, the only mother he had ever known, having been abandoned by his own.

Gráinne stood as a silent witness. Neither of them seemed aware that she was there and she was afraid to move in case she disturbed them.

"Scath the Druid cannot tell me. None of the Elders know, nor will they let me near Donal." Lugnae's body shuddered against Emer. "I – I wish Cromlach was here. He would know. He always knew everything but I drove him away too."

Gráinne was surprised at the admission from Lugnae and it gave her some hope for Cromlach's acceptance at the Dún in the future. She could no longer listen to the couple's grieving though, so she backed away, then turned and tiptoed out quickly.

She needed cool air. Her body was flushed in a wash of unbearable heat. These rushes of warmth for the last two moons had been insufferable, the only discomfort of her entire child-carrying, that and the increasing weight which she thought made her look like a goose-egg on legs.

Gráinne was weary and needed to get away from the Dún for a little while. To get away from it all seemed a desirable diversion. She opened the door of the Dún Hall and walked out on to the raised mudstone which separated the Dún from the other *bothāns* and *crannógs*. The utter devastation that greeted her as she carefully picked her way down the bank made her gasp. She followed the path of the much swollen river and watched the men clearing away the debris. They were deliberating on where they should start building the new dwellings. A temporary long-hut was to be erected and then the separate *bothāns* would be constructed. One good thing about the storm was the amount of timber now available from the fallen trees. Lugnae had ordered the burning of the oak that had killed his son, so that was one tree less for the building, but no one in the *rāth* wanted the wood that had embraced Donal Rua. No dwelling was ever again going to be erected so close to the river either. The long-hut was planned far away from the inundations, beyond the flood-plain, on the other side of the Dún.

Gráinne was out of breath when she reached the copse of trees on top of a small embankment. This was where the Brigh-dal *bothān* had been . . . still was!

101

She could not believe it! The gods had preserved it.

It was somewhat battered, a little lop-sided on one end, but nevertheless it stood like a shrine amongst the tortured terrain around it. Some of the trees in the copse were also left standing, tall, proud of their guardianship.

As Gráinne looked at the door, she wondered if Cred was in there now with Serb. Last evening he had looked so pale when he returned to the Dún Hall and then after the dusk turned to night, she had been so busy comforting Emer, controlling her own shock and organizing the feeding and bedding of the Clan that she forgot all about Cred and Finann. Later, she was exhausted, retiring to her quarters with some children bedded down on her floor for the night. She had no idea where Cred slept, nor did she care.

Mora nee Derga suddenly came out of the Brighdal *bothán*, as much surprised to see Gráinne as Gráinne was to see her.

"Well, we have a calm dawn, Gráinne, thank the gods for that at least. How is it at the Dún? Did the children sleep?"

Gráinne nodded. She wondered what Mora was doing here, then she saw Finann leading his goats out, with Misha prancing along in front. She smiled at the little goat, happy to see that Finann's favourite had lived.

Finann looked shocked when he saw Gráinne. He glanced from her to Mora and back again.

"Aah! Mora came to check out my kids. One of them was a bit on the slow side." Finann rambled on too much, backed up by Mora at every second word, so that Gráinne became suspicious. Something was not quite right. None of the goats or kids appeared too slow to her way of thinking. She wondered if Finann was having a tryst with Mora but thought it very strange that they would share the Brighdal *bothán* with Cred and Serb. It was sacred ground and therefore no coupling, other than the mating of the chosen ones, was permitted. She was thoughtful and idly wondered if the coupling of goats counted.

"So, most of your little goats survived, Finann. Well, that is grand, is it not?" Gráinne said, as she patted Misha on the head affectionately.

"I lost a few babes, Gráinne," Finann said, sadly, but then

he forced a bright, optimistic smile on to his face and added: "but the gods looked after most of us, and every year I lose some of the new kids to wolves or bears. I have to look on the bright side, for you see, the ones that survived the storm were all in fine shape too!"

Finann was puffed up with pride, then realizing what he had just said, he hurriedly tripped over his words and tried to change it.

"Except, that is . . . I mean . . . except for the one Mora had to heal," he blushed, "the one that was slow."

Gráinne knew now beyond the shadow of a doubt that Mora was not there for the goats. She let her mind slip through the veils of Untruth, probing, probing, like the bee sipping on a delicate flower, like the sea-hawk tapping the shell, feeling for the morsel, prising it out.

She got it and she did not like what she was seeing. She wished she had never come here, wished Cromlach had not taught her the ways of bending the mind to see an Untruth.

"Curve your sight, Gráinne, curve it. You can see behind the Untruth. If you will it, dare it, you can know it!"

She could hear his voice clearly in the nether regions of her head.

Her vision was clear. Cred was injured. Something to do with his arm. She flinched at the brief sight of a deep wound. Instinctively her hand went over her belly as if, in some way, she could shield the image from her child.

"Are you well, Gráinne?" Mora asked anxiously, putting her hand under Gráinne's elbow to support her. "Is it near your time?"

The touch immediately dispersed the image of Cred but just before it left, she thought she saw another image overriding it. A *scian*. A *scian* she had seen somewhere before. It was a very quick glimpse that faded rapidly and she could not be sure of it, but the moment was lost to her now and she could not retrieve it.

"I – I am faring well," she murmured softly to Mora. "Just somewhat heavier than most days. I doubt if I will carry for much longer than the full moon."

Mora placed her hands on the tight swell of Gráinne's belly and smiled warmly, forgetting the embarrassment of Finann's remark that had almost given them away.

"The head is still high, Gráinne. I think you will make it to the new moon, maybe even the sickle moon. A boy?"

Gráinne nodded, flushing with pride and suddenly feeling a closeness with this gentle woman. She knew that Mora was not only a kindred spirit and probably a Druidess, she was also a very fine healer. That was obvious. Rushes of warmth and coolness alternated in her hands. So this was the reason that Mora nee Derga was at the Brighdal *bothán*. She was caring for Cred. Gráinne was glad about that. She did wonder why Morann, the physician, had not been called out but she decided not to say anything just now.

Finann suddenly asked her if she would like to walk with him to the stream that was the pathway up Knocknarea. She smiled at him, relieved to have the excuse to leave the vicinity of the Brighdal *bothán*. She did not want to see Serb or Cred. Bidding Mora a good day, she headed off in the direction of the mountain with Finann. His goats were quite happy to frisk around in the copse and Mora said she would keep an eye on them until he returned. There was very little damage they could do, and the few trees that were down between the copse and the Dún created a natural fence to keep them from heading towards the river.

Gráinne spoke first as the two set off with Knocknarea in sight.

"Finann, where do you think Cromlach might be? I am afraid for him. When did you last see him?"

"For two days, before I saw the goat's hair in the sky, I did not see him at his *bothán*. He did not say he was going anywhere but I know the mountain and he was not on it, not on this side of it anyway. The Elders do not know either . . . but then, Cromlach is Cromlach, he keeps himself to himself . . . I think he has the means of making himself unseen." Finann chuckled. "I mistook him for a bush on many an occasion up there, with that old bracken-brown cloak of his. Mind you, taking all that into account and suchlike, I would still say he is not on the mountain."

Gráinne was relieved to hear this from Finann. She clung to any little bit of information she could glean from anyone willing to give an opinion. At the Dún, none of the stern Elders had been forthcoming with any news at all but one of the trappers had said he had seen tracks of feet and a stick heading eastwards. Cromlach always carried a stick when he was gathering herbs and wild berries, mostly to push back the thorny branches and nettles, so Gráinne did not think this was relevant to his disappearance. However, it had given her solace during the storm, to think of him being more inland in a sheltered place.

As they climbed the gradual slope that led to the stream which was the gateway to the mountain, Finann felt uneasy. The way was very muddy before them. Gráinne and Finann both gasped aloud when they saw what was happening.

"Mud-slides! Gráinne, we must get off the slope!" Finann grabbed her hand and bade her turn round to go back down the mountain. She saw the big, silent, slithering mass of mud pushing its way towards them slowly, menacingly. Gorse bushes, heather, bits of broken trees and what looked like the rags-bush from the Healing Well were dancing the slow dance down the hill. There was something else, too, something familiar which tugged at Gráinne's insides so that she pulled against Finann, her feet dragging and rooting her to the ground.

"Finann!" she screamed. "It's Cromlach's *bothán*! His things! Look! Even his hearthstone!"

Finann tugged on her with all his strength to stop her from ploughing straight into the river of mud. He knew the danger of being sucked under a mud-slide. He had lost some goats in the past like that, and the heavier the goat, the more difficult to get it out again. Gráinne was heavy in her child-carrying. If she started sinking and being sucked under, he was not strong enough to get her out by himself.

She was struggling with all her might, desperate to get over to Cromlach's belongings, her eyes wide and wild.

"Stop!" Finann shouted at her. "Cromlach is not there! Gráinne! We must get back!"

She was not listening, yelling hysterically, her eyes never

105

leaving the slow tumbling of Cromlach's poor broken dwelling. It was as if she saw him.

Finann gripped her tightly with one hand. She was almost free of him. Drawing his other hand back, before she could prise herself free of him, he slapped her sharply across the face. Her eyes widened, shocked at the impact and that he had dared to hit her but she realized that Finann would never do such a thing unless he really had to. Her blue eyes softened when she saw how appalled he was by his own behaviour.

"Cromlach is not there, Gráinne," repeated Finann, slowly. "I have no wish to hurt you, but if you get sucked into a mudslide, then we might both perish. You must think of yourself and your babe. Now, come back to the Dún. We will be safe there on flat ground well away from the mountain. As long as we stay here on the slope we are in danger."

Gráinne's voice was small and broken. She hung her head.

"Finann, you are right. I am just so distressed about all the happenings of the last few days . . . "

Finann interrupted her as he gently steered her down the slope, out of danger.

"Gráinne, not just the last few days but for the last three or four moons. You were so happy here on the mountain when you were with Cromlach that day, you remember? And then, after Baltinne you changed. Everybody changed. The gods have not been kind to us, what with the storm and the tragedy of Donal Rua and . . . well, and everything . . . Now I cannot take my goats back to pasture on Knocknarea. It has been denied to me. Maybe the higher slopes are still grassy, who knows? But it will be a time before I can find out."

Gráinne was thoughtful. She knew he was right but she did not want to hear it all. She felt somehow responsible but helpless. Helpless in the face of the Truth. If only Cromlach had taught her to curve her mind to see through a Truth. It would have served her well, now.

Gráinne quickly bade her good wishes to Mora and Finann, then hurried into the Dún, straight to Emer's quarters.

Emer was robed and sitting in front of her mirror, trying to dress her hair. Her face was tear-stained and bloated.

"Gráinne, Lugnae wanted Donal Rua's *scian* for – for Donal to take with him. We – we could not find it in his quarters and I cannot bring myself to go back in there to search again. Have you seen it, by any faint chance?"

Gráinne shook her head but she promised to go and look for it right away.

She entered Donal's quarters hesitantly. His scent and his spirit permeated everything. There were furs and unwashed linens scattered untidily everywhere. Skulls of deer and fox hung on the walls and bone implements were strewn on the floor. A few bowls were left lying around with the half-eaten food still in them, growing on the top a faint greenish mould.

Gráinne was afraid to touch or disturb anything, lest it draw the spirit back there, but her eyes scanned the room, searching for the *scian*.

She saw something glinting in the bedding on the pallet and she stretched out her hand to pick it up. As she grabbed it, a chill chased down her spine. It was the knife right enough, but she saw it covered in blood for a long moment. It was difficult to understand how Lugnae or Emer had missed it unless, of course, someone had put it there after they had searched. Now, here she was, holding it and seeing that something was not quite right. For the second time that day she began to use her powers to see into the Untruth.

All at once, Gráinne felt very small looking out of her body, which seemed very large. There was a lightness, an airy sensation within her and about her, subtle yet demanding. The image of Cred's injured arm filled her head. It was as if the goddess were trying to tell her something. Her mind clicked into place. This was the *scian* then, which had injured Cred! She almost dropped it but knew she had to keep it in her grasp to glean the rest of the information she sought. It belonged to Donal Rua, that she was already aware of, and as she gripped the handle the searing emotion which had driven the wielder of the knife to use it also swamped her. A raging hatred, a feeling of disloyalty, and an intense awareness of pain and loss. This loss was similar in nature to the loss which haunted herself but much, much more intense. There was something else too though, a guilt. An act of wrong had been perpetrated by the wielder which was the cause of this guilt and the resulting blame he had rained on his victim.

Gráinne tried to probe further but there was an invisible shield. She wanted to sense where the shield was, who was placing it before her, and she saw the distinct image of Serb. It was totally unexpected and vivid but because of her own fragile emotions at the sudden confrontation and because it personally affected her, she knew she could no longer grasp at the Truth. It shattered before her. Someone had placed the *scian* back here in Donal Rua's quarters. It could not have been Serb: she was afraid of her bruises being seen. It was not Cred: he was injured. Finann had been on the mountain with her: therefore it must have been Mora. For some reason, there was a secret. Cred did not want the Clan to know that Donal Rua had tried to maim him, or kill him, and this was now apparent by his calling for Mora and not for Morann the physician, or even for Fergus with his physic finger. Fergus would have had to record the disaster truthfully. That, Cred could not have risked. Gráinne knew that there was more but she was aware of a powerful cocoon spun around the Truth, something she could not get through. The knife dropped from her hand just as the babe kicked out fiercely from within her, jerking her out of her reverie, just as Lugnae entered the room. He saw the knife falling to the floor and watched as Gráinne clasped her belly.

"You found it! Oh, Gráinne . . . are you well, *a stór*?"

Gráinne was surprised at his use of the endearment and at the concern in his voice. She sensed a change already in Lugnae. He was more withdrawn, but at the same time a harsh tone in his voice and a brusque attitude to others which had always been a trait of his and accepted readily by those who knew him well, was now gone. Whether this was a good thing or not would remain to be seen.

"Oh, it is nothing, just my child kicking hard. It is almost time. I – I found the *scian*. It was in the bedding."

She changed the subject away from her child, being acutely aware that Lugnae had just lost his own son. She saw the pain in his eyes as he lifted the knife from the floor and held the blade to his lips. He turned on his heel without saying more, and walked towards Emer's quarters.

Meanwhile, Finann told the trappers about the mudslide on the mountain. It was too far away and flowing in the wrong direction to damage the Dún, but, because of the inundations of the river, it might join up further with the water, making the flooding backlash towards the Dún or it could even change the whole course of the river.

One of the trappers wisely suggested digging a ditch at the bottom of the mountain to drain some of the mud down on to some flat, barren fields. If twenty or so of the men started the task now, they could accomplish it before the mudslide reached the swollen river. They grabbed as many digging implements as they could from the Dún and set off to accomplish the task. They would have it done before the morrow.

# CHAPTER 11

# THE DIRGE

*As the soil is turned for the seed*
*As death moves to life*
*As the seed turns to the soil*
*As the wheel moves, so do we.*

There was a fine drizzle and a faint mist on the day. The Clan stood silently in the *Koad*, the Grove sacred to the Dead.

"Dig the *fert* and raise the wail," Lugnae said quietly, his voice unsteady.

It was the day of the interment of Donal Rua's body. He was at last being committed to the Great Mother, having been swaddled like a babe to be placed in her arms.

As he lay on the burial slab, completely swathed in fine linens, there was a plaited silk cord attached from a gold belt around his body to a belt around Emer's waist.

Emer tried to close her mind to the sharp sound of the spades thudding into the ground, the slice of the blades through the clay and the swish as the soil was flung aside. It became an ominous repetitive melody she knew she would never forget.

Fergus donned the mask of the Divine Midwife and started his oration for Donal Rua. He extolled the virtues of the boy, the goodness of the family, the beauty of Donal Rua with hair as red as the *Phagos*, the beech. The words rolled off Fergus's tongue like the waves lapping against sands. He praised Donal for his courage in his living and in his dying. Then he called upon the Great Mother to accept her new child.

One of the Elders stepped forward and used the gold sickle to cut the cord which attached the child to Emer. Emer wailed with the keeners when the cord was cut. She was relinquishing her claim to him now in this world. Emer had been denied her

110

last kiss before he was to be laid to rest and so her loss seemed twofold because of this. The Elders had forbidden her to look upon him or to touch him, due to the nature of his injuries, which distressed her. Now she could not kiss him, as was her right, before he was passed over to the Great Mother.

Donal Rua was placed gently in the shallow grave, into the arms of his new Mother. Emer kissed a white blossom and threw it on top of him. The first part of the burial ritual was over.

Lugnae then moved to the side of the grave and bent over his son, tears slithering down his face and dropping on the linen-clad body. One poor crushed hand of Donal Rua's was wrapped in linen, except for one finger, upon which Lugnae placed a beautiful marriage ring of gold knotwork. Lugnae bit his lip hard as he barely touched the stiff cold blue finger. His hand trembled. Fergus placed his own hand over Lugnae's and gently drew him back.

Then, Fergus still holding on to Lugnae to impart some strength to him, called upon Brighde to accept her new husband. He began his oration to Brighde telling her what a handsome young man Donal Rua was, how brave he was in his hunting, and how he had the makings of a fine warrior. He spoke of the fertility of Donal Rua's seed and the fine seeds that had been spawned in the generations before him. Fergus was careful to speak of Donal Rua in the present, never in the past. It gave comfort to Emer and Lugnae to think of their son going forth into marriage with the goddess.

The Arch-Druid placed a cup beside the body and sprinkled grains upon it, then gave his blessing for the journey ahead.

Donal Rua's siblings, looking white and frightened, were led up to the grave. They scattered flower seeds and petals on him, gingerly dropping their offerings and pulling back their hands quickly. They ran back to be embraced by their mother, and Emer hugged them to her tightly, afraid to let them go again.

Scath came forward and handed the *scian*, sword, hunting spear, staff and shield to the Arch-Druid who placed them at Donal Rua's feet. These were all to aid him on his journey to Í-Bhreasail.

Fergus, still holding on to Lugnae, began the chant to call

111

upon the gods and goddesses to lend their limbs to make a barque, a boat in which to carry Donal Rua with the three goddesses of Brighde to the Land of the *Sidh*, the beautiful isle of Í-Bhreasail.

> Dagda Mor, Rig na n-Dul, Dulem,
> Lend your back for the hogging-beam,
> Brighde, the fire that is good to seal the seam.
> Ana, your ribs for the skeletal timbers save,
> The strength to combat the seventh wave,
> Luga of the Long Arm, stretch up for the mast,
> Manannan, your mantle for a sail you must cast,
> And the wind of the breath of Enbarr will you blow.
> Buanann, your shanks for the oars to row,
> Coll, the hazel that is hewn for the oars,
> Grian, the sun, guiding light that soars,
> Cecht, the plough for the rudding blade,
> Danann, your hair to bind all that is made,
> Nuada of the silver hand, steer a course straight,
> Badb, Macha, Morrighan, the three wings of Fate,
> Balor of the one eye and Neith, the course will plot,
> Nemain, your ears to hear the wind-voice that is not,
> Lir, surging sea embracing Banba, Fodla, and Eire,
> Bear Donal Rua to the kingdom of Í-Bhreasail fair.

Now everyone stood in shocked silence, the keeners unable to raise any more of a lament.

The Arch-Druid covered Donal Rua in the dark blue cloak of concealment for his journey with the crone through the dark world. Emer had requested that purple should not be used. It was the colour that marked the beginning and the end of life but she did not want to use it on this day.

Gráinne was led before the Clan by Fergus. He wanted her to sing the final dirge now. It had been decided that, on account of Gráinne nearing the end of her child-growing, she should not sing the dirge on the march to the *Koad*, but after Donal was covered with the cloak of concealment. Fergus said this would aid the spirit to leave the vicinity, to go onward on its journey with the three goddesses.

Gráinne's voice quivered on the opening words of her song. It was no more than a whisper as she tried to contain her own grief. She stumbled to a stop, her words incoherent. Emer's keening had touched her greatly. She saw all the years of devotion and love that Emer had bestowed on her son, from the crib to the grave, years that were cruelly halted by one mindless act in one day.

She stared around at the throng of people before her and saw Cred at the back, watching her. Mora nee Derga and Finann the goatherd were on either side of him, very close to him, probably supporting him. Serb was nowhere to be seen.

Gráinne thought to herself that she could not go through with this. She was going to let them all down. A wave of panic threatened to envelop her and then she saw, distinctly, standing behind Cred, standing behind all of them, something she did not expect to see at that moment: *the light ones*, the glowing ones. Their tall shimmering figures took her breath away. She distinctly saw Cred nodding to her, urging her, willing her with his grey eyes which, she knew, were filled with intense pain.

She knelt on the ground and closed her own eyes to keep the image of *the light ones* before her. They were still there, in front of her. She could see them with her eyes veiled, could feel their strength within her. Her hands clasped them to her breasts.

Gráinne lifted her face to the sky. The rain-mist that fell on her was their kiss on her cheeks, the slight breeze was their breath, the warmth of the peeping sun their embrace. Her voice was swelling and stretching for the reaches of their world, and suddenly, she had no fear any more.

Her song poured out, like a newborn spring, trickling its way down a hill, easing itself into a flowing river, merging with a tumbling sea, rising in mists into swollen clouds and falling as gentle rain. Her lucid tones carried all alike who listened to her into a different way of *seeing*.

When she sang of the seeds bursting to life, striving to get through earth and stone to reach light, the Clan experienced the urgency, the persistence, and then the final sigh as they bathed in the brightness.

When she sang of the tight flower-buds opening with the new

dawn, their minds seemed to unfurl like the delicate petals to absorb the rays of the sun.

She sang about the bees and the butterflies, the honey-makers, the cocoon-spinners, the birds and the night-moths, the wolves and the playful cubs. And the Clan stayed with her, rising with her joy.

Then came the winds, fierce and relentless, the wind of the North with its icy fingers dusting the leaves of the trees.

Her song told of the trees, the panic, the fight for survival, the sucking back of the force of the sun, being lapped to the feet, feeding the roots, crystallizing the sap deep, deep inside the hearts of the trees. She named them for their strengths:

*Beith*, the birch, hailer of Samhain, first white moon.
*Luis*, the rowan, diviner of metal, charm against harm.
*Fearn*, the alder, strong in the water, tree of Bran.
*Saille*, the willow, tree of Brighde, water and woman.
*Nuin*, the ash, past, now, and to be, small and great.
*Huathe*, the hawthorn, spans dark and light, day and night.
*Duir*, the oak, King of all, prime strength and wisdom.
*Tinne*, the holly, no fear in battle, father of the spear.
*Coll*, the hazel, divining wand, salmon of wisdom.
*Muin*, the vine, seal of the seer, speaker of truth.
*Gort*, the ivy, inner and outer, mover and seeker.
*Ngetal*, the reed, ruler of destiny, sight and skill.
*Ruis*, the elder, the end in the beginning in the end.

The leaves scattered to blanket the earth, to protect the Mother, to feed the roots.

And they, the Clan, as one, felt their souls being sucked back to the Dark Mother, being carried by the crone, into the darkness of winter, deep, deep . . . and they knew that the soul of Donal Rua was with them, but he would not be returning as they had known him. Neither would they stay with him there. It was not their time.

They felt the anguish of the Light Mother, searching the Earth for that which was lost, laying barren the land in her sorrow. They knew her distress.

Gráinne then sang of the vivid colours of the rain-arch, of the fiery sun-wheel, low and distant, preparing for its new journey. The seeds, restless in the cradle, were ready to begin again, the hope, the spark, the new souls returning to the light, the old souls in their new garb, bodies fresh and young.

The Clan saw the boat on its way to Í-Bhreasail, saw the shimmering goddesses of *Brighde* as they followed the path of the moon, a silver track on the water.

Gráinne opened her eyes. She did not stop singing and she could see that she was lulling them all. They stood mesmerized, their eyes opening wide in disbelief as they came back to the present. Many were silently weeping.

Gráinne looked at Cred as she was reaching her final notes and saw the tall shining light-forms still behind him. Her heart soared with happiness as she saw, beyond them, three wonderful familiar figures approaching the Dún but from a long, long way away. She was being given a vision. She continued with her song and Fergus strummed the harp, not wanting her to stop singing, never wanting her song to end. Her voice was full of passion and love, and all who heard her believed that Donal Rua had been accepted in the Land of the *Sidh*.

Emer rushed over as soon as the last chords of the harp echoed into silence. Gráinne rose, inclining her head shyly in front of everyone, and Emer threw her arms around her, tears flowing freely down her face.

Old Tachta came over and said: "Gráinne, I am old and tired. Soon it will be my turn to pass over, and I thank the gods they sent you to give us hope, to let us *see* with our own eyes . . . that which cannot be seen. I will sleep happy now, until the time comes, *a stór*."

Gráinne smiled, glad to have been of help to the old woman, but her eyes searched the path out of the *Koad*, knowing now, *knowing* that Cromlach was returning. She had seen him plainly. He was about a day away. Tomorrow, he was coming back to the Dún. Tomorrow, with her father, Olc Aiche, and her mother, her dear mother, he was coming home. Gráinne's eyes misted over. They, *the light ones*, had shown her. But she also knew that *they* were there because of Cred.

Cred had turned to walk away. Mora and Finann were helping

115

him back to the Brighdal *bothán*. He was shaking. He had seen *them* behind Gráinne, in all their beautiful white forms, a host of them. He was sure that no one else had noticed but *they* had appeared for him. Her song had taken him to places he had never been before, let him see things he was aware of but had never really known. She was a Druidess of the highest order. He had seen it before in the sacred Grove and he saw it again now.

Even the Elders had stared at her aghast, knowing that she had not joined the orders, nor taken the vows. Cromlach had trained her, they knew that, but they could see also that she was surely her father's daughter and naturally born to the ways of the Druid. Her blood was his blood, the same river flowed in her veins. She was bound by the same Laws.

Olc Aiche was a fifth-generation Druid, Gráinne was a sixth, and the child that Gráinne carried was the seventh, the most powerful of all. The Elders suddenly had a great interest in her unborn child.

Lugnae grabbed Gráinne's hand and squeezed it. He could not speak and neither could she. Both of them were silent for their different reasons, but Gráinne felt that a barrier had fallen away. She hoped with all her heart that she was able to give some solace to this good man, repaying him for his kindness, generosity and love to her. Impulsively, she kissed him on the cheek. He was still unable to utter any words to her but he smiled warmly. All was as well as could be expected.

# CHAPTER 12

# BIRTH OF A KING

*And so the chord of Life is strum*
*In the darkness of time, in the deeps of years,*
*In the changes of things he shall sleep as a god*
*And the world shall forget him for a king.*

Donal Rua's shallow grave had been filled in, and, on top, a cairn of stones was erected. The Arch-Druid had kept one of the stones back, to carry up the mountain later, to place with all the other ancestral stones.

Lugnae planted an elder tree himself, by the cairn. He vowed, as soon as the tree bore fruit, he would drink the wine from the berries every year, for the rest of his life.

Lugnae withdrew into himself. Nothing seemed to matter much any more. He was not ready yet to face up to the responsibility of ruling the Dún. He took no interest in the rebuilding of the *botháns*, the diverting of the swollen river, the draining, digging, and replanting. He heard of the wonders Mora nee Derga was doing for his terrified horses. Emer told him of the great rescue operations for stranded people and livestock on nearby *crannógs*. But he had no mind for such prattle. The constant whining and crying of his own children was a bother to him but he could not comfort them. He constantly searched for Emer so that he could bury his face in her breasts and forget the world. He became solely dependent on her comforting pats and strokes, not wanting to share her even with their own children.

Gráinne was aware of this, so, when she was not too tired, she played with the children and told them stories. She hoped the couple would soon recover from their intense grieving. The Dún desperately needed to get back to normal again.

117

Gráinne was trying to get over her own disappointment. She had been so sure that the vision of Cromlach's return was true. The day after the burial, she had continually ventured out to the boundaries to search the paths leading to the *ráth*. She longed to see her mother and father again, even though in spirit she knew herself to be closer to Cromlach. Her mother, Dairine, was a very bright-natured woman, slight in build, and had a way about her that reminded Gráinne of feathers . . . light and airy, always uplifted and smiling in the face of all adversity. It used to annoy Gráinne greatly at one time but now she welcomed it. She needed someone sunny and gentle around her. Her father, on the other hand, was everything upright and fierce and stern. Somehow, Gráinne knew she needed his strength and sacred powers too. And of course, her dear Cromlach, her teacher, guide and friend . . . she desired his presence most of all.

That night, after supper, Gráinne tucked Emer's children into their bed-boxes, and had just decided that she was going to retire early to her own pallet when she felt a twinge in her back. Her babe was not too active inside. For the past two days he had been very quiet, so much so that Gráinne thought about alerting Carmel the midwife. She decided against it though, until she knew the pains were definitely starting. The idea of going to the birthing hut just yet frightened her. She did not want that isolation.

Gráinne could not sleep. She decided to walk for a bit. Maybe the stiffness in her back would disappear. She was going to wait for a while before calling upon Carmel. It might not be the birthing time just yet.

The air was crisp and the night sky a myriad of stars, bright like jewels on a dark mantle. Gráinne half-closed her eyes in ecstasy as a cool breeze caressed her face. She looked up at a sickle moon. Mora nee Derga was right about that. The thin sliver of a sickle moon had arrived and the birthing still had not begun.

Gráinne did not venture too far. She walked to the area where Cred used to have his forge. The forge was gone, perished in the storm, the inundations still covering whatever might be left of it. She turned and wandered slowly in the opposite direction, not wanting to think of Cred too much. She heard chattering and laughter coming from the far side of the *ráth*.

Upon closer scrutiny, Gráinne realized it was the voice of a woman, but there was no answering voice. It was coming from the direction of a small wooded area not far from the Brighdal *bothán*.

Gráinne did not mean to spy, and she did not particularly want to meet anyone, but she crept close enough to enable her to satisfy her curiosity about the woman's identity.

Keeping close to the boundary bank, she merged herself into the night and the shade of the trees until she could make out who it was. She saw the long silver blond hair, white as the moon, pale as the sand, and she knew immediately that it was Serb. Just as Gráinne had known, there was no one talking with Serb nor answering her, yet Serb was holding a conversation as if she was with someone.

"They told me you were gone but I knew they were lying. They think I do not know better, but I do. I knew you would come back . . . You were afraid, after that night, were you not? . . . I was afraid too, I thought they would kill you. They will, you know, if they find out. We must keep it from the Elders. It is our little secret, is it not?"

Gráinne craned her neck, peering into the shadows, to make sure that no one was there, maybe whispering to Serb.

She suddenly felt a little chilled and decided she did not want to know. She pushed a thought away in her own mind that she did not want to think. Neither did she want to stay.

As Gráinne turned to go, someone came rushing down the slope from the Brighdal *bothán*. Finann's voice started crooning and soothing as if he was tending his goats but he was speaking to Serb, coaxing her back to the *bothán*. She did not want to comply with his wishes at first, and then Finann said that Cred was looking for her and immediately she jumped up in a panic and ran towards the Brighdal *bothán*.

Gráinne bit her lip in anguish, to stop herself from crying out, as a stabbing pain ripped across her back. She gasped as it subsided and she knew she had to return to the Dún. Someone there could alert Carmel for her.

She had no time nor the inclination now to think about Serb, but maybe the girl had run back up the slope to the Brighdal *bothán* out of fear. After what Emer had told her about Serb's bruises, Gráinne tried her best not to bring the incident to mind. She did not like to think of Cred ill-treating anyone, could not imagine it! But Emer had seen the marks and Emer was rarely wrong in her assumptions. It seemed completely out of character and very strange to Gráinne that Cred could do such a thing.

Another pain arose and crashed like a wave, making Gráinne double over sharply. She knew she had to get somewhere quickly where she could get assistance. She was frightened.

One of the new *botháns* that had been erected after the storm was near by. There was a dying light from a torched bog-spail on the outside, and a faint warm glow from a lit beeswax honeycomb from the inside.

She made her way unsteadily to the door and tapped gently, afraid of awakening any children that might be inside. When there was no answer, and she felt another of the rising pains, she banged louder.

"Please! Please let me in!" she called out, small beads of moisture breaking from her forehead, as she leant against the wicker framework and tensed her body to absorb the searing stitch.

Someone was coming to the door. She could hear the light footfall disturbing the rush-strewn floor from within. She sighed with relief when Mora nee Derga opened the door to her.

"Gráinne!" Mora was surprised. "What are you doing here in the night? Come in, come in. What is amiss?"

"I am labouring, Mora. I – I think it is time now for the birthing."

Mora hurried Gráinne into the *bothán*. There was no time to get Gráinne to the birthing hut or back to the Dún. Mora did not think there was even time to run and get Carmel, for she could not leave Gráinne alone. By the look of pain on the young woman's face and by the shape of her belly, it looked like she was going to have a fast, intense labouring.

Mora knew that she herself was the only other capable woman besides Carmel, Emer and old Tachta, who could assist expertly with the birth. Had she not delivered many a young bull and horse into the world? Her instinct and herbal prowess had saved many an animal babe that would have otherwise passed over because of birthing hardships.

She led Gráinne over to the hearth, then dragging all the bedding off her own pallet, she laid it on the floor on top of the rushes. Mora did not have furs in her *bothán*. All her bedding was woven from linen and wools and stuffed with soft fleece. There were no animal skins anywhere. Neither did she use the boar or seal oils which Lugnae provided for the ornate bronze lamps. She preferred the honeycombs which she collected herself from her beehives and made into candles. Mora did not eat the flesh of any creature. The only parts of animal she used were the fine bones of fowl that she needed for stitching. Even then, she did not kill the fowl in order to take these bones but only used of that which was dead already by natural causes. The leathers she wore on her feet in the winter time were taken from the older cattle which had passed on.

Gráinne suddenly felt very safe and in the right place. She exchanged a knowing smile with Mora and then surprised herself by bursting aloud with laughter. The two of them giggled as her laughter turned to small indrawn breaths, as if she was supping hot broth, when another shockwave hit her. This time, she had a popping sensation deep within her and a deluge of waters poured from between her legs. Her eyes widened in disbelief. It seemed very funny. All this relief and pain and laughter and secrets, all at the same time, and on top of that it was like she had just wet herself and it was not stopping either.

They giggled and mopped, Mora grabbing linens to try to absorb the waters, Gráinne bundling the skirts of her robe between her knees. There was a sweet-salt aroma in the air.

"*A stór*! This is worse than any brood mare! We have another flood! I lose one *bothán* to water and now it seems to be my lot to lose another!" Mora said woefully.

Gráinne was howling with pain and laughter.

"No – no! P-please, Mora, do not make me laugh so much! I have never birthed a babe laughing before . . . I – I mean, I have never birthed a babe before, but I never thought it was . . . it was a matter for laughing!"

"Oh, it is not! Not at all!" said Mora, in a mock stern voice. "We women must not laugh at such things. We must retire obediently to our birthing parlours and not laugh. Oh, dear, no. We cannot find such things amusing. It is far too painful a matter. We must not practise our mirth at times like this. It would be an abomination. Yes, yes! I can hear them now! Those fat old Brehons!"

Gráinne knew in that moment that she had a new friend for life, someone like herself who was free, free as a bird, not bound by the Laws of men but by the Laws of nature, the Laws of Brighde.

"Do not send for Carmel or Morann, Mora nee Derga. I want to birth my babe with you. You told me he might last to the sickle moon and you were right. This will always, for ever more, be my moon."

"And his moon, and my moon," whispered Mora, kissing Gráinne on the forehead. "It represents the cutting of the cord, in life and in death. Gráinne, it is a very fitting moon for the birth of a king!"

Gráinne was surprised.

"You know?"

Mora was equally surprised.

"He is? I – I just said that. Every babe to me is a king or a queen."

"Sshh!" said Gráinne, happily. "It is our secret, one of our many secrets!"

That started them off again but this time a pain, such as Gráinne had not felt before, wrenched through her.

"*A stór*, we must stop our jesting," Mora immediately said, jumping into action. "Come here, lie down for a moment. Your labouring is going to be short but intense. Let me get you a shorter tunic which will be more comfortable for the birthing. Stay by the hearth and keep warm but take off your robes."

Gráinne did as Mora said. As she lowered herself down clumsily on the bedding, she felt a sharp thrust up into her rib bones. She put her hands on the top swell of her belly and felt a little lump jerk against her rib again. His tiny foot was using her rib to push himself forward.

She lay quietly, hoping she would not have another spasm just yet.

Mora returned and slipped a sun-coloured short tunic over Gráinne's head. It was very loose. Mora positioned herself in front of Gráinne, between her legs. She then bade Gráinne draw her knees up, pushing the tunic back to her breasts. Mora heated her hands at the fire and began to warm some oil in a small black pot. The oil smelt of the field daisies, a sort of mouse smell. She mixed it with some wild-rose oil which had a more pleasant scent, then gently she rubbed it around the opening, the gateway through which the new soul would enter their world.

"So you will not tear," she said gently, massaging the oil around the petals of the young woman's flower. Then she massaged Gráinne's belly also with the oil, careful not to get any on the breasts, where the babe would suckle.

She bade Gráinne turn on her side and she rubbed the rest on to her lower back, just as another pain caused Gráinne to double up into an unborn position herself. She concentrated on Mora's hands, which were soothing, and a warmth spread quickly over her back, easing the tightening spasm.

Once it had passed, Mora stopped and made some herbal broth in a pot of hot water which was always kept on the boil.

The yellow flames licked the bottom of the pot. Gráinne became mesmerized just watching the fire and the curling smoke. After a short time, the soft white steam shooting from the sides of the lid took her mind temporarily off her aching body. She hoped that whatever was in the pot was going to alleviate these dreadful spasms.

"Never . . . never again," she mumbled as her body prepared for the onslaught of yet another severe cramp.

She gritted her teeth, tossing her head from side to side. Her beautiful raven-black hair was wet and plastered to the back of her neck. Dark tendrils spiralled against her flushed face, trapping the beads of moisture that rolled off her forehead. She felt the urge to push but Mora had both hands on her belly, probing, feeling, putting her head down to listen.

"Not yet, Gráinne, not yet. Try not to push yet. Hold back, *a stór*, and try to rise up. It is not good to birth lying down. Inhale deeply with one breath. Now, like the waves of the sea, short ebbs and flows for six breaths, then on the seventh, like the seventh wave, take a deep breath through your nose and let the air out through your mouth, a long, tumbling wave. Hear it, like the sea rushing to the shore, lapping the sands. Keep this rhythm as you move. First, I will get you on to your knees then on to your feet and we will walk."

"Walk? Mora, are you mad? I am not a horse. Oh, Dagda! I cannot bear this."

"Breathe, breathe like the sea. Yes, you have it now, fast for six, slow on the seventh wave. Good girl."

Mora clicked her tongue, as she would with an animal. It was oddly comforting and Gráinne did not object, only too pleased that Mora was there.

She managed to get to her feet, the tunic loosely falling over her belly again. Mora made her walk back and forth from one curved wall to the other. The pain seemed to subside a little. The weight and pressure of the babe shifted slowly, further down, but it eased the cramping in her back. A dull ache had shifted to the front. Back and forth, the ebb and flow, back and forth, breathing in and out. She suddenly realized what Mora was doing.

Gráinne had no idea how long she paced the floor, her bare feet gracing the rushes. She listened to the waters of the sea in her breath, the rhythm of her walking back and forth on the rushes merging with her mind so that at times she forgot she was in Mora nee Derga's *bothán*. She was in the hands of the goddess guiding her, like the moon that draws the tides. Mora kept giving Gráinne some sips of the herbal broth. It warmed and calmed her, sometimes giving her the sensation that she was far away from herself and therefore far removed from the worst pains. She was glad she was not at the mercy of a strict midwife attending her in the birthing hut. Her babe was going to be birthed here, in a humble abode bereft of killings, the home of a healing woman.

Her cries were now sighs as she rode each pain like a seal riding the waves, like the white beards tumbling on the crests.

Mora gave her a last sip of the herbal brew. It was time.

Mora guided her to the bedding and made her squat. She then made a bed of soft fern below her and dragged an oak settle over so that Gráinne could support herself on one side. Kneeling in front of her, Mora urged Gráinne to lean her hands on her shoulders if she needed to do so.

"On the seventh wave, Gráinne, press on my shoulders and bear down hard with your whole body."

She counted and then Gráinne pushed. The babe surged down, dragging her very soul with him. She stifled a cry.

Mora's hands cupped below the opening, waiting for his head.

"Bear down, *a stór*, on the seventh wave. Pass him over into this world."

Mora began to chant softly, the lilt of her voice rising and falling with Gráinne's breathing.

They counted to seven. Gráinne was bearing down again, her legs aching, her calf-muscles bulging with the strain. She leant heavily on Mora's shoulders, salt-sweat falling like a thin mist on the auburn hair of the other woman.

Mora suddenly stopped chanting.

"I feel his head!" she squealed excitedly. "Come, Gráinne, as the earth bears the flower to the light, push! As the river flows to join the sea, as the sea surges to the shore, push!"

Gráinne inhaled deeply and expelled the air long and loudly. Her hair was clinging to her body like a drape, the fine down on her arms and legs glistening. Every vein in her body strained for the bearing and the birthing.

As the babe's head emerged, Mora supported it quickly. Some drops of crimson blood fell on the fern, followed by another fall of waters.

"Again, again, Gráinne. He is beautiful, he is veiled. He has the cowl of a *rí* upon his brow!" whispered Mora nee Derga, her tears falling on his small head, dropping on the thin veil which covered his face.

Gráinne bore down with all of her might, her shanks like

125

pillars embedded in the earth, rigid and solid with her effort, her breasts sore and her face distorted and pink.

She cried out in pain as the babe slid through, then she unexpectedly soared up on the crest of a wave of pure ecstasy, her heart pounding fit to burst.

The son of the fallen *Ard Rígh*, Art the Lonely, was borne into life on the seventh wave upon a bed of fern.

The squirming, slithering infant slipped into the arms of Mora nee Derga, his little fists uncurling and tightening up again as they came into contact with Gráinne's hair. He clung to this great dark rope as Gráinne blessed him with her kisses and tears.

She shakily bent over his head and carefully brushed his veil aside, vowing to keep it for ever. Then, she licked the little soft dent on the top of his head as if to seal his spirit in.

As her tongue came into contact with him, his little woad-blue body suddenly gasped the first unveiled gulp of air and he opened his mouth wide, his healthy cry ringing out and bringing to the new *bothán* a new sound. Once his lungs filled with that first breath and bellowed out that first yell, his body changed to a warm rosy hue.

Gráinne and Mora were laughing and crying all at the same time . . . and then they heard it . . . the long, low soulful cry of a wolf outside, a cry which merged with the cry of the new-birthed babe.

Gráinne felt a chill of excitement chase down her spine. Cromlach had said the babe would have the totem of a wolf. Cromlach was right.

Mora made Gráinne lie back on the bedding and placed the squirming bundle on the mother's soft belly.

She waited until the life-cord stopped throbbing, then she pulled out a miniature golden sickle, of the rarest beauty, out of her physic bag and sliced through the cord with it in two places. Tying a loose knot on the babe's belly, she nipped the end tidily with her teeth.

Gráinne felt a rush of warmth for Mora, knowing she would never forget the intimacy they both shared this night. She could not believe the presence of the new babe on her own belly or

the slight mournful feeling that he was not still a growing part
of her. She experienced another cramp suddenly and her eyes
widened in alarm.

"Do not worry, *a stór*, it is only the after-birthing," Mora
said softly.

Gráinne expelled it and Mora wrapped it carefully and took
it away. Tomorrow, the mother must plant it where she wished,
to mark a sacred place for her babe. A *coll*, a hazel sapling,
would mark the spot.

Gráinne's hands stroked the infant tenderly. He was stretching
his body out, trying to move forward. She helped him. His little
fingers of one hand were still clinging to her hair. She smiled,
lifting him up to her breast. The tiny rosebud mouth opened
and closed but he did not clamp on to her breast-bud. She was
disappointed, urging him again.

"Not until after his first slumber," said Mora nee Derga,
coming over with a bowl of warm, scented water. "But we must
bathe him and wrap him, then I will wet his lips with the first
cream from the heart-breast."

Gráinne watched Mora fondly, as she came forward and began
to bathe both mother and babe at the same time. She used a
soft fleece dipped in the scented water.

"You know everything, Mora," said Gráinne wistfully.
"Maybe you will teach me some of it one day."

"We can teach each other, *a stór*, and this little one will teach
us even more."

Gently squeezing Gráinne's left breast-bud between finger
and thumb, she watched as a creamy substance oozed out. She
swept it up on her little finger and put it on to the babe's tongue
and lips. Several times she did this, until she thought he had
had enough.

"He has soft white down for hair, Gráinne. He will have hair
like corn silk . . . and his eyes, just look at those eyes, blue as
the summer sky, blue as the wayfarer's flower."

Swaddling him in some soft linen lengths, she tucked him
gently into his mother's arms and crooned them both into a
peaceful slumber. The light of the flickering fire in the hearth
cast a golden glow on them, the sight of which caused Mora nee

Derga to catch her breath and wipe away some tears of sadness. She hurriedly turned away, chiding herself, as she prepared a small bedding box for the babe and gently separated them, so that the babe had his own crib beside his mother, and Gráinne would sleep restfully.

"You had your chance, Mora nee Derga," she said, quietly to herself. "But now it is too late in your moons to ever have a child. You have to be content to be mother of them all and appease yourself with the occasional borrowing."

She sighed. It did not take away the small hurt. To think about it merely emphasized it.

# CHAPTER 13

# THE VIGIL

*To watch and wait and bide the time*
*Until Love sips from these lips of mine*
*Will she ever see me, guardian that I am,*
*Guiding her slumber and my own heart to calm?*

For the second time that night, Mora nee Derga heard a tapping at the door. She hoped it was not another birthing. Usually night-calls for animals were birthing calls.

She opened the door to a worried-looking Cred.

His arm was in the sling Mora had made him wear. His face was white, pale as sun-bleached grass, his eyes grey and vacant.

"Mora, please help me."

"Are you ailing, Cred?"

"No. It is Serb. Something is wrong with her. She is muttering, feverish . . . and I – I cannot calm her. She heard the wolf howling and is convinced it was . . . it was Donal Rua calling to her."

"Where is she now?" asked Mora, a frown creasing her brow.

"Finann is humming to her at the Brighdal *bothán*. It seems to calm her but she needs a draught to make her sleep. We cannot stay awake to watch her and we cannot seem to stop her wandering." Cred bit his lip in despair. "After all that has happened, Mora, I am afraid for her."

"She is still in shock, Cred. I have something, something that will work well but I must administer it myself. It is forbidden for someone who is not a healer to give it to others. I use it to calm the wild animals. There is only one more problem. Some-one must stay here with my mother and new-birthed babe."

Cred smiled wanly. His face was showing signs of strain and fatigue.

"In the *bothán*? Is it a new calfling or a foal? Mora, this place is too small for a horse or a herd. Where are they? Or, don't tell me, it is a mouse?"

Mora pursed her lips and then raised her eyebrows.

"Ah, so we are now fit to quip . . . That is a sure sign of recovery, Cred. Come, I will show you . . . You will be the first to know, but shush, I do not want them to awaken."

She led him through the porchway and over to the hearth.

Cred felt his heart jump into his throat and his pulse thudded until he thought Mora must hear it. He knew that dark draping of hair, black as the raven's wing, black as the night. Had he not imagined it spread across his bedding, ever since he first saw her?

"Gráinne?" he asked softly. Mora stared at him quickly. She saw the gentle look in his eyes as he bent over the sleeping woman and child, and she thought it strange, this sudden fleeting warmth, not meant for her eyes but she had witnessed it and that look could not be denied. It was a look that was missing when he stared at Serb.

Cred saw Mora watching him with a great deal of interest in her expression.

"She – she is my foster-sister. I – I am as a brother to her," he tried to say with conviction but he knew that Mora was not convinced.

Mora hurriedly got her physic bag and a small dark box off an oak shelf. She left Cred with instructions for him to stay there until her return, then she blended into the night, glad for the fresh nip in the outside air to clear her head. She stretched her legs into long strides as she climbed the small incline to the copse and she wondered idly if Gráinne knew how Cred felt about her.

Cred pulled off his leather sandals and leggings, put some extra kindling on the fire, and sat down on the oak settle that Gráinne had gripped on to during her birthing. He could not take his eyes off the mother and child. Gráinne's face was flushed, her hair like a dark mantle thrown over her.

As if she felt she were being observed, she drew the covers up over half of her head, tossing her hair back as she did so, and the dark waves fell over his feet. The covers she had pulled up exposed her legs. They were white and shapely, her thighs hugging together tightly, the calves firm and muscular. She was lying on her side, curled towards the crib wherein lay her babe.

Cred drew his breath in sharply. He could not move. Her hair lay on his feet, like the caress of silk on his toes. He was helpless, not only afraid to move in case he disturbed her slumber but not wishing to shift position either. He wanted to reach over and cover her legs again. It did not seem right that he could feast his eyes on them without her knowledge of his doing so. It did not seem fitting when she had just birthed her babe, but he could not help the tremors of desire that surged through him. He bent forward, not moving his feet or her hair, but he grabbed one of the sheetings of linen beside her and gently draped it over her pale legs. He could no longer bear to gaze upon them.

Cred was unaware of how much time passed. He was only conscious of the caress of her hair on his feet. He fell into a fitful doze, mostly to escape into some dream place where his wishes came true and temptations were fulfilled.


Gráinne awoke to the strange whimpering sound beside her. As if at some signal from the babe, her breast-buds tightened into a hard wet knot, leaking milk juices for the hungry youngster. Gráinne remembered suddenly and she immediately leant over the makeshift crib to calm her son.

"My son," she whispered to herself, her eyes dancing with the sheer pleasure of hearing those words.

She reached for him and lifted him carefully out of his box, into the bedding beside her. She stripped off the short yellow tunic, which had two wet patches on the front of it now. Propping herself on one elbow, she rested her body on her side, her round, swollen breasts desperate for relief. Little drops of the first watery cream plopped down on to the babe's face as she curved her body over him. She smiled as he blinked his blue eyes, the long dark eyelashes fanning his pink cheeks. He had big, bright eyes, beautiful when they gazed up at her, wide open like this. He was no longer crumpling his face to cry, being now aware that his mother was beside him.

She helped him as his mouth opened instinctively for the bud. He clamped on and immediately sucked, no trial and error this time. He was hungry for his first food.

As he supped, she very lightly stroked the side of his soft velvet cheek with one finger. It made him stop for a second and then suck harder and faster. She was aware of a tightening sensation, which was not unpleasant, in her belly. The healing of her womb was already commencing. She marvelled at the perfect design of nature.

It was then that she noticed the bare feet sprawled to the side of her. Shocked, she almost pulled away from the babe. She quickly followed the curve of the man's legs up to the splendid torso, clothed she was relieved to see, lying in an awkward position on the oak settle. Cred was asleep, his face peaceful but etched with lines of fatigue, dark rings circling his eyes. One arm was caught in a woven linen sling.

Gráinne was startled by his presence. She wondered how long he had been there and where Mora nee Derga was. She was afraid to waken him if she called out for Mora but there was nowhere in the *bothán* where Mora could not be visibly present, so it was apparent that Mora had gone out somewhere.

For the moment, at least while he was asleep, Gráinne was able to gaze upon Cred and imagine this was as it should be. She was surprised to discover that this might be what she truly wanted. She remembered the day she had been confused to find that he had chosen to stay with Serb. It was the day of the storm. He had said that the reason for his choice was not as she thought, but she had not given him a chance to explain.

Then, on the day of Donal Rua's burial, she knew Cred was feeling the same way she did. *They, the light ones*, were there that day for both of them. Gráinne knew that no one else witnessed them but everyone was aware of some change in the nature of the event, especially after she sang her song of the *ogham*.

As she watched him now, Gráinne was acutely aware of the intensity of her feelings for Cred, though she could not be sure that his emotions were running along the same threads as her own.

However, he had chosen to stay with Serb, and Gráinne could not deny the fact that Serb had been badly beaten, according to Emer. She wondered if Mora nee Derga was at the Brighdal *bothán* now, maybe treating Serb, but she knew that Mora would never leave Cred here with her if there was any danger. Something was not quite right though. Serb was talking to herself or to a spirit. Gráinne felt chilled at the thought that it might be Donal Rua.

The babe, noticing the change within her, felt the ripple of her fear and suddenly unclamped his lips from his food-source. He opened his mouth wide, his little face crumpled up and he let out a gusty cry, more plaintive than angry.

Cred stirred, his slumber disturbed, and realized before he opened his eyes that his body was in an awkward, cramped, uncomfortable position.

The cry that drew him from sleep suddenly came to the fore of his thoughts and he sat bolt upright, rubbing his grey eyes with one hand.

He stared incredulously at the scene before him, feeling that he must pinch himself as he was sure it was part of his dream.

Gráinne was soothing her babe and attaching him to her other breast. She was smiling tenderly. The babe, restored to his feasting, contentedly curled and uncurled his fingers in the fall of black hair.

Gráinne's eyes were soft and proud as they met Cred's.

"He is here, at last," she whispered. "I can hardly believe he is real. And Mora nee Derga has been a gift to us all, it seems."

Cred did not know how to face the Truth of her words. He became flustered and ran his fingers through his hair then rubbed his grey eyes again as if he was trying to wake himself up properly, but really he was trying to hide his embarrassment. The sling on his raised arm hid his face.

"Mora nee Derga is a good woman," he agreed. "She asked me to stay here with you while she went to my . . . the Brighdal *bothán*." He lowered his arm, unable to hold it aloft any longer.

"Serb?" asked Gráinne, noticing the genuine surprise in his eyes as she dared to say this.

"Yes," he answered honestly, somehow knowing that he

could never tell her an Untruth. He had the feeling that she knew how to see through them. He did not venture any more information but she still probed, anxious for some answers to put her mind at rest.

"Is she injured?"

Cred shook his head. She quickly tried to test if this was an Untruth but there was no resistance in the words. She could not pierce them. So, he was telling the Truth.

"Cred, I – I saw Serb earlier. She was talking with someone . . . but there was no one there. Finann came and took her back to the Brighdal *bothán*. I wanted to help but . . . I could not, this babe decided it was time. Neither of them saw me watching them."

Cred put his head into his hands in despair.

"Gráinne, I want to tell you everything but I cannot. My lips are sealed by Serb. Mora is with Serb now. We think she is just in shock, because . . . because of the events of the last moon. We are all in shock . . . but Serb is young in mind, she . . . she . . . "

Gráinne regretted that she had said anything. She deftly removed the sleeping babe from her breast and put him over her shoulder, patting his back until he passed up wind. She then laid him down flat and tore off some strips of linen which Mora had left for her to make a nappy for the babe. Wrapping it between his legs, she tied it on both sides, then laid the babe down to slumber peacefully in his crib.

She pulled the tunic over her head again to cover her body, suddenly aware of her womanhood in the presence of Cred.

"Cred, do not say more. I am aware that Serb was once in love with . . . with Donal Rua. It will be particularly hard for her and for you. It is difficult to live with one who carries another's spirit into the *bothán*."

Cred desperately wanted to explain to Gráinne but he knew he could not. He had to let her think what she willed. His silence reinforced what she had just said to him.

They were both quiet, their unspoken words weighing heavily in their minds, unaware of the sounds outside the door, until the taps became louder, and they had to do something about it before the babe woke up again.

Cred jumped up and opened the door to Finann.

"Where is Mora nee Derga? Is everything fine at the *bothán*?" Cred asked anxiously.

Finann struggled through the door with a hearthstone in his arms and a woven bag slung around his neck. He was smiling from ear to ear as he nodded to Cred.

"Serb is restful. Mora says she will sleep through the night. Mora wants you to go back up there, Cred, as she has some herbs she needs to show you how to brew if the need arises again. I came here to share something with Gráinne." Finann's voice ended in a whisper. "I have the hearthstone that belongs to Cromlach."

Cred patted Finann on the back, then he assisted with the carrying of the flat grey stone into Mora nee Derga's *bothán*.

"I made a boon with you, Gráinne," Finann said proudly. "I have returned the stone. I thought that the new babe should be near to the hearth of Cromlach. Mora does not mind having both stones here for the night."

Gráinne's eyes were moist with sudden tears as she stretched her hand out to touch the stone. It was a clean, cold slab. Finann must have washed it in the mountain stream.

"You have the thoughts of a good and kind man, Finann. I hope I am deserving of such friendship."

Gráinne looked at the two men shyly.

"I am happy that my babe has been birthed, with those I have love for around me."

She lowered her gaze quickly and drew Finann over to peep into the crib. Cred hurriedly drew on his leggings and sandals. He could not trust himself to speak, such was the torment in his head, so he left, to make his way back to the Brighdal *bothán*, alone with his joy and his grief.

Finann pulled a little brown bottle out of his bag.

"I think this may belong to Cromlach too."

"Finann! Cromlach will be pleased. This is very precious for the Elders, a very special medicine only they may use. I know, because my father has the same. You will be blessed, Finann, by the gods. I know it."

"I wish he may return to us soon, Gráinne. It is a lonely mountain without him," said Finann, his eyes wistful as he thought of Cromlach pottering around outside his *bothán* or walking the hills with his staff.

"Oh, Finann, do not wish him back upon the mountain. He is becoming old. We want him here at the *ráth* or in the Dún."

Finann bent down and whispered in Gráinne's ear. "I have a surprise, *a stór*, but you must not reveal it to anyone. I have a new *bothán* crafted. It is not on the mountain but at the foot of the mountain, a place that is hidden, a place only I and the gods know of, that Cromlach will like. It is not far for either of us. I am very happy because it is attached to the mountain, you are happy because it is not on the mountain, and maybe Lugnae is glad it is not in the Dún."

"Oh, Finann!" Gráinne embraced him warmly, laughing as his face reddened like a fallen apple.

Mora nee Derga walked in and laughed along with them.

"It is good to hear the chattering and laughing of good spirits in my new home but, Finann, I must send you back to your hut and your goats and I must share some of your bedding, Gráinne, before my poor eyes close of their own choosing and I fall down."

Finann disappeared into the night.

Gráinne gave some of her bedding to Mora nee Derga who arranged it on the floor beside Gráinne, then both tired women settled down to sleep until dawn, or until the babe awoke to break his fast.

# CHAPTER 14

# HE RETURNS

*He returns so that my heart leaps high*
*Soaring up purple mountains*
*To dive down deep green valleys*
*And I yearn for the naked Truth of it all.*

The blanket of night was folded tidily away and a fresh light bathed the settlement.

A strange trio approached, followed by a small party of helpers and horses laden with goods.

The hounds barked like good guarding curs, and the children, squealing and running around barefoot, suddenly stopped in their tracks to stare.

One of the hounds began to bark and whimper excitedly, his tail almost wagging off. He leapt forward and threw himself against one of the hooded figures who immediately bent down to fondle the dog's ears.

One of the trappers, Devin, dropped the pile of wood he was carrying and ran to meet the arrivals.

"Cromlach!" he said. "My hound greets only Cromlach in such a way."

"Cromlach has returned!" he shouted to the children. "Tell Lugnae that Cromlach has come back to us!"

The children scattered, each one eager to be the first to break the news at the Dún Hall.

Before long, nearly the whole Clan had gathered to help the weary travellers to the Dún.

Lugnae did not appear, but Emer came out nervously and stood waiting for the three people and their party to reach the Dún.

She extended her hand to Cromlach.

"We bid you greetings but we are in mourning, Cromlach. Lugnae is not coming out of his quarters. I – I . . . I have sad tidings . . . Donal Rua is gone."

Emer lifted the ends of her skirts and buried her face into them. Cromlach immediately came forward and wrapped her in his arms. He did not ask her any questions. Later, one of the trappers would tell him what had occurred in his absence.

"Emer," he said gently, "I have Olc Aiche and Dairine here to see Gráinne and the new babe."

Emer hurriedly wiped her eyes and then extended her arms to Dairine who hugged her warmly. Olc Aiche patted her on the back.

Emer smiled tremulously and shook her head.

"Cromlach," she said, "Gráinne has not birthed her babe yet. She is in her quarters and by the looks of her, she will be birthing any day now."

Cromlach was surprised.

"The babe is not here? Are you sure, a stór? Well, of course, you must be, Emer, you dwell in the same Dún," he said quickly, not wishing to cause offence.

"Come, come, I am not offering you the hospitality you deserve after such a long journey. It will be good to have company and to converse about other settlements. We are rebuilding at present, because of the storm, but we will manage to accommodate you all." Emer had suddenly brightened into a clucking hen again. She was fussing, like her old self, anxious to mother everyone. Her children, sensing this, moved closer to her skirts, glad to glimpse their beloved mother again. The past moon had given them a stranger, indifferent and untouchable, and because of this their sense of loss was twofold. They felt that they had lost a brother and a mother.

Emer called upon Devin the trapper to get the ostlers to see to the horses, then she invited the guests to step over her threshold.

Just as they entered the Dún Hall, they heard a voice shouting and squealing excitedly. Cromlach turned at the sound of his name and saw Finann running, as fast as his legs could carry him, from the direction of the Brighdal *bothán*.

"Cromlach! It *is* you! I knew you would return!" Finann yelled. "The babe is birthed. He is here! He is here, Cromlach!" Finann was breathless when he reached them. "Emer! I – I beg pardon of you, Olc Aiche and . . . and . . . "

"Finann, this is Dairine, spouse of Olc Aiche, mother of Gráinne," said Emer.

Finann inclined his head to Dairine and Olc Aiche.

"I bear you good tidings. Gráinne is delivered of a boy, a grand boy with eyes of the sea and hair of the sun!"

Emer was surprised.

"When? But Gráinne is slumbering in her quarters!"

"Not so, Emer," said Finann. "She is at the new hearth of Mora nee Derga and the old hearth of Cromlach. She has birthed a fine boy."

Emer could hardly believe it but Cromlach was smiling knowingly. By the light of a sickle moon, Gráinne had birthed the new King-boy. A growing moon was a sign of a growing wisdom. A King, with the totem of a wolf, was a god-given gift to the land. Things were bound to change.

Olc Aiche and Dairine rushed forward.

"Boy," said Dairine, "take us to our daughter and her son. We will bathe and feast and sleep later, no mind how weary we are now. Come, Emer, we must all welcome the new spirit."

Olc Aiche's face was aglow with pleasure. His King-calling had worked. He blessed the day that Art the Lonely came to his dwelling. He blessed the night that Gráinne had lain with Art the Lonely.

When they reached Mora nee Derga's *bothán*, Finann rapped at the door with his knuckles.

"Mora, it is Finann. I have some guests to see the babe!"

Mora came quickly to the door, lest they knock again and wake the babe.

"Shush, Finann! Cromlach! And . . . and is it the father of Gráinne I see before me? Oh! It is her mother also. I welcome you into my dwelling. Gráinne will be so happy and glad to see you. She . . . she is out finding the sacred ground to give the source of life back to the Mother as it was too late last night to do it. Enter, enter! See the babe, slumbering with a very full

139

belly!" Mora giggled, "Gráinne's babe likes his milk . . . thrice through the night before dawn and once this morn . . . enough to make one want to return him! And what a lusty cry, better than the cock that hails the day!"

"Oh, oh, I can wait no longer," whispered Dairine, as she clasped her hands together under her chin and shuffled her feet forward to get into the *bothán*.

Once inside, she and Emer rushed over to the makeshift crib and cooed until Olc Aiche warned them not to waken the babe. But he could not stifle the proud smile that stole over his face as he gazed into the crib himself.

"Unblemished, as a true King should be," he muttered under his breath.

Cromlach watched and waited. He knew he was going to be a special guide for the child in his King-making, so he stood back and let kin greet kin. He wanted desperately to go outside and seek Gráinne but knew he must not. His presence could not be seen to be intrusive, or treading on the toes of Olc Aiche. Cromlach knew that he was very dear to Gráinne as her mentor, and she was like a daughter to him. He was also aware that Olc Aiche was astute enough to know this, even to encourage it, as in his own absence he knew Gráinne had the special protection of a Druid Elder. Nevertheless, he probably did not wish to see too much of a show of affection between the two of them. Cromlach thought it was right that Gráinne should greet her parents and himself together. He had thought of going to the Dún with Emer and seeing Gráinne later but was wise enough not to, lest she display too much excitement and affection then, in front of her father and her foster-father. It was a very delicate situation and best dealt with in this way, in the presence of the new child which helped to divert some of the attention, the rest hopefully being diffused by Gráinne's own pride in the babe.

They did not have long to wait. Gráinne was humming to herself when she returned, unaware of the visitors in Mora nee Derga's *bothán*.

She flipped the latch of the door and entered, surprised to see Finann jammed almost to the portals of the doorway. Then she saw the plump sturdy body of Emer, who had moved back from the crib and now stood in front of Finann. Gráinne's heart suddenly started thumping wildly. She could smell familiar scents, a certain musty heather smell of travelling cloaks and of a sweet fresh blossom she had grown up with. She could not see beyond Emer but she hoped that what she was thinking was true.

"*Máthair*? Mami, is it you?" she called out timidly, afraid that it might not be her.

"*A chuisle!*" Dairine smiled as her daughter hurled herself through to grab her. The two of them laughed and cried and crushed themselves to each other, Gráinne uncaring of how tender her breasts were or how her body ached. The pain seemed to glide through her body and stay in her throat, a bubble of deep hurt that almost took her breath away and made the salt tears chase down her face.

She saw Olc Aiche and Cromlach at the same time and squealed her joy, trying to grab all three of them to her, with not enough arms or enough room to do it. Emer watched silently, happy for Gráinne. She was having a very difficult time holding back her own tears. Reunions of foster-children with their blood-kin always made her cry. She remembered that this was never going to happen now with Donal Rua and some strange little thought placated her. Somehow, in his passing over, he was with her always. If he had lived, and of course she wished he had, she would have faced the dreadful torture of separation due to his fosterage somewhere far away, even with her own relatives. She could not bear to be parted from her children. Emer determined in that moment to renounce the Brehon Laws of fosterage. She was going to keep her remaining children at the Dún. Not one of them was she ever going to be parted from, ever.

Gráinne caught the glazed look in Emer's eyes and smiled warmly at her. She was very close to Emer now and looked upon her as the Clan-Mother. It tore at her heart to see her suffer but somehow, today seemed lighter.

All voices started chattering excitedly at once and then, as one, stopped in shame when they heard the little frightened cry of the new babe.

Gráinne immediately rushed to soothe him, her blue eyes shining and bright, her mother close on her heels, clucking her tongue and making funny endearing noises.

Olc Aiche stood close, his fingers nervously rolling a tassel from his cloak in his hand.

Emer, Finann, Mora nee Derga and Cromlach realized that the *bothán* was too small for the comfort of many visitors and so they each started to excuse themselves.

Finann took the lead and tugged on Cromlach's cloak.

"Cromlach, I have somewhere to show to you."

Gráinne anxiously looked over the babe's fair head. She desperately wanted to talk with dear Cromlach but knew in her heart that the time would come later. Of course he was not going away again. He had fulfilled his boon. Had he not said he was going to return to the Dún when her son was birthed? And he had. She was glad.

Her face relaxed and she nodded to them all as they bade their farewells until later. She was pleased to have some time alone with her mother and father.

Emer wanted to return to the Dún to have preparations started for the Feasting. Also, she needed to find quarters for everyone.

Finann caught her gently by the arm and whispered: "I have somewhere for Cromlach, Emer, do not fret, *a stór*."

Emer was grateful. She was not sure that Lugnae would yet accept Cromlach under the same roof. Cromlach was also relieved that he was not residing at the Dún and he exchanged a knowing look with Emer, forging a stronger bond of mutual respect than had been there before.

Cromlach was aware that not much had survived the storm and assumed that his old *bothán* at the Dún and his simple dwelling on the mountain were both gone. He would start again. Had he not done it many times in his life? This time, he had his hearthstone, rescued by Finann or so he presumed. He had seen it in Mora nee Derga's, and now knew what Finann meant when he said Gráinne birthed her babe by Mora's new hearth and his own old one.

Mora nee Derga linked her arm with Emer's.

"Come, Emer, we have to feed the Clan Beag and we have no boiling pot big enough!"

Emer laughed, for the first time relaxing a little since the passing over. She warmed to Mora nee Derga and her easy way of making people smile.

"Indeed, the Clan Beag is nothing when I have Dagda's Cauldron!" she quipped back, surprising herself as wit never came easily to her. Everyone knew Dagda's Cauldron was bottomless in its never-ending source of food supplies.

Mora laughed heartily. The Clan Beag was a Clan created by the imagination of Fergus the poet which caused great merriment because of the rampant fertility of the tribe and the vast numbers of children birthed every moon. Long and wonderful stories about the Clan Beag were related at feasts and gatherings, elaborately embellished tales that kept men and women happily awake into the small hours of cold winter nights, listening to the stories of their antics.

"Emer, I know you are wondering where you will put everyone. Well, Gráinne and the babe can stay with me another few nights," said Mora. "I will love to have their company and although my *bothán* is small, we will manage well. Olc Aiche and Dairine will, of course, stay at the Dún. And Cromlach is going to set up his hearth in a dwelling Finann has found for him. We are, all of us, content. I am thinking that the bondmaid and helpers who arrived with Olc Aiche and Dairine may be able to stay near by, perhaps at those large new stabling quarters by the old horse-sheds. The horses still have not been moved over, as I suggested they stay in their familiar surroundings for now. Cathbar, Lugnae's favourite, though, is causing me some concern. He is fretting too much. It may help if our Chieftain, Lugnae, would see him. Do you think that is possible, Emer?"

"Possible but not probable," said Emer, then she completely changed the subject, not wishing to dwell on anything which dampened her spirits. "Mora, we have some wild suckling-pigs which perished in the storm. They are not the 'pigs of Asal', gone today, back tomorrow, but we must be thankful Devin found them and I had them cured and salted, so we can have a roast tonight with some apple falls I have stored. Do you realize, Mora, that the Fire of Dagda is almost upon us and the trappers have not yet made the Fire-Wheel? Never before has it been forgotten."

"Nor shall it be this time either." Mora hugged Emer to her. "Cromlach has returned and I have a feeling that it will be good for all of us; yes, Emer, even for Lugnae." She nodded to reassure Emer. Something about the tone of her voice or the certainty of the words gave courage to Emer, who held her head up high and strode back to the Dún with determination, chatting and laughing as she eagerly thought of the feast ahead.

Mora thought of the Fire Festival of Dagda and the great celebrations that were held every midsummer for *Ollathair*, All-father. A burning wheel was rolled down Knocknarea on the gentle slope of the mountain. All the young boys in the settlement ran and squealed after it as it tumbled and gathered speed on the hill. It was a great time of hilarity and games and marked the beginning of the descent of the sun from its highest peak in the sky. No one felt like celebrating this sun-wheel though, at least not so soon after the passing over of Donal Fer Trí, but maybe the birthing of Gráinne's son would help ease the pain in the Clan. He was a sun-child, with blue eyes and corn-silk hair. It was fitting that he arrive at this season to hail the Fire of Dagda.

The Hall was a hive of activity that evening. Although the throng of people were subdued, they were happy to see some semblance of normality in the Clan again. Emer was bustling about making sure that everyone had enough to eat, and her children were hanging on to her skirts again, as they had always done before. The feast was sumptuous, roast suckling-pigs with sliced apples, which Mora nee Derga could not bear to look at, served up with skillet mushrooms and nuts, which she and everyone else devoured heartily. There was a fine broth made from the trotters and a variety of roots and shoots fried with

corn-mush. Mora made some extra flat-cakes stuffed with cream-
ed cheese and apple, a favourite with Finann, Cromlach, and
the children. Some venison was cooked on the huge spit over
the hearth and the trappers ate well of this, satisfied to eat their
kill and fill their bellies with that familiar taste. Lugnae was
fond of venison, especially from a fine stag. He sat at the table
quietly, avoiding conversation and eye-contact with almost
everyone. He knew that Cromlach was there and he was civil
to him but did not show any outward signs of emotion towards
him. Mora nee Derga watched him with interest. When Cromlach stretched out his hand to pat Emer's hand as she gave him
some hot drink, Mora was sure that she saw Lugnae's dark eyes
soften, almost wistful that the gesture had been towards himself.

Olc Aiche was also watchful, totally oblivious of the playful
banter and idle chattering of Dairine, instead wishing to observe
the unsaid feelings between Cromlach and Lugnae. He determined to do something about it before the night was through.
Just as he decided to take Cromlach aside and request a meeting
with Lugnae in private, the door opened and in walked Gráinne
with her babe, followed by Finann carrying a slumber-basket.
The room hushed in reverence for the babe and Gráinne walked
straight over to Lugnae Fer Trí, not to Cromlach or himself,
but to Lugnae. Olc Aiche praised the gods for his daughter's
good sense. Lugnae's eyes were sad as he gazed at the babe but
he acknowledged Gráinne and covered her hand with his own.
He could not bring himself to touch the child and hoped she
would understand. She turned to the Clan and suddenly
announced: "My son is to be named at the Fire of Dagda, as
his father would surely have wished."

There was a murmur in the Clan. Cromlach and Olc Aiche
were both getting to their feet, afraid of what she would say
next but she motioned for them to sit down and then turning to
Lugnae, she said, "Foster-father, it is my wish that you will give
him his first name."

Lugnae was taken aback. It was not usual for someone who
was not kin to name a child. He immediately looked to Olc
Aiche who smiled and nodded his assent, thereby giving his

blessing. Cromlach also inclined his head to him. Only Emer and Dairine sat down with their mouths open in disbelief.

Gráinne waited breathlessly, suddenly afraid that Lugnae might refuse her but he stood up and raised his goblet to her and to Olc Aiche and Dairine, and then to Cromlach.

"I bid my guests well and hope the Dún is hospitable to them. They do us a great honour and give us comfort in their presence here at this time of mourning. That you chose this Dún, above all others, Olc Aiche, and there are many of them, for the teaching and fostering of your child, I am happy and I speak also for my dear spouse, Emer. But it has lain sorely on my mind for many, many moons that Cromlach felt the need to exile himself from the Dún and therefore from my heart which had hardened against him. Remorse, regret, and guilt have been my constant companions for many nights and I wish to see the back of them. Cromlach, we need you here at the Dún, and if I am to name the new babe, I will be in sore need of advisers. Perhaps I may take leave of the company here this night and give you into the capable hands of Fergus whilst we retire, Olc Aiche, Cromlach and myself, into my chamber for the sole purpose of name-hunting!"

Gráinne felt that persistent lump come into her throat again. She did not want to burst into tears in front of everyone there nor did she wish to upset the babe. It was difficult for her to do anything other than stand there, still, completely overcome by the turn of events, and bury her face into the babe's head. She drank in that sweet-sour smell and poured all the love in her heart into him. After all, he was the one who had saved the day and brought them all together again. Soon, very soon now, he would have a name. Dairine came over and hugged her daughter.

"Gráinne, I always knew you had a charm for the men and I am glad to see you use it wisely," she murmured into Gráinne's ear so that no one else could hear.

"Mami, that was the first lesson you taught me." Gráinne's eyes twinkled.

"I did?"

"I just observed you, from an early age. Only the finest,

wisest, and most patient woman in the land could have managed to snare and keep content my father."

"Wisdom had nothing to do with it, Gráinne. I made the best flying-potions and I had the best legs!"

Gráinne stared at her mother and, for the first time in her life, she saw another side, another facet to this lovable, light-hearted woman. She had never considered that her mother might be a Druid priestess but she knew that the flying-potions, the medicines that gave one access to the spirit-world, were only draughted by very skilled hands, the ingredients consisting of many dangerous poisons. Only someone with great faith and love was capable of learning this Craft.

"Come! You look like you have seen the otherworld! Let us rejoice in the birth of our new *rí*!"

Gráinne's eyes widened.

"You? *Máthair*, you? Tell me something, I must know . . . that night I lay with Art the Lonely . . . the milk my father made me drink, did you draught that? I had no will, only the will to lie with Art."

Dairine cupped the babe's head in her hand.

"And if I did, you will not be angry?"

"So it was you! Oh, Mami, how could I be angry? You have given me the greatest gift of all, the most precious treasure ever. *Máthair*, I want you to teach me, please. Cromlach has given me knowledge of many of the plants and herbs but I want to know the secrets of merging them and how to prepare them. I had no notion all this time, no notion of you as a Druidess at all!"

"Do you think your father would have been content with someone who did not know the Craft? No, Gráinne, *like* must wed *like* amongst us. We are a race unto ourselves. In time, you will get to know all the secrets if you take the vows. Now is not the night for us to talk, *a stór*, now is the moment to attend to the needs of the babe, kin and friends about. Gráinne . . . " Dairine paused, then asked suddenly with interest, "who is that becoming young man who has just entered the Hall?"

Gráinne turned her head and then felt a rush of warmth invade her cheeks.

147

Cred's eyes scanned the room to alight on her.

"Gráinne?" Dairine questioned. "You have a suitor?"

Gráinne immediately retorted, "Nonsense! You mean Cred?" She laughed tensely. "He is my foster-brother. Mami, he has no interest in me. He belongs to another."

"You could have fooled me," mumbled Dairine but she did not pursue the issue as she did not want to embarrass her daughter further.

Cred came over, which made matters worse. Gráinne's face flamed as she made the introductions between her mother and Cred, both of whom smiled and nodded cordially to each other. Then Cred asked urgently of Gráinne, "Where is Mora? Is she here? I need her to come with me."

"She is here somewhere, Cred. Is anything the matter then?" Gráinne did not like the worried look on Cred's face.

"Serb is ailing again," Cred answered shortly.

Gráinne looked across the room.

"Morann the physician is here. You know Fergus has the physic finger? But he is story-telling so I doubt if he – " she began.

"No!" Cred said sharply, then pulled himself together. "No," he repeated softly, "Serb will only see Mora nee Derga. Mora has good medicine and I do not want to cause too much bother."

"Can I be of assistance maybe?" asked Dairine shyly. "I last saw Mora making flat-cakes for Emer's children and telling stories of injured wild animals. It may be difficult to prise her away but I may be able to help your friend."

Gráinne added proudly, "My mother is skilled in the Crafts, Cred. She will take care of Serb."

It was a moment of mutual respect between mother and daughter. Dairine glowed as Gráinne acknowledged her as someone other than just *Máthair* at last.

Cred hesitated only for a brief moment, then his immediate desperation got the better of him and he nodded, anxious to get back to the Brighdal *bothán* before Serb made her way to the Dún.

Dairine went off to grab a beautifully dyed woven bag of woad-blue, which Gráinne, when she saw it, guessed that it contained dried herbs, potions and totems for healing. She shook her head and smiled. Dairine had kept the secret well from her daughter.

Gráinne wished she could leave and go with them but knew she would not easily step over the threshold of the lovers' Brighdal *bothán*. Besides, she had her babe to care for. Instead, she watched as Cred called to Finann to escort him and Dairine to the *bothán*. If anyone wondered where they were going, no one made any comment. They gathered around to ooh and aah over the babe and Gráinne had a difficult time concentrating on all the questions and answers. Emer eventually came to her rescue.

"Gráinne, the babe must slumber away from the noise and the crowd here. Come into my quarters. I had Finann place the slumber-basket in there when you first arrived."

Gráinne, much relieved and grateful for her foster-mother's intervention, left the noisy Hall for the peace of Emer's quarters.

Emer came straight to the point. "*A stór*, why did your mother leave in such a hurry with Cred and Finann?"

"Serb is not too well," Gráinne answered casually. "I told Cred that my mother is good with the herbs, so instead of bothering Morann or Fergus, and before I could say anything at all, she was off. She is like that, Emer, always willing to try her cures on anyone, any time of the day or night." Gráinne hoped she sounded convincing. She wanted to give the impression that Dairine was dabbling in handed-down women's remedies rather than that she might be a skilled Craftswoman.

Emer's voice was stricken with fear. "But Serb is the chosen May-Queen. It is not seemly for her to sicken. We must get Morann to see to her. We cannot have any more ill fate at the Dún!"

"Oh, no," Gráinne said hurriedly. "It is probably just women's moon-pains or aches in the head or some such thing and Mami has the cures for all those little upsets. Do not fret, Emer. If it was serious, Cred would surely have insisted on searching out Morann or taking Fergus away from his storytelling!"

She hoped this was true.

"Ah, we will see soon enough," said Emer, as she lifted the

babe from Gráinne and laid him down in his slumber-basket. He was fast asleep and not due to feed for a while yet so Gráinne decided to go into the Hall and eat some of the delicious fare. Emer beckoned for her to leave and told her she would keep an eye on the babe for her. Her eyes were tearful as she peered into the basket and Gráinne left quickly, knowing that Emer needed time to be alone, and she was also aware that a new babe can heal great sorrows.

The evening was long and everyone was loath to break it up as it was some time ago that talk and laughter rang through the Hall. There was a hum of idle chatter that soothed the ears with its familiarity and made the Clan feel like one large family again.

Gráinne listened intently to Fergus's wonderful stories and allowed herself the pleasure of being carried away to distant lands and the world of giants and little people. She shrieked with the trappers and the children when he scared them and laughed heartily when the hero won the day. The tumblers came in and somersaulted down the Hall, and Mora came over to speak with Gráinne.

"You realize that all this entertainment is just for us. No one seems to be aware that none of our honoured guests is here to see it!" Mora smiled. "And the name-making . . . well, all I can say is: your babe is going to have a very long one, if indeed they have been name-making all this time!"

"Just what I was thinking, Mora!" Gráinne whispered. "Still, let them all talk it out, feast, and be merry for it is good that the Dún is alive again. I think it is time for me to retire though, as I am sure I shall not slumber the night away, not with a sweet hungry little mouth to feed."

"Devin the trapper will help you, Gráinne. I will come back later after I have seen Cathbar, Lugnae's steed. He may need something to calm him through the night."

Gráinne went into Emer's chamber and swaddled her babe with a soft woollen blanket ready for the walk back to Mora nee Derga's *bothán*.

Just as she was about to approach Devin for assistance in carrying the slumber-basket and extra food, which Emer had lavished upon her before retiring for the rest of the night, Dairine arrived back with Cred, not Finann as Gráinne would have expected.

Dairine said that Serb was slumbering peacefully, and Finann had gone to feed and tend to his goats now as he was going to return for Cromlach later to escort him to his new dwelling.

Olc Aiche, Cromlach and Lugnae were still in Lugnae's quarters. Gráinne thought bemusedly that Mora was right about the name-making.

Then, before Gráinne could object, Cred stooped and lifted the slumber-basket containing the sleeping babe and stated he was going to walk Gráinne back to Mora's *bothán*. Gráinne noticed that his good arm held the basket but he was not wearing the sling tonight. She knew though that his injured arm was bound in soft linen beneath his rough-woven cloak. She looked around for Mora so she could appeal to her to accompany them, but Mora gestured for her to go on, as she was in deep converse with one of the trappers about Lugnae's horse.

Dairine kissed Gráinne on the forehead.

"Rest well, *a stór*. We will see you in the morn."

Gráinne had no excuse to stay and it seemed, whether she willed it or not, she was to share Cred's company alone for a second time.

The night was crisp and bright with a myriad of stars, the moon a thin sliver curved in a pale light and a soft plumage of cloud. Gráinne surveyed the vast expanse of sky for sight of the great ploughshare and the seven sisters. It gave her comfort somehow to see these formations. Olc Aiche showed them to her when she was a little girl and she remembered her first ecstasy of the discovery when she sighted them now.

"It seems I am destined to share part of my nights with you, Cred," she quipped bravely.

"Would they were all with me, Gráinne," he answered bluntly, shocking her into silence. They walked side by side, both intent on carrying their burdens, hers the food, his the child. She was glad it was dark enough for him not to see her discomfort. She did not trust herself to speak at first but then, unable to bear the weight of the silence any longer, she blurted out: "Cred, you are with Serb! Do not speak against the goddess like this!"

He did not answer but kept walking, tense and tight-lipped, until he reached Mora nee Derga's *bothán*. Opening the door, he set the basket down, then reaching for the faintly glowing bog-spail that burnt outside the portals, he lit a beeswax candle on the inside and returned the bog-spail to its rightful place. Carefully he moved the slumber-basket to the hearthside, beside the pallet. Gráinne set the food down on a small wooden table. Then, heart pounding, she broached the subject again.

"It is not right that you talk with me like this, when you are with Serb. We have suffered enough. It will anger the gods and cause naught but pain."

Cred strode over to her, towering to his full height.

"You said that once, Gráinne. Once is enough!" he snapped suddenly, frustrated and unable to bide his tongue.

She flinched as if he had struck her. His tone made her step backwards and brought to memory Emer's description of Serb's bruises.

Cred saw the flash of fear in her eyes and felt like someone had speared him. He stretched out his hand contritely, ashamed of himself for speaking so harshly to her but she misunderstood the gesture and side-stepped to avoid his touch.

Cred could not believe she recoiled from him.

"*A stór*, I will never harm you. Why do you look at me like that?"

She realized the absurdity of her behaviour and relaxed.

"Please, Cred, do not raise your voice to me again. It . . . it is not good for the milk," Gráinne gasped, crossing her arms protectively over her breasts, which were rapidly rising and falling as she tried to catch her breath again.

Cred could no longer bear or control his feelings. He wrapped his arms around her gently, heeding not the pain that seared through his injured limb, and trapped her against him, her hands still folded across her breasts. She looked up, startled. Then he pressed his mouth to her parted lips, soft yielding petals that they were, and crushed them gently, probing until she had to respond and hesitantly moved her own lips in unison until she felt the tip of his tongue enter. Her lips closed and then half-sobbing, she moaned as her hunger gripped him to her like a leech. His body was hard against hers but she struggled to loosen her hands and buried them in his hair, her arms locked around his neck.

Her swollen breasts squeezed wet to his chest and she thrust her belly, round and soft, firmly towards him. She desired him desperately but knew it was too soon and too late, too soon after her birthing and too late because he had chosen Serb. Her despair draped over her, making her even more fervent so that he, sensing her desperation, wanted only to stay like this for ever, protecting her from the anguish he knew he was causing. He wanted to take it away but the more he devoured her, the sharper the pain for both of them, and reluctantly he eased himself from her and drew back.

For a long moment he gazed into the hazy blue of her eyes, drowning in the pools of her mind, knowing now as he had always known that he had to have her for his own, that they belonged together, somehow, some way, some time.

Cred found his voice. He said hoarsely, "Do you think this angers the gods, Gráinne?"

Tears welled in her eyes. She could not answer, feeling that this was how it should have been, how it could not be now because of Baltinne. Serb had chosen unwisely and a great penance had been paid all round.

Gráinne's arms slipped down from Cred's neck and she lowered her head, resting her forehead briefly against his chest, her hair silk on his throat.

She withdrew herself abruptly when the babe cried out. Cred watched her move quickly over to the slumber-basket. He was conscious of an intense feeling of loss, an unkind helplessness that descended upon him, as if he were losing himself in a blanket of fog. His heart was thudding in his breast, beating a war-drum of his churning emotions. He wanted her so badly, wished her for himself for one whole night and then one lifetime of nights, but it was not to be. He had to serve many moons yet with Serb before he was free again.

Gráinne sat on the pallet and cupped her breast, offering it to the babe in her arms. She shivered, trying to still her trembling body and fluttering heart. Cred came over and stoked up a fire in the hearth, assuming that she was cold. He then sat crosslegged on the floor in front of her, thinking he had never seen a more beautiful sight. Her skin was white like milk, her exposed breast the orb of the moon, the long black night of hair giving her the appearance of a goddess, fertile, fruitful. The golden head of the child clasped to her breast made him feel humble. Cred could no longer look at her. He sank his head into his hands.

"Gráinne, *a chuisle*, I cannot begin to tell you what . . . what you do to me. I must have you for my own . . . "

"Please, Cred," she interrupted, "you are with Serb and you chose to stay with her after the first moon. Why?"

"I cannot answer that, Gráinne. In time, maybe, you will know, but I made a boon with Serb."

"Has she fallen with child?" Gráinne was afraid.

"No, no, that was not possible. I . . . I could not fulfil the great rite. Please, I implore you, do not ask any more questions. I am aware that you are a powerful Druidess, Gráinne, but enough ill-fate has come to the Clan. It is best not to see all the Truth sometimes." He gripped her hand and held it against his cheek. "I want you to know that I share only my *bothán* with Serb until next Baltinne. Then, I shall claim you, if you will still have me. We will have served our fosterage by then too and I will take you and your babe anywhere you would like to live. This is my last word on it until then, *a chuisle*."

Gráinne's heart was bursting with happiness. She believed him and she was going to put her trust in him, despite her curiosity about his decision to stay with Serb. She did not have to be a Druidess to read the Truth in his sincerity. It was obvious that he felt the same way about her as she did about him.

She turned her palm in his hand where he held it against his cheek, and she gently tilted his face towards her. Her breast fluttered at the smouldering intense look he gave her. He was making it so hard for her to speak. All she wanted to do was melt into his arms again and alleviate the agonizing pain of desire that seared through her.

"I will wait," she whispered softly, closing her eyes to blind herself to him. She could no longer bear his body so near to hers. It made it difficult for her to breathe. "N-now go, please go, before Mora comes back and sees that you are still here. No one must know. It would not look good nor fare too well with the Clan, especially after the cold destruction of the storm and the loss of Donal Rua. We must not be seen to be breaking the rules of the Elders or going against the gods . . . even if it is our belief that we are not. Please?"

Cred got to his feet, forcing himself to take his leave of her. He bent down and sipped her lips once more, a soft, fleeting gentle coming together, the memory of which would seal the promise of their future during the long moons apart.

After he had gone, she hugged her babe to her, stroking the down of his fair hair against her chin, a teardrop of bliss rolling down her cheek and wetting the top of his head.

Cromlach had returned . . . but so had Cred.

# CHAPTER 15

# FIRE OF DAGDA

*To dance within the sacred flame*
*And tumble with the Wheel of Fire*
*It is time for him to call your name*
*And pluck Hope's string upon the lyre.*

The Fire-Wheel rolled down the slope of Knocknarea, on the far side where the grass still grew, away from the mudslide which had stunted the year's growth.

Everyone was dressed in saffron- and mustard-dyed garments, some orange and others flaming red, including those worn by the younger children.

The Elders wore beautiful patterned robes, embroidered with orange serpents and huge suns. They each wore the *niam-lann*, a band of burnished gold worn around the forehead. Some of the women Elders had twisted ribbons of silver or findruine, a splendid white bronze, woven around the gold.

Lugnae was true to his word and all the Clan had their *botháns* rebuilt by now, on new sites, away from the banks of the river. Their wealth and tools were replenished. Cred had a new forge. Lugnae traded for some gold-ore from Laighin Theas, sending out his traders to find good bronze, copper and superior metal ores in exchange for reams of fine woven linen, some of his own pots and implements. Cred set about making new tools for himself, and salvaged some of the old ones from the brown mud-flats left after the swollen waters of the river receded.

He was glad to work again to get away from the Brighdal *bothán* during the day, and to dream of the time Gráinne and he would be together.

His first task was to help make the Sun-Wheel with the wheel-wright and the carpenter.

156

It turned out to be a splendid wheel and after the fires were lit all around it, the squealing and laughter of the men and boys who chased it down the hill echoed over the mountain.

Cred decided that, loath as he was to leave the Dún and Gráinne, he would have to sojourn to one of the larger settlements on the coast where the ships came in from other lands. He needed to do some trading of his own with some of the pieces he had artificed himself and stored at the Dún during the storm, for raw materials, ore, and unpolished jewels to begin the crafting of the Chalice he saw in his vision.

He knew that during his absence he could rely on Mora nee Derga and Finann to keep an eye on Serb, who had taken to avoiding people and wandering about talking to herself. He worried about her. Sometimes she called him Donal Rua which made a ripple of fear pass through him, making him feel uneasy for the rest of that day. Scath the Druid, her father, saw her once but did not seem to want to come back to visit her again. He sent little gifts now and again, which she hid in a corner of the *bothán* or even buried outside.

Gráinne climbed the slope with Olc Aiche and Dairine, Lugnae and Emer. Her father, Olc Aiche, carried the babe as he intended to bestow upon him the name of Lugnae's choosing, at the Fire of Dagda ceremony.

Cromlach was already waiting for them at the top of the first slope where the fire had been lit for the event.

Half the Clan were breathless after the Wheel-chasing but they climbed back up for the name-giving ceremony.

Cred could not take his eyes off Gráinne, although he stood with his arm linked with Serb's. Everyone had to be there for the name-giving, and the only way Cred could keep Serb from wandering off on her own was to link his arm through hers. She seemed to like that and remained calm throughout the ritual.

The Elders and the Clan all sat on the grass at Olc Aiche's command. Only Cromlach, Olc Aiche, Lugnae, Gráinne and the babe stood beside the fire.

Dairine and Emer sat on the grass beside Fergus, who was there to record the event in poetry and strum soft music on the lyre. The lyre was easier to haul up the mountain than the harps he usually played.

"Lugnae Fer Trí, Chieftain of the Fer Trí Clan," boomed out Olc Aiche's voice, "in sight and in sound of all the Hosts, here at the Fire of Dagda, we ask you, do you bless this child with a name of your making?"

"I do," answered Lugnae, "in sight and in sound of all the Hosts, in obeyance with the Laws of Brighde and of Dagda, I bless this child with a name of my making."

Cromlach passed a small urn of water to Lugnae, who sprinkled some on to the babe's head.

Cromlach then offered a handful of earth from the ground which Lugnae rubbed into the babe's hair.

A little wooden box containing precious salt was put before him next and Lugnae dipped his smallest finger into it, then placed some of the salt on the babe's tongue, whereupon the child let out a lusty cry.

Cromlach lifted the babe from Olc Aiche and the crying stopped right away. Gráinne was asked to disrobe the child. Olc Aiche, meanwhile, removed the top of his robe, exposing his upper body which was firm and muscular.

The Clan was awestruck, one and all, when he lit a bog-spail in the fire and passed it all over his own body. Gráinne's heart went into her mouth as Olc Aiche placed the burning torch in Lugnae's hand, then holding Lugnae's hand with his own, he passed the flame of the torch over the babe's skin, up and down the body and over Cromlach's hands holding him, without any scorching on the flesh.

"Name him! Lugnae Fer Trí, in the presence of Dagda and Brighde, name this babe!"

Lugnae said, "I name this child: Cormac mac Airt! Son of Art the Lonely, Art mac Conn who was the son of Conn of a Hundred Battles."

The crowd gasped in disbelief. Gráinne fell on her knees at Lugnae's feet.

"You have named him for a *rí*," she sobbed with relief. "The Truth is out, at last!"

The Clan rose to its feet, almost as one, still in awe and

unable to comprehend what they saw and heard. Mora nee Derga and Cred were smiling, happy for Gráinne, happy for Cormac the babe.

Before the silence broke, a shout went up from one of the trappers.

"A messenger! Riding to the Dún!"

On the way to the Dún, travelling on the Bréifne road, was a horseman on a steed galloping along at a great pace, clouds of dust rising behind him.

Devin the trapper raced down the slope to intercept the traveller before he reached the Dún. Gráinne wrapped the babe and held him close to her as she watched Devin run, slipping and sliding down the slope. The Clan were tense, fearful that the messenger might be bringing tidings of war. Maybe the *Ard Rígh* needed men and women for battle or some such grave event.

They saw the horse pull up in a shower of brown dust . . . and then Devin was jumping up and down, arms flailing excitedly. He ran back up the slope, gasping and breathless when he reached the Clan again.

"Lug . . . Lugnae," he spluttered, "tidings from the Briugu . . . your herd at Bréifne has produced twin . . . twin white bulls. Twin white bulls have been birthed!"

"No!" Lugnae was astounded. "Surely not! Yes? . . . oh, Emer, we have been blessed this day . . . Though I would trade them both for the return of my son," he added sadly. Then brightening up, he turned to his Clan and announced the tidings to them.

The Clan gave out a great roar. Fergus began the music and people danced and wept and leapt about with joy. This was a grand sign and meant untold wealth for the Clan. It seemed that Queen Maev had blessed them from her tomb on the top of the mountain. Queen Maev once owned the finest prize white bull ever reared and now the spawning from that same strain had rooted in Lugnae's herd.

Cromlach put his arm around Olc Aiche.

"He is here. We are now assured that Cormac mac Airt will be *Ard Rígh* one day. A deed well done, Olc Aiche, well done."

Above the noise, loud and clear, another sound rang out and echoed on the mountain, that of a baying wolf in the distance.

When he heard this, Olc Aiche's face was grim in the midst of the gladness around him.

"Cromlach, our work is only beginning. There are those who will know by the omen of the white twins, that an *Ard Rígh* is birthed . . . and there are those who will not want to acknowledge it. We must read the signs. When the time comes, Cromlach, take Gráinne and Cormac away from here. I will send word when I find a safe place. But, for now, all is good, the gods favour us," his tone lightened, "and good times are to come."

He then quietly dropped some corn and ground it into the dirt with his feet, as he had done at Gráinne's name-changing. Cromlach helped him, then looked for Gráinne.

Serb meantime was with Finann on her way back to the Brighdal *bothán* as the noise on the mountain troubled her too much to stay there.

Cromlach reached Gráinne at the same moment as Cred did. From the description that Gráinne had given him many moons ago, Cromlach knew that this was the metal-artificer she had spoken of in great detail.

"Cred, well named for Creidné, goldsmith to the Tuatha De Danann," he said politely.

Cred was startled.

"This . . . this is Cromlach, Cred," said Gráinne shyly, "my mentor, my Draoi, my friend . . . and Cromlach, this is Cred, my . . . my foster-brother," she finished lamely.

"Indeed?" said Cromlach, as he inclined his head. He did not miss the exchange of unspoken feelings that passed through their eyes to one another.

As soon as Cromlach embraced him, Cred knew him for one of *them*. He saw *the light ones* immediately around the Druid and felt himself go lighter within his own body. Their eyes held, an instant respect for each other bonding them together, they knew each other for the great love for Gráinne and the desire that they both had for the well-being of the babe.

Cred then embraced Gráinne, his eyes twinkling. "Foster-sister, I offer my blessings on the birth of an *Ard Rígh*," he whispered, loud enough for Cromlach to hear but not within ear-distance of anyone else around.

Cromlach then knew that Cred was one of the chosen ones to care and protect the mother and child. So, it seemed that his old hunch that Cred was gifted was right. Had Cred not fashioned a buckle worthy of an *Ard Rígh* and given it to Finann the goatherd? The workmanship in that was far too superior not to have had some help from *them*. Only a very gifted or inspired man could do such a thing, or one not knowing the true quality of his own fine work, and Cromlach did not believe that for one moment. He wondered if this Cred realized he came from *them* or if he was merely susceptible to *their* manipulations. Time would tell.

Gráinne could not stand the close proximity of Cred's body. It was just like it was the other night. Again, she thought she was going to lose her breath. Gazing into his eyes, she whispered, "For someone who never used to utter a word to me, you are certainly making up for lost time now, but please . . . go from me. I – I cannot bear your touch."

He raised his eyebrows at this.

"Come now, sister, that is an Untruth, if ever there was one. Shall I attempt to see through it?"

Gráinne wriggled free, with the babe, and pushed Cred away. "No, no. Go . . . go before everyone knows!"

Dairine watched the couple with interest, unaware of the light banter between them but knowing of their feelings. Now she was disturbed with the knowledge she held within herself. She pondered on whether to tell Gráinne or not but knew that this was not the time to do it; later, much later, before she returned to go home again with Olc Aiche and their entourage. She did not want to be the chosen one to mar the happiness of this day or any other in the immediate future.

Mora nee Derga was also watchful, thinking much the same thing.

As soon as Cred reluctantly turned to leave, Cromlach hugged Gráinne.

"If you would like shelter and a quiet place to feed our Cormac mac Airt, my *bothán* is just at the bottom of this hill."

She leant against his cloaked form gratefully and nodded, drinking in the familiar smell of heather and smoked herbs, unable to speak after her encounter with Cred.

He steered her through the crowd and as they made their way carefully, unbothered, down the grassy slope, Cromlach was pleased with the timing of the announcement of the birthing of the twin bulls. It put the name-giving ritual into the shade. Later, Lugnae's words would burn in their minds and realization would dawn on the Clan, but for now, they were intent on celebrating and it gave Gráinne plenty of opportunity to get away and avoid the inevitable questions.

Out of sight of the Clan, Cromlach made a turn at the bottom of the mountain, parted some branches across a rockface, and lo and behold, to Gráinne's surprise, there was a perfect cave opening in the rock. It was narrow, but when Cromlach ushered her inside, she gasped at the large beautiful room before her. Beeswax candles and small bronze oil lamps cast a warm glow against woven mats which were gracing the rock walls. There was an inner chamber further back, which Gráinne rightly guessed had been turned into sleeping quarters. The hearthstone, which Finann collected from Mora's *bothán*, was near the entrance, so that the smoke could escape easily enough, although there were plenty of cracks in the roof of the cave which drew the smoke into other sub-caverns above.

"Perfect! Perfect for you, Cromlach! Finann did this?" she asked incredulously.

"Finann and Mora nee Derga. It is a fortress for a king, is it not? Gráinne, *a stór*, you are invited to come here often and stay with me. We can continue our studies."

"Cromlach, I have to tell you something . . . Mami, Dairine, is a Druidess, a priestess of some renown too, as I have just found out. And yet she kept it a secret for all these years from me. She . . . she told me that she can make the flying potions. I desperately want to learn how to do this but she says I must take my vows first. Please, Cromlach, tell me no. I swore in the name of Brighde to remain free in my solitude and learn every-

162

thing I could fill my head with, from a Draoi such as yourself and from nature and my own instincts . . . but the queen poisons . . . I cannot learn these from self-study, this is a knowledge which is part of the sacred and divine mysteries, known only to the few. I cannot return home with Dairine for her to teach me these things, not now when I have Cormac to care for and keep safe. Do you have the knowledge of these potions?"

Gráinne bit her bottom lip as she waited for his answer. She sat down on a fur-covered settle and offered her breast to the babe to suckle. He was ravenous and she felt he was studying her face as he nestled down for his supper.

Cromlach did not reply for some time, then he said simply, "This is something you must ask of Mora nee Derga, *a stór.*"

Gráinne's eyes flew wide open. "Mora? No, surely not!"

Cromlach smiled, his weathered face crinkling with amusement.

"Do not be so surprised, Gráinne, Mora has the hidden knowledge as you do too, passed on through the ancestry. It merely takes a few nudges to awaken it. She has stretched her mind to the limit of her abilities and still found more. Never give up, never. And your son will have it through his ancestry and his other lives, we must not forget those. Perhaps you and Mora will teach me one day."

Gráinne laughed. "Oh, come now, you are jesting, Cromlach. I cannot envisage anyone teaching you anything!"

"Earlier today, I thought to myself that time will tell, and now I find myself saying and thinking this very thought again. I am longing for this child to grow," he said warmly, suddenly changing his patterns of thought and gazing at the back of the babe's head. He stroked the fair tufts of hair with his fingers.

"Unmarked, fair, tall, and comely, his wisdom will be the envy of all learned men, his noble voice will be heard for generations by Truth-seekers and he shall be remembered when we are gone, Gráinne."

His words passed a chill through her but she knew she was going to lock them into her heart for a long time to come. "Much as I desire your company here, *a stór*, once the babe is

163

fed and you are rested, I am instructed to escort you back to the Dún. Lugnae has requested it."

"He has? Whatever for? Do you know?"

"I do, Gráinne, but believe me, it is not to your disadvantage; quite the contrary, indeed. That is my last word on it, so please do not try to coax it out or attempt to Truth-read. Lugnae is merely bestowing a gift on you for the birthing."

Gráinne relaxed. Usually the birthing gifts consisted of gold, woven blankets, beautiful carved cribs, baskets, food, clothing, maybe even a bowl or some such useful object. She looked forward to receiving a gift but right now, all she wanted to do was stay with Cromlach. There was so much to catch up with and so little time in which to do it.

"Cromlach," she murmured as she caught his hand, "you are not going away again, are you? I – I cannot bear to think of such a thing."

"Put it from your head right now, *a stór*. I will not have you clutter your mind with such sadness. I have made a boon with your father, and several others we cannot see, that I will never leave your side unless you ask it of me. I told you before that I was going to return to the Dún, after the babe was birthed, and I kept my word, did I not?"

She nodded, withdrawing her hand so that she could wind the babe. He burped his approval of his supper, and she made herself ready for the journey back to the Dún with Cromlach.

A great feast was prepared for the Clan and everyone ate and drank their fill. Fergus sang a song for Cormac mac Airt and the Fire-Wheel ceremony of the name-giving. He sang of the beauty of Gráinne, the mother, and the heroic last stand of Art the Lonely, father of Cormac and the *Ard Rígh* whose life had been lost in battle against Lugaid. Gráinne lowered her head as her cheeks flushed pink with all the attention she was getting.

The Clan cheered and applauded, then Fergus chanted the story of the traveller riding fast on his steed over mountain and vale to bring tidings of the birthing of the twin white bulls.

The Clanspeople jumped to their feet, raised their mead-filled goblets and hailed Lugnae Fer Trí and the traveller who sat beside him. Lugnae gave the man some gold bracelets for himself and his wife, and then requested that he stay the night at the Dún and return tomorrow to Bréifne with more gifts for the Briugu, the nobleman who reared and looked after the cattle.

Lugnae stood up and announced that it was gift-time for the new babe.

He asked everyone to follow him outside, linking his arm through Gráinne's to lead the way. Dairine held the babe, cooing and aahing and smiling proudly to all as she traipsed outside, wrapping a cape around his tiny form.

Lugnae went behind the large building of the Dún Hall and there, behind the Dún Fort, in the shade of two oak trees which survived the storm, there were two adjoining beehive huts making up a large splendid new *bothán*. It was still within the Dún walls.

"Gráinne, Olc Aiche has requested," and Lugnae nodded in the direction of Olc Aiche, "that you may continue your fosterage with us, until such time as you may want to study elsewhere, if, for example, you take your vows or if you send the boy, Cormac, to fosterage at Teamhair. It is our pleasure to honour you with a dwelling, suitable for the rearing of your son, still within the fortress of the Dún."

Gráinne threw herself at Lugnae, delighted at the prospect of her privacy in a *bothán* so adequate for her needs. His words had rendered her speechless, first that he bothered to think of her taking vows as a Druid priestess was a very high compliment indeed from Lugnae, who generally thought women unfit to teach; and second that he thought Cormac would eventually serve his fosterage in what was surely to become his enemy camp! His name could never be revealed to Lugaid, the *Ard Rígh*, who had wrenched Teamhair from Cormac's own father, killing him in the process!

Lugnae continued: "We have built extra quarters, as you can see, for the use of Olc Aiche and Dairine when they visit, or for the Draoi who will come to teach your son." Lugnae smiled at Cromlach as he said this, having a much greater understanding now of the role that the Druid must play in Gráinne's life. The talk with Cromlach and Olc Aiche, which Lugnae himself instigated, helped put things into a better perspective and Lugnae now realized that he also played a prime role as Guardian to a future *Ard Rígh*. It would serve him well one day.

Gráinne entered the *bothán* and could not believe her eyes. There, before her, was the most beautiful, ornate, full-length bronze mirror. She swung around, searching out the one who had bestowed such a gift upon her, her beautiful eyes softening as Olc Aiche came forward.

"Gráinne, *mo chuisle*, so that you will see yourself as others see you."

"You carried this all the way from Cruachu?"

"With the help of our servants and the horses, of course."

Gráinne hugged Olc Aiche and Dairine to her, planting a kiss on Cormac's head as she did so.

"Cormac, you will see yourself grow and grow and grow and still the looking-glass will be too big for you!"

There were many gifts from the Clanspeople, well-crafted bowls and spoons, woven linens and silks and soft wool blankets for the babe from the women. Old Tachta had made a splendid wall-hanging for the *bothán*, spending many days stitching a spiral motif which was very soothing for the mind to look at. Emer gave several pots and cups and a burnished copper kettle, the envy of all the women there who would love nothing more than to grace their hearths with such a kettle. Cromlach and Finann each carried in a lovely flat hearthstone for the two dwellings. As they were put into place, Gráinne squealed with delight.

Mora gave her some baked-clay herb jars filled with all kinds of healing and cooking herbs, and Devin the trapper helped position the pallet and crib which Olc Aiche had had the carpenter craft out of the finest bleached oak.

There was another little chamber at the back and when Gráinne walked in there, she was surprised to find an older woman sitting on a settle, her belongings already stored in the room. The woman smiled a lovely friendly smile at Gráinne and Dairine, then immediately came forward to take the babe from Dairine who introduced her to her daughter. She was mouthing the words slowly and carefully.

"Tula, this is my daughter, Gráinne," she said, then turning to the puzzled Gráinne, she continued, "and this is Tula, a bond-maid for you. She is going to stay here until you no longer need her services, in which case she will then return to Cruachu. Tula is without family. She is a Fomorian, orphaned in war. Her brothers were killed in battles against marauding Danes and she thinks maybe she has a surviving sister somewhere who is bond-maid to a Pictish king. Her other sisters did not survive the winters in hiding. Gráinne, Tula has lost her hearing."

Gráinne's eyes widened and she stared at Dairine in surprise. "Without hearing?"

Dairine covered Gráinne's hand.

"Ah yes, *a stór*, but she is blessed with another sense of knowing. Never fear."

Tula nodded. She seemed either to be able to read what Dairine was saying by studying her lips or else she just sensed the converse between the women.

"I hear nothing and see all, even as I slumber," she said, her voice strangely accented.

Gráinne liked her immediately and realized by the way she was already tending to Cormac that she was going to be a very special gift indeed. Somehow she felt they would manage, despite the affliction. At least Tula had not lost her hearing until after she learned to form words in the language of Éiriú and somehow she did not forget the way of speech.

She warmly embraced the woman, overcome now by all the wonderful gifts from her kin, her foster-kin and the Clan. Only two people were missing from the gift-time: Serb and Cred. There was only one present Gráinne would have gladly bartered all the others for, and that was Cred himself. She realized though that he could not be there because Serb was ailing. She had seen someone ail like that before, someone who wandered off and talked to the spirits, someone who later became a great *seer* at Teamhair. Gráinne wondered when the time would come that the Clan noticed the strange behaviour of the young woman. An acceptance would take place once Lugnae acknowledged and embraced it. But, for now, only those who were *seers* themselves or healers could protect her.

Gráinne hardly believed that she could move into her new dwelling immediately. She invited Olc Aiche and Dairine to share it with her until their departure, which they were only too glad to do, having made up their minds to stay only until the next circle-moon.

That same night, after they had supped at the new hearth, there was a knock on the wooden-shuttered door. Dairine answered and called out for Gráinne to greet the late guest. It was a shock and a pleasant surprise to find Cred making his way into the room, carrying a linen sack. He nodded to Olc Aiche and Dairine, and smiling at Gráinne he proceeded to lay open the cloth before them on the floor. There was a gasp of admiration from Dairine. Olc Aiche stretched out his hand to touch the beautiful workmanship of the pieces, and Gráinne stared in awe at the gifts.

"For Cormac?" she whispered.

"And you," he replied, not even bothering to try to hide the affection in his voice.

She could not raise her eyes to his but looked anxiously at Olc Aiche who was now surveying Cred with great interest.

There was a small golden cup, encrusted with amber around the belly and carved with tiny coiled serpents holding the pieces of amber in their mouths. The base was studded with gold rivets, also enclosed by coiled serpents.

Beside the cup lay a stone of black onyx wrapped in a cradle of the finest spun gold. There was a small *scian* with a wolf's head beautifully artificed on the handle, which was only surpassed by the bronze arrow with the threads of gold woven on the shaft of it, to spell out the *ogham* to protect the bearer of such a weapon. A small gift wrapped in a separate piece of yellow silk was lying beside these works of art. Cred lifted it up and passed it to Gráinne who peeled back the silk gently, fearful lest her trembling fingers dropped the gift. She could not believe what she was seeing. No one had ever given her anything like it in her life and she doubted if they would ever do so in the future either. Her fingers danced gracefully over the white bronze of a *delg*, a brooch, unequalled by any she had ever seen, even on the women in the Halls of Teamhair. The face of

168

the brooch and the back were overlaid with intricate patterns so fine that Dairine looked sharply at Cred's hands, disbelieving that those large fingers could ever have wrought such a thing. Amber, glass and enamel pieces were inset between the patterns, of which there were many, spiralling and weaving in perfect design in filigree on both sides. The side that would lie against the breast was as splendid as the surface, which would be appreciated by every eye that fell on it.

Olc Aiche knew that this work was not the work of any *céird* he had ever come across. This man was sent by *them* to care for Gráinne and Cormac. He felt this in his bones, a sudden excitement making his own heart race and flutter as he observed the kinship which was forming before his very eyes.

Dairine was aware already of the growing love between her daughter and this young man but her heart was sore with the knowledge of what she knew of Serb. She decided in that moment not to say anything to Gráinne, not now, not yet, not ever. The sight to *see* would be there soon enough.

Gráinne thought she would pass over with happiness. She looked up at last, breathless, wordless, and not even the presence of her kin could deter the feelings that poured from her and rained over him, making the air breeze and dance between them. Their pulses beat as one, their bodies glowed with every fresh wave of desire that flowed through them. Nothing was ever going to take this away. Gráinne hugged the *delg* to her breast, squeezing it so hard against her that her milk leaked through her robe. She lifted her hand away and smiled as the pale droplet fell on the brooch. Cred stretched out his hand and very gently scooped up the drop with his heart-finger. He then, without taking his eyes off Gráinne, placed his fingers to his lips and sipped the sweet-salt taste of the essence from her body.

Gráinne laughed suddenly, a tinkling, wonderful, joyful sound that made Cred jump and before he had time to compose himself, he could feel that joy rolling over him also, so that his own laughter rang out, strange and unfamiliar at first and then totally senseless so that they rocked with each other, tears rolling down their faces as they realized they could not hide themselves from the Truth nor hide the Truth from others.

Dairine and Olc Aiche sat, unable to move for fear of break-ing the spell they could see being woven before them. They exchanged a smile, remembering their own first days and know-ing now that they could soon leave the Dún. Gráinne was blessed and protected . . . blessed and protected by Love. Dairine pushed away any other wayward thought that tried to make itself known to her.

# CHAPTER 16

# THE PARTING

*Sweet sorrow wets these eyes of mine*
*And my lips sear with your parting kiss;*
*My pulse beats a path to you in time*
*To seal our love in secret tryst.*

Drawing her cloak tightly around her shoulders, Gráinne clasped the precious *delg* in one hand, intent on reaching the Grove without mishap. She was very fond of the gift, making it her token of safety and well-being.

The blanket of dark lay dense and still, enshrouding the Dún and the other dwellings of the *ráth* with a thick broth of fog, so that the night air was cold and wet to breathe and the way was difficult to see. Pit-holes and banks of leaves slowed the journey.

Cormac was safe in the *bothán* with Tula. Gráinne thanked the day that Dairine, her mother, presented her with Tula, gentle, quiet Tula; she adored Cormac and he, small as he was, seemed equally to adore her. He was a contented babe, wanting only to eat, sleep, smile, and play. He liked being outside and would happily lie in his crib, gazing up at the canopy of leaves on the twin oaks outside the dwelling. His hands continually reached up to grab the movement, his little head turning at every sway and squeak of the branches. It was the time for the leaves to be shed and his eyes would follow the tumbling colours as they fell. Tula usually sat near by, spinning wool or weaving cloth.

Gráinne saw Cred when she could, calling in at the forge occasionally to exchange soft-spoken words and hold hands; but despite their desire for each other, for three moons now, since the gift-giving, they had been unable to express their love fully to one another. Serb was getting worse and had to be constantly attended. Gráinne had not seen her since the Fire-Wheel of Dagda but Mora nee Derga hinted that Serb was ailing badly and, because of this, Mora herself spent a lot of time at the Brighdal *bothán*. Serb did not want to see Morann the physician or Fergus the poet with his physic finger but always wanted Mora to be there. Mora knew the plants that made her feel good, it seemed.

Now, at long last, Gráinne had word, through Finann the goatherd who arrived at her door before the moon was up, to say Cred wanted to see her in the Grove. She had to give Finann enough time to get back to the Brighdal *bothán* to take over looking after Serb who had recently taken to night-walking. Cred could then make his way to meet Gráinne in the Grove.

She slipped through the trees and followed the sound of the little brook that fed the sacred well. A faint glow bathed the circle within the Grove and she hurried towards it, her feet rustling through the crisp, dry leaves.

He came towards her as she entered the *Koad* and wrapped her warmly in his arms.

"Gráinne," he whispered into her hair, the silk strands caressing his lips. Her breast beat like a captured bird's against him.

She felt his body tense and heard the grind of his teeth as he fought something within himself. Gráinne drew back to try to see his face by the light of the small bronze lamp he had brought with him.

"I am leaving on a journey," he said quietly. She stiffened, afraid to move, afraid to hear what else he was going to say.

He seemed to be trying to tell her something but, being unable to get it out, he merely held her tighter while she thought her heart would bleed, such was her pain at his words.

"Will you return?" she asked, shutting her eyes tight as she waited nervously for his reply.

He nodded and she relaxed against him but he remained tense against her.

"I am going to Laighin Theas for more gold and then I will visit the islands in the South to see my kin and meet the trading ships. I – I have to tell you something, Gráinne . . . "

"Hush, hush." She placed her finger on his lips.

"No, it is important, *a chuisle*, you should know . . . "

"Nothing is important, except that we are together at last."
She nuzzled her head into his chest and covered her ears with
her hands as if to shut out anything else he wanted to say.

After a moment of silence, he withdrew them gently.

"It is about Serb," he started to say, but she again pressed
her fingers to his lips.

"No, no! Do not talk about it. I know."

His eyes flew wide open, incredulously.

"You know?"

She nodded. Did he think she had not eyes to see, that Serb,
even as far back as the Fire-Wheel of Dagda and before that to
the passing over of Donal Rua, was surely becoming a spirit-
seer, less attached to this world and more of the other?

He caught her head between his hands, unable to believe
those clear blue eyes. Shadows cast by the flickering lamp played
across her face but there was no pain reflected there. She knew
and she accepted. He was overwhelmed.

Gráinne inhaled shakily.

"When will you return?"

"In two moons. I – I have to come back by then."

She understood. He could not leave Serb for too long.

She drew his head down to hers and he plunged his lips over
her own, sucking her feverishly to him, unwilling to let her go,
wanting to take her with him.

Crumpling against him, her breath quickened as he drew her
underneath the willow tree, sat in the glade and pulled her
roughly down with him.

"Gráinne," he whispered hoarsely in her ear as they lay down
together, his body fused against hers so that her belly ached
with the need to have him, "I want you."

She struggled to talk but words failed her. She was in a
state of near ecstasy but for some reason her throat rasped and
Gráinne felt only like weeping. It was something she had not
anticipated, now that they were to be together at last. Shocked
by her own reactions, it became impossible for her to contain
herself and she found that, instead of giving herself freely,

173

something was holding her back. She wanted him to take her, desperately she desired it, but somehow, not like this.

Cred pulled back suddenly, being aware of her silence and sensitive to her feelings.

"Gráinne, are you all right?"

"Yes. I – I just feel . . . " She could not continue. Instead, she broke into sobs, unable to control herself any longer, her shoulders shaking with her grief.

"What is wrong, *a chuisle*?" His tender voice made it worse. She clung to him and he rocked her gently until she stopped, caressing her neck quietly as she spoke again.

"Cred. We do not have to put into words what we feel for each other . . . but . . . I want it to be right. I do not want us to have to slip out of sight in the middle of the night on secret trysts, not when . . . especially not when Serb is ailing. I – I want it to be pure, acceptable to others, to the Clan. Please, Cred? Please understand."

He lay beside her, confused and frustrated, but knowing how she felt. He had thought that their love for each other would conquer all obstacles, in fact he tried hard not to see them and yet, had he not arranged to meet her at night, away from prying eyes? He leant over her and brushed her lips with his own, his eyes intense, sad.

"I cannot keep away from you for all that time. I could not endure the torture. It is better I stay away from the Dún, go elsewhere."

She was unsure, her thoughts wildly trying to control her emotions and the threatening hollow emptiness that seemed ready to engulf her. It was not in her plan for him to leave for the duration of his time with Serb. The fact that he was leaving for just two moons was difficult enough to endure. Any longer would be impossible. It surely made sense for them to meet in secret and consummate their love. Gráinne suddenly thought of something else which added to her misery. If the Clan discovered their secret trysts and then realized the extent of Serb's ailing, they might indeed decide that the punishment meted out to the Clan by way of the storm, and in the ensuing passing of Donal Rua and now in the cause of Serb's ailing, might well be the consequences of their illicit love. After all, Serb had chosen Cred in the sight of the gods at Baltinne and Cred also chose to remain with Serb after the first moon. Was this extra year and a day not proof enough that their union was well blessed by the Mother? If the Clan thought that Cred and Gráinne's secret love had been going on for longer than it actually had, the ill-fortune which befell the Clan would definitely be blamed on them both. Suddenly the danger was only too apparent to Gráinne.

"Cred, we cannot see each other at all for the sake of the Clan. The Truth is not theirs to know yet. We shall be held to blame for the misfortunes so far and if anything else should occur, we shall be held responsible. We – we cannot take the risk."

"I cannot bear not to see you, Gráinne. We must think of something. If it means that I have to stay away longer, I shall, but to be here and not to see you or acknowledge you and yet to feel your presence would surely be the death of me. It is more than any man could bear."

"Perhaps I should be the one to go, Cred. Dairine, my mother, would be only too pleased to have Cormac and myself to fuss," she said, her lips trembling, "or maybe if I do not go to Cruachu, we—"

"No! You cannot leave here, a stór. You must not!" he said in desperation. "Cromlach is here. I want you to stay here with him until I return." He cupped her face and pressed her lips with his own. "We will both be strong in the knowledge of our love, a chuisle. The moons will pass quickly enough and then at last we will be together. I cannot possibly stay away too long, because of Serb and her condition and most of all because I cannot bear being parted from you for too long. Our time will come just as the seasons do."

She nodded, her fears allaying somewhat at the surety in his voice. He got up and drew her to her feet, crushing her suddenly to him so that she gasped for breath and stifled a cry of pain. Her body slumped against him.

"When do you leave?" Her whisper was warm on his neck, causing shivers to ripple down his spine.

"On the morrow." His own voice was harsh across the top of her head. The words echoed in her mind. Clinging to him, speech was no longer relevant. Nothing she could say would seal the yawning gap that lay before her. The thought of his long absence was like a gaping wound. No words of his could heal the pain of his impending departure.

Several long moments went by, their bodies deadly still and transfixed in immortal moment, motionless in their clinch, each more fearful than the other to break the spell.

At last, Gráinne began to tremble. Cred reluctantly let go of her but wrapping her cloak around her and with his arm holding her close to his side, he guided her from the Grove and back to the Dún. Tonight was theirs. He did not care who might see them. She felt warm tears slither down her face and neck into her hair, a wetness that cooled quickly in the night air. The *Koad* glowed faintly behind them with the flickering flame of a forgotten bronze lamp. They passed the Dún Hall and reached her *bothán* as the moon rose high in the sky.

"If anything should happen—" she started to say, but he pressed his fingers to her lips.

"Have faith, Gráinne. Not a night will pass I will not think of you, nor day when I will not carve your name in stone, small stones of the *ogham* writings that I shall bury in each place I stay."

He was leaving on the morrow against his will and because of *them. They, the light ones*, had come to him in a dream and shown him once more the Chalice that he must make for a king, and the place had been revealed to him where he would find the gold and precious metals with which it must be crafted. It was imperative that he leave as soon as possible, at first light.

She smiled. "I will scratch the *ogham* of your name here too in stone, small stones which I will keep until you return," she said shyly. "My pulse will beat with yours, *a chuisle*, wherever you are."

His heart thudded at her words. Neither of them could speak again. He kissed her fleetingly, his lips burning to possess her, but he strove to contain his passion.

His fingers strayed through her hair and he lifted it to his face, deeply inhaling the sweet apple smell that always seemed to be there, hidden in the strands of silk. It was something he would remember on the lonely nights of his long journey. Cred watched her hair flow from his fingers, then abruptly let go of her.

He heard the broken sob escape from her lips.

It was the most difficult thing he had ever done, to turn and walk away from her; and the journey to the Brighdal *bothán* was the longest one he had ever made. Cred did not, could not, look back.

# CHAPTER 17

# THE KNOWLEDGE

*As the moon waxes and wanes, so do we,*
*As the new moon grows, so do we,*
*Enveloped in the darkness of the womb*
*To rise again, and grow and grow and grow.*

Gráinne awoke and knew that he was gone. She found a small stone outside her *bothán*, in the shade of one of the oaks, and scratched Cred's name upon it as she had promised to do so, then stored it away in an oak-carved box along with the first sheddings of Cormac's hair and his tiny crescent fingernails.

Several days and nights passed. She spent her time gloriously happy with her little child, and harboured her own secret passion for Cred. Each precious stone was lovingly inscribed but she soon realized that she would need a much larger container if he was indeed to stay away for two whole moons or more.

Cromlach came to see her, not surprised by the far-away look in her eyes or the vague answers he received to some of his questions. He worried about her and decided it was time to resume her studies. She agreed readily to continue her learning. Something had to occupy her mind and still the burning thoughts. Cromlach decided to start her first learning on the new moon, the hidden moon. Tula was adept at keeping Cormac happy, so between feedings, Gráinne was going to study.

The first day of the new moon, Cromlach led Gráinne to the Grove and they sat under the willow tree, the same willow that had cradled Cred and herself when they spoke of their love for one another.

As she sat down, Gráinne gasped when she felt something hard beneath her. She pulled the small bronze lamp from under

178

her and cupped it longingly in her hands. Cromlach looked surprised. "You are familiar with it?"

Gráinne smiled and answered: "Yes, Cromlach. It belongs to Cred." She could not give Cromlach an Untruth.

"Ah, well, *a stór*, then you must take it home and light it often to guide his way."

It was a simple working that fishermen's wives often used, and Gráinne was grateful for the encouragement. She hugged Cromlach impulsively.

"Now, now," he said in mock stern tones, "we are here to learn, not for you to turn the eye of an old man!"

She laughed and settled back to enjoy her morning with her teacher.

As the moon waxes and wanes, so do we,
As the new moon rises and rests, so do we,
Enveloped in the darkness of the womb
To seed again, increasing in light, a sapling, a sickle,
To grow and grow and grow;
And so the waters of the Earth succumb to this growth,
Rising and resting, ebbing and flowing,
For ever and ever, so do we.

Gráinne studied all morning with Cromlach on the ways of the moon and the effects of its draw. Some of this she knew already from her own moon cycle and from intuition, but it was good to have it confirmed. He talked about seedlings being planted on the hidden moon and watered on the sickle moon and how they should be planted in circles. Then he told her that the next lesson was going to be about Earth-pathing and she looked forward to this, knowing it was something given only to the Elders, so her surprise and joy was apparent. Cromlach fervently hoped that something new and forbidden would heal her lovesickness, but it proved not to be.

Gráinne pined away the long sad nights, sleeping fitfully, tossing and turning, dreaming strange dreams of people and places she did not know. She awoke one night, uneasy, unable to recall the vision but knowing that the amber eyes of a wolf had stared back at her, glowing, burning into the recesses of her mind. It was after spending another such disturbing night with the same wolf that made her go in search of Mora nee Derga the very next day.

Mora was delighted to see her and badé her come into the *bothán* right away.

"How is Cormac, Gráinne? It has been some time since I saw him, *a stór*, that I am sure I would not recognize him now. Has he grown? Oh, come in, come in. I am starved of the company of women."

"But, Mora, have you not been looking after Serb?" Gráinne smiled. "Cormac is a young man to be reckoned with . . . You must come and see him . . . But tell me, what of Serb? Is she well yet?"

"*A stór*, I despair of ever healing Serb again. She has now retreated into herself, making it almost impossible for me to reach her mind. She speaks in tongues constantly, occasionally reverting back to her old self and throwing one off-guard . . . and the things she speaks of are strange, not relating to this time or place. I know the herbs to calm her but I have to be careful what I administer because she is—"

"She is becoming a *seer*, Mora!" Gráinne interrupted. "We had such a one at Cruachu and now she resides in special quarters at Teamhair, or nearabouts, consulted by the Arch-Druid there, when Lugaid, the *Ard Rígh*, wants to go to battle or conduct a raid. Serb will go through the seven sicknesses before she accepts her role as seer. Why did I not think of this before? My father told me of these ailings when it happened to Bláth, the young woman in our tribe, at Cruachu."

Mora looked at Gráinne in amazement.

"You know the nature of these sicknesses, *a stór*? Why did I not seek you out before?" she said in exasperation. "I should have known you would have the answer. Oh, Gráinne, I have been to the end of my wits and back a hundred times over, searching, searching for the cause, for only then can I effect a cure. There have been stages in the development of her ailment that I managed to fathom. First she wandered, night and day, straying to odd and dark places, in her waking time and in her sleeping time, chattering to ones I could neither see nor hear."

"Aye," nodded Gráinne, "that is most assuredly the first sickness: *the wandering*. The second is what my father, Olc Aiche, called *the gathering*."

"Aah! That is right!" Mora was excited now. "She started collecting stones and sticks and feathers, bringing them all back to the Brighdal *bothán* and then jealously guarding them in a dark corner. We had to screen off the room and give it to her. Finann, Cred and I took turns in watching her."

"Mora, has she taken on *the smell* yet? There is a peculiar scent, similar to milk on the sour, and warm and musty like the hide of a corn-mouse. It will permeate and scent the room in which she lives. This is the third ailment."

"Yes! When she took on the smell, that was when she started speaking in tongues. Oh, Gráinne! I am so happy to know and share all this. So, *the speaking in tongues* is the fourth. What is the fifth then? It seems she is about to have another change and I will know how to deal with it accordingly if I know what to expect."

"*The bones*. This one is not too pleasant, Mora. She will search for bones and, not finding them, she may kill small animals to get them or desecrate the cairns for the bones of the ancestors. Olc Aiche left deer bones and the bones of cattle and fowl around, at Cruachu, to stop our *seer*, Bláth, from disturbing the cairns."

"Oh, dear, I shall have to get poor Finann to deal with this one. I certainly cannot take the bones of a hunter's kill to scatter around the vicinity of the Brighdal *bothán*! Well, this is one to look forward to, is it not, Gráinne?" Mora looked tired, fatigued from the responsibility she had taken upon herself for the welfare of the young woman. "And the sixth? What is the sixth ailment, *a stór*?" she asked wearily.

"*The callings*. She will copy the animal calls, the bird calls, the human cries. She will want to leave her scent everywhere, passing her waters on the ground outside the *botháns*, inside the *botháns*, anywhere she sees as her territory. She will lust and mate with, or at least attempt to mate with, whomsoever she desires. This is the most difficult one to cope with. I think by then it may be wise to let Lugnae know, Mora. Maybe it is time for all of us to take care of her."

Mora's face was white. She sat down, trying to digest all that Gráinne was saying. Shaking her head, she covered her face with both hands and murmured: "And the seventh?"

"*The sorrows and the calming*. They are one and the same. Serb will at last accept the role of *seer*. Her keening, weeping, and wailing will be for the passing of the old self within herself. Then the new *seer* will emerge. It is both a sad and beautiful birthing. Never again will she be Serb as we know her because she will be constantly traversing the worlds. She will be unable to communicate as Serb would, but her *seeing* abilities will bring through many great spirits and many voices. We must nurture her and help her through this, Mora, when the time comes. I think it is time for Cromlach to see her and aid you through it, Mora. I will help you all I can. Cormac is good and does not cause me bother, but I fear that Serb may not wish me too near . . . "

Mora's cheeks were wet with tears.

"Gráinne . . . you have helped more than you will ever know. Now, I have only one more worry and this will take all our strength to conquer. I wish Cred had known all this before he left but naught can be done about that now. I am afraid for Serb but most of all I fear for her . . . "

At that moment, there was a terrible banging and sounds of squealing and a scuffle outside.

Finann shouted: "Help me, Mora! Quick!"

Mora and Gráinne raced outside and there was Finann struggling to get Serb into the *bothán*. She was covered in dirt, the brown clay smearing her face and hands but Gráinne hardly noticed that. There was something else . . . Gráinne's face was ashen.

"Her unborn . . . her babe . . . that was what you were going to say, Mora," she whispered, as her spirit seemed to leave her head, winging its way to some dark corner of her body, leaving a half-empty shell in its wake. "You feared for her babe." Her mouth was parched, her tongue lying dry and clumsy behind clenched teeth. She stared, transfixed, at the swollen mound of the belly twisting before her. Rooted to the ground, unable to move, she watched as Finann and Mora tried to calm the agitated young woman.

Suddenly, Serb also became aware of Gráinne. Serb stopped all movement immediately, then her face contorted, changed, her eyes hardening into dark jet beads.

"Black Crow!" she hissed. She spat, her spittle landing at Gráinne's feet.

Shocked and distressed, Gráinne found her legs moving of their own accord and she ran and ran, as fast as she could, down the hill, her breath catching in her throat, her heart bursting with pain as she was chased by the sound of harsh cawing and hollow laughter.

Gráinne reached the *Koad*, without breath, without presence of mind. She collapsed beneath the willow tree and was sorry she did not have her *delg* with her, the gift that Cred had given to her. She would have flung it to the far corners of the land. What had he said? He could not serve Serb. No, he had not spilled his seed within Serb. That was it! He had been unable to perform the great rite. An Untruth! Had she not seen with her very own eyes the cradle-mound of his offspring?

Her eyes were dry. No tears were going to wash away this sorrow. She angrily pulled her breasts out from her bodice and began to squeeze them, one at a time, pressing the flat of her hand in a downward stroke to express her milk. She squirted it on to the ground, spraying it back to the Mother, knowing that Cormac could not drink of this milk while her thoughts were in turmoil and her body was in shock. She was going to feign being unwell and Emer would find her a wet-nurse for the next day or two until her emotions were stilled.

It was some time before she stirred to return to her *bothán*, by now feeling very unwell. There was no longer any need to feign illness.

Tula saw that Gráinne was pale and immediately led her to her pallet. Cormac was asleep, seemingly unaware that he had missed a meal, so they did not wake him. Tula left to fetch Emer, who came right away and took command of the situation, sending for a wet-nurse for the babe and then summoning for

Mora nee Derga. Emer intuitively knew that Gráinne would not appreciate either the presence of Morann the physician or Fergus the poet with his physic finger. Cromlach was in his own *bothán* on the mountain, too far away to be of immediate assistance but, no doubt, he would be visiting before long.

Mora had sedated Serb and as soon as Serb was washed, fed and put to bed, Mora immediately set out to find Gráinne. She was not surprised to meet the messenger on the way.

"Gráinne," whispered Mora, as she stared down at the young woman whose head was turned to the side, her hair falling over the edge of the pallet like a raven's trailing, broken wing. Her eyes were like blue glass, cold, sad and lifeless. There was no soul shining through.

"Gráinne, *a stór*, you are in shock. Please let me help you. You must suckle your babe, you must, to keep the bonding and to ensure the milk-flow."

Gráinne squeezed her eyes tight to prevent any tears from dropping out. She swallowed hard.

"I know I have to nourish him but I want no part of my own sorrow to spoil or sour the milk for him," she said, then suddenly opening her eyes wide and grabbing Mora's hand, she implored Mora to stay with her.

"Do not leave me, Mora nee Derga. You and Cromlach are my only friends . . . please tell me . . . why did he tell me an Untruth? Why?"

Mora paused, thrown by the question, wishing that she knew the answer.

"I do not know what he said to you, Gráinne, but this I do know . . . he has never yet uttered an Untruth in my hearing and if this has anything to do with Serb being with child, whether he spilt his seed in Serb by his own knowledge, by error, or by divine intervention, means naught in the long run. Serb will not be a fit mother if what you say is true. We will talk to Lugnae Fer Trí when the time comes. Cred is not yet bound to Serb, whether his seed be in her or not, and I have some notions on that . . . but I do know that his heart-stem is coiled with your own and that is a blatant Truth, *a stór*. Lugnae will be fair and just . . . perhaps he will allow you to be . . . "

"No! No!" Gráinne shook her head. "I will not be bond-maid or second wife to Cred. How could I live with a woman who spits her bile at me and calls me Black Crow! No! I would rather die. As a *seer*, she will curse me with great spirits. I might die anyway! Then Cormac would live with her? No!"

"Gráinne, stop upsetting yourself! Serb is ailing . . . Have some compassion on her. You are a well woman! You will not die! Cormac will never live with her. Are you mad? She will not be able to rear her own babe, never mind yours. I was going to say that maybe Lugnae will allow you to be first wife to Cred, although this is not usual if Cred and Serb chose to stay together for a year and a day and she spawned a babe of his during their time in the Brighdal *bothán*. It would not look good for him to deny the child then . . . but I think, because of Serb and her condition, that Lugnae will embrace her back into the Clan and the child will be cared for . . . I will care for the child myself, and Serb too, if that is what is needed of me."

Gráinne looked deeply into Mora nee Derga's eyes, surprised to see the far-away look and the desire which kindled therein. She had never thought of why Mora had chosen not to take a mate or have a child of her own but now she could see the hope in her eyes. It was clear that Mora was worrying her powers, coaxing the situation to unfold the way she wanted it to. Gráinne was a little troubled though, as something wanted so badly with a desire born of an unfulfilled wish, or with such blind, urgent emotion, was usually thwarted, or a hefty price paid in its coming. With confused thoughts spiralling in her head, she saw the solution that Mora desired but she dared not hope for such an ending herself. It was not right that she should fuel the wishes of Mora. Serb might even yet recover, or fate take a twist in some other direction. She was afraid and still saddened that Cred had uttered an Untruth to her.

"Mora, we will let be what will be. I will feed my babe but I will veil my mind and try not to think of . . . of Cred until his return."

Mora smiled. "And boars might climb trees! Now, make me a boon, *a stór*, that you will come to me if you have any difficulties or need to talk or sleep soundly. I brought a draught to help your milk and another to calm your mind."

"Mora, you are a *seer* yourself! This was why I went over to your *bothán* before. I have been unable to sleep without dreams of a wolf disturbing my night. Cromlach told me that Cormac had the totem of a wolf, so it pains me that I feel threatened by it."

"Then Cromlach is the one to put your mind at rest, *a stór*. No potion in the land will prevent visions such as these but it is better to confront them with strength and well-being than from a position of weakness and being ill at ease. These messages are better slow in their coming and swift in their passing. It will be revealed to you soon. I think it is time for you to use the adjoining *bothán* and invite Cromlach to your home. Anyway, the mountain and he tire of each other from time to time."

"Not only do you heal, Mora nee Derga, but you have the knack of lifting the spirit and for this I am indebted to your goddess!"

Mora flushed with pleasure and embraced Gráinne.

"When I am with you, *a stór*, I am inspired to utter wise words."

# CHAPTER 18

# FROM BEYOND

*And so the search begins for the new one*
*As hailed by the prophecy untold*
*And countless eyes and ears are closed*
*To conceal the way by which he goes.*

Cromlach was very happy to stay near Gráinne. He was perturbed by her wolf-dreams, which still occurred from time to time. Cormac was growing every day and Cromlach was pleased to observe that the babe was of a quiet disposition. He did not seem to suffer any of his mother's troubled thoughts. Very often, babes reflected the anxieties of their kin, but this child was gentle and playful, always smiling. Cromlach thought about the day of the name-giving and remembered what Olc Aiche did as he laid his hands upon the babe. No one had heard the mutterings but himself. Five protective bands were bound ritually around Cormac by a simple gesture to protect him now, and later when he became *rí*, against slaying, drowning, fire, sorcery, and wolves. Gráinne was unaware of this charm but Cromlach hoped that, as Cormac's mother, it extended also to her. The wolf of her dreams did not seem very friendly, though, and anything which frightened Gráinne disturbed him. He still had some corn-grains from her name-changing and decided that when the time was right he would again look into her destiny. He knew that by Samhain he would also have the corn-grains of Cormac which Olc Aiche had flattened into the ground with his feet. Cromlach checked on their growth when he could, as he knew how precious they were. They sprang up faster than other grasses, being imbued with otherworld powers and the incantations of Olc Aiche, for whom he had now the greatest respect. He looked forward to reading those one day but, for now, it was only his dear Gráinne that he wished to protect.

Things were much as they used to be. Cromlach was still teaching Gráinne, who had great intuition and a profound understanding of the workings around her.

One day, it became clear to Cromlach that his teachings were going beyond Gráinne to the child. He had spent the morning showing Gráinne the ancient art of mastering the burning flame but her confidence was not yet strong enough for her to lift the burning sod. Later that day, Gráinne nourished her babe and then sent Tula over to Emer with a hot-pot she had cooked from some wild turnips and barley-corn. Cromlach, on impulse, offered to care for Cormac for a while to give Gráinne time to rest after her rather frustrating morning.

Cromlach was sitting in front of the hearth with the babe on his lap. The child kept tugging on the end of his beard and tried to put it in his mouth to chew on. Cromlach chuckled and told him that it was none too tasty, then he gave him one of his little carved wooden tokens to play with. Cormac swayed back and forth, making babe-noises and dribbling as he gnawed on the token with his gums. His first teeth were already sawing their way through.

The effigy dropped from the babe's tiny hand and rolled forward towards the fire, just falling short of the flames. Before Cromlach could move to prevent him, Cormac lunged forward, hand outstretched, to grab his new plaything, when his gaze seemed suddenly arrested by the dancing flames eating up the peat-sods and sticks on the hearthstone. His little hand stole into the fire and grabbed a small flaming stick, which he removed and held for a moment, much to Cromlach's shock and astonishment. Then he passed it over to Cromlach, whose presence of mind immediately had to sharpen to override the danger of being burnt. He only just managed to concentrate in time. Accepting the gift, he remained unscathed and handed it back to the babe, who rewarded him with a beaming smile, and then threw the stick back into the fire, causing a shower of sparks to leap high. Cormac retrieved the wooden token from the hearth-side and continued playing with it, totally unharmed by the episode with the flames.

Cromlach was thoughtful, wondering if for a moment he had visualized the whole thing as a sort of day-dream. He realized that his own teachings were somehow getting to Cormac from Gráinne. Maybe the babe was picking up Gráinne's thoughts, or the information was being bled to him through the milk. The child had been nowhere near Gráinne or himself during the actual passing over of the teachings and, even if he had been within close proximity, because of his tender age, he could only have acquired it by thought-reading.

Cromlach marvelled at this and decided to keep quiet about the incident for the time being. Gráinne would find out soon enough, and Tula had spent adequate time with Olc Aiche and Dairine to know she could expect anything of the ways of the Druid. Olc Aiche and Dairine obviously chose her to be here precisely for that reason.

Cromlach enjoyed the rest of the day with Cormac, Gráinne and Tula, and he ate the rest of the hot-pot with great relish. Living alone by the mountain, he did have to admit that as he got older, he certainly appreciated the home comforts of being with a family.

Several days later, Gráinne was thoroughly enjoying Cromlach's teachings on Earth-pathing, having sufficiently recovered from her failure to master the fire and being more at ease with the Mother than any of the other gods or goddesses.

Cromlach had a forked rod of *coll*, the strong sapling of the hazel branch, and with it, he proceeded to demonstrate to her the means of detecting the Earth-paths of the Mother.

"These are the spirit lines of the Great Mother, *a stór*. You see how the branch jumps? Here, take it from me. Now, stand back and walk towards this point again . . . hold the rod in front of you, straight out like so . . . that is right. Slowly, now slowly . . . you see? It is moving! There! You have found the path. As you can also see, this spirit-path is directly in line with the *Koad*, our sacred Grove. Now you know why the Elders chose that particular place in which to have the Grove. Our cairns are all on spirit-paths, and even some of the dwellings, especially the Dún Hall. This, of course, means that your own *bothán* is in line too. These lines spiral across the Earth and cocoon the Mother energy."

"Cocoon? But the land is not round." Gráinne was puzzled.

Cromlach smiled. "There is that which is deep and that which is wide. There is that which is high. The sky arches over us and I believe cradles us also . . . we cannot assume that such a vast making should all be in a straight line. But these are the thoughts of an idle hermit. Let none of it worry you. The task at hand is enough, *a stór*, without cluttering our minds with the riddles we can never unravel." He paused suddenly, squinting up his eyes against the light and peering into the horizon. "Who is that running so fast from the mountain? Is it Finann?"

Gráinne turned and stared at the figure racing towards the Dún. She instinctively dropped the hazel fork and, lifting up her skirts, she began to bound over the grass and through the trees to meet him. Breathless, she slowed down as soon as she realized it was not Cred. Her heart pounded painfully and she shook her dark head angrily at herself for being so foolish. How could she even think of running to meet him after he had told her such a grave Untruth about his relationship with Serb? She had stopped scratching the *ogham* of his name on the stones after she discovered that Serb was child-growing. She no longer kept the flame burning in the bronze lamp to guide his way home. And now, here she was, trying to recover her breath after leaving Cromlach and taking off like a deer on the run, only to find that it was Finann who was in such a hurry.

"Wh-what is ailing you, Finann? You – you seem alarmed."

"Gráinne, there is a messenger approaching. I cannot tarry. He has the – the flag of the *Ard Rígh*. I must find Lugnae Fer Trí!"

"The *Ard Rígh*? Oh no. Are we to battle?"

"No, I do not think so. Lugaid has so much heavy foreign assistance for his raids, he no longer needs the allegiance of minor Clans. We are more likely to bear the brunt of the greed of his men seeking to raid us."

"No! Do not utter such words lest they have Truth in them,

Finann. Now, go find Lugnae. Do not mind me. I will catch up in time, for I am quite winded after my race to meet you."

She watched him disappear into the Dún Hall and, within moments, some of the trappers, mounted on their steeds, made their way out of the *ráth* to meet the stranger.

Cromlach slowly walked back to the Dún. He was thoughtful. As he reached Gráinne, he very calmly told her to remove all traces of the babe from the *bothán*. She was shocked.

"I want you to accompany me to my abode in the mountain. We will go by the back way with Cormac. Gather all his belongings and as many of yours that will fill Misha's creels."

Gráinne stared at him aghast.

"Why? Cromlach, tell me, who is coming here? Do they wish to harm Cormac?"

Cromlach put his hands on her shoulders.

"Stay calm, *a stór*. It is just a precaution. The tidings of the birth of the twin white bulls will have travelled far by now. It will have reached the ears of the *Ard Rígh*. Gráinne, the birth of twin white bulls is the hailing sign for a great King. Any Arch-Druid or Elder knows this. Think, *a stór*. This means that Lugaid is aware that a birth is imminent, or has already taken place, of a babe who will one day usurp him. He will not be happy. It is best we prepare to leave. I will send Finann to ask all the Clan to keep quiet about the child, and I will alert Lugnae Fer Trí about the danger. The trappers who are to escort the messenger and, no doubt, the party which will be following, will not speak of any matters until Lugnae Fer Trí sees the Elder who most certainly is part of that party. We have a little time, but not too much. You see, the messenger usually arrives before the others to warn the Dún King of the impending visit. We probably have until sundown this day or sunrise on the morrow to get Cormac to the mountain, well away from the eyes and ears of the visitors."

Gráinne was suddenly afraid and she bolted away quickly to begin preparations to get Cormac out of there. She could not speak, such was her terror. Lugaid could only do one deed to keep Cormac from claiming the position of *Ard Rígh* one day. He would have to prevent the growth of the child's body and mind. Gráinne began to shake and shiver uncontrollably as she seized all his little clothes and his tokens and wrapped them in a large woven plaid. Tula sensed the urgency and helped her. As they waited for Cromlach's return, Gráinne carefully explained to Tula all that was happening, forming the words well so that the deaf woman could read her lips. She understood that she was to stay at the *bothán* and pretend to be Cromlach's aid. It was usual for some of the Elders to have a woman helper live near by, so no one would think it was odd to see them set up with adjoining *botháns*.

Cromlach arrived back with Finann and Misha, the goat.

"We have warned everyone except for Serb, but Mora will take care of her, and Finann will be back to help later. Now, come, Gráinne, let us be on our way. You carry the babe while Finann and I pack the creels. We will make sure that you have food brought to you every day until the visitors leave. Do not worry, *a stór*," Cromlach said, being aware of how fearful she was, "I will see you often. You will be much safer in my abode than anywhere else in the land. Trust me."

She knew he was right but she still felt an uneasy sense of foreboding. She glanced around quickly, just to make sure there was nothing which could imply that a mother and babe had lived in her *bothán*. Hugging her child close to her, Gráinne slipped behind the dwelling and waited until little Misha had her creels filled, then the party set off towards Knocknarea.

"Why did we not use a horse or a donkey?" she asked Cromlach.

"Because if, by some remote chance, we meet someone on the way to the Dún, they will not expect the new-birthed King-boy to be travelling with a goatherd towards the mountains. Neither will they pay too much notice to a babe when they spy a goat carrying creels . . . something which they will not have seen before. Also, if we were travelling far, we would have had horses . . . so they will merely think we are mountain-dwellers or traders from a nearby *crannóg*."

Finann smiled. "Gráinne, he thinks of everything. This is why he is your Guardian."

"Hush, Finann," scolded Gráinne, "mind you do not utter

such Truths in front of Lugnae Fer Trí. He will not thank you for it." But she was secretly pleased to think of dear Cromlach as her Guardian.

They reached the mountain safely without meeting any stranger and Gráinne breathed a sigh of relief when she slipped through the concealed entrance into the cavern. It was cold but a fire would soon take care of that. Soon she had it cosy and warm. She spread a rug in front of the hearthstone so that she could attend to her babe in the warmth. He fell into a deep slumber after he suckled his milk, and she swaddled him with fresh linens and laid him in his wool-lined crib, which Finann had carried over for her.

She vowed that she would make this abode much more comfortable for Cromlach. If she had to stay here for a whole moon, she would have to do something to relieve her boredom. Cromlach said he would try to find out how long these visitors intended staying at the Dún. It might only be a matter of days if they realized that no new babe was there, but if they were suspicious that something was amiss or being hidden from them, they might indeed stay longer.

That night, after Cromlach and Finann had long gone, Gráinne settled down to sleep, curled up in her old plaid beside the fire, with Cormac near her, in his crib.

She immediately fell into dreaming and visited a place she had never been to before. There was a man there, with a long grey beard, who was very kind to her and seemed to be very fond of Cormac. She knew that she had been on a long treacherous journey to get there. She felt safe and sobbed with relief. Her own weeping and the wet tears on her face made her sit upright. She came out of the dream, alarmed that it had awakened her. The face of the man was etched in her mind and she wondered who he could be or where he lived. It was a long way away, over great mountains, somewhere in the North. She did not know how she knew such things, or even why, but she was sure that the dream was a message.

Gráinne was disturbed. She did not want to leave the Dún. Tossing a peat on to the dying fire, she stoked it to life and huddled closer. The sound of a wolf baying in the distance made her even more anxious, and the dangers of the night closed in, suffocating her. She was glad the babe was sleeping peacefully. He did not need to share her fears.

Cromlach arrived early the next morn. It was obvious that Gráinne had not had a restful night. Her eyes were dark-ringed and she had not bothered to comb her hair. She had attended to the babe, who was lying on a plaid rug and playing with his tokens. Cormac smiled at Cromlach, making little chuckling sounds and reaching towards him with delight. Cromlach was touched. Usually he did not spend much time with babes but this one was special. If Cromlach had ever desired a son of his own, he would have wished for such a child as this.

"They arrived?" Gráinne was anxious.

"Yes. They arrived just after sundown. There was not much time between the arrival of the messenger and the coming of the visitors. An Elder, escorted by two warriors and a woman, is now at the Dún."

"A woman? Is she an attendant for the Elder? Or a warrior's mate?"

"No. She is a *seer*."

Gráinne was horrified. "Bláth! It is Bláth. She knows me. She will find me, Cromlach. There is no place here I can stay. She will hoke me out, believe me, she can find that which is lost with great ease."

Cromlach held Gráinne's trembling body steady.

"You know of her, *a stór*? You know the *seer* for the *Ard Rígh*?"

Gráinne nodded. "Yes! She was at Cruachu. My father knew she was a *seer*. She trained with one of the Elders and then she went to Teamhair. Once, when she was at Cruachu, I – I hid from my father one day. It was a place only I knew of, a little crevice within a rock that only a child could crawl through. It was my special place. My father, Olc Aiche, who has great knowing, could not find me. He sent for Bláth, who led him straight to me. Bláth also is aware I am serving my fosterage here. She will wonder why I am not at the Dún."

"She knows you not as Gráinne, though. She is probably not

194

aware of your foster-name, knowing you only by the name of Achtán. But something of interest has happened at the Dún, something which has greatly angered Lugnae Fer Trí and poor Emer. The cairn was desecrated last night. The stones were moved off the cairn and, although the body of Donal Rua was not touched, an attempt had been made to get him. Something or someone must have frightened the robber away. Mora spoke with me this morn and now I know that it was probably young Serb who was searching for bones. I only wish I had known of these things before. Of course, Lugnae was raging at the strangers who arrived, swearing that no one within his own Clan would do such a deed. Then their *seer*, this Bláth, went into a spirit-seeing, and began to point blindly around her, spinning and spinning, until she came to a stop and she was pointing directly at the Brighdal *bothán*. Lugnae would not believe it, and Scath the Druid became very angry. Never have I seen him like this before. I had to step in and calm everything down before heads went flying, or the *Ard-Rígh's* warriors became sufficiently insulted to warrant them taking the offending words back to Lugaid. I drew Lugnae Fer Trí aside and explained as much of the Truth as he could tolerate. He asked a great pardon of the strangers and bade them welcome to the Dún."

"So now he knows of Serb. That is good. She will be embraced by the Clan and cared for, as she surely deserves. Bláth is aware then of Serb. For the time being, this will keep her mind off me."

"I have work to do, Gráinne, and I must work fast. Give me some of your hair and some of the sheddings of Cormac's first hair. I have to go out to get something on the mountain. There are some crane feathers in a pot by my pallet, *a stór*. Bring them to the fire but do not put them on it yet until I return. I will not be long. Just remain in here, calmly and quietly. Try very hard not to show any emotions or feel fear, as this will make you even more vulnerable and easier to find. Think of the oak tree, sturdy and strong like your back, and the willow, soft and flowing on the outside, like your hair in the wind. Keep these images within your mind. Do not think of Bláth, for that is how she will find you."

Cromlach left quickly and Gráinne went to his pallet and brought the pot, containing the feathers, to the hearthstone. She built the flames up with the peat and bracken that he had stored in his dwelling, then she awaited his return, thinking all the while of a strong oak with willow fronds. She visualized the leafy fronds hiding the babe within them, positioning herself over the child, so that her long black hair trailed on either side of his body. He chuckled gleefully, grabbing handfuls of her hair, and she smothered his little face with kisses, dropping them like rose-petals on to his soft, warm cheeks.

Gráinne did not know how long she remained like that, but Cromlach's return startled her out of her reverie. He had a little bag with him, full of precious grains, the corn-grains of Cormac which were planted at his name-giving. There was another crane-skin bag tied around his waist, which he emptied out on to the floor. Some willow frond tips, oak leaves, birch bark, pink fingers of wild rosebay, and a scarlet and white mushroom, the spotted red-cap.

Cromlach set to work immediately. Peeling off the white beard on the stalk of the fungus and throwing it on the fire, he then laid the red-cap to dry out on an iron hob. He boiled up some water and made a tea of the rosebay. Ideally, he would have liked to have made a fermentation of the wild rosebay but there was not enough time for this. Neither was there enough time to dry out the fungus completely. He knew, from past experience, the toll on the body when the dark spirits in the fungus had not had enough fire.

He placed the willow fronds, oak leaves, and birch bark in front of him.

"*Saille*, *Duir*, and *Beith*. Why are you arranging them so, Cromlach?"

"*Saille* is for you, *a stór*. The woman, the moon, the willow, the water-seeker, Brighde, and the *seer*."

"Even Bláth? Nay, surely not."

"She is a woman, Gráinne. And so, we must use the woman-spirit to gently divert her somewhere else."

"And *Duir*? Why the oak?"

"I would rather have had *Uilleand*, the honeysuckle, but I

could not find it on the mountain, not at this time of year. It is ideal for what I need to do. You see, *a stór*, the lapwing is sacred to *Uilleand*. She hides the secret of her eggs by means of distraction, which is what I intend to do with you, to hide you from Bláth. I do not, though, have lapwing feathers or honeysuckle, so now I intend to use *Duir*, the oak. Strength of a boundary is my plan. The oak gives strength and protection. I will build a spirit-wall which Bláth will not get through. She will not find you, *a stór*, and you will be shielded on all your journeys."

"What about *Beith*, the birch?"

"It is not quite Samhain, Gráinne, but you know why I have chosen the birch, do you not?"

Gráinne inclined her head, ashamed of her slowness of thought.

"You taught me well, Cromlach, and I am not thinking like the hare, am I? *Beith* will stand tall above the thorns and shrubs and guide the way. *Beith* is the pathfinder, the pointer, the purpose, and the one to make pure. The way of the new is found in the old. This is why it is the start of our year . . . the first moon of the cycle . . . Samhain, which is almost upon us."

Cromlach lifted the infusion of rosebay off the fire and left it aside to cool.

He closed his eyes for a moment and deliberated whether he should scry into Cormac's name-grains. He decided against it and placed them in their little bag on the shelf beside his nightberry oil. Later, when Gráinne was asleep, he might scry with them. Now, he merely wanted to build a protective veil to hide Gráinne and Cormac from Bláth.

He held the crane feathers and plunged them into the glowing peat. They at once began to smoke, their light grey-blue pungent tendrils causing Cormac to screw up his face with distaste and Gráinne to blink her eyes rapidly. Cromlach himself spluttered as he waved the feathers through the air inside the cave, weaving a soft haze around them all.

Reaching for the red-cap, he bit off half of it, chewing and chewing the bleeding fungus, forcing himself to swallow the damp mixture. It was a vile thing and he tried not to worry that it had not had enough fire. Gráinne watched, anxiously. She was curious about the whole procedure, mentally taking in all that Cromlach was doing. One day, she wanted to try the different plants which contained the special spirits for *seeing*.

She saw Cromlach's face change and contort as he fought against the spirit of the plant at first. Then she sensed that it must have taken over his body. His hand reached out for the rosebay tea, but it looked like he was going to spill it. She gently guided the pot to his lips so that he could drink. He seemed surprised at her presence, jumping when she moved, but he smiled towards her as she settled back and drew Cormac to her breast to sup. She was afraid that the babe might cry out suddenly and startle Cromlach.

Cromlach felt himself drifting into the shell of himself, the exquisite young woman before him fading as the woody scent of the fungus invaded his nostrils, coupled with the smell of the smouldering feathers.

He resisted the temptation to slip back to the roots, to study the sigils, to find the teachers he knew were there, on many different layers. He had work to do.

His eyes focused on the sheddings of Cormac's hair and the strands from Gráinne's black mane. He clumsily plaited the two together, mostly binding Gráinne's longer locks around the short, fine silk of the babe's hair.

Taking the willow fronds, he began to wind them around the hair, invoking the spirit of *Saille* to envelop the mother and son.

Gráinne began to feel drowsy, as if she were being wrapped in a moth's cocoon, so she lay down on her soft pallet with her babe who, by now, had fallen into a deep slumber. She felt herself slowly spiralling into a dreamless, mindless grey fog. It was neither hot nor cold there, wet nor dry, light nor dark. She was no longer aware of Cromlach, or the cave, the Clan or the Dún or anything else. Her mind was adrift, swimming in a sea of forgetfulness.

Cromlach breathed a sigh of relief at his first accomplishment. At least the girl was safe from the *seer*'s eyes for now, but not for long if he did not reinforce the spirit-wall with the oak leaves.

Quickly rubbing the leaves to a powder between his fingers and thumb, he packed it into a little clay pipe and lit the mixture from one of the crane feathers. Inhaling deeply, he felt the smoke searing through him, filling his lungs with a choking, dreadful taste and smell. Then he expelled it, long and slowly, into the dwelling. Several times he repeated the pipe ceremony, uttering an enchantment as he did so, invoking the god of the oak to strengthen the spirit-barrier between Bláth and Gráinne.

His head was unbearably light, spinning and making it very difficult for him to form thoughts. He knew that this was due to the damp fungus he had ingested earlier. It was now time to take the rest of the spotted red-cap and finish off the enchantment. This was going to be probably the most difficult part and the most dangerous.

Cromlach gagged as the fat, bulbous substance bled red-black juice into his mouth. He swallowed. It felt as if the tail of a venomous serpent had just slithered down his throat. He tried not to recoil as he did not want to anger the spirit.

Stretching towards the birch bark, he began to scratch into the underside of the bark with the pointed end of the singed crane-quill. He wrote, in *ogham*, the names of Gráinne and her babe. Then, on impulse, he inscribed the name of Cred also, and sealed the bark, along with the hair in the willow cocoon, into the crane-skin bag. No *seer* could undo an enchantment which was sealed in the crane-skin bag. This was the domain of Manannan mac Lir, the great god of the sea, and no one dared challenge the protection that he gave to a wisdom held within a crane-skin bag.

As he tied the bag, Cromlach suddenly felt himself being thrown into the depths of his own mind, back, back.

"No! Not now, please!" he implored, knowing he was not going to escape the penalty of partaking of an ill-prepared potion.

He was sucked viciously through a black gap, black as a starless night. A great pressure began in his navel, making his belly cave in suddenly. He crawled and stumbled in the direction of the cave entrance, needing to breathe some fresh cold air. His chest filled with a burning, hot pain, stabbing him again and again. Slow-crawling and clinging creatures dragged at his legs so that he could not move. Winged serpents flew from his mouth, unfolding their wings in his throat and flying out. Their smell was foul, their taste atrocious. His belly heaved and he spewed them out as he fell heavily on the cave floor. Eyes, beady and darting, watched him from all sides. Slimy, wart-covered toads croaked as they tumbled from him.

Cromlach fought the dark ones, desperately recognizing his own repressed fears as he was confronted with them, one by one. The teachers, the Elders, the Brehons, all hissing and pointing the finger at him. His ways were the cause of their anger and disgruntlement. He saw a forked road. Down one lane were the Clan and the Druids, the Dún and all the home comforts of tribal life, and on the other path he saw clearly himself, Gráinne, Cormac, Mora, Finann and Cred, Olc Aiche and Dairine. Someone else was there too . . . a man, with a long grey beard and kindly eyes . . . someone he did not know. The way was cold, mountainous and rocky. There were wolves and unseen dangers lurking. Cromlach stared long and hard at this road, where the crawling things and the winged serpents and the toads lay waiting, but everything he had ever loved was also on this road. He compared it with the path to the settlement, where the sun shone and the Dún of Lugnae Fer Trí seemed warm and inviting, but it was a lonely way amongst the rules and teachings of the Elders. He knew he did not want it, no matter how cosy the hearth seemed there. It was time, even in these advancing years, for him to make the final break from all the traditions of the Clan and from his own hermitage. If he stayed, he knew the Laws would gradually creep upon him again, and he would succumb to the ways of the Elders. It was time to go.

As Cromlach made his decision, he saw *them*, tall, bright and beautiful. It was a fleeting glimpse . . . but he felt that he had made the right decision. If only this searing pain and terrible sickness would pass. If only he did not hurt so much.

# CHAPTER 19

# BLÁTH

*It is a lonely way, the seer's path,*
*Unmarked, untrodden, long forgotten,*
*To will, to dare, to know, to keep the faith,*
*To seek the signs, and to be silent.*

Emer was as shocked as Lugnae to hear the news of Serb. Mora
had explained to them the nature of Serb's ailing and they tried
to understand that the searching for bones was part of this
sickness. Emer knew how Donal Rua had felt about Serb, and
somehow the need for Serb to have his bones was completely
acceptable to Emer. She forgave the girl and thought com-
passionately about the poor babe who was soon to enter the
Clan. Serb was not a fit mother for a babe. Serb was becoming
a *seer*, or so they said, and if she was going to end up like this
Bláth creature, who had appeared at the Dún with the visitors
from the *Ard Rígh*, then she definitely would be an unfit mother
for any child. Emer determined that she was going to make sure
the babe was well cared for.

This Bláth was curious about Serb also, and Emer was worried
about the interest that the Elder, the warriors, and Bláth were
bestowing on Serb and her child-growing.

Some questions had been asked about Achtán, which Lugnae
had answered directly, saying that she had gone to the mountains
with her Draoi for some teachings. This Truth was accepted
readily. Many Druidesses and others who were interested in the
Crafts would go off for several moons at a time to learn these
teachings. It was fitting for Achtán, or Gráinne as she was
known to the Clan, to learn about these things. After all, she
was the daughter of a very powerful Druid.

It was not until later that same evening, when the sun had set and the moon was rising, that Bláth decided to *see* for the babe growing within Serb. There had been an instant recognition between herself and Serb, and Bláth needed to get closer to the girl before she could use her powers to Truth-*see*. Serb was drawn to her, and despite the eagle eye of the woman Mora, she managed to creep out and meet Bláth in the Grove. Mora was in the Brighdal *bothán* in a deep sleep of exhaustion, aided by the enchantments of Bláth.

The air was cool and crisp. Bláth, her tawny hair wild and unkempt, her black-sloe eyes prominent above her hollowed brown cheeks, stretched her hands out to the wary girl, who took them in her own willingly enough. Serb knew that this woman was very powerful but she could also sense that, somehow, they had a similar thread running through them. Their destinies were locked in the same pattern.

Bláth then placed her hands on Serb's belly and drew in her breath, exhaling slowly. She concentrated on pulling her own spirit back from her hands, making them icy. Her spine was hot, like a fire-iron. The babe within Serb kicked out at the icy touch of the woman's hands. Bláth opened her mind and enveloped him.

She saw a tall, ruddy-faced handsome man with a mane of shocking red hair. He was of a quiet, gentle nature. His hands were big and white. He certainly had the stature of a *rí*.

Bláth watched him softly stroking a splendid black steed, murmuring all the while and making crooning noises to the animal. This man was a great lover of horses. She saw him hitch his horse to a splendid golden chariot, a chariot fit for an *Ard Rígh*.

It was then that she recognized the terrain around Teamhair. So, he would get to Teamhair! He would usurp the King!

She looked at *botháns* which were unfamiliar. The place was so grand, and there must have been at least seven Dúns there! A great wooden-built Hall, a splendid Hall of vast dimensions took pride of place. She gasped at the beauty of it. Lugaid, the battle-mongering *Ard Rígh*, had surely not erected such a Hall?

Maybe this tall, gentle giant had built it.

He turned at that moment and looked straight towards her.

She gasped when she saw his full face. One side of his cheek had a mark on it that she had not noticed at first glimpse . . . an unmistakable dark reddish-blue mark, like a black night-berry stain smeared down his face. She could not believe it! An *Ard Rígh* with a birth-stain! It had never been known before. An *Ard Rígh* must be totally unblemished.

Bláth continued to observe him with great interest.

He busied himself filling the chariot with different goods, not the kind of things that are put in a battle-chariot, but little baskets of food and flagons of drink, gourds of milk and a box of green apples. There were no weapons, no shields, only a couple of woollen plaids and a wooden staff.

He signalled to a small boy near by, who ran off towards the Hall, laughing and shouting. Out of the Hall strode a magnificent god of a man, with fair curls the colour of sun-bleached corn, and eyes blue as the sea. Bláth had seen eyes like this before somewhere, but she could not recall for the moment. The man was smiling. On his forearm was a brown leather wrap, strapped at his wrist and elbow, and perched on the wrap were two hooded falcons.

Bláth knew that this man, this splendid god, was indeed an *Ard Rígh*, and the red-haired one who grew within Serb was going to be a friend and champion to a king.

Where was Lugaid? Or, for that matter, where was she, herself?

Bláth suddenly snatched her hands away from Serb's belly. She did not want to know the answers.

So, this babe growing within the fair young woman was not the King-boy.

Bláth became aware that Serb had withdrawn into herself again. It was apparent by the change in the air around her and by the complete stillness of her body and spirit.

Bláth could feel that the young girl, although not having physically moved, had cowered back within herself, probably frightened by the sudden snatching away of Bláth's own hands.

"Serb, do you understand me when I speak with you?"

Serb's eyes were staring straight ahead. She was wary as she nodded with an almost imperceptible inclination of her head.

"Serb? Listen carefully. Is there another babe birthed at the Dún? Or another woman who is child-growing?"

Serb's eyes remained stony, her lips firmly sealing her voice within her.

Bláth reached towards her, but Serb recoiled, backing away and crouching in the far corner of the Grove.

Bláth sat crosslegged and straightened her head, keeping her body as still as Serb's. She closed her eyes, and then did what she had not wanted to do . . . she stared into her own destiny, curving her mind to look again towards Teamhair.

The chariot was being driven into the distance, clouds of dust billowing behind it, the red hair of the Champion like the fox's russet brushtail, and the long flaxen curls of the *Ard Rígh* blowing in the wind, like strands of spiralling gold.

With great effort her mind came back to the long Hall, which had been built, in all its splendour, on the prime site at Teamhair. She wanted to explore the Hall, drink in its beauty, but did not need the distraction to weaken her.

Taking a deep breath, she called upon her guides to help her absorb any shock she would encounter looking into her own destiny. It was forbidden territory, avoided by most *seers* and Elders, but now she was anxious to *see* if she herself would stay at Teamhair.

Beyond the Hall, on the top of the hill overlooking hills, plains, forests, and woods, as far as the eye could see, there was a *bothán* flanked by two blackthorn trees. Ah . . . *Straif* . . . her friend.

She glided into the *bothán*, which was on the same site as her old one. Bracing herself, she dared to know her destiny.

Desperately rooting herself to the centre of the *bothán*, in the protective shield of her guide, she stared aghast at the shadow of herself, emaciated, withered and unkempt, lying on a pallet of beautiful carved wood, strewn with furs, and with circular gold posts at each corner, reaching to the roof of the *bothán*. There were colourful woven cloths of the richest textures everywhere. A woman was bent over her, an exotic woman with fair-white hair, plaited into many plaits over her head, all sealed with gold balls. She had that same vacant look about her, a stance that Bláth knew she had herself.

The old woman on the bed croaked, her voice cracked and hard as she spoke, and with a limp gesture she beckoned feebly to the younger one.

"It is time," she whispered, harshly.

Bláth was afraid as she watched, but then, as she slid into the mind of her older body, absorbing the racking pain, she was shocked to look out of her own eyes and see Serb there, an older but unmistakable Serb.

Bláth's breath was staggered. She felt a stinging sensation within and without her body sweeping over her.

Serb bent down and placed her mouth firmly over the older woman's yielding lips. Bláth began to breathe in as Serb breathed out, then exhaled as Serb inhaled. They shared their breath.

Bláth felt all her knowledge gathering at her navel. She made it soar with one huge effort, a supreme last effort, up into her throat, where she savoured that sweet, sweet nectar. The tears ran down her wise, withered face, as she gave it up and passed it through the soft pink lips of the younger woman who inhaled and sipped it readily.

Then, she was looking out of Serb's body. They were now one and the same. She stared at the shell of the old woman in front of her who had passed over her knowledge and herself, discarding the robe of her worn body. There were tears of sorrow and joy on her cheeks.

It was a lonely world, the world of the *seer*. Now, she was only one.

Bláth snapped abruptly out of the vision and returned to the Grove, alarmed to find the girl Serb rocking her and holding her tightly against her child-growing body. Serb must have *seen* too, or at least sensed their shared destiny. Serb knew then that she was to be the chosen one.

Bláth could not speak. Neither of them was aware of how long they stayed in the Grove, clasped together like that, unwilling to let the other go.

Eventually, Serb spoke suddenly, shattering the silence.

"Her name is Gráinne. It is she, she who is the Black Crow, who has grown him."

Bláth tried to ask Serb for more information, but noticed the vacant look in her eyes again.

"Where is she, Serb?"

Serb did not speak. Bláth stood up, took her by the hand and led her back to the Brighdal *bothán*.

"On the morrow," she said softly, "on the morrow, we will find them."

Serb nodded meekly and went inside.

Bláth returned to the Dún where Emer had arranged some quarters for her.

Emer was a little afraid of her and earlier in the day had kept shooing her children away if they ventured too close to Bláth, but the *seer* was used to this. Children usually giggled and pointed their fingers at her, whispering to each other and running away if she stared back at them. They were both fascinated by and frightened of her, unused to seeing the tattered dress of the old ways.

Now she lay on her pallet and thought of the night's visions. Teamhair was to be a prosperous and wonderful place with maybe as many as seven Dúns upon it. This new *Ard Rígh* used battle-chariots to take his falcons hunting, and his Champion's hands were smooth and unscarred, indicating that he probably had not fought a battle in his life! Compared with the present *Ard Rígh*, Lugaid, whose Champion had few fingers left and sported a twisted jaw, the result of an axe wound, Bláth knew that her loyalty now favoured the new one. But Lugaid had given instructions to seek out and kill the new-born babe.

Bláth thought of Lugaid, who was always coming home from surprise raids with the smelly prizes of men's heads strung on his belt by their bloodied locks. The chariots would be filled to the brim from the pilfering, but despite the great wealth attained by foul means, everyone lived much the same in the settlement at Teamhair, except for the fighting men. They were mostly foreigners and Lugaid had much respect for them, but regarding his own, Lugaid was not a generous Rí and would kill a man for speaking of his smallest complaint. It was a rulership of fear and dread. Only Bláth did not fear him, for she could strike him dumb with a word or two about the ancestors, for whom he had an immortal fear. She had had to *see* for her own survival, when she first arrived at Tara, what was Lugaid's weakest point. Only then could she wield power over him, if she needed to do so, although she knew the penalty on herself could also be dire. Many times she had suffered the spirit-sickness gladly to either save herself or another from being killed or banished.

Yes, she would have no difficulty in switching her loyalties to this new King-boy. She worried about the Elder and the warriors whom she had accompanied here to the Dún of Lugnae Fer Trí. The Elder was a perceptive and cruel Druid, worthy of his namesake. He was named after one of his ancestors called Dorcha, meaning "dark". He, most certainly, would not wish Serb or her unbirthed babe to live. Bláth could not let that happen. Before this night of *seeing*, she might have let the Fates decree the destiny of the girl and her babe, but not now . . . not now when her own spirit was coiled with Serb's. If Serb was killed, it would destroy Bláth's passage into the coming generations. It was not easy to find an heir to such a lonely existence. Her own destiny at Teamhair would end abruptly with her passing over. So, on the morrow, Bláth was going to tell the Elder that Serb was not the one. In his limited way, the Elder was able to *see* a little, at least through an Untruth. He most certainly could tell that Bláth spoke a Truth in this. She hoped he would use his Druid powers of perception to *see* this Truth at least, and save Serb from an untimely passing over.

Bláth thought about the new *Ard Rígh*. He had beautiful blue eyes, the palest blue she had ever seen . . . and yet, she had seen eyes like this before, someone she could not recall. Her mind sailed through her past, the men and women at Teamhair, the children she knew with blue eyes, green eyes, brown, hazel, grey . . . none like his. She went further back to Cruachu, to Olc Aiche and Dairine, to the people at Cruachu. No one with eyes so pale . . . and then, she remembered! A child, with a look of smouldering resentment, a child who could happily have seen her drop dead, pass over, such was her fury at having been discovered. Achtán! Daughter of Olc Aiche, who had hidden from the prying eyes of those who searched for her, who had managed to escape the eagle eye of Olc Aiche himself, but had been unable to conceal herself against the sorcery of Bláth!

"My sorcery! She was unable to conceal herself then, and she will not hide from me now!" whispered Bláth, suddenly sitting upright with great excitement. She hesitated as she thought of something which Serb had said: "*Her name is Gráinne. It is she, she who is the Black Crow, who has grown him.*"

"Gráinne?" Bláth murmured. She was confused. Could Serb be wrong? Serb was becoming a *seer* like herself. No, she was not wrong. Achtán must have changed her name when she came into fosterage. Yes, that was it! But why? Achtán was a nobleman's daughter but she was still only the daughter of a smith, even if he was a Druid. There had to be a good reason for her to have her name changed. Bláth wondered if Olc Aiche knew, or if indeed he had anything to do with it, and for what purpose.

She decided that he must have known, maybe even planned it, that Achtán would birth a king, far away from her home, in fosterage, where none would know of her. Maybe he had changed her name to aid her concealment. He had not thought of the signs, the omens, that came from the other worlds, when great events were taking place, the sign of the twin white bulls, for instance, which always hailed the birth of an Ard Rígh, and which had now led herself, the Elder, and the warriors to the Clan of Lugnae Fer Trí.

Bláth gave up concentrating her mind. It had been an effort all day long to keep occupation of her own body, to keep the *others* out. She now let herself fade into a well of light and the *others* came to dream their night stories and they rested with her, but she did not share with them. On the morrow, she knew they might still want to be there, but she would have to be strong and so, for now, she must rest.

# CHAPTER 20

# HE IS GONE

*He is gone, and I was not prepared,*
*He is gone, and my heart can bleed no more,*
*I am as a shell, with no living thing within,*
*I am as one demented, lost in a shadowed world.*

Finann picked up some food from Mora and packed it into Misha's creels, then headed out in the direction of Knocknarea.

It was cool, with a sharp breeze blowing from the north, unusual for that time of year, too early in its coming. The winds from the north brought the bitter coldness and the snow. Finann did not like it. If the long arm of *Lúgh* stretched out at this time to bring the frosts, it was only because he had not been properly placated at the time of his festival. This was true. Usually the Clan went to the fair at Crom Cruach to implore the giants in the land to relinquish the harvest and to eat the first breads from it. There were games and horse-races and everyone had a great time. But this harvest was quiet. Lugnae Fer Trí decided that as the giants of the land had taken his child, Donal Rua, into their keeping, then there was no cause to celebrate a harvest when his own son had been a sacrifice for those same gods. It had been a sombre *Lúghnasadh* for all at the Dún. Finann had not felt right about it. He knew there would be a fierce winter ahead. One could never take revenge on the gods.

As he reached Cromlach's cave, he was surprised to see a wren perched sentinel on the top of the cave opening.

"*Drui-én!*" he exclaimed. The bird of the Druid, the soul of the oak . . . why was it here? And a north wind too? Finann began to feel uneasy. Something was amiss. He left Misha grazing outside and entered through the narrow crack in the mountain. He tripped up and almost fell over something near the entrance.

It was dark and the air was thick with a curious-smelling smoke inside. Finann choked and reached around to find the bronze lamp he knew was kept near the hearth. He fumbled for a piece of fire brushwood and pushed the spail into the barely glowing embers. After the third attempt, it began to flame, and then Finann lit the oil-wick in the lamp. There was a diffused glow which did not quite pierce the haze within the cave. It seemed empty. Finann called out, his voice resounding back at him from the walls.

"Gráinne! Cromlach! Are you here?"

There was no answer, only the song of the wren from outside.

He turned towards the bird-sound at the entrance, and then realized that the crumpled heap that he had earlier tripped over was Cromlach, who appeared to be sleeping.

"Cromlach?" Finann rushed to his side. He touched the weathered face. It was cold. He laid his head against the chest and listened to the faint drumming of a heart-beat. Finann knew that he had to get the old man into the warmth, away from the cave entrance. He wished Mora was here, or Gráinne. Where were Gráinne and Cormac the babe?

He set to work, building the fire, working as quickly as his shaking hands allowed. Then he somehow managed to get his arms under Cromlach and carry him over to the hearth, laying him down gently on a wool-spun rug and covering him with a plaid. There was something peculiar about the hearth-side. The walls seemed to have closed in. He could have sworn that the space within the cave was much larger before, but he thought he must be imagining it. How could a cave shrink in size?

Finann chafed the old man's hands, rubbing them to make them warm again. He did the same with his feet, cupping the gnarled toes between his hands and blowing warm air out from his mouth on to them.

"Cromlach? What ails you? Cromlach?" He shook his shoulders gently, trying to make him stir. Desperately, he searched around for some clue, smelling the woody scent of the dreggings in the pot. His mouth grimaced and his nose wrinkled with distaste. It was a foul smell. There was also a pungent scent of burnt feathers. He knew this was so because of the times he had smelled the preparations of birds, plucked for broth. The women usually burnt the feathers afterwards.

Finann decided to fetch Mora immediately. Something was not quite right.

He quickly unloaded the creels and brought the food into the *bothán* in case Cromlach should awaken. At least there would be some nourishing food to hand. He then set out to find Mora, taking Misha with him so that he could leave her to graze back with the herd.

Finann was afraid. Maybe the warriors had found Gráinne and the babe. Maybe they had poisoned Cromlach. The dreggings in the pot had the odour of something bad.

He began to run, little Misha prancing along beside him, eager not to lose him. It was an unusual sight and one which did not go unnoticed.

The Elder, Dorcha, screwed up his piggish little eyes, and stared at the odd twosome who appeared to be in a fierce hurry.

Dorcha had just returned from the *bothán* of the mad girl, Serb. He was not happy with the findings in the Brighdal *bothán*. The place had a strange scent, not unlike the smell that pervades the *botháns* of the old hermits, the old ones who are unable to control themselves and pass their water anywhere. The woman, Mora, was there, trying to banish the odour by burning sweet oils and pine sap, but to no avail. Bláth, the *seer*, had been stranger than usual, mumbling and muttering to herself. She was not good company this morn.

Dorcha had questioned her about Serb. Bláth shook her head wildly, circling her own belly with her hands and violently moving her head from side to side.

"She is not child-growing? Tsh! Woman, do you take me for a fool who is without sight? Of course she is child-growing!"

Bláth's eyes were wide and smouldered with dislike. She was not fond of Dorcha, nor did she care for any of the Elders with their false spirit-powers and their limited *seeing*.

'She is that . . . but she does not swell with an *Ard Rígh*."

Dorcha was surprised. He immediately searched her words

for Truth, struggling to *see*. He could not fault what she said. His lips tightened into a grim line of determination.

"Then our search is not yet over."

He called to the warriors who were standing with their arms folded, watching Mora prepare a broth at the hearth.

"Stop thinking of your loins! I will wait by the Grove. Bring the girl, Serb, to me – without her minder!"

Mora swung round, perturbed, but she did not say anything. She did not like the way the warriors never took their eyes off her.

Bláth became agitated, which surprised Mora.

"No! She is ailing!" Bláth blurted out, before realizing that she should not have spoken. She shrugged and turned her body away too suddenly. The Elder's eyes narrowed. The *seer* was hiding something. He was sure of it.

"Bring her to me!" he said shortly, his curtness disturbing Bláth even more. He marched out and went to the *Koad*.

Serb was brought before him. She cowered back, wrapping her arms around herself protectively. She was frightened by the presence of the warriors and the imposing bloated face and body of the Elder. He had little darting eyes of stone that seemed to bore through her.

As Dorcha towered over her and began to interrogate her, she passed her waters with the terror of it all. It dribbled down her legs, puddling on the ground in front of him. He stepped back, curling his lips with disgust and shaking his head. He was as repelled by her as she was by him.

Bláth tried to will her to silence but could not combat the fear within the girl. It was no use. What was to be would be.

The Elder's eyes pierced Serb's.

"Is there another who is child-growing?"

Serb was silent. Bláth was relieved.

Dorcha caught Serb fiercely by the arm. Bláth leapt forward. This was forbidden: a woman who was child-growing must not be touched like this, it was bad for the spirit of the babe.

The Elder pushed Bláth roughly aside and did not let Serb go. Bláth screeched at him, a loud wailing screech that made him immediately withdraw his hands. He looked around, fearful that anyone had witnessed the little episode. No one else was there.

"Is there another, child-growing?" he repeated, hissing menacingly at Serb.

She shook her head. He *saw* the Truth of this.

"Is there a new babe birthed at the Dún of Lugnae Fer Trí?"

She glanced wildly around, seeking Mora or Finann, but they were nowhere to be seen. Bláth saw the fear in her eyes, felt the tremors emanating from her. She reached out towards Serb who recoiled from her, thinking herself tricked by Bláth also. Bláth was stung by the rebuff.

The Elder was relentless.

"You will go before Lugaid, the *Ard Rígh*! We will take you away from the Dún of Lugnae Fer Trí. Now, answer me – is there another who has birthed a new babe here?"

Serb's whole body shuddered. It was difficult to control the trembling. She closed her eyes, wanting to shut out everything that was happening. There was no place to run to and nowhere to hide, neither could she understand why she did not want to answer the question. The Black Crow had taken *him* away. Cred's heart was not with her any more because of the Black Crow. Donal Rua's heart was not with her any more either. The Black Crow was not good. They were going to take herself away if she did not tell them. Serb did not want to leave the Dún.

Bláth followed Serb's feelings with shock. She tried to get through to her, tried to overcome the girl's fears and angers so that she could calm her, make her silent, but Bláth knew as she watched her that Serb would betray the Black Crow, Gráinne . . . Achtán.

The Elder pressed further, this time quietly reinforcing his words to rock Serb.

"You will leave the Dún. You will not see it again. We will take you away."

"Gráinne! The Black Crow! Her name is Gráinne . . . the babe, Cormac mac Airt, has been birthed!"

Bláth, the Elder and the warriors, stared at Serb with astonishment on their faces. This, they had not expected. The name of the babe was Cormac mac Airt! Son of Art the Lonely, the slain

*Ard Rígh* of Éiriú, killed by Lugaid himself at the battle of Mag Muccrime . . . Art had sired a son? This was the twist of the serpent's tail for Lugaid then, the blood of Art the Lonely coming to haunt Éiriú.

Bláth knew in this same moment that she had made the right decision to honour Cormac mac Airt. He was now in great danger and she was going to do everything in her power to protect him. It was going to be vital to win the trust of both Serb, and of course Gráinne, if they ever found her. The animosity that Serb held for Gráinne had to go. Bláth determined to work on this, once she regained the trust of Serb. A very difficult task lay ahead. Dorcha and the two warriors would not hesitate to kill her if they found out her allegiance was now with Cormac mac Airt, babe though he was. Bláth also had to hope that she did not disclose the secret while she was speaking in tongues. Such things had happened before.

They returned Serb to the Brighdal *bothán*, where she flung her arms around Mora and hid her head. Bláth watched enviously.

The Elder spoke with Mora.

"Do you know where the girl Gráinne is?"

Mora was aware then that Serb had spoken of Gráinne. The seal of silence in the Clan was now broken.

"She is with her Draoi, learning . . . in the hills somewhere." This was partly true.

"When does she return?"

"That I know not."

"Where is the babe . . . Cormac mac Airt?"

Mora could not speak. Her feet were like clay, heavy and stuck to the ground. She did not think she could ever move again. Her face was ashen. Serb slid to the floor, curling up like a child and clinging to Mora's legs. Mora felt like kicking her aside but knew she must not even think like that. Serb was ailing, so maybe she was not aware of what she had done.

Mora inclined her head. Her breath quickened as the Elder grasped her arm, pinching her.

"Maybe you did not hear me? I asked of you where the babe is?"

"A babe should be at the breast of his mother where he belongs," she retorted softly, "and may he stay there, well away from thieves and tyrants!"

Dorcha's eyes were cold, although his face flamed red at her impertinence. He was bruising her arm and he did not care. One of the warriors laughed raucously, only to fall silent at the stony look which fell his way.

Dorcha flung Mora's arm away from him, then turned and strode out of the Brighdal *bothán*. That was when he saw the curious twosome leaping and running towards the Dún.

He watched as the goatherd banged at the door of one of the *botháns*, calling out for someone who was either not inside or did not want to answer. Then the young man was running up the hill towards them. Dorcha quickly urged Bláth and the warriors to hide behind the trees. They waited.

The goatherd called for Mora, urgency and fear lacing his words.

Mora came out to Finann, who was breathless from his run and could hardly speak.

"Cromlach! He – he is ailing . . . at – at the cave!"

"What about Serb? Can you stay, Finann? I am afraid that the tyrants from the *Ard Rígh* will come back here." Mora glanced around but did not see them in the copse of trees. She assumed they had gone back to the Dún Hall. "And Gráinne?"

"I did not see her, Mora . . . but I think you may need to make haste. Cromlach does not look himself."

Mora ran inside and gathered her medicine bag and some dried herbs, which she placed in a basket. As she rushed to go, Serb became hysterical, clinging on to her.

"I will come back soon, Serb. I must tend someone who is ailing. Look, Finann is here! He will keep you safe."

"They hide and wait!" screamed Serb.

"No, there is no one there, Serb. You are safe. Finann is here, he will protect you . . . and Misha is here. See, she wants to play."

Serb became at once like a child, leading the little goat into the *bothán*, so they could play together.

Mora nee Derga let out a sigh of relief, embraced Finann,

and then hurried away from the Brighdal *bothán*, in the direction of Knocknarea.

Had she taken notice of the signs, she might have realized she was being followed. Some crows noisily winged the air behind her. A hare raced across the plain in front of her. A wolf howled in the forest on the other side, but Mora thought only of Cromlach and wondered why he was ailing. It was not usual for him to do so.

She also thought of Gráinne and Cormac, hoping they were far away by now. There was nowhere safe for them here. Indeed, there were few places anywhere for them to go if Lugaid set a large hunt in motion.

As Mora approached the hidden cave, she noticed the little wren perched at the opening, chirping a calling song, and knew that Druid spirit-powers were at work. If that was so, and sickness had come of it, then Mora doubted she could heal such an affliction.

Entering the cave, she saw immediately that something was not quite right about the interior but could not determine what was wrong.

Rushing over to Cromlach lying by the blazing hearth, Mora became aware of the strange smells within the cave: burnt feathers, a stale smoke, and the unmistakable woody scent of the drying procedure for the spotted red-cap, *Beith Rua*, the red one who hugs the birch.

Mora felt Cromlach's pulse in his wrist and in his neck. She started counting the beats against her own rhythm. They were very weak but slow and fairly steady. Then she saw the pot with the dreggings in it. She sniffed at the pot.

"Ah . . . rosebay – I knew it!"

There was only one plant that complemented the rosebay. So, Cromlach had ingested the spotted red-cap. He had obviously eaten it in a hurry, before it was thoroughly dry. At least he must have removed the white beard, or by now he would have had no pulse. The rosebay itself should have been fermented, but some urgency or desperation had made Cromlach fight against time to work his power. This was strong spirit-work, crafted at great risk. Mora started preparations immediately. The only strength to combat this ailing was a strength equal and opposite: that of the deadly black night-berry, the dark-shadowed one.

Mora removed Cromlach's plaid and robe. He did not stir. She took a dark glass bottle from her medicine bag and, smearing some sweet-scented oil from the bottle on to her hands, she worked quickly, rubbing the oil into his body. She knew it would take time for the spirit of the plant to penetrate the seven layers of skin, but there was no other way to do it. She hoped it was not too late. In his deep dreaming state, she could not give it to him by mouth. He could not retch it back to dispel the darker forces, so the safest way was through his skin which accepted the spirit slowly and filtered out the unwanted terrors.

She waited for a few moments and wiped off the dirt residue left on his body, then she wrapped him in his plaid and stoked the fire into a blaze to keep him warm. Cromlach did not stir. Mora was so anxious by now that she forgot to wash her own hands.

By the time she thought of it, the elixir of the berries had already penetrated her own flesh.

"Oh, no . . . Brighde . . . this I could have done without!"

She stretched across a starlit sky to throw a peat-sod on the fire. Mora panicked as she scrabbled in her medicine bag for a dried red-cap. She started chewing on it right away. It was ironic that she had to take the same medicine as Cromlach to counteract the effects of the medicine she had just administered to him.

Before long, she was rushing to the entrance of the cave and retching to throw off the dark poisons. Her throat burned and her belly heaved. The taste in her mouth was bitter-sweet, her thoughts spinning and diving in painful slow motion as she fought against the shadows. She gulped great mouthfuls of fresh air as she knelt on the ground outside the cave, unable to stand up. Everything had slowed down unbearably. Her heartbeat was pounding one moment and then murmuring the next.

Mora doubled over, leaning her forehead to the stones, being unaware of much of the noise around, although the wren still perched on the rock and sang, observer of all at the entrance of the cave-*bothán*.

There was a footfall beside Mora's head, and then she was wrenched to her feet, the act of violence like a lightning bolt charging through her. She was shocked to the core, the waves of fear rippling over and out from her being. The warrior's laugh echoed in her head, his lewd eyes sweeping over the fine figure of the woman and burning into her.

She shuddered as she stared at the man before her. He was a beast, a primitive horned beast with a tail which had wrapped itself around her arm. Mora screamed, only to have a claw clamp over her mouth.

He was biting, nibbling at her shoulder, eating her. She struggled wildly and looked about her. There they were, all four of them, the beast that held her and his three accomplices. One was female. Sometimes it looked like the visiting woman, Bláth, but mostly it was some thin, scraggy, sly hunting animal, pathetic to watch.

The fat one, Dorcha, *the dark one*, the Elder, the Brehon, who looked like a boar, was vicious, a killer who lusted after blood, the blood of a babe. They were here to kill Cormac mac Airt.

The tailed beasts, the warriors, dragged her into the cave.

Mora was aghast. There lay Cromlach beside the hearth, still in his dreaming, but, beyond him, lying curled in an unbirthed babe position, was Gráinne. Beside her slept the infant, Cormac.

"No!" she screamed, tears springing from her eyes when she saw the babe lying with his mother.

"Please, I beg of you, do him no injury. Do not kill him," she implored, knowing as she said it that they would not hesitate to do so.

"What are you gabbing about, woman? We have no cause to harm an old man who is sleeping."

Mora was confused and alarmed. She searched their eyes, scanning their expressions one by one to see why they were pretending not to see Gráinne and the babe. With a great effort, she remembered that when she first came into the cave, it had lost its dimension in size. Of course!

Cromlach had put an enchantment on Gráinne. Mora could no longer control herself. She began to laugh and laugh and laugh. They seemed so strange, these beasts before her who had been tricked. Cromlach, dear ailing Cromlach had shielded Gráinne and the babe from these killers. Without the plants for *seeing*, Mora had not been able to detect the mother and babe sleeping there right under their noses!

A sharp slap across the face made Mora intake her breath and stare in shock at the small, wizened Bláth. Bláth was looking hard into Mora's eyes. There was a Truth here somewhere that Bláth wanted. She struggled to *see* but could not. A fog surrounded that which she searched for. The cave was under an enchantment. She knew that. The only way to *see* was for her to get somehow into the mind of the woman, Mora, but try as she might, she could not penetrate the slow tumbling thoughts and mirth which spilled from the woman, despite the shock she had received from the slap.

There was a secret here but Bláth was not able to unravel it. It frustrated her but there was nothing she could do about it. Dorcha was watching out of the corner of his eye.

"What do you *see*?"

"I *see* that Gráinne is not here with us, neither is the babe, Cormac mac Airt."

"Any fool knows that!" retorted the Elder.

"I *see* that the man by the hearth is ailing from the dark spirit of the spotted red-cap . . . and the animal-healer, Mora nee Derga, has administered the deadly night-berry to heal his ailing."

Mora was suddenly interested. This Bláth knew her name and knew her Craft. What else could she *see*? The woman had snakes growing for hair, but for some reason Mora was no longer afraid of her.

This was when the visitor, Bláth, caught her relaxed and off guard. Immediately Bláth *saw* through Mora nee Derga's eyes. There was the cave, much larger than before, and there, in a soft hazy cocoon, were the mother and child, Gráinne and the new-birthed *Ard Rígh*! Through her own eyes, she could not have *seen* it, but the man by the fire who had cast the enchantment could not have foreseen that his healer would have taken the herb to *see* and then had the misfortune or fate to meet herself, who could only break through the charm with Mora's eyes. Now it was vital that Dorcha the Elder should not guess what had happened.

As Bláth continued to stare at the cocoon with Mora, who now realized that the *seer* knew, and hoped fervently she was not going to say anything, a strange event occurred which happened so fast that the women could not and knew not how to prevent it.

"Where have they gone?" asked the Elder abruptly, now becoming irritated by the sight of Bláth gazing into Mora nee Derga's eyes, and Mora nee Derga in some dreaming state, staring blankly into the cave, beyond the ailing one.

Into the haze of the cocoon, something grey streaked, a grey-blue animal with an underbelly of swollen milk-filled teats . . . a she-wolf, who opened her jaws wide and, just as Bláth and Mora screamed together for fear the babe was going to be devoured, the wolf gently licked Cormac, then picked up the infant by his swaddling linens, and there was the child dangling from her mouth when she disappeared as quickly as she had appeared. A flash of grey fur and amber eyes, and the she-wolf was gone with her prize.

Both women, looking terror-struck, separated their spirits with a jolt, neither one able to speak with the other. Mora was weeping uncontrollably. She rushed towards Gráinne, only to slam against the wall of the cave, the spirit-wall that Cromlach had built.

"He is gone! He is gone!"

Mora panicked, not knowing where to go or what to do next.

The warriors were taken aback. They did not really like these women with their strange powers. It made them feel uneasy in their company, but one of the warriors, the tall, dark one with the deep battle-scar etched down one side of his face, badly wanted a release. He had been away from a mate for too long. This woman, Mora, despite her rantings and ravings, had not an unfriendly face. She was all curves with a great behind. Her hair was dark russet auburn. It reminded him of the time of the falling, when the leaves scattered on the ground. She was over-ripe for this time of year. He vowed to have her soon.

"The child is gone from here, Dorcha," said Bláth. "We waste our time. Neither is he with the woman, Gráinne, the Black Crow."

The Elder searched for the Truth again and *saw* it was as she said.

"Where is he?"

"Maybe in the land of Í-Bhreasail, who but knows? He is not here at the Dún of Lugnae Fer Trí. The mother, Gráinne, sleeps somewhere without her babe. She does not know he is gone yet. He has been taken by greater forces than you or I."

Bláth looked sideways at Mora nee Derga. It was the Truth she spoke, but a veiled Truth.

Dorcha became enraged with the *seer*.

"If we return without him, we are in Í-Bhreasail ourselves!"

"He has been spirited away, Dorcha. We will not find him here, nor in any land we know. Lugaid, our *Ard Rígh*, must accept a Truth. I will bear his rage for you. Have I not done so many times before? We will leave on the morrow."

Bláth was determined.

"No!" said Dorcha, "Lugaid wants a body and he shall have one!"

"You would slaughter an innocent?"

Mora was as pale as a bone as she listened to Bláth's question. Her heart raged and thundered as she read the intent upon Dorcha's brow. He was going to kill a babe, any babe, to save his own hide!

His next sly words burned into her.

"When will the girl, Serb, drop her wain?"

Something snapped in Mora and in Bláth at the same time. A bond of mutual respect forged them together as they reacted in their separate ways.

Bláth glared at Dorcha, then suddenly whirled around and around, calling upon afflictions of the darkest nature to make themselves known to the Elder.

He yelled at the warriors to seize and curb the women, to silence their mouths from their vile curses.

Mora felt the snakes, in the snake-pit of her groin, uncoil and unleash their fury and venom, as she spun and shook and hissed with that fury, her face contorting as a screech rang out from her, piercing their beings.

The warriors did not obey Dorcha. They ran for the cave entrance as the Elder, seeing their cowardice and definitely not wishing to confront the women on his own, backed also towards the opening. All three collided as they made their escape. Bláth began laughing and speaking in tongues, all the spirits now awakened within her. Mora nee Derga caught Bláth's arm to try to shake her out of the spirit-talking.

"Bláth," Mora spoke firmly, "go to Serb! They may harm her. I have to stay here with Cromlach."

Bláth's eyes were wildly rolling as she gibbered on and on, unable to control the stream of words that poured from her.

Mora pinched her, sorry that she had to hurt her.

"Bláth, go to Serb! Go to Serb!" she screeched in the same way she had shrieked at the men, *the dark ones*.

She repeated herself over and over again until Bláth nodded suddenly, stopping in mid-sentence, and then ran towards the entrance of the cave, without saying another word.

Mora hoped that Bláth understood. She thanked the goddess that the woman was in favour of keeping Cormac alive.

Mora nee Derga glanced over at Gráinne. She was still sleeping. It was true . . . it had really happened . . . Cormac was not there. Mora wished that Cromlach would awaken. She prepared herself for a night-vigil if he did not stir, but she wished he would. It was difficult for her to bear this knowledge by herself.

The medicine was still quite strong inside. Her eyes were constantly adjusting to focus on objects as everything had such movement. Even the rock surrounding her in the cave was undulating in great waves, like the sea. There was too much movement and danger in it.

She became aware of something out of the corner of her eye, something at the cave opening. Before she realized fully what was happening, she was pinned on her belly to the ground.

The tall, dark, scarred one had returned. The black-horned one, whose tail wrapped itself around her again, now tossed her to the rush-strewn floor. A rampant stallion, a bull with rippling muscles forced her to prostrate herself, to hug the ground, its breath panting in the back of her neck, blowing her hair. She felt teeth nip her shoulder. She knew she could not struggle against such a force. It was better to go with it, to blend and merge herself so that she felt the least pain. Her robe was cast aside. Sweat poured off her brow as she was forced to kneel up on all fours, her legs parted roughly and hastily. He entered her, one hand grasping a handful of her hair, a hoof digging into one buttock. He charged into her again and again, snorting and bellowing his triumph as his seed spilled. It was over very quickly.

She was surprised at how gentle and quiet he became afterwards, fondling her, almost as an act of worship. He turned her over on her back and caressed her so that she felt a great stirring within her loins and it was as if he was aware of her aloneness, her path of self-denial. His black horns were no longer there. She danced her fingers over the scar on his face, wishing him healed. His hazel eyes registered surprise at her tender touch and he collapsed suddenly upon her, weeping for all women, his sister, his mother, his mate. His shoulders shook. This woman was the goddess incarnate, all embracing, all forgiving. His shame was his alone. He wept and accepted her, the soft arms enfolding him, holding him close to her heart, which purred against his head. He dared to touch her. He dared to feel a yearning, a love for this Mora, the embodiment of all women. He asked a pardon of her, as he brought her to fulfilment, his long fingers quietly kneading her to greater and greater pleasure, and her pleasure was his pain. She found herself weaving words in and out of his thoughts, softly threading a pattern he would take with him.

The warrior left, stunned by what he had undergone. Somehow, going back to the Dún of Lugnae Fer Trí, being in the presence of Dorcha, was not what he wanted. Neither did he desire to see Teamhair again. He wanted not to battle or kill again, but to have a quiet life, making his woman happy, producing strong sons and daughters. He wanted a new land of growth, not bloodshed. The warrior quickly mounted his steed and rode away, away from the Dún of Lugnae Fer Trí, away from the road that led to Teamhair, and he headed north to embrace a new life elsewhere. If Cormac mac Airt still lived, he hoped he would grow up to bring peace to Éiriú. In his heart, the warrior swore an oath of fealty to the chosen one.

Mora lay near Cromlach, unable to move except to throw peat upon the fire to keep it alive.

Cromlach was sleeping. Mora wanted nothing more than to escape into sleeping. The bird still chirped outside. Mora wondered when the enchantment would end and how much longer Cromlach and Gráinne would remain in the land of shadows. She wanted Cromlach back. She wanted Gráinne and the babe back but she knew in her heart of hearts that Cormac was gone.

Mora turned and buried her head into the musty plaid which covered Cromlach. Mora nee Derga wept for them all, all the loved ones who were parted from each other, even the warrior who had just left her, Cred who was away from Gráinne, Serb in her own *seer*'s world, Gráinne in her cocoon of forgetfulness, Cromlach who was ailing from the enchantment, and most of all, dear little Cormac who was abducted by the she-wolf.

"He is gone, and I was not prepared," she whispered. "He is gone . . . and my heart can bleed no more. I am as a shell, with no living thing within. I am as one demented, lost in a shadowed world."

She echoed all their thoughts. The tears fell upon her lips and she licked the salt-taste, closed her eyes and tried not to think of the morrow or what it might bring.

A wolf bayed mournfully on Knocknarea but the sound was comforting to her.

# CHAPTER 21

# THE AWAKENING

*She wanders in an endless sea of forgetfulness*
*Like a new-birthed one, pure of thought,*
*Innocent of deed, knowing and all-knowing;*
*She is at the heart of the seed of it all.*

It was bitterly cold. Cromlach did not awaken until the day of
Samhain. Mora stayed by his side, custodian of the sleeping
ones within the cave. She wrapped furs around Cromlach to
keep him warm and even pulled the skins around herself,
although she was loath to do so. She wished she was back at
her own *bothán* but knew she had to stay here. Every day she
rubbed some of the dark night-berry oil on her arms, or nibbled
some of the spotted red-cap, just so that she could keep a
watchful eye on Gráinne. It was impossible to *see* her without
the aid of the special plants.

Finann came by each day with fresh roots, vegetables and
goat's cheese so that Mora could make a hotpot or two. She
usually cooked one to be taken back to Bláth and Serb, the
other she shared with Finann. There was always extra food left
over because she hoped every day that Cromlach would awaken
and Gráinne would return.

Finann filled little Misha's creels with peat-sods and bracken
to keep the fire going on the hearthstone.

"Mora," he had said, on the day after her encounter with
Bláth and the warriors, "Dorcha is ailing. Fergus the poet was
called out with his physic finger, and Morann the physician
attended him all night. Fergus told him that the cause of his
ailing was a charm which could only be lifted by the one who
placed it upon him. Morann the physician did not agree and
began to leech him for bad blood, which he said was down to

225

bad thoughts having rotted the rivers of his body. I dare say he was not far wrong there!"

Mora had smiled then, amused by Finann's comment.

"No, I dare say he was not," she said, thinking to herself: If only you knew the half of it, Finann.

Several days after that, Finann came back to say that the warrior and Dorcha were returning to Teamhair. They were fretting about the disappearance of the other warrior. The Elder Dorcha was slightly better now but much subdued. He was anxious to return to Teamhair. Bláth had warned him that she would curse him with fevers and afflictions if he dared to kill an innocent to take back to Lugaid. She made a boon to the remaining warrior that she would cause his manhood to wilt, his seed to become stale and any mate he chose to become barren, if he as much as thought of harming Serb or slaughtering a babe. The much frightened warrior could not wait to get back to Lugaid and engage in some serious battles and skirmishes, man's work. He did not want to deal with mad women or the bother of abducting babes. It was too fraught with dangers.

Bláth urged the two to return to Lugaid, the *Ard Rígh*, and inform him that she was going to bear the news to him when she returned. She was going to Truth-tell. They had to say that he should not worry about it, that Bláth told them to say that the ancestors had taken care of the new-birthed babe. She would tell him this Truth and he would know that there was nothing he could do about it.

Lugaid had such a fear of the ancestors that he would not do anything rash for a while, maybe long enough for the enchantment to break and Gráinne to leave and go far far away to rear the babe.

Bláth needed to have the trust of both camps to enable this to happen. She already knew that Mora nee Derga and Serb were with her in this.

Dorcha was nervous about returning but knew that the wrath of Lugaid soon passed but that the wrath of Bláth was likely to have a lasting effect. He had never ailed so much as in the last few days and could not risk a lifetime of ailments brought on by the vile curses of women. He assumed that the other warrior had run away for fear of the same curses. Maybe this warrior, one of Lugaid's favourites, was already at Teamhair. Dorcha would have to tell the Truth as this one might have spoken to Lugaid and given him the tale.

As the Elder and the remaining warrior hurriedly rode away from the Clan of Lugnae Fer Trí, they were watched by an anxious Bláth. She hoped they would convince the temperamental *Ard Rígh*. It was Samhain, the time of the new beginning, the new year, story-telling, the lighting of the beacons upon the hills and, of course, the arrival of the beautiful exotic foreign women Lugaid summoned to Teamhair every festival. Maybe with his heart in his groin he would not be raring for blood. There was still some time.

Bláth turned to the task at hand, that of controlling Serb, sweet little Serb, so vulnerable and full of fears, who was about to birth her babe but could never care for him as a mother. Bláth looked upon Serb as her successor and heir to all her own wisdom as a *seer*. The young woman was going through the sixth sickness and was very difficult to manage. She lusted after all the men and boys in the Clan. Bláth often found her gone and then discovered her in the midst of a circle of laughing boys who always ran when Bláth appeared. Serb was always sitting with her legs open, pointing and offering herself to any and all around. She displayed herself to the trappers, none of whom took advantage of her because of the taboos on the Brighdal *bothán* and the fact that they thought Cred had chosen Serb for his own. The gods made her child-grow. It was not right she should offer herself in this way.

Serb would scream, frustrated, tear at her hair and claw at herself, yearning for the fulfilment that was all part of her sickness.

Bláth usually soothed her with both the male and female spirit-voices, ancient and now familiar to Serb. She would lead the girl to the Brighdal *bothán*, lay her down and then fondle her to help her over this part of her sickness. Serb writhed with the rhythmic movement of the *seer*'s hand which took her to the heights she desired and caused her to rise again and again until she collapsed exhausted into a deep slumber, soothed by the spirit-voices. But it was now becoming more strenuous for Bláth, who was not used to such responsibility and who had to watch Serb all the time. It made no difference to Serb which was night and which was day, when to sleep or when to wake. A sleeping draught was of no use as it might harm the babe who was preparing to awaken to this world.

Bláth tried to persuade Finann to touch Serb in the same way she did, but Finann could not bring himself to do so, not when the girl was child-growing. Serb sometimes even attacked him or tried to grab his manhood. He was glad that Bláth was there and that poor Mora had not had to deal with this part of it all.

Mora Nee Derga was sad to miss the eve of Samhain. She always enjoyed the great festival, the gathering of the Clan and the simple people of the *crannógs* who came to the Dún Hall in their colourful clothes. The Elders revered the ancestors on this night. Beautiful carved effigies were exchanged as gifts and the new year was called in by the light of the moon. The beacon-fire was lit on the top of Knocknarea and torchlight processions around the Dún were wonderful to behold. Men, women and children chanted the marches to the reverberating sound of the special drums, *bodhrans* made from the stretched skins of old goats who had passed on. The men wore antlers. Masks and headdresses were especially made for the event. There were contests and games of strength for the body, the walking on flames, the swallowing of the fire, and there were chess-games for the mind, played with the movement of human chess figures on a large, squared maze, formed by digging out alternate blocks of sod and turning them over to make a contrasting squared patch. It was played by the light of all the torches which were stuck into the ground. All night long, everyone laughed and sang, children falling asleep where they dropped with exhaustion, mothers wrapping them in furs to keep warm until they could be carried to their pallets later. Men and women danced and tumbled until they too needed to lie down. Much loving went on in the *bothåns*, deep in the furs, into the small hours.

Mora heard the laughs and cheers, the pipes, the harp and tympan sounds echoing across the plain between the Dún and

Cromlach's cave-*bothán*. Mora nee Derga sighed, a long weary sigh that betrayed her loneliness.

Finann came at early dawn and brought very appetizing food including some of the last fall of apples for her to eat. He had a torch with him with which to light the first fire on her hearth for the new year. He told her he had already gone into her *bothán* at the Dún and lit a fire on her hearthstone there. She felt an ache for her own fireside again.

Finann then gave her a crudely carved wooden likeness of what was supposed to be Danann, Mother of the gods. He had made a skirt out of goat's hair for it. Instead, it looked more like a poor little wanton babe with no mother, but Mora nee Derga laughed and hugged Finann. He loved to see her happy again and wished to hear her laugh some more. So he told her about the antics of Serb and Bláth and how Serb had been trying to bed him every time he went past her. Mora was astonished to hear of Bláth's remedy for Serb's behaviour, whooping suddenly, doubling over, a long-needed release of hysteria overcoming her, so that the tears rolled down her cheeks. Finann tittered, then fell about laughing himself. They hugged each other in their mirth, Mora clinging to Finann, who never quite shook off the smell of his goats, but she buried her face into the familiar scent on his shoulder and her cheeks were wet from the tears of laughter and sadness that engulfed her. He clumsily stroked her hair back from where it had fallen in her eyes.

"When? When will they return? Oh, Finann, how much longer must I be a Guardian of the shadows?"

Finann heard the despair in her voice but he was unable to speak so he held her against him, hoping his presence was enough. In the same moment, they both became aware of a small movement in the cave. The space within had suddenly become wider and grown in depth.

Mora gasped as she watched the stirring of the figure before her.

"Gráinne!" she whispered, moving towards the woman who was trying to rise but who was too weak and fell back upon the furs.

The enchantment was broken at last!

Finann stared incredulously.

"Where is the babe?" he asked suddenly. Mora put her fingers against his lips to hush him. She rushed towards Gráinne's side and cradling her head, she put a horn-cup of water to Gráinne's lips and urged her softly to sip it slowly. Gráinne gulped down two mouthfuls, then she licked her lips and smiled at her friends.

"Have I been slumbering?" she croaked.

Mora nodded, urging Gráinne to wet her lips some more.

"I am famished, Mora. The food smells so good."

"No, Gráinne, you have been sleeping long, so we will break your fast with some goat's milk first," said Mora, then turning to Finann she gestured for him to get the milk. Mora also quickly put some crushed oats on to boil.

Finann carried the urn over and Mora dragged a wooden bowl through the milk in the urn, scooping up just a small amount at first.

As she placed the bowl to Gráinne's lips, the girl became startled by something. Mora suddenly froze with fear and Finann jumped back alarmed when a little wet nose nuzzled out from under Gráinne's tunic, pushing its way up from between her breasts to get to the cup. It was a soft ball of fur, a little wolf-cub, which clumsily lapped at the milk, its paw plopping into the bowl and spilling the milk over Gráinne.

"Oh! . . . Look at him, Mora!" squealed Gráinne with delight when she sufficiently recovered from her surprise. "Where did he come from? Does he belong to Cromlach then?"

Mora was speechless. Finann was white, fear of unwanted spirits sending shivers through him.

"Wh— where is Cormac? Is – is this the work of Samhain spirits? Gráinne, where is Cormac?" he babbled.

Gráinne seemed puzzled.

"Who? Mora, what is Finann talking of?"

"The . . . the babe!" said Finann, his voice high-pitched. This was a madness. Why did Gráinne not know of her own babe?

"Babe?" she giggled, "I have no babe, Finann. I am not much more than a babe myself." She caught sight of the figure lying by the hearth. "Is that Cromlach over there? Is he slumbering too, then?"

Mora nodded, afraid to say anything. The wolf nuzzled her hand and she snatched it back suddenly.

"Mora?" Gráinne raised herself on her elbow. "What ails you? You, who are a healer of animals, back away from a helpless wolf-cub. Look at him! Come here . . . sha, sha, sha," she said, talking babe-talk to the little furry animal.

Mora quickly found her voice again. "He startled me, that is all," she murmured with false lightness in her tone.

Gráinne was engrossed with playing with the wolf-cub and trying to get him to lap some more milk which Mora gave to her. She drank some herself and then offered the rest to the cub. He sneezed, unable to lap it properly.

"What are we to do?" wailed Gráinne. "He is too little to lap. What are we to do?"

Finann looked helplessly at Mora who shrugged and then took Finann aside and whispered: "The babe is safe, Finann. Gráinne is not being herself because she is under the enchantment of forgetfulness for now . . . The wolf-cub is a . . . special gift. It seems we must care for the wolf-cub to ensure the safe return of Cormac."

Finann nodded, no less scared but relieved that some sort of explanation had been given to him. He watched Gráinne dip her finger into the milk and offer it to the cub who could not suckle the milk off her finger.

"Finann, what are we to do?" pleaded Gráinne.

Finann thought of something, mulled it over in his mind and made a decision, although he was not sure how Misha would like it.

"Misha has milk," he said. "Her kids are weaned but I kept milking her. She has good milk. Let us see if she will allow the cub to suckle her."

Misha shied away from the inside of the cave as soon as she smelled the wolf-scent. She began to tremble and her eyes widened with terror but Finann stroked and soothed her. She jumped back and tried to rush for the cave-opening when he brought the cub over. Finann realized he could not hold the wolf and the goat at the same time, so Mora caught the goat by the horns and led her back. Misha was kicking and butting.

One would have thought that it was a pack of wolves she was confronting instead of a little ball of fluff not much bigger than would fit into the cupping of two hands.

Mora began to blow her breath into the goat's nose, then made clicking noises against the roof of her mouth, whereupon Misha immediately calmed down and let Mora lay her upon the rushes, not far from Cromlach and the hearth.

Mora nee Derga started the flow of milk by pulling on and squeezing the goat's teats. All the while, Mora clicked her tongue. Finann placed the wolf-cub beside the teats. Misha tried to get up, but Mora blew in her face again and laid her back down. Misha's eyes rolled anxiously to glance sideways towards the wolf-cub.

The cub smelt the milk immediately and struggled to get at it, his little mouth opening to grasp the teat. After a few failed tries, with Finann's assistance he at last managed to get his mouth latched over the large finger-like teat, without choking, and began to suck the milk.

Mora soothed the goat who allowed the cub to suck on her.

Gráinne laughed gleefully.

"Look! A goat giving suck to a wolf! What do you think, Mora, shall we name him *Gabhar* or *Gadhar*?"

"A goat or a hunting dog? I think whichever name you choose will be the right one, *a stór*, but why not call him *Cú*, for surely he is not an ordinary wolf, but a hound and a gift from the gods."

"Aye! He is Cú! Mora, Finann, we have a new friend . . . Cú!"

Mora was finding it difficult to accept the new Gráinne. She had to keep reminding herself that Gráinne was in the sea of forgetfulness and that the girl was not being a bad mother for not thinking of her babe . . . she just had no memory of him. And yet she remembered who Finann and Cromlach were, so only part of her memory was being veiled.

Mora's attention turned to Cromlach. She knew it was he who was keeping the enchantment intact. It was he who spun the cocoon and stayed in his dreaming state to keep the threads safe. Mora wondered if Cromlach knew of the wolf or the

232

abduction of Cormac or indeed that Gráinne was no longer under the enchantment. She thought of alerting Lugnae Fer Trí. Should he know of what had occurred? How was she to explain that Gráinne was well, but without memory of her babe, and that a she-wolf was taking care of the babe? She hoped this was possible and that the child was safe. This was no ordinary she-wolf who had pierced the veil of enchantment and left a cub in place of the babe.

Mora wished that Cromlach was awake or that Olc Aiche was here or someone with whom she could confer. Finann was a blessing and a comfort but he was unable to make a decision about Gráinne or Cormac. His fear of the spirit-world was too deep to overcome.

Mora was worried. Cromlach should have awakened with the breaking of the enchantment . . . but then Mora recalled that Gráinne was still in between worlds. Only at the time of Samhain could such a sorcery be possible, as Cromlach obviously had known.

The cub fell asleep. Finann disengaged the goat's teat from the relaxed and milky mouth of the cub and then drew Misha away from him, taking her to graze outside. She was only too happy to leave.

Gráinne cradled the wolf, Cú, and snuggled down beside him on the furs again, but Mora did not let her fall asleep again just yet. She passed a small bowl of the boiled oats to Gráinne and urged her to take a little at a time and chew it well, then advised her to relieve herself afterwards outside the cave before she settled down to a natural slumber.

Mora helped the girl get her shaky body outside and waited until she was finished before helping her inside again. She bathed her face and hands for her and coaxed her to sleep, hoping that maybe everything would return to normal by the time she awakened.

Mora went over to Cromlach. His breathing was shallow as usual but his body seemed very cold and clammy. She did not like this new development. Something was wrong.

"Finann!" she called out. He was still with Misha, but he

heard Mora summoning him and reacted immediately to the urgency in her voice.

"Finann! Go and get Fergus quickly. I need his physic finger to detect the cause of Cromlach's ailing so that I can treat him safely – but please hurry, he is losing warmth, Finann. I need help. Do not alert Morann. He thinks my healing is only good for horses, deer and beasts that graze and suchlike. Fergus, on the other hand, is a poet and therefore a man of Truth. He is skilled with finding the flowing rivers in the body which are blocked, diverted or dirtied in some way. He can tell me where we must work on Cromlach to save him."

"To save him?" Finann was disturbed. He had not fully realized the danger in Cromlach's sleeping state. Cromlach looked so full of peace.

"Aye, to save him. Hurry, please, Finann, hurry!"

Finann threw one worried glance at Cromlach and then ran, ran as fast as he could to find Fergus.

Fergus was at the harp, making a song, when Finann burst in and interrupted him. This was something which was never, never, done. No one on the face of the land was allowed to stop the poet's flow of thought and action, but Fergus took one look at the breathless young man in front of him, listened to the desperation in his voice and did not hesitate to put his beloved harp aside.

Fergus mounted his horse, pulled Finann up behind him and galloped towards the mountain.

Mora waited solemnly. She noticed something suddenly . . . the wren had stopped singing but the silence seemed all the more deafening to Mora's ears. So! She was right, the enchantment was over and therefore Cromlach should also be back. Why was he not here? Why? She heaped more peat-sods on the fire to keep him extra warm but his body was cold to the touch. Mora was afraid.

Fergus arrived, surprised at the cosy *bothán* concealed within the hermit's cave, even more surprised to see Gráinne sleeping with the wolf-cub curled up beside her. The sight stirred his thoughts. It created a beautiful scene, the cave, the fire, the woman with the long, black hair trailing out across the furs, and the wolf-cub.

Fergus felt the words spinning in his head, the harp-song echoing from deep, deep within himself. It excited him, the glow of the red and amber fire, the man slumbering by the flames, the fingers of light playing on the weathered face . . . it was fodder for great mind-play.

He then saw Mora's pale face, her russet hair wild and uncombed like tangled brushwood, her green eyes, the still waters of a rush-pool, the green rushes mirrored in the water, but her face was drained of all colour, white and mild, settled snow. Anxiety reigned there, spreading its shadows on her furrowed brow.

Fergus could not speak with the awe of it all. He was glad that Finann had interrupted him to bring him here.

Mora led Fergus by the hand to the hearth-side.

"Fergus, Cromlach has taken the *seeing* plants, many nights ago, but he is not back with us yet. I have administered the potion to help him but, you see, the plant he ate was taken in a hurry, ill-prepared. Even so, he should have returned by now. I fear that his spirit is being prevented from returning because of some disorder of the body. I – I need your assistance, Fergus."

"Mora nee Derga, my fingers itch to pluck my harp but now I find one string broken. Let me see if we can mend it between us both."

Fergus peeled back the furs and the plaid, both of which were not adequate now to keep Cromlach warm.

He then began to divine with his physic finger by holding his hand out gracefully, spreading his fingers and thumb, and then dropping the third finger so that it glided lightly over the surface of Cromlach's body. First, he traced the line of the head, then circled the face and went down the forehead, over the nose and over the mouth, up again to both of the eyes and ears and then swept over the entire head once more. He started on the torso but as he traced the hollow in the throat, he stopped suddenly.

"Aah!" he whispered, "I think I have found you."

Fergus placed his ear to Cromlach's throat and then coursed his physic finger across the shoulders, over the chest and down to the navel, tapping gently along the way, all the while listening to something of which neither Mora nor Finann had knowledge. His finger came back to the throat region. He was fine-tuning a harp, the harp of the spirit, and he was listening to the reverberation of a sound known only to himself.

"It is as I thought," he said, sitting up and stretching his spine, then stretching his neck first one way and then the other, until the bones cracked.

"What is it?" asked Mora urgently. "Will Cromlach come back to us?"

"That I cannot say, but we can make it easier for him to return, less painful for him to come back to an ailing body. What brings the most relief to a painful throat? Whatever that is, prepare it quickly, Mora nee Derga, we have not much time."

Mora immediately went to her medicine bag and took out a precious salt-block which was wrapped in a woven pocket of fine silk. She heated the salt on a skillet and then packed it back in the woven silk and placed it gently around Cromlach's throat.

"Mora nee Derga, do you have something in your bag for the afflictions in the belly, something to soothe?" Fergus asked.

Mora nodded and urged Finann to bring over the urn of goat's milk and pour some into a pot so she could heat it over the fire. She then scraped some soot off one of her black cooking pots and a little ash from the bottom of the fire. She mixed them both together and sprinkled them into the warming milk. Testing the milk with her elbow, she got it just at the right temperature and poured it into a drinking horn.

"How will I get him to swallow?" she asked anxiously.

"We must!" said Fergus grimly.

"Maybe we can use a long rush-straw if we bend it and place it down his throat, past his passage for air," suggested Mora. "I did that once for a babe . . . a – a cub who could not be given suckle."

Fergus nodded with great respect. This woman was a good person and a worthy healer. He helped support Cromlach in a sitting position while she placed the dried rush-straw into the horn of milk, then sucked on it to get the flow going and quickly squeezed the end and pushed it down Cromlach's throat, letting go when her fingers came into contact with what she called the small tongue at the back. She hoped the rush was far enough down as she tipped the horn to continue the flow of milk.

A small amount was all that was needed for now. Mora was wary of giving him too much. Although Cromlach did not appear to swallow the milk, it was going down too fast for Mora's liking, so she withdrew the rush-straw and the horn and put them aside.

Fergus nodded. The more he watched this woman work, the more he wished it was she and not Morann who was the physician at the Dún. Morann was too much under the influence of the Brehons and their precise Laws for everything, even the healing arts. Mora nee Derga was bound only by the Laws of nature and the spirits. Her ways were the correct ways for the Clan. She practised her Craft with love. He had watched her selfless caring for Serb when it was obvious that Serb was ailing in her mind and would not heal easily.

Fergus determined that his next poems were going to honour these gentle people within the Clan who kept the old ways. His eyes misted over as he felt the great love which surrounded him within this cave and he wished to go no further than these walls for this day. He had discovered another Clan within the Clan of Lugnae Fer Trí.

"Fergus, you are a Truth-seeker and a speaker of Truth," said Mora, startling him from his reverie, "and I wish to know if you may also withhold a Truth, I mean, in the way of keeping a secret."

"That is not the way of the *filé*, Mora nee Derga. Veiled Truths reveal themselves in time and even if it is thought to be the best time, it may not always be the appropriate time they unveil themselves."

"But if the veiling of the Truth saves the life of an *Ard Rígh*, I mean an *Ard Rígh* who is birthed and chosen to usurp an existing one?"

"Then, Mora, if the existing *Ard Rígh* is not a just man in word or deed then the spirits of the land will bring about the birthing of a new *Ard Rígh*. This King is in danger if he is the chosen heir to usurp a tyrant. He must be protected but only with a Truth. Cromlach drew the veil on the Truth to save the life of Cormac mac Airt, did he not?"

Mora's eyes filled with tears at these words.

"Aye, he did. Oh, Fergus, must he forfeit his own life now because he protected an innocent unable to defend himself from the tyrant?"

"He is suffering a fate now, Mora," said Fergus gently, "but he has drawn the veil on the Truth many times to protect the innocent from the harsh Laws of the Brehons and, well, he paid the trade then with his own exile and his hermitage . . . It is my belief that he has veiled the Truth for Gráinne too. But Cromlach works the Craft in the ancient ways – he knows what he is doing. Do not fret, *a stór*, it is not time for him to pass over. It is my belief that his greater work is only beginning. He is the victim only of his ill-prepared medicine. You have healed his belly and his throat. Soon he will be with us."

As he said this, Fergus looked towards Cromlach and he could have sworn that he saw a frog come out of the older man's mouth but this surely was not possible. Fergus thought the flickering firelight had cast a shadow, that was all.

He yearned to have his harp with him, yet he did not want to leave. Reluctantly he got to his feet. The poem he was about to create and sing as a chant was going to be one of his best efforts. One day he would chant it at the Court of Cormac mac Airt at Teamhair. He promised this to himself. Fergus smiled. He was not only a Truth-seeker, he was also a Truth-*seer*. Mora nee Derga knew this now. He was glad. No longer did he have to veil his own Truth.

As he bade his farewell to Mora, glanced longingly at the beautiful Gráinne curled in slumber with the wolf-cub, and stepped over a sleeping Finann at the entrance to the cave, Fergus saw a brown toad hop over the threshold to the cold outside. He was not surprised.

Cromlach was healed by Mora nee Derga and he, Fergus, had been a small part of that. A great contentment swept over him. The spirits had allowed him to *see*.

# CHAPTER 22

# REMEMBERING

*Deep in the salmon pool of forgetfulness*
*Lie the nuts of knowledge from the hazel tree*
*And little by little the salmon of wisdom nibbles*
*And little by little she remembers the sea.*

Cromlach was with them once more, his voice feeble, his throat still a little sore. He marvelled at the changes which had occurred whilst he slept his dreaming sleep.

Bláth the *seer* now looked after Serb. Samhain came and left and he had missed all the feasting and celebrations. Gráinne returned with a wolf-cub and she was still wrapped in the cocoon of forgetfulness, and Cormac, her babe, was with the she-wolf. Had he, Cromlach, not *seen* the wolf with his own eyes come to take the babe? No craft in the land had power of concealment from the spirits of the gods. He remembered the amber eyes and the gentle way in which the she-wolf took the babe into her care.

He also remembered his own struggle to return, the guidance of Fergus the poet and the skill of the healing woman, Mora. The pain had swamped him so that he did not wish to come back, but she soothed his pains so that they were tolerable.

Now he was a little weak but with the people he loved around him Cromlach knew he would not be ailing for long.

Misha the goat got used to Cú the wolf-cub, giving him suckle during the day. At night, Misha stayed at the back of the cave as it was too cold for her to be outside but the cub never bothered her when it was dark, preferring instead to sleep with Gráinne.

Finann kept the other goats in the lower pastures but soon the snows would come, and the herd of goats, for their own

239

survival and to keep them protected from the wolves, would then enter the winter enclosure. The sheds were beside a new *bothán* at the Dún which had been built especially for Finann for the duration of the winter. In the meantime, because Finann was spending so much time with Cromlach, Mora and Gráinne, a new goatherd boy, Ben, grandson of the old woman, Tachta, stayed at Finann's *bothán* and cared for the herd in Finann's absence. Old Tachta was pleased because the boy had no crafts or skills to speak of, but he did have an uncanny way with the animals, especially the goats. Tachta liked the extra milk he brought home and she spent most of her time making cheeses and sour-doughs for the Clan. She liked to keep busy when she still had light in her life.

The wolf-cub lay with Gráinne at night, curled up beside her, his nose buried under her arm, but Mora saw him crawl and push under Gráinne's tunic and she realized what was happening. She had known for a time that he was too young to survive the night without his mother's milk at least once or twice during the long darkness. She had also wondered if Gráinne's own milk supply for her babe, Cormac, had dried up, and if so, then they would need a wet-nurse when he returned.

Now she knew and understood. With quiet fascination, she observed the sleeping woman and the little furry bundle moving at her breast.

The gods had provided the remedy. Mora was going to let it be. Gráinne's ignorance was her bliss indeed.

Two whole moons went past with little changing except the size of the wolf-cub. He was still a playful, furry cub but now he was chewing everything, although he still had some difficulty lapping and preferred to be suckled by Misha. She butted him now if he became too boisterous. Poor Cromlach was still weak but he enjoyed the caring of the two women and the company of the goatherd.

The mid-winter fires were lit on the Solstice but, again, they all missed the Clan gathering, with the story-telling and the singing and poetry all going on in the Dún Hall. The gathering of the holly, *Tinne*, and the mistletoe was always a great occasion, the bright red berries of the holly representing the moon-blood of the woman, and the white berries of the mistletoe the child-growing seeds of the man. There was much hilarity and drinking of the special mistletoe brew. Emer mixed a mulled mead for all, with special spices sprinkled in it, which was sworn to make the long night, the last long night of the year, a special one for the women. A yule-log was replaced on the hearthstone in the Dún Hall, a new oak-trunk which was to stay there until the next longest night. Rowan circles were hung on the cattle and goat sheds to protect the animals for the winter. Finann did this every year with great reverence and this time he showed Ben how to do it.

It was not long after this that Finann returned one morn, excited and obviously bursting with tidings.

"Serb has birthed her babe!" he yelled as he entered the cave, dishevelled and out of breath. The cub scampered under Cromlach's plaid, not used to such noise.

"It was terrible! There was much screaming and terror in the night. No one at the Dún managed to close their eyes to sleeping. Weeping and wailing she was! It was more like a passing over than a birthing, what with Bláth the *seer* speaking in tongues! Emer and Carmel the mid-wife were there to assist at the birthing!"

"Was it a boy or a girl?" asked Mora. "By the way she was child-growing it looked like a boy."

"Aye! A boy! But he is marked . . . he has a berry-stain on one side of his face . . . and there is something else, something no one expected!" Finann paused dramatically.

Cromlach, Mora and Gráinne all waited to hear what Finann had to say. They thought maybe the babe was not formed right or some such thing. Serb was ailing during her child-growing so such a maiming could have occurred, but even they were not prepared for the next shock. Only Gráinne looked a little vague.

"He has bright red hair, red as the fox's brush, red as the Samhain sun! And didn't Emer collapse, such was her shock! Lugnae Fer Trí was called in to the Brighdal *bothán* and he had to carry Emer home. Then a wet-nurse was called because Serb rejected the babe, seeing him as a spirit who caused her too much pain. She spoke in tongues for most of the time, clinging fearfully to Bláth who announced she was taking Serb to Teamhair with her, once she was able to travel."

"And – and the babe?" Mora's lips quivered tremulously.

Finann did not notice.

"Oh, the babe! Well, it seems he is the spawning of Donal Rua – that is why Emer collapsed – it was like his return to her, you see. Scath the Druid was called in to see his daughter. Well, he was shamed for Serb because the Laws of the Brighdal *bothán* had been broken. Lugnae and Emer were also shamed because they now know that Donal Rua broke those Laws. Both Donal Rua and Serb have been punished enough by the gods . . . so declared Lugnae Fer Trí. Then the decision was made that the babe was to be reared by Emer, with a wet-nurse to stay with him for the first year until next Samhain!"

Mora was trembling. Her tongue was firmly squeezed against the roof of her mouth as she gritted her teeth together. A knot formed itself in the pit of her belly and a lump in her throat almost choked her. Tears welled in her eyes.

Cromlach stretched his hand out to comfort her. She turned and ran out of the cave, sobbing as if her heart would break.

Finann stared after her, shocked.

"Did I bring her sorrow?"

Cromlach patted Finann on the back.

"Finann, Mora is saddened because she had set her heart on rearing Serb's son. She has no babe of her own. Her heart is big, Finann, and no one knows better than yourself how much time and devotion she has bestowed on caring for Serb when the rest of us were living our own little lives. We are all responsible for her sorrow now because we did not share the task of caring for Serb during her child-growing. Mora was attached to the notion of Serb's babe replacing the babe of her own, which we know she cannot have. Now, she comes to care for us and Serb births the babe and rejects it, which Mora thought might happen – Serb is an unfit mother – but Lugnae Fer Trí has not turned his back, despite the shame his son brought to the Brighdal *bothán*, and the child will be reared by Emer, as is right and proper. Mora knows this but she still mourns the loss of what she never had and never will have. Help me up, Finann. It is time for me to brace the cold and smell the outside air. I will go to her."

Gráinne was sitting on the floor, rocking the cub in her arms. She was disturbed by Mora's reaction to the news of Serb's babe. There was something that Gráinne thought had been left out, something she thought she ought to know.

Finann knelt beside Gráinne.

"Are you feeling well, *a stór*?"

"I do not know," she said in a small voice. "I feel like I have lost something . . . but I do not know what."

Finann put his arm around her shoulders. It was a clumsy gesture but she rested her head against his shoulder.

"Gráinne, we all feel this way when one of us is pining. Do not fret, *a stór* . . . all will be well."

Gráinne sighed, "You are right, Finann, but I still cannot help feeling that something is hidden, or lost, or else I have forgotten something."

Finann whistled and clicked his tongue for Misha to come in and suckle little Cú, who was restless and trying his best to escape from Gráinne's arms. The she-goat lay down obediently on the rush-strewn floor. This was not the way of the goat, who normally stood to suckle her own young, but she was so used to lying down like the she-wolf now that she did so without having to be coaxed. Gráinne smiled at the cub's enthusiasm and the great amount of tail-wagging as he latched himself on to a teat.

"Finann?" Gráinne twiddled with a rush from the floor, then inclined her head to the side and hesitantly asked, "Why is everyone so shocked that the new babe has red hair?"

Finann wished Cromlach was back. He could not believe that Gráinne remembered so little, but she was looking for an answer now and he had to speak.

"Because no one expected the babe to be sired by Donal Rua, especially not when Serb had chosen C-Cred at the festival of Baltinne, and then after the first moon, Cred chose to stay with Serb. Donal Rua must have taken Serb when she was

243

in the Brighdal *bothán* under the eye of the godd⌐ . This is forbidden."

"I know all about Donal Rua and his love for Serb, but – but Finann, I do not remember Cred . . . who is Cred?"

"You do not remember Cred?" Finann asked softly. "Gráinne, *a stór*, I cannot help you in this. You must ask Cromlach who knows everything."

Finann then began making a fuss of Misha and he played with the cub, letting him nip his hand until it hurt, then he squeezed the cub's jowls between the wolf-teeth to let him know how it caused pain so that it would deter him from biting them as the moons passed. Finann did not want to meet Gráinne's sad blue gaze again. He wished Cromlach would return with Mora.

When Cromlach and Mora came back, it was obvious that Mora nee Derga had been weeping a lot. Her face was tear-stained and her eyes were red and puffy.

Cromlach made her sit down and wrapped his plaid around her.

"You would not thank me, Mora, if I placed my furs around you."

She smiled at his Truth.

Cromlach then called them all together. Even Cú ventured over and tugged at the end of Cromlach's robe, worrying it with his teeth and rumbling in his throat to form a growl. Gráinne tried to rescue Cromlach's robe but he gestured for her to leave it be.

"I have just had a long talk with Mora, my friends, and now has come the time for us to care for her as she has for us. She protests but I insist . . . we have come to rely on her presence and her work too much. It is time for us to return to the Dún dwellings. Finann needs to attend to his goats and train the boy, Ben. Mora needs to put her *bothán* in order and be alone for a while. Our caring for Mora will be in respecting her solitude. We will all be close to her if she needs us. And I will stay with Gráinne and Tula and Cú in the *botháns* beside the Dún Hall until the time comes for us all to leave."

"To leave?" Finann and Gráinne chorused together.

"Aye, I have had a vision of us travelling north. We will wait until the time is right but we must prepare ourselves to leave at the turn of a night if we have to!"

Finann stared down at the cave-floor and he felt himself trembling with awe.

"I – I have never been anywhere other than the Dún of Lugnae Fer Trí," he said. "I know only how to . . . how to care for my goats. Ben is helping me now, but . . . " Finann stammered and was silent.

"But what, Finann? We are not forcing you to come with us but I have seen the road and you are there. I have seen a Truth," said Cromlach kindly.

Finann's heart was pounding. Cromlach had seen him on the road north but his goats were like his babes: he knew them each by character, by name. How could he leave them? He felt miserable. "I cannot go," he said simply. "I cannot leave my goats."

"The time is not yet, Finann. Put it from your mind for now."

Gráinne got up suddenly. She did not want to think about leaving or travelling, not now in the winter.

"Come, let us gather our belongings together and do as Cromlach says. I wish to go back to my *bothán* and I want to see Emer and Lugnae and the new babe!"

Mora thought of Cormac. She hoped the wolf would not return the babe to the cave when they were gone, but Cromlach seemed to know what he was doing. He did not seem unduly worried about the babe for now. She noticed, however, that he reached for his little special bottle and his crane-skin bag to take with him.

Finann went to get a horse and trap from Lugnae so that they could carry everything they needed in one journey. By nightfall, Misha had her creels packed, a little furry head peeping out of one of them, and Finann walked alongside, making sure the cub did not jump out. Mora, Cromlach and Gráinne rode in the trap filled with their furs, food and cooking pots and other bits and pieces they had taken with them. It was a short journey back to the Dún but one filled with tension. Cromlach knew he would have to have counsel with Lugnae Fer Trí soon, as the Chieftain had a right to know what was going on.

They had settled in their respective homes for a day when Cromlach came across Gráinne sitting under the oak with her mantle wrapped around her. She was hugging herself, rocking back and forth and looking very sorry for herself.

"*A stór*? What is wrong? You look very sad."

She turned a tearful face up to Cromlach.

"I cannot remember. Please, please, Cromlach, tell me why I cannot remember everything. Tula handed me something this morn and I – I do not know who gave it to me. I was afraid to ask her."

A tear hung off her eyelashes like a droplet of dew then slid down her face and into her cloak. Cromlach bit his lip. He felt that he was responsible for her confusion and sorrow, but if she had not been placed within the cocoon of forgetfulness, her anguish would have been ten-fold when she realized her babe was gone. Gradually she was going to remember. He hoped that Cormac would be returned by then.

"What did Tula give to you, *a stór*?"

Gráinne pulled an oak-carved box out from under her cloak, put it on the ground in front of her, then wiping her eyes with the corner tail of her mantle and sniffing pitifully, she proceeded to open the box. She took out seven stones and laid them side by side.

"They are inscribed with *ogham*. You see the name on them? It is Cred. Why have I scratched his name on these stones, Cromlach? You must remember for me, please."

Then her voice cracked as she picked up a piece of silk and unwrapping it, placed some delicate little thing on to the palm of her hand. "See, Cromlach. It is a crescent fingernail and there is some hair, but wh-where is the babe, Cromlach? Is – is he in Í-Bhreasail? Please, I have to know. I – I cannot bear it any longer. Have I been ailing?"

Cromlach's heart went out to her. He knew he could no longer withhold the Truth from her but neither did he wish to hurt her by giving it all to her at once. Where could he start? He no longer knew where the beginning was. Cormac's crib and other items had been stored at the Dún to save Gráinne from anguish. But there was always some way in which a veiled Truth revealed itself. He could not blame Tula. She was now working with the Truth.

Gráinne was quiet as she put the little crescent back with the others and wrapped them once more in the silk. She placed the lock of hair back also, fingered the stones for a moment and then tidied everything away into the box and closed it. Her breath was catching in her silent weeping as she then drew something else from beneath her mantle. It was a woven plaid wrapped around some objects which she placed one at a time in front of Cromlach. He was tormented by her distress but let her go through all of the little tokens before he spoke.

Gráinne held out a beautifully artificed golden cup, wrought with great skill and obviously the work of Cred. There was a bronze arrow, a stone of black onyx and a *scian* with a wolf's head carved on the handle and a *delg* worthy of display upon a Queen's mantle. As he looked at these gifts, Cromlach realized the great love Cred had for Gráinne.

"*A stór*, Cred is a *céird*, one of the finest smiths I have ever come across. He was chosen by Serb at Baltinne as the Corn King but his heart was with you, Gráinne. You were child-growing the spawning of Art the Lonely, the deposed *Ard Rígh* who was slain in battle. You birthed a son to him. Donal Rua, the red-haired son of Lugnae Fer Trí, had his heart set on Serb and so his spirit was broken when she chose Cred. He violated the goddess and took Serb, whether by force or consent, it makes no matter, and she has now birthed a boy with red hair, obviously the spawning of Donal Rua. This has surprised us all, and yet it now makes sense, for the Clan have been punished by the gods and Donal Rua forfeited his life. Everyone thought that Cred chose to stay with Serb because she was child-growing his babe, but now we know he was really protecting the name of Donal Rua and the face of Lugnae Fer Trí. Cred is a good man."

"I remember Emer speaking of the bruising on Serb's face. She saw it in the Phoenician mirror. Serb must have been taken by force . . . No wonder we had the storm which destroyed all! But, Cromlach, I know not why I remember everyone around but Cred . . . or my babe! How can I not remember a babe or what happened? Did – did he pass over?"

Cromlach caught Gráinne's hands in his own and gazed into the blue pools of her eyes.

"*A stór*, it is my error. I veiled the Truth to protect you and the babe, Cormac, from the tyrants of the *Ard Rígh*, Lugaid, who slew the father of your babe and would not hesitate to slay his son. I placed a protection on you which made you slumber in the sea of forgetfulness. This protection I placed upon Cormac and Cred also. It means that you will not remember them for a time and neither will they remember you. This was to prevent the babe crying out, or Cred, if he returned, looking for you and leading the tyrants to you. Cred is guided by *the light ones* so they will take care of him . . . '

"Where is my babe?" wailed Gráinne, beginning to panic now. "I want to see him!"

"He is safe. You must believe me, Gráinne . . . he is safe but he cannot return yet."

"Why not? I demand to know where he is, Cromlach! He is my babe!" She was tearful and angry at the same time.

"He belongs body and spirit to the land and the spirits of the land will bring him back when the time is right," said Cromlach quietly.

"How will he live without his mother's breast to suckle him? Has he a wet-nurse then?"

Cromlach was at a loss for the first time in his life. He realized it was impossible to reason with a mother who has lost her child. How was he going to make poor Gráinne understand that the earth-spirits were caring for Cormac until it was safe for him to travel north? Cormac's own destiny for the first years of his life lay in the northern part of the land. Cromlach knew not where, but he felt sure the path would be revealed to him in time.

Gráinne suddenly thought of something.

"My breasts are not dripping milk. How is this so, Cromlach? I have had a babe but I have no milk?"

"It will come back in time," he assured her. He did not want to tell her what he had witnessed and knew to be true, for he saw also that Mora nee Derga had witnessed the same. Both

248

were going to keep quiet about the silent feedings which went on in the dead of the night. It was not that Gráinne would begrudge her milk to the wolf if there was no other way, it was just that she would never accept the replacement of the wolf-cub for her babe.

Gráinne had to be content with Cromlach's answers for now. But she was vexed, even more so because she had no real emotion for the child, having no memory of him. She was afraid to ask Cromlach again where the babe might be, for fear he said he did not know. Cromlach had never been wrong before in all the years she had known him. She decided to put all her trust in his judgements.

But the days went past and little by little memories came back to her. She went to see Emer and the new babe, and as she leant over the crib, her hair falling on either side of the babe, she felt a sharp pang of longing deep within her for another time when she did exactly this . . . but then, the child was older and chuckled and caught hold of her hair in his little fists. She remembered him! A glimpse, but none the less, an important memory. She had a hope that when her memory returned, so would Cormac.

Emer chattered excitedly about the new babe.

"We are naming him Luis, after the red rowan berry. I wanted to name him Ruadh, because of D-Donal Rua, but Lugnae said it was best not to disturb Donal Rua's spirit by giving his name to his son. He said the calling of the name would not give him peace. I do not agree but I will not go against Lugnae. Luis is a good name, it is one of our sacred trees." Emer spoke softly, her eyes misting over as she thought of Donal Rua. But somehow, the pain was lessened now that she had his offspring to care for, and the other siblings were happy to have another babe in the Dún. Emer was now her old self again. They had truly got their mother back.

Everyone was used to Gráinne being there without her own babe. Cromlach had simply gathered them together one day and explained about the sea of forgetfulness on Gráinne and said that the babe was being cared for. Everyone just assumed that Cormac was with Olc Aiche and Dairine at Cruachu and for a time they felt sorry for Gráinne, but now they watched her playing with her wolf-cub and ceased to worry about her. She seemed contented enough.

*Imbolc* was almost upon them when one day the Elder, Dorcha, arrived back at the Dún of Lugnae Fer Trí. He demanded to see Bláth, who was in no hurry to see him. She knew she was being summoned back to Teamhair and she had no intention of leaving without Serb. Serb was well enough to travel now, having recovered from the trauma of birthing a babe, but she was going through the seventh sickness, *the sorrows and the calming*. There was much weeping and wailing and she still aped the animal cries, making the trappers run to see if they had caught rabbits or hares in their snares, and then she would laugh at their frustration when they realized she had tricked them. Bláth was thankful that the birthing seemed to have stopped the insatiable lustings. She no longer had to placate the girl to try to stop her trying to bed every man and boy in the Clan. This was the time for dealing with the long sorrows, terrible keening, made more poignant by the emotional and bodily changes which occurred after the birthing. Bláth was not getting much rest and, although Mora nee Derga came to help her often, Bláth was very jealous of the affection Serb displayed for Mora and could not rest for very long before wanting to take over her charge again.

Bláth knew she could not leave for Teamhair until Serb had begun *the calming of the sorrows*.

Dorcha was also creeping around Gráinne's *bothán* one night to see if the babe, Cormac mac Airt, had returned. Cú growled a low, deep growl which startled Cromlach and Gráinne from their slumber. Cromlach immediately went outside and demanded to know who was there. He saw the hooded figure disappearing into the Dún Hall. He knew it was Dorcha and he was thankful that Cormac was not here but it disturbed him that Dorcha had been sent back to the Dún of Lugnae Fer Trí. Cromlach was sure that it was not just the deliverance of a summons for Bláth to return to Teamhair that brought Dorcha skulking back here.

Three days later, Serb was beginning to enter *the calming*

and Bláth immediately prepared for them both to journey to Teamhair with Dorcha. Bláth did not like Dorcha being around any more than did Cromlach. She knew that the babe should return soon. Already Gráinne was beginning to remember. As soon as her memory returned fully, the wolf would have to bring back the babe. It was best that Dorcha the Elder was well on his way back to Teamhair before this happened.

Lugnae Fer Trí gave Serb and Bláth horses and a cart for their belongings. Everyone came to see them off and gave them presents and food for their journey. Scath the Druid embraced his daughter but he knew that she was gone from him for ever. Only his *knowing* helped him overcome his own sadness. He was glad Serb's mother was not alive to see her now. She would never have desired the life of a *seer* for her daughter, but Scath, although disappointed, was also secretly proud of the worthy position his child was to hold in the future. He knew that Bláth had found her successor and that his lovely daughter was, one day, to be the *seer* for a great and noble *Ard Rígh*, Cormac mac Airt.

Mora nee Derga fought back tears as Serb singled her out and clung to her, kissing her neck. Then Serb whispered something into her ear and pressed a token into her hand. Bláth looked towards the ground, her knuckles white as she clenched her fists to her sides. She could not watch easily as Serb whispered to Mora nee Derga.

"You will be the one to tell my son who his mother truly is. I will meet him again at Teamhair. You, Mora nee Derga, will become a renowned healer with a school at Teamhair for the healing arts. Give this to Luis when the time is right. It will protect him from harm when he truly accepts I am his mother."

Mora nee Derga was astonished at the way Serb spoke to her. She knew she had been given a Truth and her heart skipped a beat at all the implications within the words. Mora could hardly believe what she heard. Her heart soared suddenly and she was filled with a great joy, tears of relief and happiness replacing the sadness she had been feeling for some time now. It was nearly time for her own journey to begin and she was ready. Wistfully, she watched as the party left to go to Teamhair. One day she would meet up with them again. She turned the token over in her hand and stared at a beautifully woven miniature corn poppet, a child's token but too intricate for the clumsy, playful fingers of a babe. Woven and stitched on to the head of the poppet were the long flaxen strands of Serb's own hair, interwoven with the unmistakable red-gold locks of her babe's hair. She had taken cuttings of the fine red hair and expertly stitched them in with her own. It was very touching. Mora nee Derga did not think she could cope with any more feelings and she hurried away back to her *bothán* to find a safe place for the token. She placed it in a piece of plaid, tied it carefully and put it into her medicine bag. She knew as she did so that she was safe-keeping the heart of Serb. Mora never went anywhere without her medicine bag. It was something she guarded with her life.

Gráinne's memory was returning rapidly, bringing her anguish. She was seeing images of her babe with his sun-coloured curls and big blue eyes mirroring her own. There was one vision of a tall, fair man with dark grey eyes like thunder clouds.

It was the day after this vision that Olc Aiche arrived from Cruachu. He went at once to the Dún Hall and demanded counsel of Lugnae Fer Trí and Cromlach, insisting it was of the utmost importance and extreme urgency.

It was the day of Imbolc, when the fire in the earth is rekindled by Brighde the goddess, and the preparation is made for the re-emergence of green growth. The first flowing of milk into the udders of the goats and lambs for their new offspring takes place on this day. The smith's forge is blessed for the making of new tools and the old ones are reconsecrated with the sacred fire. The serpent uncoils itself and the animals rouse themselves from their long winter slumbers.

Cred the smith was not yet back from his travels, so one of Lugnae's own sons, who liked to potter in the forge and had been making tools in Cred's absence, now took over the task of making the new implements. He was just a young boy but he showed promise in working with the fire and he had a great love for it.

Olc Aiche stood before Cromlach and Lugnae Fer Trí. He

was going to see Gráinne afterwards, but now it was her Guardians that he wished to speak with.

"Lugnae Fer Trí . . . Cromlach . . . my good friends, Imbolc is the day which has been chosen for the goddess to begin the uncovering of that which is hidden. Cormac has been resting and growing in the womb of the winter, slumbering with and being suckled by the wolf. Now it is time for you, Lugnae, to use your knowledge of tracking and take your trappers, the most trusted ones to do your bidding, and find the den of the wolf. She will be where the wren sings. Do not try to harm the wolf.

"Cromlach, it is time to take Gráinne to the north, as soon as the babe, Cormac, is found. Go to the Dún of Fiachrae Cassán, foster-father of Art the Lonely. The babe must be concealed from the tyrants of Lugaid, the *Ard Rígh*. You will cross the mountain, Sliab Conachla, and many things will happen on the way so be watchful at all times. You will always be one step only ahead of those who seek you and your lives will be forfeit if the tyrants sight you. Once the mountain is crossed, the rest of the way will be safe . . . but already Lugaid and his tyrants are on their way to Cruachu to look for Cormac mac Airt. I must return there to waylay them from coming here until you have time to find the babe and go north. Please, Cromlach, bring Gráinne to me so I may bid her a good journey."

Cromlach arrived with Gráinne and the young wolf, both of whom greeted Olc Aiche with great affection. Cú wagged his tail and leapt about, barking and panting while Olc Aiche ruffled his fur with one hand and gripped Gráinne to him with the other arm. She was so pleased and excited to see her father that Gráinne hardly noticed that Cú was being so friendly towards Olc Aiche. But Cromlach noticed. He knew the wolf was attached to Gráinne but shied away from those he did not know, his hackles rising and a low growl making itself known which was fierce enough to deter the biggest of men. The wolf was growing fast but although a goat was easy prey for him, Cú had never once tried to attack Finann's goats, and even though he could lap milk easily now, he still tried to get Misha to suckle him. Misha had no fear whatsoever of him and would butt him away when he annoyed her. They often lay down together to sleep and sometimes they played but always it was Misha who chased and butted Cú.

Olc Aiche sat down and explained to Gráinne why he was there. She listened intently to all he had to say but broke down when he told her that the search was started for her babe. She wept silently into his cloak, relieved that the long enchantment was coming to an end and overcome with a longing to have her babe again. Olc Aiche warned her that she was going to be shocked by his size. She had to understand that as the wolf-cub was much bigger now so would be the child.

"It is not safe to travel with just the babe and Cromlach," said Olc Aiche. "It is important to have others with you . . . and dress like peasant serfs, not as befits a noble family. Do not take the bronze looking-glass with you. I know it was a gift from your mother and myself, but it does not belong on the road with you. It will have its place. You will see it again, so never fret, *a stór*. Finann, the goatherd, and the healing woman, Mora, should also accompany you to the North. She is a fine Druidess and you may have need of her healing herbs. You will need milk, so take a goat or two. They will graze by the wayside and give you drink."

"Finnan did not want to leave his goats if we travelled north, Father, so he will be happy now to come with us," said Gráinne.

"Finann knew you were to travel north?" Olc Aiche looked incredulously at Gráinne, then he abruptly turned to Cromlach and offered his arms. They embraced.

"Forgive me, Cromlach, I should have remembered that you are an Elder . . . no, you are superior, for you can *see* clearly and with little effort and already you knew where to take my daughter to a safe part of the land."

"Nay, Olc Aiche, I only *saw* the direction, but although I had a vision of the man, I knew not where he had his abode," Cromlach said humbly.

"I have tried to *see* the den of the she-wolf, Cromlach, but the goddess refused to reveal it to me. We must rely on the tracking abilities of Lugnae Fer Trí who has rounded up his best trappers and they are already on their way to search for her. I have done all I can for now and if I may change my horse and have some sup, then I shall be on my way. I have to reach Cruachu before Lugaid tries to speak with Dairine, who knows not the way of turning Truth. Gráinne, our love goes with you, before you and behind you, and I urge you again: do not fret, your mother and I will seek you out when the time is not wrought with dangers. Truth and Law will be your constant companions . . . heed them well, *mo chuisle*, and there will be no mistakes."

Gráinne hugged her father tightly. She was astounded and filled with awe at his words. Burying her fingers into Cú's ruff she held him tight to her side as she watched Olc Aiche depart. Then she hurried to her *bothán* to prepare for her journey. She was going to take Tula along too to help with Cormac. She was afraid and did not know why she should be afraid of the return of her babe. Was this not all that she ever wanted? She wished Dairine was with her. A wave of longing for her own mother made itself known to her.

Cromlach went to Mora nee Derga's *bothán* first and then braced himself to talk with Finann. He hoped Finann would know how to divide his goats.

# CHAPTER 23

# THE QUEST AND THE CONQUEST

*He is mine again, all mine and no other has a claim.*
*Who dares to say he belongs only to the land?*
*Let them challenge and stand before me now*
*If there is contest, it is I who will win the game.*

Lugnae Fer Trí thought long and hard about the role he played now. He had to find Cormac mac Airt, son of Art the Lonely, son of Gráinne, his beloved foster-daughter. The finding of Cormac mac Airt meant the losing of his foster-daughter, Gráinne. He wondered if he would ever see her again once she travelled to the North. Lugnae Fer Trí knew he had to come to terms with what he was really thinking. If Gráinne left, so would Cromlach who, Lugnae accepted now, was her true Guardian, but Lugnae also realized that if Cromlach went, so would Finann and Mora nee Derga, and when Cred returned, he was bound to want to find Gráinne when he knew that he was free of Serb. Lugnae was feeling very low in spirit. After the passing over of Donal Rua, when the storm almost destroyed everything, the Clan came together to rebuild the Dún. Cromlach came back, Cormac was birthed. There was a merging of minds to make the place whole again, but now it seemed that the people who mattered the most were going away, the strength and backbone of the Clan was leaving. Or had he just placed too much import-ance on the strengths they had each given to the life of the Clan? Others were going to rise up within the Clan, some would leave, some stay. He had to think this way. In order to be a good Chieftain he must balance carefully the weights of his attachments and keep the ways open for all to come and go as they must. He had chosen to make the *ráth*, the Dún, the home for them all. It was his duty to stay there and hold the core of the wheel, to build a place they could return to, a place they thought of as home. Lugnae wanted Gráinne, Cromlach, Finann, Mora and even Tula and Cormac the babe when he grew up, to know that there was always a place for them at the Dún of Lugnae Fer Trí. He thought it and he wished he could say it. He hoped they knew it.

He pulled his horse gently but firmly in to rein and he bade the other trappers do likewise. They were at the stream at the bottom of Knocknarea.

"I think we waste our time looking on the mountain," he said. "It is cold and there are sharp winds there and not much food. The deer will have come down to the forests and near to the grasslands and the wolves will follow. We will try to find the tracks of the wolves, any fur snagged on brambles, or bones of a feast left anywhere at the foot of the mountain. Be careful of the wild hogs or the sows with young piglets if you wish not to be gored to an early passing over. Do you have your horns with you? Good, then use them if you find the den. I want to take the babe to the arms of Gráinne."

"The babe?" asked the trappers in unison, their eyes wide with astonishment.

"Aye! Gráinne's babe was spirited away by a she-wolf. It is now time to find him and bring him back. If any man wishes not to go on this quest, then he must leave now and not utter a word about this to any ear."

There was a lot of mumbling and two of the trappers asked to leave, saying they were not going to search for a spirit-wolf, that this quest was for much braver men than they and that they wanted no part of hunting for that which came from the other-world. As soon as they spoke their minds, three other trappers did likewise, claiming that their families were too important to them and that they would not risk going to Í-Bhreasail, even to save an *Ard Rígh*.

Lugnae Fer Trí spoke softly as he stared at the rest of his men.

"I will not hold it against any man who decides not to go on this quest, if he is not ready for the challenge. It does not mean that you are any less of a good trapper or that your loyalty to myself or the Clan is lessened in any way. This quest calls for more than the bravery of stalking the most fearsome of beasts, or of being in the front line of battle or even of facing the passing over of one's kin. This calls for something more, being able to confront the goddess and demand her prize, without fear, without shame, without violence, but with integrity and honour and strength, even knowing that she can tear one asunder if she so wishes. If there is any other man who cannot accept this challenge, then let him leave now and no more will be said, neither shall I hold it against him."

Lugnae was disappointed when over half the trappers tipped their foreheads to him respectfully and then turned on their horses and rode back to the Dún.

At least Devin, his favourite, had stayed with him. Lugnae did not think he could have coped if Devin, dependable rosy-cheeked Devin, had forsaken him. The right trappers were with him. He counted the heads before him . . . seven, only seven of his trappers had stayed but Devin was one of them!

"Divide into twos and begin tracking, men. Devin will come with me. Spread out as far as from here to the lake. Blow your horns if you find the tracks of a wolf and a wren singing near by for I have been informed that a wren will lead me to the den."

They set out, two at a time in all four directions and then Lugnae suddenly stopped and, turning to his sturdy companion, urged him to stop also.

"Devin, the she-wolf abducted Cormac mac Airt and it is my opinion that she left her cub in his place. If we are to find the babe, it is also my opinion that she will want her cub returned to the pack."

"The wolf will not run with us, Lugnae Fer Trí. He will frighten the horses and will be more of a hindrance than a help."

Lugnae thought for a moment, then hesitantly suggested something which came to mind, something which he did not think was altogether wise but he had to say it.

"What if we take Gráinne with us? The young wolf, Cú,

already rides alongside her when she rides – it lies with the goat too, in the name of all that is sacred! Gráinne should maybe come with us."

"We should try stalking the wolf ourselves first," ventured Devin, unsure if he should speak his mind against what his Chieftain wished to do. "It seems to me that involving Gráinne is a last desperation . . . she may show too much emotion or rage with the she-wolf and endanger the life of the babe and that of herself. I do not think she will part easily with her new companion nor he with her either."

"What? Even in exchange for her babe? Nay, Gráinne is devoted too much to her child."

"Maybe," said Devin, "maybe."

Lugnae looked at him sharply but then realized he could not have known that Gráinne had the sea of forgetfulness around her. It must have been somewhat of a shock for Devin to discover that the babe was not indeed safe with Gráinne's father and mother in Cruachu but had been spirited away by a wolf. Gráinne must have seemed too cold about the situation, not appearing to think or talk about her missing babe, but instead playing and fussing with a young wolf-cub who was so obviously attached to her now. Lugnae said nothing but signalled for them to start the hunt again. If all else failed, they would return for the wolf-cub, and if they did that, they would have to take Gráinne along as well. Lugnae hoped it would not come to this.

It was very cold but the snows had not yet descended upon them, though Lugnae could tell they were not far away now. By the next moon, he was sure, there was going to be snow. The wind was too bitter, biting into the face and stinging the eyes. The clouds were big and fluffy and rounded and they floated heavy-laden and slow, getting ready to drop their cold treasure. Maybe the time was sooner than he thought.

He was searching the ground carefully, his eyes seeking any hint that wolves had passed this way. Usually they hunted in packs but Lugnae Fer Trí knew he was more likely to come across the tracks of a lone wolf in this instance. He listened for the chirping song of the wren as Devin and he entered a small wood near the lake.

They dismounted to search the ground where many prints criss-crossed, and tried to define if those of a wolf were there. As they did so, the sound of the cow-horn rang out from the far side of the lake.

Lugnae's sharp ears picked up the precise direction whence the deep sound came. He mounted his horse and motioned for Devin to follow and they rode fast around the side of the small brown lake, all the while listening to the intermittent blows on the horn.

It did not take them long to reach the far shore, where the two trappers knelt by the side of the lake and a small wren sang its sad song from a nearby tree. This was the sign they had been searching for. Lugnae's heart began to jump as he dismounted and looked at the ground. There were the unmistakable paw-prints of a wolf but there was something very odd about them which caused a shiver to ripple down Lugnae's back. They led to the water as if the animal needed to drink but they did not lead away from the water again. Whatever sort of wolf would come to the water, enter the water, and not return from it, was a strange animal indeed unless it had been attacked here.

There were no bloodstains, no signs of anything having been dragged back from the water, nothing but the prints distinctly leading into the lake.

"Did she swim the lake then?" asked Devin, perturbed, and wondering if indeed he should have come on this quest at all. He wanted to hunt the wild boar or the stag. This was not his notion of proper hunting. It made a man too ill at ease and there was no pleasure or pain in this kind of chase, with no kill to take home for his platter at the end of it all. Devin wanted to return to the Dún. What kind of wolf could swim this lake with a babe in tow? He did not like to think about it but he showed Lugnae he would stand by him and he intended to do just that.

Lugnae looked out across the lake at the large island in the middle, the Isle of Inis Freya. The she-wolf was over there, somewhere in that dense forest, and they had to find her – but how were they to cross the lake? There were no boats, no coracles near by that they could use. All of the seven trappers had gathered now at the sound of the horn and three of them decided to go no further. They asked a pardon of Lugnae and pleaded to return to the Dún. He let them go, then turned to the other two besides Devin and himself and asked them to skirt the sides of the lake to see if they might find a vessel to take them to the Isle.

Lugnae and Devin knelt and fingered the prints and as they did so, a wake of water rippled to the shore, startling them. They looked up and their eyes followed the rings of water lapping up and over the prints, washing back and completely obliterating them. Every print was wiped away. Devin jumped up, afraid, but Lugnae stared at the boat being rowed towards them from the Isle. He was mesmerized, watching the hooded figure leaning forward and drawing backwards, pulling the oars of the coracle through the water. The sound was constant, slapping the brown lake.

Devin backed away as the boat neared the shore and he was even more afraid when the horses bucked and whinnied, their ears pointed back, their eyes round and wild. The horses were not tethered and as the boat reached them, they turned and bolted back in the direction of Knocknarea and the Dún.

There was no retreat now. Devin panicked as he watched an old woman silently get out and wade, tugging her coracle towards Lugnae Fer Trí where he was still kneeling in the dirt, unable to move. Her hood had fallen back from her long grey hair. She was an old hermit, a hag, and when she opened her mouth to speak, most of her teeth were missing, the rest broken. She cackled and pointed a gnarled finger towards Devin, who tried to keep calm.

"Ha! He is afeared of an old woman! You think I am from the *Cnoc Sidhe*, eh?" she asked, her voice wavering and high-pitched. "What way is this to greet a woman who seeks only to trade you some fish for a trinket or two . . . see . . . I have fine salmon, some trout, a perch or a bream. What will you give me, young man?"

Devin was so relieved he would have given her anything she asked for at that moment. She was not Macha, Badb or the Morrighan, nor any of *the dark ones*, she was only a fishing woman, a hermit of the lake, probably living in the forest on the Isle.

Lugnae found his voice at last.

"I will give you five pieces of gold if you will take me to the Isle of Freya."

"Give me five pieces of gold for my fish, and, if you please, the jewel from your mantle if I take you to the Isle, and his friendship if I bring you back again," she said, pointing again at Devin.

"Friendship cannot be traded or bought, old woman. He gives that with his own freedom or not at all," retorted Lugnae.

Devin suddenly got angry, his face red, his eyes soot-black as he seethed: "You old hag, be off with you! Five pieces of gold are given freely, too much for a poor catch! But the jewel from a Chieftain's mantle is not for to grace your rags . . . and my friendship cannot be bartered at any cost for the likes of some toothless crone who dares to insult my Chieftain! Be off with you!"

She laughed and leant on one of her oars as she addressed herself to Lugnae again.

"He is of a loyal nature, is he not? But he will have a lonely heart if he does not mend his ways with women. His friendship I can live without, Lugnae Fer Trí. Only your good self will I take upon my boat and Devin Grec mac Arod, of the dark hair and apple cheeks, will not find a welcome on the Isle of Freya, nor will his kin who come after him for three generations hence! Come aboard, Lugnae Fer Trí. It is time."

"Lift your curse, woman," replied Lugnae. "Devin is a good man who does naught but protect me. He is not deserving of such a curse as this!"

"This is spoken in true friendship, Lugnae Fer Trí. Your friend would be wise to defend you without insult to those who mean no harm. I lift my curse that falls on his kin and he may come to the Isle of Freya when he wills but he must not sup or eat, even though he be dying of the *dreuth* and hunger, and if he should kill anything even by mishap upon the Isle, so shall he be killed. That is my last word."

Devin was very badly shaken. He should have stilled his

tongue. The old woman was indeed the Morrighan. He had insulted the goddess and almost brought shame upon his kin. Now he could not accompany his Chieftain to the Isle of Freya for fear of losing his own life if he accidentally slew something there. Devin realized the extent of his friendship, for he was not prepared to risk his own life to protect his Chieftain. The old woman had taught him a hard lesson about his own fealty to Lugnae Fer Trí, but worse than that, Lugnae was now also aware of it.

Devin watched as the boat pulled away from the shore, his mind in a turmoil. He was a coward. He had to face himself at last and he was shamed to his core. Suddenly, Devin threw himself into the water, calling out Lugnae's name as he swam towards the boat, but the old woman laughed and slapped her oar on to the water, causing a wave to toss him back to the shore. Lugnae looked back and smiled and Devin knew then that Lugnae Fer Trí saw that he, Devin Grec mac Arod, was now a true friend. A great lightness came upon him as he scrambled back on to the bank but he could never be sure if the curse had been lifted or not. What did it matter? He never went near the Isle of Inis Freya anyway. He threw his head back and laughed with the cackling old woman . . . never at her, no, never would he laugh at her.

Lugnae was with the hag, who led him into the deep forest and gave a whistle as she neared a bank of tall pines.

Out of a den in the bank came the she-wolf, one of the most beautiful wolves the Chieftain had ever seen. She was grey, and yet, when he looked again, she was golden or dappled or the colour of cream. Her eyes were amber, glowing like fire-sods, sometimes like the haw-berries, sometimes like the beech leaves at their falling or even the hazel-nuts at their ripening. She was a magnificent beast, with muscular legs. The ruff around her neck was full and fluffed, a deep fur that circled her face, accentuating her fiery eyes. He thought of warmth and honey.

When she saw Lugnae, she stopped and snarled. The hag cuffed her affectionately.

"A friend, Mil, just a friend. He has come to take your fosterling back. Oh, but he does not return your babe, Mil."

Lugnae whispered quietly to the old woman: "If we have to return Cú, we will do so."

"The time will come, Lugnae Fer Trí, when Cú will have to choose for himself whether he returns to the pack or not, but it is not here and not now. Mil would not accept him back with her litter. She has weaned them and is now throwing them out to sire their own packs. I think the fosterling is the last to go. Come . . . take him. She will be glad of her freedom again."

Lugnae stepped forward gingerly and peered into the den. His breath caught in his throat as he reached in and lifted out the squirming, happy bundle of babe. Lugnae was startled by the godly beauty the child possessed, his fair, golden curls, his eyes pale blue as the corn flowers that darkened to the azure of the skies before a storm, and the tiny teeth like pearls in a clam shell. He smiled and chuckled gleefully and the sound was that of the missel thrush and the lark and the linnet. He was clean, naked and unblemished, perfect in every way. Lugnae held him with reverence and was unafraid when the she-wolf came over to smell his scent. She caught the scent of Cú. Lugnae thought so because her tail wagged and she became excited, licking his hands, licking the babe and then panting with her tongue lolling so that she seemed to have a smile about her jaws. Lugnae Fer Trí thought that if ever he hoped to be touched by the gods, this was the moment. Being a hunter and trapper mostly to feed his Clan, he made a boon to himself to ban any man from hunting or killing the wolf for sport.

The old hag said it was time so he reluctantly left the forest, wrapped his mantle around the babe and followed her to the boat. He did not look back but he knew that the amber eyes of the she-wolf, Mil, followed him and would continue to follow Cormac mac Airt for the rest of his life.

Lugnae offered to row the old woman across the lake, while she held the babe, but she refused, saying her duty was not yet done.

As she rowed, Lugnae unfastened the jewelled *delg* on his mantle, reached over and fastened it to her rags. He gave her the five pieces of gold and told her that when she had his friendship, she had the friendship of all within the Clan and that included the good wishes of Devin. She cackled again but this time Lugnae detected the soft chiming of bells in her voice, a sweet music to his ears. There seemed nothing harsh at all and he could have sworn that her hair looked long and flowing like the water, the sun glinting through it, making it shine and sparkle. For a brief moment, she let him glimpse that precious being, that light that is within all.

He stepped out of the coracle and waded through the water to the shore, pausing only to look back at the boat but the sun was shining in his eyes and he thought he saw the shadow of the boat somewhere within it but he could not be sure.

Clutching the child to him carefully, Lugnae was proud to be the Guardian of the babe for Gráinne. Soon she was going to leave the Dún, but for this one act, he knew she would always remember him most and he was glad to be of service.

Devin arrived with horses to take them home. He had sent the other trappers home who had managed to find a boat but discovered it was too late . . . Lugnae was already on the Isle of Inis Freya.

Devin travelled home in silence beside Lugnae and the babe. They rode, each immersed in his own thoughts.

As they reached the Dún, the entire Clan was gathered to meet them at the gateway.

Gráinne ran forward, Cú at her heels, and she had her hands outstretched for the babe even before Lugnae dismounted. Devin helped Lugnae down and Gráinne lifted the babe gently out of his arms, her hair swinging forward so that the infant gripped it and pulled it to his mouth, chuckling and chattering the talk of a babe. Gráinne wept, her tears falling on his cheeks and staying there like dew on a rose. She rubbed her face into his head, drinking in the smell of the babe and that of the she-wolf too. Cú nuzzled in and Cormac caught his ruff gleefully. Cú also smelt the familiar scent of his own mother, and the child and the wolf accepted each other, bonded as they were.

Gráinne raised her eyes to Lugnae. The gratitude and love that shone from them was overwhelming and more than Lugnae could have wished for. He felt a tightening in his chest and could no longer bear to see her there, knowing that soon she was leaving and he had hastened the day by returning to her the most important thing in her life. Lugnae strode quickly back to the Dún Hall, back to Emer and Luis and all his other children, but he still felt he was losing a daughter, the pain was no less than the pain of losing his son, Donal Rua.

Gráinne hugged the babe to her as they walked back to the Dún, everyone putting their hands out to touch the girl and the child, their eyes misting over as they beheld the reunion, but Gráinne was not aware of them.

She whispered into his ear: "I was so afraid. You are mine again, all mine and no other has a claim. Who will dare to say you belong only to the land? Let them challenge and stand before me now, for if there is contest, it is I who will win the game. Cormac, *a chuisle*, you are mine again, all mine!"

# CHAPTER 24

# THE PARTING OF WAYS

*Many ways north and many south,*
*Many ways east and many west;*
*And all ways leading to the centre*
*But only one to reach the heart.*

The journey was going to be a long one, so Gráinne began packing everything in plaids to go in two covered *vardas* which Lugnae gave to them. She had been released from her cocoon of forgetfulness, her joy at knowing her babe and finding him again being unequalled by anything else in her life. She was afraid to leave him out of her sight for even the shortest length of time in case he was spirited away from her. Tula was glad to have the child back, not really understanding fully where he had been, but it took her the best part of a day to get used to the animal smell of the wolf which seemed to be in his hair and on his skin. She knew it was a wolf because the scent was also peculiar to Cú. Gradually, over the next night, Cormac's scent changed as he supped at Gráinne's breast again. The milk was now flowing freely, for Mora nee Derga had given Gráinne some herbs to increase it.

Cromlach was surprised at how eager Mora was to begin the journey over the mountains. She wanted a change, needed to find herself too. The warrior who had taken her at the cave was prominent in her mind. Something was restless deep within herself now, something she had to face that was unavoidable. He had fired a hunger in her which caused her to examine the limitations she had placed upon herself. She yearned for change, knowing that she was alone despite being surrounded by friends and the Clan. She wanted a mate, but one who was not going to encroach upon her privacy and who would respect her solitude at times but be available when needed. It seemed selfish, though Mora knew that hers was the way of the Druidess, whether she had taken the vows or not.

Finann did not want to leave his goats, but the thought of living at the Dún without the presence of Cromlach, Mora and Gráinne was daunting. And Cred? Where was Cred? Cred did not know yet that Serb had birthed her babe nor that the Clan now knew the babe was sired by Donal Rua. Finann was happy for Cred but he knew that if Cred returned and found Gráinne gone, he would leave the Dún to go after her. Finann had to go. He loved his friends. They were the only family he had but he was broken-hearted to leave his goats behind. The Clan needed the herd for milk, curds and the making of cheese, so Finann knew he could not take the goats with him.

Cromlach put his arm around Finann's shoulders.

"Finann, my friend, I know you are tearing your heart out because you may have to leave your goats . . . but not all of them, Finann. We can take Misha with us and a he-goat for her company and to start a new herd elsewhere. More than that we cannot take with us because they must ride in the *vardas* sometimes. There will be room for Misha's creels in there too. It will be a new life for you, Finann."

Finann was stricken with fear. He did not know the cause of it or why he was feeling this way but the thought of leaving the Dún did not excite him. Strangers made him uneasy, enough for him to retreat out of their way but the physical effect on his body was what disturbed him most. He would break out into cold sweats, his heart thudding uncomfortably and his tongue was as if in a vice, unable to move or form words. After several long days it passed. Then he was able to converse with ease, almost forgetting the initial terror he went through. When Bláth and the warriors arrived with Dorcha the Elder, Finann kept out of their way at first until he got used to them.

Now he was actually going out from the Dún to meet them!

Cromlach saw the flicker of fear in Finann's eyes and he knew what was worrying him. He had studied the strange reactions of Finann for too long now not to know his innermost thoughts.

"Finann, when you go to a strange land, then you are the

stranger. They have to get to know you. It is different, you will see. At the Dún, Finann, because of the unrest in all of Éiriú under the rulership of Lugaid, a stranger coming to one's *bothán* is a possible tyrant before he proves himself otherwise. These are the times in which we live and a reversal of our true nature which is to greet everyone as a friend until they prove to be otherwise. We will be too busy proving ourselves as harmless travellers and friends when we travel, that really, Finann, you will have no time to think about whether they are hostile or not. Furthermore, it is highly unlikely they will be hostile, as they will be paying too much attention to trying to make a life in their own dún. To them, we are more likely to be the invaders. I will speak for us whenever we arrive at a settlement. Anyway, you have the strength of Gráinne and Mora nee Derga with you also, both of whom are excellent Druidesses, if I may say so. They work for the goddess, Finann. It is important to know that nothing will happen to you."

"Cromlach, you know me better than I know myself. But my fear is not that something will happen to me. I know only this place and this is the land I love . . . every blade of grass on the mountain is known to me, every shrub, every tree has its place in my heart. I cannot remember not knowing this place. How can I leave it to go elsewhere? I am wary of the strangers who come here only because they may separate me from the land and the land from myself. It is a madness I have never been able to conquer. And now . . . and now it is my friends, the only people I truly know and love, who are doing just that," he said miserably, his voice catching on a sob.

Cromlach realized for the first time how much the land meant to Finann, not just the Dún but the land itself.

"Finann, you are a true worshipper of the goddess and of everything the gods have offered you. I feel humble now in your presence, for in all the days and nights of my life, I have not had such a reverence for my land as you have . . . you, a simple goatherd upon the mountain . . . Even my exile and hermitage was one wrought with many frustrations and hostilities in hard winters. Still, with all the fierce beauty surrounding me and the calm of the peaceful days, I did not find the love for my land that you have, Finann. But you only know one small piece that is part of something much greater. If you feel like this about your patch of land, think, Finann, when you have all of Éiriú as your goddess before you. I envy you that ecstasy, my friend. If only my heart and head were as content with nature as yours and did not speak to me in so many tongues. I am striving for the simple ways you earned as your birthright." He said this with such passion and pain that Finann looked at him in wonder. How could such a great Druid wish to be like himself? Finann could hardly believe that Cromlach had spoken to him like this, yet he knew the older man uttered a Truth. Never had Finann known him do otherwise. Maybe Cromlach was right. He would look at the rest of the great land he travelled on as just being an extension of the land he already lived on. Was that not all it was anyway?

Finann made up his mind. He embraced Cromlach with a great surge of warmth in his heart for him.

"I will pack my baggage, little as it is, and I will leave with some longing but without remorse. When are we to go, this night or the morrow?"

Cromlach patted him on the back.

"Olc Aiche will delay the warriors of the *Ard Rígh* for a day or two more, but we must go as quickly as we are ready. I think we will all be fresh after a good night's rest. So, let us leave at dawn with the new sun."

Gráinne turned at the sound of a footfall behind her and saw Cromlach's smiling face and figure.

She clapped her hands together delightedly.

"He is coming! He is coming, is he not?"

Cromlach nodded but he was too tired to tell her about it now.

"Finann is a good spirit, devoted and loyal to his land. It was difficult to sway him but it is done. I am fatigued, *a stór*, so forgive me if I rest and not help you at present."

"Of course, of course, Cromlach. Go inside. Cormac is sleeping and Tula has some brew on the hearth for you to drink. I will finish this first cart by sundown. When do we go?"

"Sunrise," he answered as he entered the *bothán*, wanting

only to put his head down. Speaking with Finann had caused him to confront his deeper thoughts. The Truth he had spoken had even startled himself. He wanted to seal up those vulnerable bits, keep them well away from the surface, for it was neither the time nor the place for them to display themselves.

Emer sent two of the trappers over to help Gráinne and Mora lift their oak-chests into the two *vardas*. They fitted neatly into the back of the wagons under the oak-carved pallets. Inside were their garments, trinkets and linens, herb and scent potions for cleansing their bodies and medicines for any and all ailments. Their pots, pans, flints and utensils were stowed away in another long box which also served as a pallet, but no matter how little they thought they were going to take with them, it soon became evident that they would need another covered cart. Lugnae obliged and it was agreed that this smaller cart was for Finann and the goats and the utensils. Mora nee Derga and Tula were in one *varda* and Gráinne and Cromlach in the other with Cú and Cormac the babe, although Gráinne and Tula were going to take turns in looking after Cormac. They were to travel in a line, always within sight of one another, as close as possible, and if one wagon had to stop for any reason, the others must do likewise. The rule was never to get parted from one another.

All of them were used to working with horses and could ride easily but Mora nee Derga was an especially fine horsewoman, able to control them with a simple clicking of the tongue. She said she would teach the others the little body tricks with which one had complete supremacy over the animal.

There was much excitement and urgency now. Gráinne wondered if sleep was going to come easy that night.

There was something she left to the very last. It had to go with her, but she wanted to have one last look in it before she packed it safely away.

As she lifted the little box up to open it, she suddenly sat down on the floor in her *bothán* and clasped the wooden container tightly against her breasts. It hurt and she did not care.

"Oh, Cred . . . what am I to do? You will return and I will be gone . . . or maybe you will not return. It is past the time for you to come back and I fear you may have found another.

271

How will you know where I have gone to if I do not know myself where I am going? I have the name of the Dún and we know it is north but that is all," she whispered in despair.

She opened the box and fingered the *delg*, tracing the beautiful gold lacework on the brooch. It was the finest thing she had ever possessed and it was hard to look at it and believe that Cred was not returning. The work and the love he must have put into it was not something he could easily forget, therefore Gráinne was sure he must be on his way back to her. She remembered how angry she had been when she thought he had spoken an Untruth to her. Now she knew he had given her a Truth. Serb's babe was sired by Donal Rua. That was quite obvious to everyone now. Gráinne thought about the marks Emer had seen on Serb when Serb told her she had the tooth-pain and then uncovered her face in Emer's quarters thinking that no one was watching . . . but Emer had seen her in the Phoenician glass. Serb was black and blue. Gráinne did a quick calculation of the moons that went by before the birthing of Luis, and now she knew! Serb was taken by Donal Rua in the Brighdal *bothán* by force. It was no wonder the goddess brought the storm! No wonder Donal Rua had passed over! And that knife wound Cred had received at the time was done with Donal Rua's *scian*. Donal Rua obviously tried to slay Cred.

Gráinne thought all these things and felt great compassion for Donal Rua . . . he must have loved Serb so much. She understood that love now. Did she not have the same feelings for Cred?

Gráinne was weary. The ways were cleared and the past was cleaned and here she was, waiting, waiting for him to come back, knowing, knowing he would not return in time. 'That would be too easy for the gods,' she thought irreverently, as she carefully packed the little box into the *varda*.

The next morn arrived before they knew it. Cromlach had rested the night before and packed his few things before the sun came up. Gráinne woke up early with the babe Cormac, and went over to see Emer in the Dún, knowing that Emer was going to be up and about with Luis. Gráinne wanted to have a bath with Cormac in Emer's lovely bath. Emer came in and bathed Luis too and Cormac put his hands out to the new babe, speaking and chattering all the while with his sweet babe-talk. The eyes of the babe stared at him in fascination. Then Cormac did a strange thing. He put his hand out and touched the red-berry mark on Luis's face, then placed his whole hand on it and closed his eyes for a moment. Gráinne was surprised at the action, almost expecting the mark to disappear, but, of course, it did not, although something passed between the two babes. She was sure of that. Emer brought linens to dry them all and wished her friends were going to stay. Cormac would have been a good companion for Luis, but they were going away and there was nothing to be done about it. After they were dressed, Gráinne handed over Cormac to Tula, then she went into Lugnae's quarters with Emer, at Emer's bidding.

"Gráinne . . . Achtán . . . " said Emer, brokenly. "We are sorry to lose you, foster-daughter, for you have been like a real daughter to us and I hope we have been good for you, *a stór* . . . I know we had our little times when we did not see eye to eye but we have always loved you and cared for you and now . . . Lugnae, you – you tell her . . . I – I am going to weep."

Gráinne felt a lump come into her own throat. She threw her arms affectionately around Emer.

"We will see each other again. I know it in my heart, Emer. Lugnae, tell her please that this is so. I – I cannot bear to see her cry."

Lugnae laughed at the two of them clinging to each other, but he was also feeling choked. This was the beginning of the scattering of the Tribe.

"Why do you bother to talk, women? Each of you asking me to talk for you! Of course we will see each other again! The fire will always be lit for you, Gráinne, if you ever wish to come back here. You are always welcome at the Dún and that goes for any of your kin and that old Guardian of yours too!" Lugnae said, his face beaming a huge grin although his eyes were sad.

"Cromlach will be pleased to hear that, my dear foster-father Guardian!" said Gráinne tearfully, hugging Lugnae as she did so.

He clasped her tightly against him, then being not one for too much hugging, he broke away and picked up something wrapped in linens and handed it to her. It was quite heavy and long and he helped her support the weight of it while she unwrapped it to see what it was.

She let out a squeal of absolute delight when she saw what it was . . . a small looking-glass for travel, not unlike Emer's Phoenician long-mirror, but one half the size. It had a highly polished metal surface, which reflected perfectly her face full of excitement and joy at having such a coveted prize in her possession. Lugnae must have known that Olc Aiche had forbidden her to take the gift-mirror with her.

"Oh, thank you, thank you! This is the best present I have ever had . . . a looking-glass for travelling! Lugnae and Emer, I shall always look into this and think of you. And – and when you visit, Emer, you shall use it. Oh, how can I ever thank you both enough for what you have given to me, not just the looking-glass but the care and love you have constantly rained upon me . . . even – even when I was not deserving of it. My gratitude swells in my heart, Lugnae, because you gave me back my babe, knowing that his return meant the splitting up of your own Clan. But he is to be an Ard Rígh, Lugnae, and I know that you were the chosen one to bring him from that . . . from that other world. May you always have peace in your home, both of you, only shattered by the laughter and games of children."

Gráinne could no longer speak, such was the misery which swamped over her. She motioned for them to help her go outside to pack her new looking-glass in one of the *vardas*, then she clung to them as if she never wanted to let them go. At last, she found her voice again.

"Lugnae, Foster-father, it is hard to ask anything else from you when you have been too generous already, but I need you to do something which will mean more than anything to me. Please, please . . . when Cred returns, I would be so grateful if you . . . "

Lugnae interrupted her immediately.

"Gráinne, it is done! Of course we will tell him where you have gone to and which road you have taken, but he will have to find out, just as you will have to, where this new Dún is situated in the North. Now, be gone with you! I – I cannot bear to look upon your sad face."

And that was how Gráinne left her foster-family. She watched as her dear Cromlach went in to say his farewell. Then Finann and Mora nee Derga went next.

The fleeces, furs, rugs and food supplies were added to the carts and they were all ready to go.

Lugnae and Emer did not stand outside the Dún to wave them off. Gráinne was glad of this, but Ben and old Tachta were there, old Tachta crying that she was not going to be there for too long now, and that she would never see Éiriú under the rulership of Cormac mac Airt, more was the pity. Gráinne reminded her gently that she might yet be birthed again into a place at Teamhair and be likely to witness it all!

The trappers and their wives and children all stood silently watching the procession of covered wagons go past and leave the Dún. Some of the women wiped their eyes on the tails of their garments. The children called Misha by name, laughing at her head peeping from the cart. The he-goat, Gab, was frightened by the cart and sat at the back, well away from Misha and Finann.

Finann's eyes brimmed tears which overflowed and ran down his face but he did not care who saw them and although he was holding the reins in his hand, he hardly guided the horse at all. It was lucky that the horse had a sure foot and knew how to keep to a trail, for Finann could not move his body. His fear and his misery had challenged his excitement and won. He dared not look at anybody, did not want to see them wave, did not want to think that he was leaving the Dún and the Clan and his goats, most of all, his goats. He had kissed and embraced them all. He had gone down on his knees to kiss the ground in his *bothán*, then his hearthstone, and lastly his goats. Never did he think he could know such sadness, such abject misery as this!

Cromlach spent some time in the Grove before he left, weaving an enchantment for the safe-keeping of the Clan left behind at the Dún, then he hoisted himself up beside Gráinne at the front of the *varda* and took the reins. Cú had his head out, resting on Gráinne's shoulder, panting and wetting her plaid but she did not seem to mind. The babe slept at her breast, wrapped well within her mantle under the plaid rug.

It was a cool morn so they all wrapped themselves well in their plaids and furs, except for Mora nee Derga who sat up beside Tula in the wagon behind Cromlach and Gráinne, Finann taking the rear. Mora had a woollen rug thrown around her shoulders. They set off on the road that led to the North, where they would go through a gap behind the mountain of Knocknarea, then through marshlands, forests, bog and hills to the traders' mountain pass, much of the territory being hostile with no trail, only the north star to guide them in the right direction.

They were silent, each engrossed in the separate dealings with their hearts. The *vardas* swayed and jolted over the terrain, settling into a steady rhythm, little clouds of dust fanning up from the wheels. As the wheels turned they rumbled, squeaking from time to time, which made the horses move their ears and flick their tails. The steady clop of the hooves crunching on the ground was a sound which would etch itself indelibly in the souls of the travellers. All day and sometimes into the night they were going to hear it as they rode on, battling the terrain and the cold, their only comfort being that very sound which told them they were moving ever closer to their destination.

Breath streamed from their mouths like puffs of smoke from a fire, this fire being without warmth, and they were reminded of the winter, the cold harshness of the goddess in winter. Only those with great courage and a special destiny dared to challenge the goddess in winter.

# CHAPTER 25

# CRED'S JOURNEY

*It is now time to remember and time to return.*
*My heart beats with yours though we are apart,*
*Your pulse hums the song that calls for the start*
*Of the wish to forget the days I have mourned.*

Cred willed his horse to travel faster. He did not like to use the whip on him. He liked to think they were friends and had an understanding of each other, but now Cred was impatient to get back to the Dún of Lugnae Fer Trí. It was past the time he should have returned.

Something had happened when he was at his father's *ráth*, something strange which had never occurred before. One evening he suddenly felt very tired and drowsy, right in the midst of rowdy festivities which his father had laid on in the Great Hall, one of many feasts which were continually taking place to celebrate the return of the wayward son. His father used every excuse he could to have a banquet, with music, dancing and laughter which lasted into the night, the dawn greeting the exhausted revellers as they made their way to their pallets. Many concubines and bond-maids flashed their eyes coquettishly at the handsome young man who had just returned, making Cred aware that he would have to bed one of them soon. There was a lovely young woman with long black hair who reminded him of Gráinne, but her eyes were brown, not blue. They were soft and inviting though, reminding him of a gentle doe's eyes, round and appealing with long, sweeping, dark lashes.

He made up his mind to have her that evening, pushing thoughts of Gráinne away. Recently, it seemed easier to do this. He wondered why he did not feel as close to the memory of his dear Gráinne as he had done previously but he assumed it was the distance or the time separating them which grew every day. It was as if she had created a wall between them which was impenetrable. He had to be sure she was the one, he kept saying to himself, and that very evening he determined to bed Úna.

Throughout the day Úna made it very plain to him that she wanted to take him to her *bothán*, touching his arm or leg if she was near him, deliberately rubbing her side against his when she walked with him to the forge to show him some article the smith was making for her. Úna's long brown fingers intertwined with his own, her index finger circling the palm of his hand. He could tell by her ragged breathing that she was becoming excited, small beads of perspiration breaking out on her forehead and a sweet damp mustiness emanating from under her arms, staining her tunic. She had a smell about her that should have made him want her even more but he remained calm and not particularly moved to do anything about her. She wanted him. That was obvious. He thought he wanted her but that remained to be seen. His fingers crushed hers as he made a fist even though their hands were still interlaced. She yelped with the sudden sharp pain and he instantly let go of her hand. He had not realized that he was hurting her. She was sorry, though, that she had cried out, knowing as she did so that the moment of intimacy was now gone, but she still pursued him until, at last, after they left the forge, he pulled her roughly against him and placed his mouth on hers. His lips moved with hers, a kiss that he knew he would forget by the morrow, but her own passion was intense and she plunged her tongue between his teeth, moving and writhing her body against him.

Maybe she was being too forward. He did not know what was wrong with him, so, being unable to respond fully, he gently freed himself from her clutches, whispering gruffly: "This night, Úna, after the feasting . . . after the feasting."

She whined but released him, licking her finger and tracing it down his cheek provocatively. She swayed her body from side to side as she walked off towards her *bothán* without saying a word.

Cred hurried back to his quarters and lay down on his pallet. He did not like being chosen by a woman. It reminded him of

Serb and the heartache that had caused. But his needs were great and the woman he had chosen was far away. What did it matter if he indulged in some coupling. There were no rules against sharing one's body with another.

That evening, the feast was well under way when Úna left her place where she sat with the other concubines and made her way over to Cred.

Her hair was braided in a number of plaits all sealed with tiny gold balls. She had ear ornaments which hung from her ears down to her shoulders. Her breasts were jutting forward, rubbing against his shoulder, as she leaned forward and nibbled his ear.

It was at that precise moment that he became aware of a curious light across the Hall. He thought Cromlach the Druid was standing there in the light, but decided that that was not possible. Then he saw *them*, bright and solitary, standing beyond the end of the table and *they* seemed to move as one body of light around him until, at last, he was surrounded and felt himself spinning into a blanket of warmth and in it there was nothing, nothing to see nor hear, nothing to think about. He felt himself keel forward on to the table, heard voices far away for a brief time, was aware of being shaken and carried somewhere, and then there was only sweet oblivion.

He knew not for how long he remained in this state, but one day he was aware of waking up on his pallet, heaped with furs to keep him warm, a blazing fire on the hearth spitting as it was being stoked to a greater flame by his mother.

"*Máthair*?" he said, making his mother jump suddenly and drop the irons for the fire. She raced over to him, wiping the ashes from her hands on her robe, and embraced him, tears welling in her eyes.

"*A chuisle*! Where have you been? We have had physicians from far and near to tend you but none knew what sickness had come upon you."

"Sickness? I was ailing?" Cred was surprised.

"Aye! You did not know? Cred, you had a long sleeping sickness. Even the Elders could not say what ailed you, neither did they know if you were in pain or needed some medicine herbs. I have taken turns with – with Úna . . . you know the bond-maid, Úna? . . . to keep vigil."

He remembered Úna, with the brown arms and legs, the swaying motion of her body as she walked, the large brown doe-eyes which were so inviting. He was to meet her later. They were going to get together after the feast. There was something else niggling at the back of his mind but he could not quite recall what it was.

"I have been sleeping long? What? One night, maybe two?"

"Nay, *a chuisle*, for two whole moons! We have been sick with worry ourselves. Every day we turned you so that your body would not get the bed-sores. We oiled your body, wet your lips, and we implored the gods to bring you back to us."

Cred was aghast. He could hardly believe he had been slumbering for all that time. Now, he intended to make up for it.

His father arrived and made a great fuss of him, calling upon everyone to celebrate, his son had awakened. Úna was smiling and tearful, caressing his face and smothering him in kisses, but he was still weak. It would take some time for him to strengthen his body again. He wondered why he had been slumbering for so long and then he remembered that *the light ones* had come and wrapped him in a cocoon of warmth. That was the last thing he recalled.

After several days, he was able to get up and walk about. Úna was constantly by his side, hanging on his arm now, whereas she had been supporting his arm before when he needed to attend to his ablutions. She was ever there. Cred was not yet fit to bed her but he had every intention of doing so whenever he felt strong enough. He had the feeling that he had to go somewhere but knew not where.

One night he bedded Úna. She flailed and thrashed her body beneath him, slapping her belly against his, yelling, biting and nipping him as she drove herself into a wild fury. She cursed him for having made her wait so long. He became caught up in her frenzy, sweat pouring off him as his muscles hardened and rippled, arching his back to charge into her again and again. Grinding into him until his pelvis rasped with hers, she at last spilled over into an ecstasy, yelling at the top of her voice so that he smothered her mouth with his own to keep her quiet. The moment was lost. He could not release himself but waited until she panted to a halt and then withdrew gently. She became angry and aggravated with him, tears slipping down her cheeks.

"Why? Why did you not spill your seed in me?" she asked, hurt by his apparent rebuff. "Is there another?"

He shook his head. He did not think so, but some vague memories were beginning to haunt him. He remembered the Clan of Lugnae Fer Trí now and he remembered Serb but he knew he did not love Serb. He thought there was someone else but could not recall her.

Úna stayed with him that night. The next day, there were sly looks and knowing smiles at the couple. They all knew Úna was a noisy lover. It was obvious though that she had her heart set on this young man, Cred, and they were interested in watching the development. Cred's father was very happy. He wanted Cred to give up his plan to be a master smith and settle down in this tribe, making fine sons and daughters. Úna was different from the other concubines, being capable of loyalty when she lived with the right person. Cred needed to be part of this Clan again so that one day he could take over from his father. Úna would be quite the queen bee.

That same day, Crèd managed to give Úna the slip for a while and he went down to the ostler to ask him for a horse and his chariot so he could take it for a drive.

As he stepped into it, he realized that it contained a trunk full of precious metals and stones. For what reason, he knew not. There was something else too. In a little skin bag were two stones, and scratched on both of these was the name 'Gráinne'.

He sat on the floor of his chariot and fingered the stones, trying to recall why he had them and why he had scratched the name upon them. Who was this woman?

He had missed Samhain and the long night of mid-winter. The only way he supposed to find this Gráinne was to return to the Clan of Lugnae Fer Trí.

Avoiding Úna for the next three nights by pleading fatigue, which was quite true, he began to plan his journey back. He awakened one morn with Gráinne's name on his tongue and a memory of a babe who was going to be an *Ard Rígh*, a babe for whom he was going to make a splendid chalice. The purpose of his journey had been to find the gold, precious metals and stones, needed to perform such a sacred Craft. He remembered trading at the ports for the precious jewels which came in on the sailing ships.

Later that day, the vision of Gráinne flooded into his head, blinding him to all else. He packed whatever he wished or needed to take with him, bade farewell to his father and mother, then soothed a weeping Úna, trying to shut his ears to her pleading, ranting and raving, before he left on the journey northwards. He bestowed gifts on Úna, tried to reason with her but to no avail. She threw a string of curses at him, vowing revenge for her humiliation, especially after she devoted so much time to him when he was ailing with the sleeping sickness. It was all for nothing. Surely she was deserving of much more than a few trinkets. These were finely and beautifully wrought to perfection by Cred's own hands, but she wanted him, not his work. Nothing would appease her, so he just had to leave when he could get away, paying the ostler not to serve Úna with a horse whereby she could follow him.

The winter sun set and the darkness descended fast upon the land forcing Cred to dismount and make a camp for the night near a river. Wolves howled in the forest but he was not afraid. He built a fire and boiled some water for a herb tea to warm himself. Hunger pangs reminded him that he must eat and feed and water his horse. He gave the horse some roots and oats, then led him to the river to drink. There was a clearing where someone had camped recently and the new grass-shoots were accessible for the horse to graze upon, the branches and brambles having been cleared away. It seemed that a sizeable party had been here maybe for a few nights. A pig-skin bag had been left behind but it contained only a mug and a poor-man's plaid, some salt and a small silver spoon. Cred wondered where the owner was now. This was the trail that led to the Dún of Lugnae Fer Trí. Cred reckoned it was half a day's journey from his foster-home. He could not wait to see Gráinne.

His mother had packed provisions for him before he left and

he sat in front of the fire, wrapped in his furs, eating contentedly. The crackling flames and the warm glow made him feel drowsy and he curled into a ball and fell into slumber.

A sudden whinnying from his horse woke him up with a start. The fire was smouldering, barely alive, its flame not throwing enough light by which to see. Cred peered into the darkness and was aware of a movement on his right. He quickly pulled his *scian* from his leggings and crept forward in that direction. This was where his chariot was, filled with his belongings and the precious metals for making the Chalice. If there were thieves about, Cred vowed to make them pay dearly.

He saw a looming figure in the darkness, lurking by the wheel of the chariot and he crept softly up behind him like a cat stalking its prey. He pounced. There was a struggle and Cred wrapped an arm around the man's throat, placing the cold blade of the *scian* against his neck.

"You are looking for something, my friend?"

"Do – do not k-kill me! I am without weapons and returned to this clearing because I – I left something behind me here," answered the man fearfully.

"Who are you?" demanded Cred, not taken with his story.

"Ferda. My name is Ferda. I am one of Lugaid mac Conn's serfs. The *Ard Rígh* is heading north-west."

Cred was disturbed and let go of the man, then lit a torch from the fire and looked upon the serf's face.

"What manner of business brings our *Ard Rígh* away from Teamhair, my friend? Are you on a raid with warriors?"

"Nay. The *Ard Rígh* is visiting a dún which is not far from here."

"The Dún of Lugnae Fer Trí, by chance?"

"Aye! Now, be a good man and help me find my booty. It is not of any worth to anyone except myself."

"Will this be it?" asked Cred, pulling the pig-skin bag from behind a bush and presenting it to the fellow.

"Aye, that it is! I had no intent to startle you, my friend, but you know how it is, a man needs his plaid and his mug on a winter's night like this."

"And his salt and his spoon too," said Cred. "Sit yourself

down, if you have no hurry, and I will bank up the fire so we can sup."

Ferda sat down while Cred made them a fire and put some food on for the man. He seemed very hungry and thirsty and glad of an ear to listen to him.

"I am weary, man. We have been traipsing over hill and dale looking for the traitors. One of our warriors never came back from a quest there before, and we believe he may be helping the traitors to escape."

"Traitors?" Cred asked, surprised.

"Aye. There are those who wish to usurp the *Ard Rígh* who are now in hiding. We intend to scour the country until we root them out. Lugaid has a madness upon him now, believing that a new *Ard Rígh* has been birthed! Two white bulls have hailed him and Lugaid does not want to chance leaving it be, even though the usurping may not take place for another twenty years or so! He thinks it is better to rid the land of the babe now rather than risk his sons or himself being killed later!"

Cred's face was ashen.

"And – and the mother?" he asked hesitantly.

"Lugaid is to judge them for their treachery. The woman who would lie with an *Ard Rígh* before battle, knowing she was to fall with child, is knowing of her plan . . . especially a Druidess. Lugaid wants only to see the land rid of those protecting the new birthed *Rí*. A new *Ard Rígh* is proclaimed after winning a battle against the old one or is a birthed or chosen heir from the old. Lugaid will see this one gone. It is not secret, so I am not gabbing a Truth that should not be gabbed. Everyone knows of his intent."

"Where is your party that I may join them?" Cred asked urgently, a plan forming in his mind. He had to get word to Gráinne to flee, had to save the babe. If he tried to pass the party of the *Ard Rígh* and go ahead, they would be suspicious of his intentions. Somehow he was going to try to delay them from reaching the Dún, so that he could then either race ahead and warn Gráinne or get a message somehow to Lugnae Fer Trí.

"The *Ard Rígh* will only be too glad of another strong and

able body. Lugaid has need of loyal warriors, and besides, he conducts a raid now and again. A fellow like yourself is quick to action and nimble with the knife. I shall gladly recommend you to him."

"You do that, my friend," answered Cred darkly, poking the fire with a stick and casting his eyes towards the ground so that Ferda could not see the smouldering hatred that lurked in his heart. Cred's blood ran cold. He wanted to kill for the second time in his life. He remembered such a day before, when he slew the pheasants. He had been looking for Gráinne then too.

There was no time to lose. He sat with the stranger until the first break of dawn, not daring to rest his head for any more sleeping, although Ferda did drop his head and shut his eyes. Whether he was really sleeping or not, Cred did not know, but he was not going to risk closing his own eyes.

They packed up the camp and hitched the horse to the chariot, then began their journey to catch up with the party of the *Ard Rígh*.

It did not take them long. Ferda made the introduction, by this time knowing Cred's name. He told a great story of how he was almost put to the knife until Cred realized he had no weapon and that he was from the *Ard Rígh*. Lugaid was pleased to hear this. His name was honoured by this man then and this man also had honour not to kill one without weapons. Lugaid looked him up and down. The young man had a sturdy body, muscular and tall. This was how Lugaid liked his warriors. He was becoming much dissatisfied with the fat bellies of some of his warriors. They were becoming too content, gorging themselves with food and the riches of their spoils, like fat cats that lapped too much cream. This man was strong and lean but he still had a sturdy look about him.

"What is your Clan, boy?" Lugaid addressed him curtly.

Cred was honest, answering the *Ard Rígh* immediately.

"I am from the South, from An Daingean, the Fort of Chúise."

"Aah! A fine Clan, the sept of Chúise, with plenty of warm women there! You are a son? Aye, then welcome. Ferda tells me your name is Cred. Cred mac Chúise . . . what brings you so far north and west?"

Cred wondered idly if Úna had ever entertained the *Ard Rígh* or his warriors.

"I am a smith and my Craft brings me here. I travel, bringing precious stones and metals for my work."

"What forge will you use?"

"The forge at the Dún of Lugnae Fer Trí for now, *Ard Rígh*. Then I shall travel to the North."

"Let me see some of your work, boy," demanded Lugaid.

Cred unwrapped one of his lesser pieces. He was afraid to impress the *Ard Rígh* too much, but even his lesser piece drew a gasp of astonishment from the attendants around Lugaid, one or two of the warriors coveting it with their eyes.

Lugaid fingered the *delg* made for a man's cloak. He could not see any imperfection on it, although Cred thought some of the filigree lacework was slightly irregular. Cred pleaded with the *Ard Rígh* to take another one of better quality but Lugaid wanted this one and that was all there was to it. Cred was pleased to give him something which was not quite perfect.

Cred was accepted into the party of travellers, Ferda riding in the chariot with him, and they set out to reach the Dún of Lugnae Fer Trí by sun-down.

Cred planned how he would delay them when next they rested.

But they did not rest, Lugaid trying to get there as soon as possible, and the Tribe being anxious enough to find a Dún with women and girls there for play, plenty of jewels and implements for them to thieve, and men to fight.

Cred was worried. He managed to delay them a little by letting the happy Ferda take the reins and then loosening and sabotaging the pin on the axle of his own chariot-wheel. He was sorry that he had to startle and jolt his horse like this when the wheel wobbled and slid to the side and they jerked to a halt. Poor Ferda thought it was his fault but Cred put his mind at rest, saying simply that the pin had loosened in the axle. This was true but he did not further elaborate upon it.

Lugaid drew up alongside the chariot.

"Unfortunate accident," he said. "It seems we are destined to rest. I think the men wish for food and we will water the horses while you repair your wheel. This is an ample opportunity for us to prepare a plan of action when we get there."

As Cred knelt on the crisp frosty ground to repair the axle, he became aware of someone sidling up to him away from the others. He was shocked to see the face of a woman, an unkempt, not old but still a hag-like figure, who peered deeply into his eyes and made him very uneasy.

'Cred mac Chúise," she said, "your Gráinne is safe. Have no fear."

Cred jumped to his feet but she put her hand out to still him.

"Nay, do not draw attention!" she hissed urgently, but it was too late. Lugaid strode over and grabbed the woman angrily away from Cred.

"What did she say to you?" he demanded.

Cred answered: "She told me to have no fear. I presume she meant of herself or of you, my King. She startled me with her presence, so all of a sudden like that!"

The sincerity in Cred's voice seemed to satisfy Lugaid who gave a throaty laugh and spat suddenly on the ground.

"That is the way of Bláth! But you have every right to fear her, mac Chúise! She is a *seer* and can *see* into any black heart!" He let go of Bláth's arm and motioned for her to go. "Be off with you, woman! This man is a nobleman. I will not have you creep up on my honoured guest like that! It does not make for a strong constitution and we need all the strength we can muster to combat this cold and these traitorous rogues."

Cred inclined his head respectfully and knelt to continue his repairs. He could not help smiling to himself. There were always those watching out for Gráinne a· ᐧ the babe, even the *seer* at the court of Lugaid, the *Ard Rígh*.

# CHAPTER 26

# TWIST OF
# A SERPENT'S TAIL

*The Truth that stares him in the face is hidden,*
*For he thinks it one way and yet it is another.*
*To go against the fate of the gods is forbidden*
*Bringing only anguished sorrow to the Mother.*

As they neared the Dún of Lugnae Fer Trí, Cred drove his chariot alongside the *Ard Rígh*'s horse and signalled that he was requesting a meeting.

The *Ard Rígh* reined in his splendid steed beside the chariot.

Cred shouted that as he had been to the Dún of Lugnae Fer Trí before, maybe it would be a good plan for him to herald the coming of his most honoured *Ard Rígh*.

Lugaid looked at Cred sharply but Cred stared boldly back, then said: "I am a trusted man at the Dún of Lugnae Fer Trí. I am a just man, good and true, and no man has any cause to fear me, but if it pleases you, *Ard Rígh*, to send someone to accompany me, then send your *seer* who can read my heart and mind."

Lugaid considered this for a moment, weighing up the young man before him, trying to read the sincerity in his voice. He called upon Bláth and Dorcha the Elder to come to his aid.

"Are this man's intentions honourable?" he asked Dorcha.

Dorcha glanced sideways at the *seer*. Bláth put her hand out dramatically and circled Cred's forehead with her forefinger.

'Well, answer your *Ard Rígh*!" she said to Dorcha abruptly. Dorcha was nervous as he answered Lugaid. "Aye! His intentions are good," he said.

He wished that Bláth was not there. She had too much of a

hold over him, over them all, if the Truth be known. He was glad to ride behind the *Ard Rígh* and try not to see Bláth and the young man, Cred, head off together towards the Dún of Lugnae Fer Trí.

As soon as they were out of earshot, Cred began to demand answers. He asked too many questions for Bláth's liking but she was patient and replied to as many of them as she could.

Cred learned that Serb had birthed her babe who was being reared by Emer. His heart was light at this news, especially now that the weight of a great secret was lifted from him, that of the knowledge of Serb's forced coupling with Donal Rua. Whether Emer or Lugnae knew this, and Cred suspected they did, it mattered not. A violation of the goddess had been perpetrated and that was scandal enough. Emer was all encompassing with her love though, and Cred knew that the babe, which had the red hair and look about him that Donal Rua had, was in good hands and with the right mother and father.

There was only one task left for Cred. He wanted to get to the Dún fast, before Lugaid and the warriors arrived there, so that he could warn Gráinne to flee. Something perturbed him about Bláth's description of Cormac in the cave and then she blabbed about a wolf saving him from warriors. In the same breath, she spoke of a wolf-cub being given suckle by a goat, and Cormac being spirited to the land of the *Sidh*. Cred thought she was touched with a madness, but then he knew that all *seers* were prone to speaking in riddles and weaving words with visions. Only Cromlach and Gráinne would have the Truth.

Cred rode the horse as if he were being chased by an army of warriors, the chariot taking off into the air over some of the bumps, and skimming potholes so that his belly lurched and his insides seemed to drop. Bláth hung on for dear life. There was a certain thrill to be had on a fast journey and an extraordinary amount of steering skill to be exercised in the driving of a chariot over such rough terrain. Bláth threw her head back and laughed with the sensation of it all.

Lugnae Fer Trí sent Devin the trapper to see who the approaching strangers were and why they travelled in such haste. He was pleased to learn it was Cred, but puzzled as to why he should be accompanied by Bláth, *seer* to the *Ard Rígh*. Furthermore, it was very strange that Cred was hailing the arrival of the *Ard Rígh* and his warriors.

Devin worried Lugnae even more when he said that Cred had suggested it would be a wise action to store anything of value in Cromlach's old cave, concealing the whereabouts of the entrance.

Lugnae gave orders to start the hiding and moving of valuables right away, then he waited for Cred and Bláth who arrived not far behind the heels of Devin.

Bláth waited while Cred embraced his foster-father, then she shrewdly suggested that the young women of the Clan should also go to the cave. The warriors would then soon tire of the display of poverty and the lack of available girls and women. They were going to be anxious to move on.

"And what about Dorcha the Elder? He will not say anything?" asked Lugnae.

"No, he will not dare to speak, for fear of my curses," whispered Bláth in such a way that it sent shivers down Lugnae's spine. "Neither will the warrior who accompanied us last time, the one who returned to Teamhair. Ach, he is afraid of his own shadow! I told them both they must prepare secretly to welcome the greatest *Ard Rígh* Éiriú ever had and that this was decreed by the Mother! You should have seen their faces! But sure how could they not know it as a Truth when it is that?" Bláth cackled loudly, startling Devin who jumped back suddenly. This made her laugh even more and she mumbled something about bears being like field-mice these days.

Lugnae Fer Trí acted quickly and did as Bláth suggested. There were protests from the young women who said it was not every day they had a visit from the *Ard Rígh* and a troop of fine young warriors. Cred soon discouraged them when he told them that the *Ard Rígh* was flanked by gross, fat-bellied men who spoke in foreign tongues and had a smell about them that would drive away wild boars.

He then went on to order them not to light a fire in the cave because the smoke could be seen spiralling from the hill-side. Lugnae provided good furs and blankets in which they must keep warm, huddling together if they had to. He warned them not to venture out into the light of day except to attend to their ablutions and only then when the way was perfectly clear.

By the time the *Ard Rígh* arrived with his men, the Dún had been emptied of its greater treasures and the place looked quite bereft of wealth and young women.

Lugaid was greeted graciously by Lugnae Fer Trí and the Clan but it was quite obvious by Lugaid's reaction that he was disappointed by the lack of finery and the shortage of females, nor were there any bond-maids or even concubines available for play.

However, the purpose of his journey was to find and rid the country of the young usurper who was decreed to rule Éiriú and not in wake of the passing over of the *Ard Rígh* either. The Druids said it was to happen during his rulership.

Lugaid wanted to turn this fate in some way. He wished the rule to pass through his own line to his son, not to be wrenched away from him and taken by this child in his later years. There was too much excitement about the birth of the white bulls. It was the talk of Teamhair before Lugaid left and although Lugaid sent his best *seer*, his Elder and his two best warriors to the Clan of Lugnae Fer Trí, they were unable to find a new-birthed child nor had they any knowledge of him. They did come back to Teamhair with another *seer* called Serb, who was jealously guarded by Bláth. Lugaid had to appoint the warrior who had returned with them and the old wise woman, Máda, to care for Serb while Bláth was gone on this second journey. Otherwise, she would never have left the girl.

"You live frugally, my friend," said Lugaid to his host. "And your women produce only strong sons?" he asked pointedly.

Lugnae smiled as he answered: "We need to live only simple lives as trappers and trappers' sons. Some of our older daughters have left the tribe, some are in fosterage and some are with the Draoi learning the ways of the goddess."

"In the barren time? You sent them away during the snows?" Lugaid asked in disbelief.

Lugnae thought fast and inclined his head but he could not come up with a suitable answer quickly enough.

Cred stepped forward.

"Our host is shamed, *Ard Rígh*, to tell you this, but it is so that this is the Dún of hardship and challenge. For this reason my own father sent me here to work as a *céird*."

Lugnae Fer Trí was grateful for the presence of mind of his foster-son, Cred. He shrugged his shoulders and puffed out his chest confidently.

"They either like it or they do not but most of them obey the Laws," he said. "Now let us go into the Dún Hall. Emer will prepare a bath for you, *Ard Rígh*, and your men may use the sweat-hut, then we will sit down to a hearty feast of some fresh venison. I will arrange quarters for all of you."

"We may not tarry for too long, Lugnae Fer Trí. We are searching for the woman, Achtán, daughter of Olc Aiche. It has been said that she lay with my father's brother, Art the Lonely, and has birthed a babe. Of course, as cousin to this child, I am honour-bound as the only living and suitable relative left to rear him as my own. It is apparent to me that you live in a very humble way, Lugnae Fer Trí. I can alter your circumstances considerably if you will assist me in finding the mother who has been child-growing."

Lugaid was watching closely the reaction of the trapper, Lugnae Fer Trí, who remained calm even though he was shocked to the core by the blatant Untruth being uttered by the *Ard Rígh*. Lugaid did not notice the flush of rage that was spreading over Cred's face nor the tightened fists that wanted to pummel the *Ard Rígh* into the ground. Bláth was equally appalled and began speaking in tongues. Lugnae Fer Trí squinted his eyes nervously but it looked as if he was merely shading them from the light or the soft drizzle of snow which had started.

"We have no woman who has been child-growing here," he said gruffly, but politely.

"Do you have a babe who was birthed within the year?"

Lugnae Fer Trí was pale as he answered: "Aye, of my own flesh and blood."

'I demand to see the babe. Bring him to me," ordered Lugaid.

Lugnae was trembling but he stood up to the *Ard Rígh* and spoke quietly and firmly. "The child is of my own blood. It is snowing, *Ard Rígh*, and the babe is slumbering. Enter the Dún. It will please me to show him to you."

Lugaid marched straight into the Dún with his warriors, not waiting to follow Lugnae, being irritated by the Chieftain's polite refusal to bring the babe to him, snow or no snow. Emer squealed when the *Ard Rígh* pushed her away from the crib when he found it in her quarters. He snatched back the blanket from the babe. This caused the child to cry out in fright, being suddenly awakened by the rough disturbance of his bedding and the noise of the warriors crowding into the room. Lugnae Fer Trí caught Emer's hand and willed her to be silent. Cred had to hold himself back from attacking the *Ard Rígh*. He swore that if Lugaid tried to harm this child in any way, he would risk his own life to do away with the *Ard Rígh*'s.

Lugaid was so sure this was the child that his hand was ready to unsheath his sword.

The shock on his face when he saw the red-berry stain down one cheek of the babe was frightening to behold. He knew this was not his usurper. The gods would not insult him by replacing him with one who was imperfect. An *Ard Rígh* must be without flaw. Yet, for some reason, he felt he had been cheated and insulted by this trapper.

"Lugnae Fer Trí! Where is Achtán, daughter of Olc Aiche? She served her fosterage here, did she not?"

"Aye, she did that, *Ard Rígh*. But she is no longer here. She left." His voice became softer and he knew not what else to say.

The *seer* Bláth suddenly came to the rescue. She started calling upon the ancestors with such a loud shriek that Lugaid and his men huddled together. She knew what she was doing. Lugaid was afraid of Conn of a Hundred Battles and the ancestors of Conn, all of whom were great and noble warriors and kings.

"*Ard Rígh*, she is gone from here! They tell me her babe was spirited away to the Isle!" yelled Bláth, cackling and throwing herself at the feet of Lugaid.

Lugaid stepped back to get away from his *seer*, but her arms clung around his legs and she was trailed along with him.

Cred did not know what to think as he watched Bláth. She

was very convincing and he knew she could not speak an Untruth without losing some of her powers so what she said must be right. Could it be that Cormac had passed on? If so, then he had to find Gráinne quickly. She must be distraught. Cred was confused.

Lugaid, at last, found his tongue. He laughed a nervous laugh.

"If what you say is true, and I have not known you to be wrong yet, woman . . . then – then my time is wasted looking for a babe that is in Í-Bhreasail, is it not?"

Bláth never let go her grasp as she said slyly: "Those who follow the path to Í-Bhreasail do not easily return, *Ard Rígh*."

Lugaid felt a chill in his bones and he shook off the woman from his feet. He was humiliated and vowed to make someone suffer for this. He turned to Emer and asked her what was her most prized possession.

"My man," she whispered, shaking with fear.

The warriors laughed uproariously, the sound making Luis, the babe, cry and scream even more. Emer rushed over to the child, forgetting her own fear, angry now that they had further distressed the babe.

"There, there," she crooned, picking up Luis and rocking him against her breasts.

Lugaid persisted: "After your man, what is your most prized possession?"

Emer placed her lips to the child's head, then she stared straight at Lugaid and answered boldly: "My family."

"And after your family?"

"The Clan," she said defiantly.

The warriors by this time were laughing and slapping their knees with their hands. They had never encountered a woman like this before who considered her man was her possession. Possessions to them were trinkets and objects of value. This woman's jewels were her man, her family and the Clan.

Emer's eyes scanned the room again. She began to lose her confidence, her fear flowing slowly back into her, and she became confused as to why they laughed at her. Tears welled in her eyes and as Lugnae Fer Trí watched her, aching to hold her tightly against him but not daring to move in case Lugaid attacked them and hurt the child, he knew now why he loved Emer above all other women. She was telling the simple Truth, something that Lugaid, the *Ard Rígh*, had not yet learned to honour and respect. Neither did it seem that he could accept it.

"Woman, I tire of this game. After the Clan, what is your most loved possession?"

"My – my looking-glass," she said, her voice trembling and her whole body flushed and hot with the intensity of being spoken to like this by the *Ard Rígh*.

The warriors whooped.

"She is a woman after all!" one of them shouted.

Cred wanted to still their tongues for ever. Emer loved her looking-glass, not because she could see her reflection in it, but because it had been a precious gift from Lugnae Fer Trí at a special time in their lives.

"I do not want your son, nor your man," said Lugaid, "but it will please me to have your looking-glass. In return for this, you will have the company of myself and my men for a hearty feast and make sure there is plenty of mead. We will need it to make up for the lack of good women!"

Emer felt as if she was withering away like a forgotten flower. They were going to take her special gift away, the only true possession of beautiful craftsmanship she had that meant so much to her. It was Lugnae's courting gift, not just a highly polished metal-surface like most mirrors but a real Phoenician looking-glass.

The babe was quiet in her arms. There was a stillness as if everything had stopped momentarily. Emer's sense of loss was almost akin to the loss she felt when her son, Donal Rua, had passed over. She thought of the Truth that had been revealed about him when she once caught sight of Serb in that same mirror during the time of the storm.

Emer was aware of Lugnae's arms about her.

"Emer, *a chroí*, we are still together. Do not fret about the looking-glass. I make a boon to you that I will find another."

"It will not be the same," whispered Emer, tears spilling down her cheeks and falling on the babe who blinked and reached up to her face with his little hands. "Anyway, how are we to explain that we have hidden the looking-glass away without revealing the whereabouts of the others?"

Lugnae had not thought of this. He called Cred over to him, then announced to the *Ard Rígh* that while his bath was being drawn and the men used the sweat-hut, he was going to show Cred the forge so that he could settle into his workplace and dispatch of his tools and metals.

Cred was as anxious to talk with Lugnae as Lugnae Fer Trí was to speak with him.

As soon as they were outside the Dún Hall and out of earshot, Cred grabbed Lugnae by the arm.

"Where is she, Foster-father? Where is Gráinne? Is she safe? Is the child well?"

"She is travelling to the North, over Sliab Conachla to the Dún of Fiachrae Cassán, foster-father of Art the Lonely."

"What madness! Who travels with her? She will never get over the mountain in the snows that are to come. Cromlach will not live through it. He is getting old."

"You forget, Cred, that Cromlach lived through his long hermitage, when the barren moons brought bitter winds and harsh snows we could barely cope with, wrapped in our furs as we were, our hearthstones never cold. Cromlach is wise and he and Gráinne have the company of Tula, Mora nee Derga and Finann . . . Aye, do not look so surprised, Finann even has two of his goats along! I have lost half my Tribe, for sure."

Cred patted Lugnae Fer Trí on the back.

"You are a good foster-father, Lugnae, and for that I will always be grateful, but you are soon to lose another of your Clan. I have to follow Gráinne. We will visit the forge as that is where we are going now, but I would ask your permission to take some tools with me that I may work my trao when I travel to the North. I have metals and stones I must take with me but I also have plenty to leave with you, if we can hide it from these tyrants somewhere."

Lugnae nodded. "We will put them in the cave. If we make haste, it can be done before the *Ard Rígh* has finished his ablutions."

Cred was surprised and pleased to see that Lugnae's son was

now working in the forge, making very good tools and implements for the cooking, the ploughing and farming. His attempts at making buckles and adornments were not quite so successful but he flushed with pleasure when Cred complimented him on his efforts and gave him some good advice. He was delighted that he was going to have more metals and stones to play with, and he did not mind losing some of his smaller tools which Cred needed.

Lugnae and Cred then rode their horses quickly across to the cave, making sure that no one saw them leave. They unloaded the small bags of precious stones and the large rug-sacks of metals that Cred did not need for the special artificing of the Chalice but which he had carried back with him for the making of better tools and swords.

The young women at the cave, wrapped in their furs, were happy to see Cred. They had always admired him but he was shocked at how forward they were now that Serb was gone. They sidled up to him and giggled with each other, each trying to stroke or touch him furtively. Lugnae bade them behave themselves and ordered them not to disturb the bags or rug-sacks which were being left there.

Cred wandered to the back of the cave, running his hand over a woven wall-hanging he knew Gráinne had made. He pressed the material to his face with both hands and drank in the smell of the cloth, hoping to inhale some of Gráinne's scent from it, but there was only a faint waft of some kind of burnt grass smell or burnt feathers . . . yes, that was it, burnt feathers. He thought this was curious but swept it from his mind and continued his search for . . . he knew not what.

Lugnae was pulling the looking-glass away from the cave-wall where it was propped up with some of the larger items which were stored, when Cred suddenly shouted from the back of the cave.

"Lugnae! Leave that looking-glass there! Look at this. Gráinne left behind something that we can use instead. I have had a thought which will help us. Poor dear Emer is distraught about the looking-glass which you gave her. It will break her heart that she has to give it away to Lugaid, so why not give him this one instead?" Triumphantly, he held up the splendid mirror that Olc Aiche and Dairine had given to Gráinne as a birthing gift for Cormac.

Lugnae gasped: "I cannot do such a thing. That belongs to Gráinne. She was unable to take it with her because of its size and its value. She is travelling as a peasant serf, at Olc Aiche's request, and so she had to leave this one behind. Emer and myself gave her a smaller looking-glass to take with her until such time she can return to claim this one."

"But do you not see, Foster-father, what better way this is to get the looking-glass to Teamhair? It is a very special birthing gift for Cormac mac Airt from one of the most powerful Druids in the land. Think of it this way: a token of this kind belonging to the child who will one day be the man to usurp the *Ard Rígh* . . . and the *Ard Rígh* himself delivers it to Teamhair! Ha! It is a rare jest which holds the twist of the serpent's tail!" Cred chuckled.

"But what if the *Ard Rígh* gives it away or trades it for something else?" asked Lugnae, seeing the humour of the situation but unable to smile back.

"You will make it so that he guards the looking-glass with his life. Think up what story you will, Lugnae Fer Trí. It is bound to have a Truth in it if I know the way Olc Aiche charms his gifts!"

Lugnae laughed at last, his belly aching with the release of his mirth. It had been a long time since he had been able to share a jest or a trick with anyone, and this was going to be a trick worth the playing. How dared the *Ard Rígh* try to hurt his dear Emer! He began to think about what he would tell the *Ard Rígh* about the looking-glass and Lugnae determined to make the story worth his while to make up for the many moments of anguish he had been put through by this tyrant.

Cred and Lugnae carried the mirror, wrapped in a long plaid, out of the cave, first carefully checking that they were not being watched. Then they proceeded back to the Dún, with Cred supporting the glass in front of him on the horse. He had to be cautious not to drop it, so they could not go as fast as they wished.

Back at the Dún Hall, one of the trappers came running out. He was breathless as he spoke with Lugnae.

'The *Ard Rígh* has been looking for you, Chieftain. He has bathed and we have detained him by telling him tales of our hunting but now he is anxious."

Lugnae turned to Cred. "We have returned within a hair's breadth of endangering ourselves!" Then he said to the trapper: "Help us get this looking-glass into the Dun Hall so that the *Ard Rígh* may no longer feel the pain of anxiety."

Emer watched Lugnae, Cred and the trapper enter the Hall, knowing by the shape of the plaid-draped object that it must be her looking-glass. Fresh tears of sadness coursed down her face. It felt like someone was taking a part of her life away. She could not believe that she placed so much importance upon this gift but obviously it meant more to her than she thought, especially now when it was being taken from her. Emer felt like she was being unjustly punished. She knew that any feelings of allegiance she had ever had towards this *Ard Rígh* were now gone. Something snapped within her and, for the first time in her life, Emer disliked someone. She was shocked to realize this, being the mother that she was, capable of mothering everyone, or so she had always taken for granted. As Clan-mother, she was there to nurture, regardless of the caste, the nature or the look of the beast. No one ever attacked Emer or hurt her in any way, no one spoke ill of her or rejected her attentions which were always given with good intent without regard for return. She was generous to the extent that Lugnae sometimes tired of her excessive mothering instincts, which embraced all, so that he had to share her time with not only his offspring but the entire Clan. He would not have her any other way though. Emer was also just a little resentful towards Lugnae now. Why was her man not defending her against this tyrant? Lugnae had watched the *Ard Rígh* push her out of the way of the crib. He had not interfered. Lugnae Fer Trí then allowed this wicked man to question and humiliate her so that she became the victim of much hilarity and jesting. He had not come to her rescue. Then, the final straw, when the *Ard Rígh* wanted her most prized possession, something which was a token of love and a gift from the heart, here was her man *giving* it away to him without any protest or attempt to trade him something else. Emer was broken-hearted. She realized the danger they were in, but nevertheless she could not be rational about the way she felt. Deep within her, she did not want to see a weakness in Lugnae, did not want to acknowledge that she was the stronger of the two. It meant that she denied herself the god while embracing the goddess. This was not a good thing.

Lugnae was unaware of the feelings churning inside Emer. He knew she was upset but he had no notion of how deeply she was affected by it all. He was happy with her confession that he, Lugnae Fer Trí, was Emer's most prized possession. Never would he forget the pride that welled within him when she spoke those words, even though the warriors had laughed. He had always assumed that their children took precedence.

The *Ard Rígh* was surprised that here these men stood before him, offering him what he asked of them. This was not what he expected. He wanted a challenge, an excuse for a skirmish, not a polite gesture from a feeble Chieftain who would give away his own woman's token of love without a fight. He was disgusted with this display of weakness but he had to accept it now, or lose face before his own men.

Lugnae then surprised him by putting his hands together and inclining his head respectfully.

"*Ard Rígh*, it is my wish that you will accept this token of our allegiance," said Lugnae, almost faltering when he heard a sob wrench from Emer, but he continued: "But – but there is something I think it only fair that you should know. This looking-glass is charmed."

Lugaid suddenly became interested and the warriors were at once quietened. He stared at the covered object, wary but with a rising excitement. Cred was supporting it in an upright position now, the trapper having gently placed his end of the glass on the ground.

"What manner of charm, Chieftain?" asked Lugaid, anxious to know if it could imbue him with even more power. This was indeed a fortunate day.

Emer was staring at Lugnae Fer Trí through a veil of tears,

mesmerized by this change of attitude and wondering what madness possessed him.

"By whom has it been charmed?" asked Lugaid, impatiently, wanting to know all the answers at once.

"Suffice it to say, a great *seer*, one who cannot be named lest we break the charm," answered Lugnae very slowly and deliberately, thoroughly enjoying the intrigue and attention he was getting. His own men looked puzzled and were curious as to what he was playing at. They had never before heard of a charm being placed on Emer's looking-glass.

"The mirror must never be broken. An ill fate will come to him who breaks it, even in error. It must be paid for with half its own weight in gold as it can never be given away freely unless it is a birthing gift. As you can see, *Ard Rígh*, I am not a wealthy Chieftain now and, in taking this looking-glass, you are impoverishing me even further."

"But what is so special about it, Chieftain, that it is worth half its own weight in gold?"

"The wisdom it reveals upon looking at oneself within it, for it always reveals the Truth. This looking-glass is really only suitable for a *rí*, or an *Ard Rígh* like yourself, who will appreciate the true meaning of that wisdom without fear," Lugaid said intently, hoping he had baited the *Ard Rígh*.

"How do I know that what you speak is not an Untruth?" asked Lugaid, suspiciously. He had the feeling that he was somehow walking into some sort of trap but he was powerless to flee from it, his curiosity drawing him into it freely.

Lugnae looked directly at Lugaid, hoping that what he was about to say was right. It was now in the lap of the gods.

"Because an Untruth cannot be spoken in the eye of this looking-glass. Ask your *seer* if this is a Truth."

Bláth stared at Lugnae Fer Trí. This was a risk indeed for the Chieftain. He knew that she could not utter an Untruth. Bláth went before the wrapped mirror and touched it with her hands, lifting the plaid so she could *see* into a portion of the glass, covering it again quickly when she got what she wanted. She spun into immediate action, suddenly whirling and pointing towards the mirror. Bláth knew that this was all the work of

Olc Aiche. She threw her head back and laughed aloud, glad to be a part of this great work. Was it possible that this glass was sent here for just this very purpose, the means of detaining the *Ard Rígh* and sending him back to Teamhair with it in the opposite direction in which Gráinne had gone? Surely, no Druid had so much power. His observations, his *seeing* abilities, were a match for her own now.

"It is a Truth that this looking-glass is imbued with a charm by an Elder of the highest order. It has the means of revealing a wisdom meant only for the eyes of an *Ard Rígh*. It will reflect the wisdom of the greatest man of philosophy that Éiriú has ever known. This looking-glass is for Teamhair, *Ard Rígh*, and you are the one proclaimed to take it there!"

Lugaid leapt forward, forgetting all else in his eagerness to possess such a token.

"Give the Chieftain half its weight in gold. I will take it to Teamhair and guard it with my life!"

"Do not unveil it until you are there and tarry not along the way," said Lugnae Fer Trí, in awe of himself, knowing that Bláth spoke only a Truth. So Cred had been right. The looking-glass was charmed after all.

Lugaid's greed for power was greater than his greed for wealth. He had to explain to his disgruntled warriors that half the mirror's weight in gold was only the accumulated pickings of the last two raids between Cruachu and the Dún of Lugnae Fer Trí, but they saw only that their booty was being reduced because of a looking-glass. Lugaid then persuaded them that this mirror would bring about even greater wealth and promised them a bear's share back at Teamhair. He reminded them that Olc Aiche had given them a substantial amount of gold, hefty enough to stop them from pillaging Cruachu or taking any of the women. It was only Lugaid's fear of the Druid that made him comply with Olc Aiche's wishes. Now he was glad he had done so, because he doubted if he would have had enough gold to trade for the looking-glass.

Lugnae Fer Trí vowed to restore the gold, which was taken by unfair means, to its rightful owners. He would visit the Chieftains of the Clans between his Dún and Cruachu and try to give them back that which had been taken from them. He hoped the women and girls were not hurt.

The looking-glass served a triple purpose. It had turned the *Ard Rígh* from his chase to find Gráinne, although he was convinced that the babe was now in Í-Bhreasail. The mirror also gave Lugnae Fer Trí the means of getting back the wealth that was stolen or forced from the other Clans during the raids by the *Ard Rígh*, and lastly, but by no means of the least importance, the looking-glass was soon to be on its way to Teamhair where it would stay, carefully protected by Lugaid for fear of breaking the charm, and there it was going to remain until Cormac mac Airt came to Teamhair as *Ard Rígh*.

Emer was thoroughly confused by the claims made upon her mirror, even those spoken by Bláth. While the *Ard Rígh* feasted with his men, she quietly cried. If Lugnae tried to placate her with this blood-soiled gold, she decided she was going to throw it in the river or give it away to the people of the *crannógs*. How could he sell off her love-token like this?

She watched in disbelief as Lugnae helped the *Ard Rígh* unload his gold from one of the chariots of Teamhair. Her heart sank as she watched her looking-glass, wrapped in its plaid, being laid on a bed of furs and then tied with hay-twist ropes to keep it steady for the journey to Teamhair.

Then they were gone. The *Ard Rígh*, ruler of Éiriú, was gone, flanked by his warriors and with them was the only precious token of love given to Emer by Lugnae Fer Trí.

And there was Lugnae, laughing and jovial, calling out to everyone to feast and sing and dance. Emer went to her quarters and lay down on her pallet. One of the older women was taking care of Luis because Emer knew she did not have the heart to play with him. She lay heavy like a stone, unable to cry any more even though the pain in her throat was searing. She had seen a part of Lugnae revealed to her that she did not love. It was of the utmost importance to Emer that she love and respect all aspects of her mate's character. He had to be hers in whole, no part of him rejected by her, and now, after all these long moons together she had discovered a side of him, a weakness, that she did not care for. Emer covered her head with a thick plaid, shutting out the light, shutting out the world from her. She did not want to hear the celebrations taking place in the Dún Hall. Emer fell into sleeping, not caring whether she awoke again or not.

She did not know how long she stayed there but when she did awaken later, her pain was still with her. So was Lugnae.

"Emer, do not be angry with me," he said softly, stroking her arm gently. "I am a man of few words but I will never do anything to hurt you."

Emer could not look into his eyes. She turned her head away, swallowing hard to stop her tears.

"Emer . . . I confess I could not have stood up to the *Ard Rígh* alone without the help of Cred and Bláth . . . but I did not want to see Luis or yourself get hurt, nor any of the people of my Clan. I am sorry you were humiliated, *a chroí*, believe me, my spirit was bleeding with yours."

Emer turned her face back towards him.

"You traded your token of love for me for – for a half-weight of – of gold! How could you do such a thing, Lugnae, and then celebrate?" she asked, brokenly. "Do you think I will cherish the gold, blood-soiled as it is?"

Lugnae was speechless. He could not believe she would think him so heartless. Poor Emer. She did not know what had occurred this day. He thought she would have guessed by what he was saying that it was Cormac's looking-glass which was being sent to Teamhair. Obviously she did not.

Emer closed her eyes and turned her head away from Lugnae.

Lugnae walked over to the screen and pulled it back. He had sent the trappers to retrieve the girls and the valuables from the cave as soon as the *Ard Rígh* left the Dún.

"Emer," he called out softly to her, "I will always feel the same way I did when I first gave you this token."

Emer was not sure she heard him right. Then it slowly dawned on her and she turned around and there it was! Her beautiful Phoenician looking-glass, intact and here in the Dún, not in a chariot on its way to Teamhair. She was glowing with a warmth which spread itself from a tight knot of pain, deep inside, right out to the smile that beamed across her face. It was a private ecstasy she shared only with Lugnae, who was across the room in a couple of strides and now holding her tight against him. There was no need for an explanation. She would listen to that later. Now, all she wanted was the security of his arms and the feel of the strong muscles in his chest rasping his rough greying hair against her swelling breasts. She strained her body towards his, melting herself with him. This was the Lugnae she knew and loved. She dismissed that little weakness she saw earlier as nothing. No, she was Emer, all embracing, all encompassing, the mother of them all. Some of her babes would disappoint her at least once in their lives but her bosom was big enough to nurture them all. She moaned with pleasure as Lugnae's mouth clamped on to the teat of her breast.

# CHAPTER 27

# THE CHASE

*Black is the night sky, sleek cat hunting,*
*White is your smile, biting, pale wet kiss;*
*I am dreaming of your snow-soft hands,*
*Light as the day, thieving my soul away.*

Cred rested for one night. Then he went to the forge at daybreak
and began to work with the fire, forging an arch of iron for the
front of his trap and an arch of beaten copper for the back.
Cred decided it was impossible to use the chariot for his long
journey. Although it was much faster than the comfortable trap,
he could not fit all his essential belongings into it. The trap,
being a two-wheeled small cart, had more room and was faster
than the *varda* which Gráinne had taken. He needed a canopy
on it for this bitter-cold and wet weather. Lugnae's son helped
him, watching and learning as the tall, pale-haired young man
worked the metals with expertise. Cred had no time to spin gold
wire around the iron to make it look better. He was anxious to
make the hood for his trap, then go.

The children, the women and the men gathered around in
groups to watch this curious contraption being erected on to the
trap. They had never seen anything like it before. Cred took
some fleeces, skin-side out, and stretched them over the framework which was now attached to the trap. He tied and stitched
the fleeces to each other and around the arches, then rubbed
the skins over with a layer of boar's lard to further insulate them
against the snows and rains. He waxed and rubbed all kinds of
unguents, tallow, daub, black pitch, anything he could think of
to keep himself and his tools dry as he sped across the terrain
to find Gráinne. He packed food, hard cheeses, grains for
making gruel, dried and salted meat strips, nuts and apples. Old

306

Tachta gave him dried leaves and seaweeds to chew on, and Emer prepared a hotpot which would last a couple of days to start with. Devin gave him bog-spails and flints so that he could have light if needed. Everyone was so sad to see yet another brother of the Clan leaving the Dún. Cred presented Lugnae with his splendid chariot and a beautiful gold *scian* that had a very sharp blade of iron useful for hunting with. Lugnae Fer Trí and Cred embraced warmly, an understanding there, as the knife passed from one to the other, Donal Rua's knife unspoken of between them. Emer rocked Luis, her face flushed and happy today after her night with Lugnae, but no matter how thankful and glad she was that Cred had assisted in the plan to keep her looking-glass, and no matter how much she cared for this foster-child, Cred, she was pleased he was leaving to find Gráinne.

Both of her foster-children, Cred and Gráinne, reminded her of the terrible pain suffered by her own child, Donal Rua. It was best that she did not have to live with them as a constant reminder of times of sorrow. Now she had her other children and, of course, Luis. Emer vowed not to let him out of her sight for a moment. A new life had been given to her to nurture and she was going to be a much better custodian this time. Her heart was not in the farewell goings-on but already back in the Dún. She did not know how anyone could leave the Dún.

By midday, Cred was on his way, following the road to the North, leaving the Dún of Lugnae Fer Trí far behind him, thinking to himself that he had never climbed to the cairn at the top of Knocknarea and probably never would do so now. He felt a certain sadness in this knowledge, but thought that maybe it was caused by the biting pain of leaving behind all that was familiar to him. He thought of the recent visit to his father's Dún, and realized he had not even gone to the familiar isles in the South where he used to swim, nor touched the sea with his feet. What was wrong with him that he was forgetting the joys of his boyhood so easily? All the things he intended to do at his foster-father's place he had thought he would have plenty of time for, like the lake islands he had wished to explore. But now he was driving his horse and trap away and the Dún was shrinking fast into the distance behind him. For a long moment he panicked and almost headed the chariot back to Lugnae Fer Trí and the security of life within the Clan. But then he thought of Gráinne and wished to bury his face in her long, black hair. He wanted to sip her lips and drink her spirit into himself. His mind ached to see her and touch her, feel her blue eyes wander over him. He wanted to make her laugh, hear her voice jest and play with his. Somewhere they were going to meet and he vowed that when they did, he was never going to let her go again. This was the chase of his lifetime.

Cred felt like he was on the hunt, out to capture a rare and exquisite animal, not to kill, no, never to kill it, but to make it his own. He would have to use the skill of a hunter to find it. A vast land of plain, forest, marsh, hill and mountain lay before him. She could be anywhere out there. The terrain was fraught with danger at this time, with the snows bringing hungry bears, wolves, wild-cats and boars to the warm fire of the camper, to say nothing of the raiders and scavengers who lay in wait for unwary sojourners. What defence did they have? The *seer* Cromlach was getting old, Finann was a goatherd who was used to keeping wolves at bay . . . he had a whittled ash-whistle which could deter them for a short time, but not if the goats were attacked by a pack . . . and then there were Mora, Tula and Gráinne with the babe. Tula, the bond-maid, was without hearing, Mora had a way with animals but only for healing, and Gráinne had certain powers, he knew that, but would they be strong enough to keep her safe?

Cred drove his horse and trap as fast as he could across the plain, spurred on by the fear that Gráinne might be in danger. There were days and nights of hard travelling to catch up with them, providing they had kept to the main thoroughfare as far as the forest. Cred knew only some of the territory from stories told by travellers and trading people who had visited the Dún. Fergus the poet was well informed of the layout of the land, so Cred had asked him some questions before he undertook the journey. He hoped that all the knowledge he had was correct.

Gráinne wrapped herself into her furs and kept the babe warm against her breasts. He was happy, chuckling softly and murmuring to himself, pulling on her hair, which seemed to be his favourite pastime. From time to time she would press her face against the top of his head and drink in the smell of him, smothering his curls with kisses so that he laughed even more. She was so weary of travelling and they had not reached the mountain yet. Several times they hid, concealing themselves in the forest away from the track, when Tula warned them of approaching strangers. Occasionally Tula sensed a vibration beneath her feet which the others could not and, despite being without hearing, she proved invaluable to them. By laying the palms of her hands or the soles of her feet to the ground, she could tell from which direction the travellers came and how far away they were. It was uncanny. Gráinne now knew what Dairine meant when she said that Tula had special senses which compensated for her lack of hearing. So far, because of them, the little group had not been confronted by anyone, nor had they been followed.

None of them felt they were out of danger though. There always seemed to be a grey cloud of uncertainty and fear surrounding them. Sometimes it was visible like a thin mist, spurring them ever onwards, pushing themselves to the limit day after day, hoping to shake it off. The blue mountain loomed large and ominous before them, when they could see it, and the smaller forest, marsh and plain seemed far behind them. But there were small hills and more forest ahead. They hoped the track continued on the mountain. Cromlach said there was a pass somewhere which they would have to find. Fergus had spoken of two great lakes beyond the pass and upon the lakes were many green islands, one for each night of the year. There was no turning back now and they knew that the more harsh and hazardous the way before them, the more unlikely they were to be followed, but if the way did become any more difficult it was likely that the carts would not make it. The track was becoming harder to discern.

They were camped at the foot of the mountain but it was difficult to say where the hill of the mountain began. Even the forest was on a gentle slope, maybe the slope of Sliab Conachla, maybe not.

Finann fed the fire with what bits of dry bracken he could find. The snows were deep and swirling drifts had prevented them from moving several times. Cú had disappeared one day, which sent Gráinne into a panic, especially when they heard the sound of wolves baying quite far away. She cried all day while Cromlach tried to comfort her by telling her it was nature's way for a wolf to run with the pack. That night he returned, dragging the haunch of a deer back with him and laying it at Gráinne's feet. Cromlach caught him by his ruff and patted his head, praising him as he would a hound. Cú's ears went flat against his head and his tail wagged until Finann was sure it was going to drop off. That night they cooked the haunch, speared with an iron over the fire, supported by forked hazel sticks on either side. Gráinne caught the dripping fat in a pot, so they could use it later, either for cooking with or for smearing on their bodies to keep warm. Mora declined to eat the flesh of the deer and made a tasty broth from nuts and herbs. Cromlach threw the left-over deer-bone to Cú, who gnawed on it contentedly. The incident made them acutely aware that Cú acted almost as if he had been sent as a Guardian to them. He had come back to them this time but Gráinne could not help thinking that one day he would not return. Cromlach tried to remind her of the teachings about attachment and no attachment, knowing they were of little or no use to her when she was at present totally absorbed by her child and the cub. How did one teach a mother or child about no attachment and the importance of maintaining loose threads to strengthen one's spirit? Cromlach decided it was nigh impossible and realized he had more learning to do himself. It made him quiet and sent him into a hermitage for a few nights. He was travelling with them bodily but his hungry mind was curved inwards as he battled with himself for answers.

Cú still liked the milk from Finann's goat, Misha, but the she-goat did not care for the young wolf trying to grab her teats any more. She butted him away angrily and he would yap until Finann drew the milk off and offered it to him in a bowl. Cú lapped it up greedily as if it were nectar from the gods, licking his lips noisily afterwards and then barking for more. Sometimes he got it but often Gráinne would cuff him and tell him to go,

310

lie down and be quiet. He obeyed her instantly because he knew that when he did what he was told, she always came over and made a great fuss of him.

Cormac loved Cú and Cú loved Cormac. Any time the child stretched or crawled towards Cú, the wolf lay down gently and allowed the child to pull or poke him in any way he wished. Sometimes the child hurt him, then the wolf would nudge the babe to let him know that he was in pain and Cormac instantly stopped what he was doing. But Gráinne found it increasingly difficult to let them play together because the air was so cold and the ground so wet. When they settled somewhere for the night and Finann managed to get a good fire going, Gráinne usually threw one or two fleeces on the ground so Cormac could crawl around and keep warm.

One such night, Gráinne and Tula were arranging bedding in the *varda*, Mora was cooking, and Cromlach and Finann were gathering bracken, all of them within range of the wolf and the babe, when suddenly they all heard the loud and distinct voice of Cormac calling: "Cú!"

It startled them because it was more like the sound of an older boy's voice than a child's. When they all immediately stopped what they were doing and turned to see what was happening, they were shocked to see Cormac standing upright, holding on to the ruff of the wolf, his legs at first a little wobbly. But as they continued to watch, Cú began to walk slowly forward and Cormac walked with him. Gráinne squealed with delight and ran forward to hug them both, tumbling and kissing and cuddling with them.

"He is walking! He is walking!" she shouted with pride. Within a sennight, the babe was indeed walking on his own, taking little babe-steps further and further each day, the wolf always near by ready to break his fall if he stumbled or to help him up again with a few nudges. It was a very cumbersome time to learn to start walking with all the thick clothing and uneven surfaces of the fleeces upon which to press one's feet but Cormac managed very well.

Food was becoming a problem, as none of them were equipped to kill except the wolf, and he brought home morsels when he could, always disappearing when he heard the call of other wolves, then reappearing later with some part of an animal, usually a deer, so that they could eat well that night. Gráinne had remembered to bring salt with her and she tore off strips of meat to dry and salt in case of very hard times.

Mora made goat-cheeses. The goat was still producing enough milk, but for how long none of them knew. Finann had brought enough dried grasses and hay mixed with treacle to keep the goats well fed until they could reach a safe dún or a *crannóg* somewhere to get food. Because of their fear of being followed by the *Ard Rígh*, they had avoided the *crannógs* in the marshlands which were too close to the main thoroughfare and too near the *Ráth* of Lugnae Fer Trí. They regretted this now, knowing they should have kept building upon their supplies of food. Water was easily come by. Mora just melted snow or they used the water from springs and streams. They could just about manage to keep their flagging spirits and bodies going by existing on the minimum amount of food they needed for energy, if the wind did not become any colder or the snows any deeper. The huge mountain lay ahead, which had to be conquered somehow.

Gráinne thought often of the Dún she left behind, and when she thought of the Dún she could not see it in her mind without venturing into the forge and seeing Cred, without wandering into the Grove and hearing his voice or without visualizing the Brighdal *bothán* and having to turn away thoughts of Cred and Serb together. She knew when the babe, Luis, was born that he was sired by Donal Rua but still she imagined Cred's powerful body merged with Serb's. It was an image not easy to dismiss, even when she tried to feel his body next to her own. Maybe she was afraid to let go of the painful images from the past because the pain she felt now would be greater, knowing he was not with her, knowing that he had not returned to her when he promised to, within two moons at the most. It was easier to think of the pain he caused her many moons ago than the pain he caused her now.

Gráinne could no longer store her feelings. They were increasing within her until she thought something would burst if she did not share them.

That night, when everyone was slumbering, except for Cú, Cromlach and herself, Gráinne went over to the fireside where Cromlach was sitting, watching and feeding the flames.

"Cromlach, I wish to talk with you. If I do not speak of this, it will grow greater within me and I shall fall to ailing before long."

"Aye, *a stór*, that it will. Is it about Cred, by chance?"

Gráinne smiled. "Is nothing sacred with you, Cromlach, that you must *see* into my very soul and then tell me about it?"

"Everything is sacred with me, *a stór*. Now, what is not so with you?"

Gráinne pulled the furs around her body and rocked herself to keep warm.

"Cromlach, he told me he would return within two moons at most. He was going to be back before Serb had her babe but he did not come. I – I am afraid." Her voice faded and she hugged herself, wishing she did not have to say these words. To speak of it made it too real.

"Afraid for him or for yourself?"

"Neither. I am afraid because I am forgetting his face. I see him all the time in my dreaming, in my waking . . . but I – I have no memory of his face and find my mind clinging to the last shreds of fleeting glimpses."

Cromlach stoked the fire with a stick which caught alight and so he threw the stick on to the flames and let it burn. The flame flickered purple and yellow and he watched the dancing colours for a moment before he answered.

"Gráinne, to have no vivid memory of the face is of no consequence, of no importance. It is something that exists within us to protect us, and the one we think about, from pain. We learn to let go. It is part of the healing time in our mourning and so we bury it deep within us or shut out that which causes pain. It is to stop the haunting by the spirits of pain."

"I am constantly trying to shut him out but he is there always," she said tearfully. "Just his hair, the colour of his eyes, his strength, but no expression, no detail of his face. He is becoming no longer solid in my mind, but drifts in and out of my thoughts at will. It – it is becoming difficult to think of anything else and I do not know what to do, where to turn for solace."

Cromlach came over when he heard her sigh. It was a sad, broken sound that made him wish he could make things well for her. He did not know how to console her with words but he put his arms around her and gently guided her head to lie against his shoulder. They sat for some time like this before he tried to find the right way of saying something which would give her comfort and hope.

"*A stór*, it is usual for us to communicate without barriers when we love another. If you are thinking so much about him, he is just as likely to be haunted by images of you. Because the thoughts bring to life the pain of separation, our minds will grow angry and maybe wipe out the face or blemish it in some way or we will find fault with the one whom we love because we feel betrayed that they are not with us. It is the same when one we love passes over. There is disbelief, anger, sorrow and then the pain of the acceptance and back to love. I have seen all these in you, Gráinne. Even though Cred has not passed over, you still mourn what you thought was the loss of his love."

Gráinne buried her head, not wanting to hear any more.

"I – I cannot accept this loss, Cromlach, not when I have waited for so long. He must have found another, he must have!"

Cromlach placed his hands on her shoulders and prised her from him, urging her to look at him. He decided that now was the time to tell her.

"Gráinne, I have something to confess to you, something which I hope will not trouble you but I can no longer hold this Truth within myself, for in doing so, I have hurt you when I merely wished to protect you from harm."

Gráinne wiped her eyes with the back of her hand and gazed at him searchingly, her blue eyes trying to read his. She felt a little flutter in her breast as her heart jumped with sudden fearful anticipation of what he was going to say to her. His voice sounded so grave and serious.

"Nothing has happened to C-Cred?" she asked quickly, gasping out the words in one breath.

Cromlach almost looked away because of the anguish on her

314

face but he knew he had to confront himself too. He never shifted his eyes as he spoke to her with honesty.

"I do not know, *a stór*. When you went into the cocoon of forgetfulness, it was my doing, my wish, to shield you from the pain that was intended for you and your son. I did not realize that greater forces were also doing the working. Cormac has the totem of the wolf and so the she-wolf came, not at my bidding, but from somewhere or someone beyond any of us. I uttered the names of those to be protected and added the name of Cred to them."

"And you did not think to name yourself, Cromlach," she said, softly, "so that was why you were ailing. Dear Cromlach, why did you not tell me of this before? I would have understood. Now I know why Cred did not return sooner . . . he was slumbering in the sea of forgetfulness, was he not? Surely he must have returned by now? But he will never find us, never!" She moaned, clinging on to the furs around Cromlach. A thought occurred to her that made her drop her hands and turn again towards the fire.

"It was a long time before I had memory of Cred again, Cromlach," she murmured, her voice barely above a whisper. "I knew the Dún and I remembered the Clan, everyone, everything except for Cormac and – and Cred. He will have had memory of all except for me . . . and Cormac. What if he met someone during that time? The memory of my love for him was not there and so he could have joined with another."

"He had no memory of you, *a stór*, but if he remembered all else . . . that would also include Serb. He was honour-bound to return to Serb who was child-growing with the child of Baltinne, a babe that he knew to be sired by Donal Rua. But because he was protecting the good name of Donal Rua and the honour of Lugnae Fer Trí, he could not speak of this. I feel that he made a sacred boon to Serb not to disclose it, even to you. It is my belief that the seed for the child-growing was planted by force."

Gráinne nodded slowly, everything now falling into place. She had wandered through mazes in her mind, trying to decipher the symbols and various signals which presented themselves to her over many moons. Emer saw the bruises on Serb's face that time during the storm, and then there was the time that Cred was injured and Gráinne sensed it was Donal Rua's *scian* which had pierced his arm. Donal Rua followed Cred out during the storm, most likely to kill him but the gods had intervened. Gráinne even remembered when Cred tried to tell her in the Grove something about Serb. Of course! He was going to tell her that Serb was with child but somehow their words and thoughts got mixed with their feelings and Gráinne now knew that she had misinterpreted what he was telling her about Serb. She thought he was referring to poor Serb's sicknesses in becoming a *seer*. All the past sorrows and angers were being washed away as Gráinne stared at the fire and far from being troubled by what Cromlach confessed to her, for the first night in a long time, Gráinne was relieved that she, at last, saw the Truth of it all.

The only grief left in her was the sadness that Cred was not with her. One day, maybe, he would find her. She could only hope he was looking.

As Gráinne sat by the fire, she heard the baying of a wolf in the distance and watched as Cú's ears pricked up, then he took off into the night. Gráinne called out to him but it was no use. He was going to run with the pack and she had to let him go. There was nothing she could do except resign herself to wait for his return. She seemed to spend her life waiting for the return of her loved ones.

Cred was considerably slowed down as he travelled through the marshlands which were treacherous in their frozen state, the ice too thin to support the weight of the horse and trap and yet thick enough to cover the track on the bank of land which led to the other side.

If it had not been for the help of a *crannóg*-dweller who was out feeding morsels to swans, Cred knew he would surely have perished in the marshes. There was no way of knowing this unfamiliar crossing without the assistance of one who had done it many times before. For his assistance, Cred gave the *crannóg*-dweller one of several fleeces he had brought with him.

The bigger forest was all uphill and Cred stopped to rest the horse continuously. Again, he would have lost his way, because the frost and snow covered up the track, if it had not been for the help of an old hermit-Druid who pointed out the direction and the different trees to guide him, then invited him to sup and stay the night. Cred was happy to spend a night in the *bothán* of the hermit, who had a large enough goat-shed which sheltered Cred's horse from the snow.

The next day seemed easier after their rest and they progressed faster and further than before, despite the cold conditions.

That night, when Cred stopped to rest, he noticed tracks in the snow and traces of ashes and blackening from an old fire. There was a deer-bone near by which was half-gnawed. Whoever was here before had a hound with them, so he dismissed the notion that Gráinne had been there. He was glad to see the remnants of a camp though. Somehow it brought him closer to finding her and showed him he was following a main path.

He built a fire and settled down for the night, falling into an easy slumber. Later, something awakened him. He jumped suddenly, his heart pounding when he saw a lone wolf lying on the other side of the fire, gnawing on the old chewed bone. There was no meat on the bone. Cred thought that it was very unusual that a wolf should return to his bone after the meat had gone. And why was he not running with his pack? For a lone wolf to venture near a traveller's camp on his own was odd enough, but to return to a bone without the pickings was unheard of. Cred wondered if it was a spirit-wolf or an omen. This made him even more wary. He had heard of such animals, shape-shifting spirits who appeared as omens of disaster or imminent danger. Cred felt a chill start somewhere in the base of his spine and travel up to the back of his neck. His hackles were rising and he dared not move for fear the animal might attack.

It only took a short while for Cred to discover that not only was the wolf not going to attack him, it looked like he was going to stay with him for the night.

He watched in astonishment as the wolf picked up his bone and carried it over to Cred's side of the fire. Cred backed away when the wolf came towards him, his light amber eyes shining eerily, reflecting the yellow flames of the fire, but when the animal lay down beside the fire and dropped his bone, rolling over playfully and submissively on to his back, Cred immediately responded and got down on his own knees to show he was not a threat to the wolf. He stretched his hand forward to scratch the animal's chest affectionately.

So, the wolf was someone's hound. Cred played with him for a while before he rolled up in his furs beside him and went back to sleeping.

The next morn he was still there and Cred knew then that it was not just a vision he had had. This was a real wolf too . . . spirit-dogs and shape-shifters had a definite habit of disappearing, neither could they be touched and played with like this animal.

When he broke his night-fasting, Cred shared his meal with him.

The wolf wagged his tail and barked when Cred packed up his belongings and began his journey on the track again. It was difficult to discern whether he was on the mountain or not yet, but the incline seemed to be getting steeper. The wolf ran at quite a pace in front of the horse and trap. Cred wondered again about the lone wolf when he realized that the horse was not afraid but, rather, seemed to be trotting along at a comparable pace with the animal.

They travelled all day, resting only twice to eat and drink, resuming their journey well into the evening until it was time to camp again.

The cold was bitter this night and Cred built up a fire with every piece of bracken he could gather, and some sticks which he had dried in the trap under the canopy. He threw a fleece over his horse, then he curled up with the wolf in his trap to keep warm during the freeze.

He fell into dreaming and had visions of Gráinne. He saw her with the babe at her breast, remembered how he felt when her hair trailed across his feet many moons ago and he yearned to be with her. If she was already across the mountains, he doubted he could pick up the trail so easily. He seemed to spend the entire night searching for her and chasing after shadows in the dark, his heart yearning to hold and caress, to be with her again, and breaking into pieces when he awoke and found she was not there. Only the lone wolf served to keep him company and it was thick animal-fur, not the long black hair of his dreams, that lay against his feet.

# CHAPTER 28

# *A CHUISLE MO CHROÍ*

*As the earth breathes, so do we.*
*As the fire leaps, so do we.*
*As the water flows, so do we.*
*As the air swirls, so do we.*

Gráinne would not break camp. She insisted on waiting yet another day to see if Cú returned. The wolves had been baying every night since he left.

"He is running with the wolves," she told Cromlach. "He will be back," she said, and she believed it.

But Cromlach was anxious to move on. The last night was bitterly cold and he knew they desperately needed to find a settlement somewhere where they could shelter from the cold for a short time. The worst of it should soon pass if Finann was reading his sky right, and Finann was very rarely wrong in matters of this kind. They hoped to find the pass to the north soon.

The main Gap to the North, which led into Emain Macha, was over on the other side of the land, many, many nights' journey away, but Cromlach knew there was a pass on this side, hidden in the mountain range of Sliab Conachla, used by the traders.

Mora and Tula were anxious about food supplies. The babe needed grains. Gráinne was still feeding him at the breast but now his little teeth needed to chew more grains than he was getting.

Finann mounted his horse and rode ahead a little way to see what he could find. It was the first time that Finann had ever ventured into strange territory alone but he was anxious now and thought he must do something to improve their situation.

He veered slightly off-track, not caring to follow the main path. He knew it was important to remember the land-markings and the trees on the way so he would not get lost. Tree after tree he traced in his mind until, only a short while later and out of sight of their camp, Finann saw a small settlement of *botháns* nestled into the mountain. He rode towards it unafraid as it looked deserted, but when he got closer, there was smoke spiralling from one of the *botháns* and the sound of goats from one of the sheds near by.

Finann dismounted and ran towards the *bothán* which was being used. It must belong to a goatherd like himself.

A man and woman came out to greet him, friendly smiles wreathing their faces.

Finann greeted them cordially, upturning the palms of his hands towards them, as he had seen travellers do at the Dún, to show he held no weapon and came as a friend.

"You journey alone?" asked the woman. She was round and motherly-looking and reminded him of Emer.

He told them he travelled with others who were camped near by and needed warmth and food and then said that they could trade some goods.

"That is why we are here, boy," said the older man. "This is a place of hospitality. We are hospitallers who give refuge to the traders between the North and the South. There is a bigger settlement on the track near the pass but we prefer to settle here, off the beaten track. We have our regular older travellers who like the peace and quiet. The other settlement is bigger, with more entertainment, bards and women of gaiety."

Finann told them he was a goatherd and liked the quiet life. He then mounted his horse and informed them he would be back in no time with the others and to prepare for a babe too. When they heard that there was a babe with one of the women, Finann saw that the "Emer" woman became very excited, planning the *bothán* that the mother should have and saying she was going off immediately to light the fires on the hearthstones.

Finann rode fast, remembering the sequence of trees he had passed before, and he soon found his way back.

Cromlach was proud of Finann and hugged him tightly. Finann's face was pink like a salmon, and he grinned, pleased that he had been able to help.

Mora and Tula started packing the wagon to move on.

Gráinne's heart dropped and she implored Cromlach to stay with her just one more night.

"He will return, I know it. Please, Cromlach, stay with me. I do not want to move away, for fear he will not find me."

Cromlach took her aside from the others.

"*A stór*, let me explain something about the wolves. They are the forefathers of the hounds and can pick up a scent better than any hound. You have seen how well Lugnae Fer Trí's hound can scent a rabbit out when we did not even realize a rabbit was there. Do you really think that Cú, a wolf, greater than any hound, could not find us? Do not forget also that Cormac has the totem of the wolf."

Gráinne reluctantly agreed, convinced by Cromlach that Cú would track them down, but nevertheless, she stopped the wagon when they had gone just a little way off the main path. She squatted down on the ground and let the waters flow from her body. Cromlach smiled to himself knowing she was not taking any chances. She was leaving her scent to make it easier for Cú.

Cred could not understand why the lone wolf was anxious to make him veer off the trail. It was almost dark and to go off-trail now would be a madness when there was a perfectly good place to camp where he was now.

Cred tried to stay in this sheltered site, pulling the horse to a halt and preparing to get down from the trap, but suddenly he stopped because the lone wolf was growling low in his throat. His long lip curled back and he snarled, becoming like a different animal altogether, wild and angry, his hackles rising up on his ruff.

Cred was both frightened and curious. This strange wolf was leading him somewhere and he could do nothing else but get back into the trap and follow. He was surprised when he came over the steep brow of the incline. There was a small settlement nestled in the shelter of the mountain.

The wolf ran ahead, yapping and barking, but Cred slowed his horse down to a walk. The cantering chase after the wolf had exhausted them both, the horse from trying to keep up and Cred from driving to hold and keep the trap steady.

Cred thought that obviously a trapper, or a trader, owned the wolf and lived at a lodge in this settlement tucked into the mountain. Cred was grateful to the wolf and wondered how many other hungry or lonely travellers the wolf had found and led to this place.

A lamp glowed within the first *bothán* and there was the sound of laughter from inside. Then an old man came out as the trap rattled to a halt and Cred jumped down.

"Aah! You are another friend of the wolf," the old man said, when Cú rushed past him and licked Cred's hand.

Cred raised his eyebrows in surprise and laughed.

"Nay, I thought he was yours, friend. I just followed him."

Then he stopped still, his heart seized with a great pain as he stared behind the old man and saw the halo of black hair, black as jet beads, black as the night, and he dared not hope it was Gráinne.

She, in turn, gasped and peered out into the darkness trying to match the stranger with that so-familiar deep voice.

"Cred?" she asked, trembling lest it was not him.

There were no other words needed. Cred was with her in two strides, his arms crushing her to him so that she thought her back must break in two. He buried his face in her hair and she laughed and sobbed all at the same time, unable to find words to say, unable to do anything but collapse against him.

Cú began leaping excitedly, yapping and running around the couple in circles until, at last, Gráinne lifted her head off Cred's chest and turned to Cú.

"Quiet, Cú. Be quiet, boy. I know you are just as happy as I am," she babbled, "though I do not know why . . . you hardly know him!"

"Oh yes he does," murmured Cred into her hair. "He has been my sleeping companion and my guide for the past two nights."

Gráinne looked up, surprised. "He has?"

Cred wanted to crush the petals of her lips with his own, wanted to drown in her eyes, forget all else and take her, right there and then in the snow. But the hospitaller was coughing nervously to let them know he was still there. He did not want to interrupt the lovers yet he had to get them inside out of the bitter cold.

"Come inside, my friend," he said, "to the comfort of a bath, a fire and some food, after your long journey. We will take care of your horse."

There was great excitement at Cred's return and Cred had to reluctantly drop Gráinne's hand when he went inside. Finann and Cromlach, Mora and Tula all embraced him warmly. Gráinne could not keep her eyes off him and her fingers burned where she could still feel the heavy squeeze of his hand.

After bathing and feasting, telling their stories and then trading some gold and fleeces with the hospitaller, it was time to retire for the night. Gráinne fed Cormac, who fell blissfully into slumber at her breast.

The hospitaller's wife led them to their warm *botháns*, each one cosy and sheltered from the cutting night air. Mora had a *bothán* to herself and Tula took Cormac in with her. Finann wanted to be near his goats so he had the *bothán* closest to the sheds. Cromlach soon saw that the wolf was following Gráinne, so he sank his hands into Cú's ruff and led him away to his quarters.

"Come with me, Cú, you will keep a hermit company this night," he said firmly.

The hospitaller then led Gráinne and Cred to the one other remaining *bothán* beside his own, and he smiled knowingly as he pushed them through the door and left. This was a special one for couples and not used too much at this settlement.

There was a pallet strewn with furs, the floor covered in goat-hair rugs and the walls hung with fleeces.

Gráinne felt a rush of warmth spread over her face. She could not help thinking that Mora nee Derga would have hated this room. Then she wondered how she could think a thought like that at a time like this. Maybe because of it, and wanting to feel free of the killings around her, Gráinne took her own plaids and woven wool-rugs and threw them on the pallet.

Cred was standing in the middle of the room, watching her, almost afraid that if he tore his eyes away she might disappear. She knew not what to do or where to look next, knowing he was observing her. She flushed with shame because she had been fixing the pallet just right for them.

Gráinne sat down on the pallet and hid her face shyly in her hands, rocking herself, frightened to look into his face. What must he think of her?

Her breath was ragged, too long in the intake and too short on the outbreath. She could not catch her air properly as she felt him sit down beside her and slowly push her back on to the plaids.

Her scent permeated everything, a musk to his nostrils that made him strain against his clothing. He pulled her hands away from her face and looked deep into the glassy brightness of her eyes. They were pools of light, drawing him closer to her. He read her spirit in them.

His mouth circled hers softly and then slowly leached the soul from her body as his lips hungrily fastened to her own.

She was helpless, powerless to move, as he peeled off her robe and threw it aside, never once taking his mouth from hers. Her white flesh tingled in the air and she felt shy and vulnerable.

Cred then drew himself up, at last unleashing her from his kiss, and he removed his own plaid and tunic. His body was glistening and strong, his muscles and wide shoulders like the powerful rippling frame of the tawny mountain lion.

He was without any mercy in his slowness and she was still unable to move, as if she had been turned into a tree or a stone or the soft yielding earth. There was light in the room. She could see it through a haze and felt that *they* were there, *the light ones* were with him, somehow part of him. She could feel their hands playing her body like the harp, making her desperately yearn for *them* to be a part of her, making her surrender to *them*, to him. Her eyes had closed in *their* presence and now she opened them as she felt a hardness against her. She knew an awe, a fear she did not mind, as his hand trailed down her pale body, down to the very pit of her soul, scooping gently and then smearing her wetness on his face, like a warrior drawing woad or red ochre from the belly of the earth to paint his face.

He was moaning like an animal. She thought she saw antlers, smelt the mouse-brown hide of a stag and felt she was being turned over. His hooves were on her back and she was a doe being taken, his body bucking and his large member charging into her brutally. He was a wild black stallion, a pure white bull, a wolf. She smelled the scents, felt the rampant hardness within her and she was sucking him deeper, deeper . . . and then she was being turned again on to her back and she was Gráinne, Achtán, the earth, the land, the grass caressed by the wind, the flowing rivers, the sea. He was the sun bathing her hair, warming the land, the sands, lighting up the oceans, hot against her skin, the wind of his breath in her ear.

Gráinne opened herself to him, her trembling intakes of breath quickening with his own.

"*A chroí, a chroí,*" he murmured somewhere far away, and it echoed in her head, over and over like the call of a bird, high in the sky, riding the air-waves.

"My heart, my heart," it sang.

"My pulse runs with yours for ever," she murmured, "*a chuisle, a chuisle, mo chroí,* O pulse of my heart!"

He swelled within her, and her belly, her snow-white belly rose with his and plunged again like the crests of the waves to the shore, chasing each other, over and over. She rose to meet him and then pulled back, the ebb and flow of tide on the sands.

Her arms clung around his neck and she flailed, thrashing against him, beating the corn, her nails gripping his back. He was rolling in sand and shingle and it was tearing into him.

Her hair, black, shining eels on the waves, water-snakes, feathers of a raven, wings unfolding around him, talons digging deep . . . deeper and deeper he plunged, the current now stronger and stronger, their bellies lapping the shore.

He rushed into her, tensing his thighs, charging to the shore, rippling through the caves and she lapped him to her, her final moans merging with his primal roar. The calls of the gulls in their ears, the shrieks of their ecstasy as they plunged and rode the air again and again.

Cred saw *them*. *They* were there, caressing them with light somewhere on Í-Bhreasail.

Her face was damp and wet, he tasted the salt on her face, licked the tears from her eyes, the dew on the grass, the smell of the flowers on her glistening body.

She could smell the scent of the stag, feel the heat of the sun on his shanks, feel the breath of the wolf on her neck.

They lay together, clasped in each other's arms at last, knowing that this was how it should have been. He caressed her breasts gently, bending his head to sip the sweet essence which leaked from them. He slid his body beside her and kissed her, his lips sealing hers, a kiss which began their healing. A long arm of sadness and a trail of tears stretched from the Brighdal *bothán* of the Dún of Lugnae Fer Trí to here. This was the true rite. Theirs was the great rite, sanctified by the god and the goddess. They now belonged together. All obstacles, no matter how big or small, would yield before them. They were now the strength of a new Clan.

Cromlach smiled in his *bothán*. It was done. He knew it. It was as he had *seen*. They were all together now, ready for that new road, that new life. There were more Truths ahead to conquer but with the love they had, one for another, they would conquer them all. The morrow was a new journey on a harsh path.

He lay down, the echo of that roar suddenly dancing in his head. A sweet and terrible sadness engulfed him as he thought of her long black hair pressed against him, her soft white hands putting a flower in his hair, tugging his beard, her laughter piercing his heart with its tumbling innocence, her lips like petals against his face. He remembered the touch of her young body curled up with his and the sweet breath of her sleeping face against his neck.

For the first time in a long time, Cromlach felt a wet tear trickle and slide down sideways to the shell of his ear. He closed his eyes tightly, his weathered face contorting with the pain of loving her. She would no longer run to his arms. Her head would lie on the chest of another and she would not think of it being otherwise. No, she would never think of it, but he was going to be there for her. Always, he was going to be there. The snake around his heart was constricting, forever constricting.

Cromlach held the little bags against him. They were tied around his waist under his robe and one of them contained the name-grains of Cormac mac Airt. The other held the remaining name-grains belonging to Gráinne. Cromlach bit his lip as he fumbled to untie one of the bags. He sat up and poured the few seeds into his hand. He could still see her blue eyes laughing, crying, glowing with warmth for him. And the snake around his chest only relinquished its grip a little as he reached over and flung the grains on to the fire. The flames blazed red like his bleeding heart. Cromlach was glad he was the chosen *seer*. Yes, he was the Guardian and *seer* of the ways. He lay down again, cradling the remaining bag in one hand while the other strayed to the ruff on the wolf's neck. The wolf lifted his sad amber eyes briefly. The Druid patted him on the head.

"You too, boy?" whispered Cromlach, wiping his own eyes quickly with the back of his hand. Cú licked the hand gently.

They fell to slumbering.

There was a sickle moon outside . . . Gráinne's moon.